I0762309

Soundscape

Soundscape

Royce Flippin

PILFROCK PUBLICATIONS
New York, NY

Published by Pilfrock Publications, New York, NY.

Cover and interior design by Susan Welt Design | susanwelt@gmail.com

Cover image credits: band, iStock.com/Leontura; figure, super1973/ Shutterstock.com; police and demonstrators, iStock.com/grynold; waves, iStock.com/-M-I-S-H-A-.

Library of Congress Control Number: 2015944011
ISBN: 978-0-9908828-1-7

10 9 8 7 6 5 4 3 2 1

Printed in the United States of America

Permissions

Fortunate Son

Words and Music by John Fogerty
Copyright © 1969 Jondora Music
Copyright Renewed.
International copyright secured. All rights reserved.
Reprinted by Permission of Hal Leonard Corporation

Undun

Words and Music by Randy Bachman
Copyright © 1969 Shillelagh Music (BMI)
Copyright Renewed.
All Rights Administered by BMG Rights Management (US) LLC
All Rights Reserved. Used by Permission.
Reprinted by Permission of Hal Leonard Corporation

White Rabbit

Words and Music by Grace Slick
Copyright © 1966 IRVING MUSIC, INC.
Copyright Renewed.
All Rights Reserved. Used by Permission.
Reprinted by Permission of Hal Leonard Corporation

"2 little whos". Copyright © 1961, 1989, 1991 by the Trustees for the E.E. Cummings Trust, from COMPLETE POEMS: 1904–1962 by E.E. Cummings, edited by George J. Firmage. Used by permission of Liveright Publishing Corporation.

Table of Contents

Prologue

Monday, August 19

THE DIAG WAS CRAMMED TO capacity. Shading his eyes from the noonday sun, the CNN correspondent counted a cross-section of the restless crowd and made a quick mental calculation. There were at least five thousand people milling around in the midsummer heat, he estimated, with hundreds more streaming into the expanse of grass and red brick every minute. Although most were conversing calmly, a sullen tension hung in the air. In one of the stone buildings along the quadrangle, someone had draped a sheet from a window with a hand-painted message: AYN RAND WAS A SELF-SERVING FOOL.

"Our political guys have been saying all summer that Fish is on the ropes," the correspondent muttered to his field producer. "It doesn't feel that way now."

"Let's shoot the interview footage and get out of here," the producer said, glancing around apprehensively. "I'm picking up a distinctly pissed-off vibe."

The correspondent nodded and turned toward the TV camera. A production assistant had selected several promising subjects and was standing a few feet away, chatting with them. As the producer waved them over, a knot of curious onlookers formed.

"We're on the University of Michigan campus," the correspondent began, "where Maxwell Fish supporters have turned out in force for the man who, just two days ago, became the Democratic Party's official nominee for the presidency of the United States. Experts give him little chance of defeating the Republicans' heir apparent, Vice President William Acton, in November—but many in this battleground state feel otherwise. Let's hear from some of them."

"I'm a junior here at Michigan," said one young woman, smiling brightly into the camera. "I'm looking for change. We can't keep going the way we have been—something has to give. That's why I'm supporting Max Fish for president. I'll do anything I can to help him get elected!"

"Fish is for *all* Americans," said a disheveled-looking man in his forties. "Except for the lucky few on top, we're all rotting on the vine. He's the only one promising to do something about it!"

"Do you sense the energy?" said the twenty-something next to him. "This campaign is morphing into a *movement,* man." He pointed to the front of his T-shirt, where a peace symbol was superimposed over a bloodied dollar sign. "I hear Fish is laying out his economic plan today. When he's through, the one-percenters won't know what hit 'em." Flashing a thumbs-up, he melted into the surrounding throng.

"We need help!" said a matronly-looking woman, tears glistening in her eyes as she grasped the TV reporter's arm. "You people are supposed to be journalists—can't you see what's happening to us?" She moved closer to him as the crowd pressed in.

"What does he care—these TV networks are all owned by big corporations, right?" cried a balding man in Bermuda shorts.

An angry murmur rose from the crush of people around the production crew. "Fucking bastards!" someone shouted.

"This is Tim Riley signing off from the University of Michigan in Ann Arbor," the correspondent said hastily, turning back to the camera, "where the support for Max Fish is strong, and the mood is... volatile."

"I don't like the look of this," the producer said in a low voice. "Let's pack it in." Four network security guards surrounded the camera crew and began forcing a path through the crowd. As they pushed their way across the quadrangle, a plastic water bottle whizzed past the correspondent's ear, missing him by inches. Cursing under his breath, he tucked his head between his shoulders and kept moving.

❖ ❖ ❖

"Sixty-four years ago, well after midnight on a cool October evening, another Democratic presidential candidate stood just a few yards away from here, on the steps of the Michigan Union, addressing another crowd of Michigan students."

In one corner of the Diag, a group began chanting: "J-F-K! J-F-K!"

The man at the microphone nodded. "That candidate was John F. Kennedy," he said, "and the short speech he gave that night laid the foundation for the Peace Corps—one of the greatest mobilizations of youthful idealism the world has ever seen."

A cheer swelled up, filling the quadrangle. Maxwell Fish, ex-governor of New York State, waited for the noise to subside, then began speaking again.

"Today, my hope is to lay the groundwork for another new initiative, one that will also renew America and the world for decades to come. For the past eight years, our leaders have told us repeatedly that the only way we can succeed as a nation is to allow the very richest Americans to amass as much money, and as much power, as they possibly can. They assert that it is the wealthy, and the wealthy alone, who make this country what it is—while the rest of us, because we don't have our hands on the levers of economic power, are mere takers."

The crowd rumbled, and a scattering of boos could be heard.

"I'm here today to tell you that I could not disagree more with this philosophy," Fish continued. "Thanks to Republican policies, the richest Americans now own virtually all of our nation's assets—leaving four-fifths of our population with almost nothing to their name other than the clothes in their closet, the car in their garage, and a roof over their heads—one that's all too often rented. Their jobs pay barely enough to cover their living and health care expenses. Why? Because most Americans' wages have not increased in fifty years, when measured against inflation! Well, I say *enough is enough*. A half-century is too long to wait for a raise!"

The crowd's reaction had grown into a full-throated growl by now, and Fish raised his voice a notch. "The evidence is in, and it shows just what our country's leading economists predicted—too much wealth, in too few hands, is strangling the very economy the wealthy are claiming to save!"

The thousands of listeners were on their feet now, clapping and shouting the speaker's name: *"Max...Fish...Max...Fish."*

"I also realize that more government institutions aren't the answer to our nation's problems," Fish continued. "That's why, if elected president, my very first action will be to propose that the U.S. Congress increase taxes significantly on the wealthiest American individuals and corporations. I do *not* propose to use this money to grow the size of government, however—or to create any new government programs. Instead, I want the U.S. Treasury to redistribute that money to the working families of America on a monthly basis in the form of direct financial grants, to be spent however you see fit."

A wild cheer went up, making it impossible to hear anything for several minutes.

"The conservatives call it Leveling," Fish added after the din finally subsided. "I call it good economics. We can only grow the nation from the middle out—*not* from the top down. As your president, I will make sure that you and your family have what you need to lead our economy forward. And if the wealthiest among us can't stomach the idea of doing with less—so that we can *all* create more wealth for everyone—then they are free to leave our shores and take up residence elsewhere!"

Fish nodded for emphasis, his face breaking into a wide grin. "I invite you to follow me forward...to victory in November, and to prosperity for all Americans!" As the candidate waved his fist defiantly, the shouting increased to deafening proportions.

"Max...Fish...Max...Fish."

A few hundred yards away, inside their mobile production unit, the CNN correspondent and his producer took off their headphones. "He's talking straight redistribution," the producer said.

"I know." Riley shook his head slowly. "Fish may have some nerve comparing himself with Kennedy, but he's got at least one thing in common with old Jack: he's not afraid to make powerful enemies."

Ten minutes after the end of Fish's speech, the crowd was drifting slowly out of the quad when the sound of a thin, insistent voice and twanging guitars cut through the humid air.

Some folks are born to wave the flag, ooh, they're red white and blue...

As the Creedence Clearwater Revival recording floated across the campus, people began walking more quickly, trying to distance themselves from its source. An Ann Arbor policeman stood by his squad car speaking urgently into his two-way radio. Seconds later, a line of black sedans appeared, driving down South State Street.

"Homeland!" someone shouted.

People began running frantically as the cars pulled up to the quadrangle entrance and squealed to a stop. A dozen uniformed Homeland Security officers jumped out, rolls of portable orange fencing under their arms.

"Over here!" yelled the local cop, pointing to a young man and woman cowering in a building doorway. The officers unfurled their fencing and swiftly linked the ends together with plastic ties, forming a single two hundred-foot section. Stretching it to full length, they encircled the doorway, penning the couple and another thirty-odd onlookers inside the plastic corral. The people trapped inside the enclosure stood in resigned silence as the officers began frisking them and searching their bags.

"This him?" one of the officers asked. He was gripping the arm of a young man wearing a backpack, fists pushed defiantly into the pockets of his jeans. The Ann Arbor policeman nodded. Spinning the man around roughly, the Homeland officer yanked the pack from his shoulders and rummaged inside it.

"What have we here?" he hooted, pulling out an old-fashioned cassette tape deck. He punched a button and the tinny recording started up again, John Fogerty's voice echoing off the building's stone walls.

It ain't me…It ain't me…I ain't no senator's son.

"I'll bet you ain't," the officer smirked, silencing the song with a punch of his finger. "But what you *are*, pal, is under arrest." He reached for his plastic handcuffs.

"Please," said the woman crouched at the young man's side. Dressed in a rainbow-patterned shift, she was wringing her hands nervously, her eyes wide and pleading. "We have a newborn baby at home. You don't really have to take him into custody, do you?"

"If you don't shut up, lady, we'll be happy to detain you as an accessory," the officer said brusquely. "What about it? You want to call your babysitter, tell her you'll both be home late?"

The woman clutched her husband's arm. "You've always wanted to be the rebel," she said in a tired voice. "Well, you got your wish!"

A few feet away, a college-aged girl began weeping as another officer plugged her iPod into a device on his belt and studied its display. On the far side of the fenced-in area, a late-middle-aged man with a graying ponytail was face down on the grass, his arms pinioned behind him. Struggling to lift his head off the ground, he opened his mouth wide. *"Set the music free!"* he shouted. An instant later, a boot came down on the back of his head, slamming his face into the turf.

Outside the fencing, a teenager in a Michigan T-shirt stood holding a poster with the words "Gone Fish-ing" scrawled in marker. Through a hole inside the letter "O," he was using his smartphone to shoot a video of the scene inside the containment. "Anyone watching?" he asked his companion quietly.

"Nah. The bugs are too busy getting their rocks off, hassling the libs."

"They're having a field day, aren't they?" the first kid said. "Okay, I've got enough." He slipped the phone into his pocket. "Let's edit this baby and slam it up on YouTube. We'll see how long it lasts before they yank it."

"Looks like the networks have the same idea," his friend said. A few yards away, several camera crews were filming the action.

"If ten seconds of this mess makes it onto the nightly news, I'll buy you a pizza," the first student snorted. "And if they *do* have the guts to show it, you can bet they'll edit the tape to make these poor saps look like a bunch of hardcore anarchists."

"Yeah, I know." His friend nudged him in the ribs. "A couple of bugs are looking our way. I think the party's over, dude."

"I hear you. Time to go-go...."

"I can't *believe* they had the nerve to come down on our people like that." Fish's press secretary stirred his glass of iced tea with a contained fury. "It was a legitimate political rally, for Christ's sake. What's next? Are they going to start tear-gassing the crowd in advance whenever Fish shows up to speak?"

"Start believing." Fish's campaign manager frowned, causing the prominent creases in his forehead to deepen further. "There's more where that came from—you can be sure of it."

The two men slouched gloomily in overstuffed armchairs, staring through the hotel lobby's plate glass windows at the traffic flowing over the Blue Water Bridge between Port Huron and Ontario, on the far side of the St. Clair River. Their mood wasn't helped by the fact that the afternoon's itinerary was now a shambles, thanks to an unscheduled meeting their candidate was holding at that very minute in his hotel suite, twelve floors above them.

"Remind me again," said the press secretary, "who is Fish talking to?"

"As I've told you repeatedly, *I don't know,*" the other man said with a flash of impatience. "I'm as much in the dark as you are. Marshall isn't sharing on this one." The campaign manager shot a dark look at Max Fish's longtime chief aide, lounging in a chair nearby. Jim Marshall had been at Fish's side since his earliest days in politics and his allegiance to his boss was legendary.

"First he blindsides us with this meeting, then he refuses to tell us what it's about. How does Fish expect us to help him get elected if he won't keep us in the loop?" said the press secretary. "Besides, what if this guy he's meeting with turns out to be a security risk?"

"Two Secret Service agents are outside Fish's room as we speak. I'm sure they did their due diligence. The Governor isn't going to get plugged in the chest with a .44, if that's what you mean—at least not today." For an instant, the operative's chronic look of worry gave way to a grin. "You're not getting out of your job *that* easily!"

"You brought the documents?"

"Right here." Balancing his briefcase on his lap, Paul Jorgensen of the Canadian Security and Intelligence Service slid a sheaf of papers across the coffee table to Max Fish.

Fish lifted the edge of the stack and withdrew a cassette tape from beneath it. It had no case or identifying label. Silently, he slipped the tape into the inner pocket of his sports jacket. "What have you got for me?" he said briskly.

"These are photocopies of the personal journal of Rick Rogers," said Jorgensen. "He mailed the journal together with a bunch of saved correspondence to a post office box in Canada, shortly before his arrest and subsequent escape in Minnesota. He passed along the whole trove to the Canadian authorities when we interrogated him several weeks later. As you know, Canada has never acknowledged its existence."

"If I understand you correctly, this will shed new light on the Boundary Water Incident."

"I can assure you that you'll have a new understanding of what took place, once you review this material." Jorgensen tapped his own jacket in the spot where Fish had placed the tape, raising his eyebrows slightly. Fish nodded and rose to his feet.

"I can't thank you enough for getting in touch," he said, grasping the other man's hand.

"No sweat, eh?" said Jorgensen. "I'm about to retire, anyway. If my bosses find out we met, the worst they can do is screw me out of my pension."

"I hope not," replied Fish. "As far as I'm concerned, you've earned every penny."

As Jorgensen walked out of the room, Fish picked up his mobile phone. "Jim, can you come up here for a minute? I need to talk to you."

Fish and Marshall were finishing a late lunch in the hotel restaurant when two men in suits approached the table.

"Mind if we sit down?" the older of the two asked. He opened his wallet to reveal a Homeland Security badge.

"Do we have a choice?" sighed Fish. He put his fork down and took a sip of water. "Isn't it enough that you harass the people who come to my rallies?" he said with a tight smile. "Are you going to start hounding me personally, as well?"

"This is a highly unusual situation," the man said quietly. "We're here to escort you to Washington. The Justice Department wants to meet with you—today."

"What about?"

"You'll be informed of the details later," the man said. "But I can tell you that it involves unapproved contacts with a foreign intelligence agency."

"I see." Fish studied his water glass for a moment, then glanced across the table. "Jim, I think you'd better put in a call to our lawyers, so they can have someone over at Justice when I get there."

"There's no hurry—please, finish your lunch," the man said. "We've got some people in your room right now, packing your things. Once you're done, we'll all take a plane ride."

"Not me, thanks," said Marshall, rising to his feet. "As the Governor indicated, I have some phone calls to make."

"Hold on a second," said the second man, rising also.

"I'm sorry—am I being detained too?" asked Marshall sharply.

"The answer is no...for the time being," said the first man. "But since you were in the room alone with Mr. Fish for several minutes following his, uh, appointment, we do need to confirm that he didn't pass along any potential evidence to you. It'll just take a minute." He nodded at his colleague, who unobtrusively patted Marshall down and then riffled swiftly through his briefcase.

"Nothing here," he said.

"Okay, you're free to go," said the first man with a wave. "We'll be in touch regarding your statement."

Marshall walked into the lobby and punched a number into his cell phone. Holding the phone to his ear, he strode out the hotel entrance and ducked into one of the cars reserved for top campaign staff.

"Jimbo! What's up?" The booming voice caused the phone to vibrate in Marshall's grip.

"Big news—none of it good." said Marshall. "Can you make an emergency session at DOJ this evening?"

"Sure, if I have to. Give me a minute to clear my calendar. Then we can talk."

"I'll hold," Marshall said. Covering the mouthpiece, he bent forward. "Detroit Metro Airport," he told the driver. He leaned back in the upholstered seat as the car accelerated out of the parking lot, then turned to peer out the rear window. Once he was sure no one was following them, he casually reached down and felt the top of his right foot, where a cassette tape was wedged firmly between his instep and the leather interior of his shoe.

ONE

For What It's Worth

Friday, August 23

DEPUTY SECRETARY OF HOMELAND SECURITY Charles "Chuck" Smyth sat behind his desk, skimming that morning's edition of the *Washington Post*. The lead story, as it had been for the past four days, was about the Fish affair. While authorities stressed that the inquiry into his meeting with Canadian intelligence was still in its early stages, Fish was now officially under house arrest in his Manhattan apartment for "reasons of national security," forbidden to leave the premises or have personal contact with anyone other than his wife, his top aide and his attorneys.

This latest development had brought the simmering political battle over Fish's arraignment to a boil: The Democratic minorities in the House and Senate were charging that the Constitution was being subverted in order to steal the upcoming presidential election for the Republican candidate, sitting Vice President William Acton. Meanwhile, the Republicans had begun talking darkly of treason.

As usual, President Tom Ballinger was staying above the fray. "I'm just concentrating on completing my second term," he was quoted as saying. "I have full confidence in the ability of our judicial branch to sort this matter out."

I'm sure you do, thought Smyth. He had personal knowledge that the decision to detain Fish and charge him had come straight from the White House—a fact that had been carefully kept from the media. He also knew that Homeland Security had been planning the operation for weeks. The day before the meeting, they'd sent a team posing as air conditioner repairmen into Fish's hotel room and bugged it with highly sensitive microphones.

The Republicans must be plenty worried to pull a stunt like this, he reflected. All summer long, Acton had held a solid 20-point lead in the polls over Fish, the Democrats' presumptive nominee. While Acton wasn't exactly charismatic, his fame as the man who uncovered the Boundary Waters nuclear terror plot had left him with an enduring reservoir of goodwill. That along with Ballinger's endorsement had combined to make him an overwhelming favorite in November's general election.

Recently, though, the tide had started to turn. A week earlier, Fish had accepted the nomination at the Democratic convention with a fiery televised speech that garnered the highest viewership of any political convention broadcast in history. Since then, the polls were indicating a larger than usual post-convention bounce that showed no signs of fading. The latest numbers had Fish within single digits of Acton, with favorability ratings approaching 70 percent among young adults and middle- to low-income voters of all ages.

The day's big news was that the Supreme Court had agreed to hear arguments surrounding Fish's legal challenge of his arrest as soon as possible. With the nine Justices just beginning their summer vacations, however, the scheduled court date was five weeks away—an eternity, as far as the final months of a presidential campaign were concerned. By then, even if Fish's detention was overturned, the damage would have been done: Tarred by scandal and unable to appear in public to defend himself or wage his campaign, the Democratic candidate would have seen his chances for the presidency melt away.

Smyth moved on to a story below the fold, about a Democratic Congressman whose teenage son had been arrested for distributing digital copies of Grateful Dead concert bootlegs. *Interesting,* he thought, *how the Dems' kids are the ones who always seem to get nabbed.*

His musings were interrupted by the buzzing intercom. "Courier from Secretary Jackson's office," his assistant announced.

Smyth groaned. Just what he needed—another one of Jackson's pet projects to manage. "All right," he sighed. "Send him in."

The courier dropped a folder on his desk. "New file, sir. Music possession. It's flagged top priority."

"Why do these cases always end up on *my* desk?" Waving the courier out of the room, the Homeland Security official opened the folder and began reading. After making his way through the entire document, he leaned back in his chair and rubbed his eyes. He sat thinking for several minutes before picking up the phone.

"Perkins? Smyth here. I was just looking through the Hawkes file. Listen, is the Secretary absolutely certain about this? I mean, the kid's a real standout—science awards stretching back to junior high school, a former track star.... And his record's perfectly clean up until now. Plus, his father's retired Navy brass, as I'm sure you know. There's potential for serious blowback here."

He listened, furrowing his brow. "I guess what I'm saying is that a more indirect approach might be preferable. If they simply gave his project a military classification, then he'd be required to proceed under DOD oversight—correct?"

He fell silent again, his eyes scanning the pages in front of him. Finally he whistled softly. "The warrant's already drawn up? Jackson isn't fooling around. Yeah, I agree, this invention could be a game-changer. And there's no question his psych profile makes him a risk. A march-to-his-own-drummer type, for sure—which could spell trouble on the arrest, by the way, if it's not handled properly."

Smyth listened intently for another minute. "Sure, I'll be glad to oversee the pickup. Tell the Secretary we'll keep it nice and low-key. That's a promise."

TWO

Tomorrow Never Knows

Sunday, September 1

"YOU'RE GOING TO BE *RICH,* man! Just remember all of us poor peons from La Jolla High when your mug is splashed across the cover of *People* magazine: Blake Hawkes, Inventor of the Year..."

Not bothering to reply, Blake inhaled deeply from the joint he was holding, then handed it back to Carter. Ever since the U.S. Congress finally voted to legalize marijuana nationwide in 2016, the California varieties had consistently ranked at the top of every survey. Still, the stuff Carter got from his licensed supplier up in Humboldt was always a cut above the rest. Blake indulged infrequently these days, but whenever he sampled Carter's stash the experience was always intense—like lying back in some celestial hammock, watching half-formed ideas rise up from his subconscious and connect in a vast Hegelian constellation.

It was another joint from Carter, rediscovered in a desk drawer, that had inspired his solution to the quantum communication problem. Other than Mel, Carter was the only person who knew about Blake's discovery. The whole story had tumbled out during their run that morning, despite his promise to Mel that he would keep it under wraps. It was okay, he knew—Blake could trust Carter with anything. They'd been best friends since the third grade, and had shared countless confidences over the years.

"Let's review," Carter was saying. "You're telling me that this invention of yours lets anyone communicate instantly with someone else, wherever they might happen to be—across the universe even, to quote the late, great John Lennon?"

"That's right. *And* the communication can't be intercepted or jammed, or even detected—because there's no actual transmission occurring between the two points."

Blake lay back on the smooth wooden planks, staring up at the blue sky as his bare chest and legs soaked up the warmth of the sun. It was Sunday morning of the long Labor Day weekend, and not a car could be heard on the surrounding streets. On a day like this, up here on the roof deck of his parents' house, it was easy to forget that he lived in the nation's most populous state. Their four-story home was built on one of the highest points of their residential La Jolla neighborhood, and the roof had a commanding view of the tree-lined landscape around them. Spending time there always left him with the feeling that the world was somehow under control.

This is what life is about, he thought: catching rays and sharing some prime weed with an old friend after a hard morning run. They'd covered the rolling seven-mile course at a good clip, too. How long was it since he and Carter and the other guys had brought home the Division II high school cross-country championship? Nine years...an eternity. His training was more hit-or-miss these days, but it was nice to know he could still turn it on when he wanted to.

He'd needed this break. Closing his eyes, Blake visualized himself detaching from his worries and drifting down a quiet river, leaving all of them far behind: the breakup with Ann, his misgivings about his post-academic career, and now this latest twist—the sudden request from the government for a meeting. He didn't mind talking with the Feds about his work, he thought, but why the mystery?

He'd gotten the phone call two days before.

"Blake? Mel here. I finally caught the video of your Zurich presentation. You were sensational! This work you're doing on random convergence is going to turn the whole multiple universe concept on its head."

"Thanks, but I had some help. You were there the day that theory hatched—remember?"

"Sure I do. I realize it's not going to cause the kind of splash your quantum communicator will, but it's a very big deal. In the long run, it could point the way to a unified theory. I can't tell you how proud I am of all you've accomplished."

There was an awkward pause, as if the speaker was searching for the right words to express what was coming next. "Actually, it's the communicator I'm calling about, Blake," he said at last. "I'm afraid you'll need to come back to campus a few days early. The Federal government got wind of the project somehow. They want to ask you some questions."

Blake was taken aback by his advisor's wary tone. Mel Morrison usually played the laid-back California surfer-physicist to the hilt ("The name's *Mel,* dude—as far as I know, Professor Morrison's still safely interred in Paris…"). It wasn't like him to sound so uptight.

"Is everything okay?" he asked.

Mel waited a beat before answering. "This was bound to happen," he said, a hint of weariness in his voice. "These days, every discovery has its price. Just stick to the science and you'll be fine." And with that, he hung up.

Blake was brought back to the present by Carter's voice.

"If what you're saying is true, you're going to have every military and spy agency in the world knocking on your door. You lost me with that last part, though. How can the two thingamajigs communicate if there's no transmission between them?"

"It's based on something called quantum entanglement," Blake replied. "The communicators use entangled electrons—pairs of electrons that are generated at the same time in a way that leaves them linked forever, no matter how far they are from each other—like psychic twins separated at birth."

Opening his eyes again, Blake paused to let this sink in.

"When you bring one of these linked electrons out of its entangled state—what they call collapsing it," he continued, "it takes on a definite spin, along either the 'x' or 'y' axis. At that very same instant its twin collapses too, and takes on the opposite spin, even it's a million light years away. Theoretically, you could collapse an electron in another galaxy and its counterpart would respond instantly back here on Earth."

"Got it. So you communicate by sending out a bunch of 'x' and 'y' messages, like Morse code dots and dashes—right?"

"It's not that easy. For one thing, there's no way to predict which spin an electron will take on. So you can't say, 'Now I'm going to do three x's and a y.' The only thing you *can* control is whether you collapse an electron out of its entangled state or not."

"Then why not collapse them in some kind of pattern—and send a code that way?"

"Because that poses another problem. Just by checking a particle, you'll automatically collapse that particle if it hasn't collapsed already. So when you look at a collapsed particle you can never tell whether you collapsed it yourself, or if your counterpart at the other end of the universe messed with it first."

"I'm having serious trouble following you, brother."

"Think of it this way," said Blake. "Imagine that I sent you a magic envelope with a white piece of paper inside. Meanwhile, I have a special matching envelope that I keep for myself. The instant you open your envelope, the paper inside will randomly turn either red or blue. At that same instant, the paper in my matching magic envelope will turn the opposite color—even though I haven't opened it yet. This means that any time you open your envelope and see that the paper is red, you'll know that mine has to be blue—or vice versa."

"Okay," said Carter slowly.

"Now, my matching envelope works exactly the same way in reverse. When I open my envelope and see that my paper is blue, I know that yours has turned red. That's pretty cool knowledge to have, right? Especially if you're in another galaxy."

"Right—an instantaneous exchange of information! And since you're a galaxy away, it's being sent faster than the speed of light, right?"

"Like I said, it's not that simple," said Blake. "For one thing, you can't control which color either paper will turn. Plus, you can never tell if a paper has already changed color inside the envelope, because you'd have to open it to check—which automatically makes the paper turn red or blue, if it hasn't already. So we can't really exchange any information. Say you want to send me a prearranged signal by opening three envelopes at your end—because we've agreed that three colored pieces of paper means send help, whether they're red or blue. There's still no way I can tell that you really sent the signal, and that I didn't transform the papers myself. To know that, I would need X-ray vision to look inside each of my closed envelopes without opening them—which is impossible."

"I get it. A Catch-22...." Carter squinted skyward. "But you found a way around it."

"Yeah, I did. The random convergence theory I developed predicts that when you bring together enough entangled electrons, it curves time slightly. It turns out you can see this time shift if you run a microwave beam through the electron field, because the shift accelerates the beam just a little bit. Then each time you bring one of these collected electrons out of entanglement it slows the beam down just a fraction, in a way that's unique to the electron's location. Using that knowledge, you actually *can* send the kind of signal we're talking about, by collapsing electrons in a deliberate pattern with a laser while someone at the other end monitors the changes in the microwave transmission."

"You figured this out yourself?"

Blake nodded. "About six months ago." As he spoke, his mind flashed back over the long weeks of calculations leading up to the breakthrough, and his feeling of euphoria when he realized that the theory was holding up.

"The thing is," he continued, "no one has been able to gather enough entangled particles together in one location to test the theory out. That was my big challenge: I had to find a crystal structure that could hold a billion or more entangled electrons for a sustained period of time."

"And you did that, too."

"Yup."

"He said modestly," laughed Carter. "I'll take your word on the science, dude. It all sounds a little spooky, though."

"It's funny you say that, because Einstein thought the exact same thing. He called quantum entanglement 'spooky action at a distance.' He didn't believe this kind of relationship between two particles really existed. He was convinced the theory was mistaken, or at least incomplete."

"So Einstein was wrong?"

"One of the few times he was," said Blake. "Anyway, after those issues were solved, it was just a matter of developing the hardware—starting with a computerized pulsed laser that could target specific electrons inside an artificial crystal lattice."

"Spare me the techno-speak," said Carter. "Can't you just show me how it works?"

"I thought you'd never ask. Back in a flash."

A minute later, Blake climbed back up the stairway to the roof with two identical black leather suitcases in his hands.

"These devices are configured to transmit and receive data from each other," he said. "I just put the crystals in. Normally I keep them in the freezer to prevent the electrons from decaying. Each one holds one crystal for transmitting and another for receiving. They're good for about a half hour's communication time apiece before the quantum effect gets too faint to measure."

Placing the cases carefully on the large picnic table at the center of the roof deck, Blake walked over to a corner section of the deck's wraparound bench. Raising its hinged seat, he removed some blankets from the storage space inside, then pried up the floorboards underneath to reveal a hollowed-out space he'd created years ago by sawing away the deck's supporting struts. Blake reached down again and retrieved a rectangular object wrapped in heavy plastic. Setting the bundle down on the bench, he peeled away the covering to reveal an old manual Technics turntable.

"Haven't seen *that* in a while." Carter gave a low whistle. "Don't tell me you've held onto your vinyl?"

"Relax," Blake said. "You know the government scanners can't detect analog."

He plugged the turntable into a weather-protected outlet, then went back to the secret compartment and pulled out a pair of flat, plastic-covered square objects. Visible through their protective plastic sleeves were two vintage records—*Who's Next,* with its iconic urine-stained block of concrete, and the Beatles' debut album *Please Please Me,* graced by the grinning faces of an impossibly young John, Paul, George and Ringo.

Carter stared open-mouthed. "Hawkman, you never told me you still had these. You are one unreconstructed classic rock fiend—I'll give you that." He took one of the albums from Blake and turned it over in his hands. "As your oldest friend, though, I've got to advise you to ditch them. Seriously...we're talking big trouble if you get caught with this stuff."

"You're being paranoid," said Blake. "You think the Feds are going to come poking around a retired Admiral's house looking for ancient record albums? Anyway, that law's bound to be repealed soon."

"You've been saying that for six years, and each year they clamp down harder," said Carter. "You're a whiz at physics, Blake, but you don't know power politics like I do. The Rock Ban is just a new version of the old War on Drugs—an excuse for the cops to keep the population under their thumb. It's a license to stop and frisk anyone they like. It's even better than the drug laws, in fact, because it also lets the government monitor everyone's computers and smart phones."

"That's easy for you to say. You've been able to listen to anything you like, over there on the other side of the ocean."

Carter ignored him. "Lately, with these wireless probes," he continued, "they can scan a whole city block in five minutes. I didn't get a chance to tell you this, but my cousin and a bunch of her friends actually got arrested last spring when some Cultural Hygiene goons did a campus-wide scan at the University of Oregon."

"What did they get caught with?"

"Illegal digital files, of course. Random stuff—Radiohead, Aimee Mann, Green Day, Beyoncé. Even some early Carole King. The point is, it was illegal, the Feds found it on their computers, and they were screwed."

"What happened to them?"

"They were eventually let off with reprimands and probation—but the government could have prosecuted. My cousin would've been kicked out of college, maybe even gone to jail. My aunt and uncle were pretty freaked out by the whole thing."

"It's so messed up," said Blake. "Remember when we were kids, racing over to each other's house to hear the newest CD or download? Or how we'd hear some great tune coming from the iPod of a kid we didn't know, and we'd just walk over and ask what they were listening to?"

"That still happens," said Carter.

"Yeah, except the only music kids get to hear now is that bland, government-approved crap. They'll never know the thrill of getting turned on to Santana, or Little Richard, or Phish."

"That's our reality. Sooner or later you've got to accept it," said Carter. "If the Republicans score another big win in November like everyone's predicting, it'll only get worse."

"Maybe Fish will surprise everyone," said Blake.

"With the number they're doing on him? Not likely."

While they were speaking, Blake had hooked an output wire from the turntable to one of the black cases. Next, he pulled a headset with earphones and attached microphone out of a compartment in the second case and connected it to an input on the case's exterior. Satisfied with the setup, he slid The Who album out of its sleeve and placed it on the turntable.

"Your cousin's big mistake was sticking with digital," he said. "There's not a scanner in the world that can pick up old-fashioned hi-fi. I've connected this turntable directly to one of the communicators, and it's going to send the music straight to the second device, where you'll be listening. There's no Wi-Fi signal, not even any magnetized tape to scan. The police would have to have a directional microphone pointed at this exact spot to hear it. Now, get ready for a treat!"

Switching the turntable on, he lowered the stylus to the spinning record. A grin spread across Carter's face as the first chords of "Baba O'Riley" hit his eardrums. Lifting the phones from his ears, he looked at Blake and shook his head.

"I stand by what I said about the risk and all," he said. "But man, do I like it." Replacing the phones, he reached for the still-smoldering joint, closed his eyes, and floated away on an ocean of sound.

At the end of Side One, Carter took off the phones and gave an approving thumbs up. "Good dynamic range. I'm impressed!"

"And you didn't have to go to Africa to hear it."

While his friend had been listening to Townshend and company, Blake had been in a reverie of his own. This would be his last visit to his hometown for a while, he knew. In two days he was heading back to Berkeley to finish his dissertation. From there, the road led straight to Silicon Valley. He'd been fielding a steady flow of inquiries from technology firms based on his earlier research work, and had even met with a few. Once news of the quantum communicator became public, that stream would turn into a flood. It all felt vaguely disturbing, like driving down a jam-packed freeway with no exit ramp in sight.

Thinking about the communicator reminded him of his upcoming meeting with Federal agents. How did they hear about the project, he asked himself for what felt like the hundredth time, when Mel had been planning to sit on the news until next week?

Slow down, he thought, recalling the words of a former meditation instructor. *Live in the moment*. He glanced over at Carter, who had moved the tone arm back to replay "The Song is Over," the final cut on the first side. The last time they'd seen each other was over a year ago, just before Carter left for his final Peace Corps posting in the Congo. The fact that they were hanging out today could be chalked up to pure fortune: Carter had been due to return Stateside in mid-September, but his paperwork had gone through faster than expected. The preceding week he'd been handed a ticket for the next plane home, more than a fortnight early.

"The bureaucracy works in strange and mysterious ways," he'd told Blake. "I've learned not to question it."

A lucky break for me, Blake thought. He had a sudden rush of nostalgia for their high school years, when the world revolved around running, music, academics and girls, all blending into what seemed now like an endless procession of shimmering, carefree days.

"I'd love to take this thing out on the street," Carter was saying. "What if we try talking over it while I make a run to my house? I can throw some beers in a cooler and be back here in twenty minutes."

Blake shook his head. "I don't think so. I'm already breaking lab rules. I wasn't even supposed to take these off-campus."

"*Now* who's being paranoid? I'm talking a quick stroll down the block!"

"We can't. It's too risky," Blake said.

Carter heaved a sigh. "Hawkman, this is like having a new Maserati and being afraid to drive it. Your invention is *begging* to be road tested! Aren't you the tiniest bit curious to see how it works in the real world?"

Blake hesitated. Fucking Carter! He knew just how to push his buttons.

"Okay," he said finally. "Twenty minutes. But don't use the headphones—they'll attract too much attention. There's a built-in microphone and speaker at one end. Just wear it like a backpack and speak normally. I'll hear every word you say." He unplugged the box from the turntable and slipped the case straps over Carter's shoulders.

"Cool. And don't worry, Hawkman. If anyone makes a move, I'll run like a snakebit coyote."

Blake picked up the headphones connected to the second black case and placed them over his ears. "Don't bump against anything, or you may throw off the computerized laser," he instructed. "I'll be listening, so keep talking as you go. I want to know right where you are, every step of the way."

"Roger that."

As Carter headed down the inner stairway, Blake suddenly heard his friend's voice in his headphones.

"This is Red Paper calling Blue Paper. Do you read me, Blue Paper?"

"Loud and clear," said Blake.

"Beautiful! Here we go...down the stairs, past the empty master bedroom—parents and little sister away for the long Labor Day weekend," Carter intoned. "The house is ours, which once upon a time would have meant just one thing: part–y! We're getting old, my friend..."

Blake listened to the sound of the front door opening and clicking shut again. "Out on the sidewalk now," Carter continued, "covering the familiar furlong to my own *Leave it to Beaver* domicile—the prodigal son, back from the Peace Corps, future unplanned, direction unknown. His progressive parents, disturbed by the situation, struggle valiantly not to show it as they gradually become reconciled to the fact that their son will *not* be following in his attorney father's footsteps."

"There's always business school," said Blake, speaking into the microphone on his own headset.

"Wow, it's like you're standing next to me! Thanks, pal, but I think I'd rather bop up to U.C. Santa Barbara and study anthropology—which is not such a bad idea, by the way. Anyhow, the old homestead is coming into sight...."

Carter's voice broke off momentarily. "What's this? We've got a *very* official-looking black sedan parked at the curb. Let me guess: the Feds are busting a meth lab. Or maybe rounding up some illegal aliens." Another pause. "Hold everything. Two guys in suits are getting out. Something's up."

Blake leaned forward, listening intently. Carter's voice had shifted gears, his easy patter replaced by the reflexive caution of someone who'd spent the past four years living on the fringe of various war zones.

"What can I do for you, sir?" he heard Carter say.

"Homeland Security," a man's voice said. "Keep your hands where we can see them. We're going to need your backpack and any mobile devices you're carrying. Then I want you to please get into the back seat of the car."

"I'm afraid I can't give you this—it belongs to a friend of mine and I have to return it," said Carter coolly. "I'll be glad to help you any other way I can, though."

"You saw his badge, and here's mine." This second voice was ice-cold. "You can *help* by not giving us any shit. The man said 'Please,' didn't he? I'll take this, thank you very much. Now *get in the fucking car.*"

"Yes sir," Carter said. His voice, more distant now, had the respectful tone of someone who had seen more than his share of violence and knew all too well what the authorities were capable of.

A car door slammed, but Blake could still hear the men talking. They were holding the transceiver, he realized, unaware that he was listening in. He quickly reached for the mute switch on his own transmitter and flicked it on, then crouched on the deck, concentrating with every fiber of his being.

"You sure this is a good move?" one of them said. "It could tip Hawkes off."

"How's he gonna know? Unit Two will be at his back door in fifteen minutes. As soon as they're in position, we ring the front doorbell and invite him for a ride. Remember, keep it polite. We just want him to come downtown so we can have a little chat about his school project."

"Meanwhile, Spencer and Torres will be tearing his place apart," chuckled the first voice.

"Things will go a lot easier without his buddy hanging around, believe me. Anyway, what choice did we have? HQ gave explicit instructions to snatch the black box at the first possible opportunity."

"You're right—we had to do it.... So, Poindexter's in for a surprise, huh?" chuckled the first voice.

"That little platter collection's gonna be his one-way ticket to Officer Training School. Hope he likes doing push-ups!"

"What about Mr. Peace Corps here?"

"We'll keep him locked in the car until right before we make our move on Hawkes. Then we let him scamper home."

"Sounds good. Any idea what this thing does, by the way?"

"Headquarters didn't say. Some newfangled radar detector, I think...."

THREE

Going Mobile

BLAKE SWITCHED OFF THE TRANSCEIVER and remained frozen in place, his mind racing. Somehow, Federal agents had discovered his record trove—probably during a secret search of his parents' house, the kind of "sneak and peek" authorized by the 2001 Patriot Act, where the subject never knows the search took place. Now they were executing the next step: Arrive with a warrant, "discover" the hidden albums, and arrest him under the Rock Ban legislation of 2017. From what the officers had said, it sounded like they were planning to offer him the option of military duty in lieu of prosecution. Lately this had become a favorite government tactic for silencing political dissidents—effectively sidelining them without the negative publicity of a trial.

He was no dissident, though. Why were they targeting *him?*

Even as the question formed in his brain, Blake knew the answer: This was about the quantum communicator, of course. The Feds wanted the technology for themselves—which meant keeping him bottled up. What was it Mel said? *These days, every discovery has its price.* The whole bit about meeting the Feds in Berkeley had probably been a ruse, cooked up so he wouldn't be suspecting anything when they made their move in La Jolla.

Blake had another thought: Did Mel know the Feds were planning this? Could he even be involved somehow? Along with Ann, his uncle Frank, and now Carter, Mel was one of the few people who knew about his stash of illegal albums.

His marijuana buzz had vanished, replaced by a mix of adrenaline and fear. The whole arrest scenario flashed through his mind: He'd be stuck in a holding cell for a day or so; then would come the formal charges, followed by months of legal maneuvering—all leading, if he was lucky, to a year of Officer Training School followed by another four years in an Army lab. Then there was the media angle: He could just picture the *60 Minutes* interview with his parents, the grieving Admiral and his stricken wife....

Fighting down a wave of panic, Blake forced himself to breathe slowly and evenly. There had to be a way out—he just needed time to figure out what it was.

Unit Two will be at his back door in fifteen minutes....

He glanced at his watch: 10:45. First, he had to get rid of the records. That wouldn't change his legal status—the searchers who had discovered them earlier would certainly have documented their findings—but he didn't like the idea of leaving the incriminating albums in his parents' house. Plus, the thought of a bunch of Homeland Security officers fingering his precious LPs turned his stomach.

Thinking fast, Blake scurried downstairs, returning to the roof a moment later with an empty backpack in his hands. He jammed the turntable and the two record albums into it, then crossed to the bench on the far side of the roof deck and lifted up another stretch of floorboards. Inside were twenty more plastic-wrapped albums, which he added to the pack. Replacing the boards, he hesitated a moment and then grabbed a pocketknife from the pack's side pocket. Using the Phillip's head attachment, he swiftly unscrewed a light fixture on a corner post of the deck and retrieved a small object from the space behind it. He shoved the object into the pack and rapidly screwed the fixture back in place.

As he worked, the outlines of an escape strategy were taking shape. The key was to make his pursuers think he'd stepped out of the house for a short time and that he knew nothing about his impending arrest. Setting the backpack on the table, he yanked on his T-shirt, socks and running shoes, then reached for the notebook and pen he always kept close for jotting down notes and equations. Ripping out a blank page, he scribbled a message:

> ***Carter—Couldn't bring myself to tell you earlier, but I'm considering a leave of absence from school. Thought I'd take one last walk through the Heights to clear my head. I'll call when I get back. Leave the case on my bed.***

Hopefully the note would send the agents to the La Jolla Heights Natural Park in search of him. Meanwhile, with any luck, he'd be well on his way in the opposite direction, bound for the desert.

Blake glanced at his watch again: 10:49. Four minutes gone. Spotting the half-finished joint resting on the picnic table, he slipped it into the backpack. *Might come in handy.*

He'd need a few emergency supplies, too, things that wouldn't be missed. Meanwhile, any personal belongings—wallet, mobile phone, laptop computer—would have to stay behind. Nothing could indicate he was on the run.

Moving at top speed now, Blake gathered up the backpack and the quantum transceiver and rushed down the steps to his old bedroom. He propped the transceiver on the bed with the note lying next to it, then rummaged feverishly through the bin of camping equipment in his closet, throwing various pieces of gear into his pack—a canteen, khaki pants and a canvas jacket, a floppy sun hat, binoculars and flashlight, a sand-colored blanket, a plastic tarp and a compass. From a drawer in his desk, he pulled out a dog-eared topographic map and stuffed it into the pack as well. Hurrying downstairs to the kitchen, he scooped up several books of matches, grabbed a half-dozen granola bars from a cabinet, then filled the canteen from the sink faucet.

His kit complete, he padded down one last flight of stairs to the basement garage that had been his personal workshop for as long as he could remember.

"I'm counting on you, old paint," said Blake, staring down at the teardrop-shaped car on the garage floor. He'd built the ultra-light hybrid as a high school senior, attaching a thin acrylic body to a pared-down aluminum chassis cobbled together from spare parts. Ten feet long and just three feet in height, it weighed less than 200 pounds empty. The car, which he'd named the Silver Beetle, was his entry in a local competition to build a street-legal vehicle with the best gas mileage. Good for well over a hundred miles per gallon of petrol at highway speeds, it had won going away.

Blake did a quick risk assessment: Would the agents notice the car was gone? For months, the roadster had been scattered in pieces around the workshop, unrecognizable as a working automobile. He'd reassembled it just two days ago, shortly before getting Mel's call, with the idea of taking it for a final drive through the hills before heading north. Except for their run that morning, he hadn't left the house between then and now. The Feds couldn't possibly know about it, he decided. With his Honda Civic parked in the driveway and his bicycle and motor scooter locked under the carport, they'd assume Blake was on foot.

He wedged a five-gallon container of gasoline into the space behind the driver's seat and used a voltmeter to check the battery. It held enough charge to get him at least a few miles down the road, where he could fire up the internal combustion engine without alerting anybody.

Showtime, thought Blake. He eased the garage door upward, steeling himself for the sight of Federal agents on the asphalt, guns at the ready. Except for the parked Honda, the driveway stood empty. His parents' lush backyard was the picture of tranquility: songbirds chirping, trees and bushes rustling softly in the Pacific breeze.

With a light push, Blake guided the Silver Beetle smoothly out of the garage, maneuvering the steering wheel with one hand as the car glided forward on its precision-engineered bearings. He closed the garage door quietly behind him, then slipped into the driver's seat and switched on the silent electric motor.

Here goes nothing. Pressing on the pedal, Blake accelerated noiselessly down the sloping drive toward the road below. Reaching the bottom, he glanced to the left in the direction of the Interstate, half-expecting to see a black Homeland Security sedan bearing down on him. Spying open pavement instead, he made a right-hand turn onto the curving two-lane road leading to the gated community's eastern security post. The rent-a-cops stationed there typically concentrated on arrivals, Blake knew, paying little attention to who drove out. The Sunday morning shift also had a reputation for catching catnaps on the job. Still, he slowed to a 10-mile-per-hour crawl as he neared the small guardhouse, sliding down in his seat so that his head was below the windowsill. He rolled quietly past, then peered back at the structure in his side mirror. Not a soul was stirring.

So far, so good.

A mile later, he flipped a switch and the four-cylinder engine roared to life. Giving a silent cheer for the primitive power of fossil fuel, Blake depressed the gas pedal and picked up speed, driven by the simple imperative of the hunted: to leave the hunter behind, as swiftly and completely as possible.

"Stephanie Montaigne. It's an honor to meet you, sir." As the young woman smiled and squeezed his hand in greeting, Martin detected a hint of flirtatiousness. There was truth in that old saw about power being an aphrodisiac, he mused.

"The honor is all mine," he said, bowing slightly. He was always amazed at how well put-together these TV personalities were—they all seemed a little better groomed, better dressed, and just plain better-looking than the rest of us, he thought. Stephanie's shoulder-length blonde hair was cut perfectly, and her tailored outfit hinted at the curvaceous figure beneath. It had been too long since he'd appeared on one of these Sunday morning shows, Martin thought. He made a mental note to do this more often in the future.

"I'd like to ask you some questions about your government work. Then maybe we could talk about your own music?"

"Of course." A lovely young woman indeed, he decided, settling into the director's chair opposite his interviewer.

"We're on in five seconds," called the producer.

"Hello everyone," said Stephanie cheerily, "we're talking on this glorious Sunday morning with Martin Bibbitt, the famous composer of electronic music, who for the past seven years has also worn another large hat, that of U.S. Secretary of Cultural Hygiene—our nation's lead watchdog in ensuring that the music and art we Americans are listening to and viewing is safe for us, and safe for our country. Secretary Bibbitt, welcome."

"Thank you, Stephanie. It's nice to be here."

"So—seven years into America's 'clean music' policy, at a time when many predicted the Rock Ban, as it's commonly known, would start to be loosened, the government actually seems to be enforcing the prohibition more aggressively than ever. Is that a fair assessment, in your view?"

"It's true, Stephanie, that we've been implementing some new technologies which are making it harder for lawbreakers to evade us. For example, as you probably know, our enforcement units now have portable Wi-Fi scanners that can enter any computer or mobile device within range, search through all audio and video files stored in them, and identify any that match our database of banned material. As a result, our apprehension rate is significantly higher than it was a few years ago. That said, we've always taken a firm approach in terms of searching out and prosecuting Cultural Hygiene violators. We simply have more cases to prosecute now."

"Wow—sounds like everyone should be double-checking the files on their old laptops! Does this mean that your mission to clean up America's music has been accomplished?"

"Our job is never done, Stephanie, but we've achieved a great deal. Working with Homeland Security and other agencies, our department's officers have confiscated hundreds of millions of illegal compact discs and DVDs, and facilitated the removal of literally billions of toxic digital music files from the nation's computers, tablets, mobile phones and MP3 players. At the same time, we've eliminated almost every trace of dangerous music from our domestic Internet."

"And of course people can still enjoy their favorite movies, simply by trading in their versions for copies with new government-approved soundtracks—isn't that right?"

"That's correct. As most people know, this is a free government service. All they have to do is bring or send their DVDs or digital video files to their regional Cultural Hygiene office. We'll provide you with a safe, alternate version within six weeks."

Stephanie glanced down briefly at her notes, then looked up brightly. "As an artist yourself, what do you say to critics who complain about the loss of creative integrity when a famous movie like, say, *Apocalypse Now,* no longer has the Doors song 'The End' as the background track for its opening sequence—but instead has an orchestral composition from Rachmaninoff?"

Martin suppressed a grimace of irritation. "I'm glad you chose that example," he replied evenly. "That particular musical passage was selected with great care. I might add that the film's director, Francis Ford Coppolla, who happily is still with us, gave the new soundtrack his blessing."

Stephanie glanced down again. "I believe his actual quote was, 'At my age, I've learned to roll with the bullets,'" she said smoothly. "Meanwhile, of course, classic rock movies like the Beatles' *A Hard Day's Night* and The Who's *Quadrophenia* have vanished from the U.S. market altogether, along with the albums by the same name."

"Ridiculous films glorifying hooliganism for its own sake. Good riddance, I say! I'm sure the vast majority of Americans agree with me."

"Yes, I see. But does it concern you that hundreds of thousands of Americans continue to travel outside our borders for the sole purpose of listening to both live and recorded music that is illegal here in the United States?"

By now Bibbitt was seething. *What's this little bitch trying to pull?* he thought furiously. *Her television station is owned by a company that does half its business with the Department of Defense. Does she think she can fuck me over and get away with it?*

"We can't control what U.S. citizens do outside our borders," he said with a forced smile. "But I can tell you that since Congress outlawed the most dangerous forms of rock-based music, America has seen across-the-board improvements in every measure of mental health. Most important of all, we've had no major terrorist incidents since then—which I'm convinced is no coincidence. We all remember what happened eight years ago up in the Boundary Waters, and we all know how important it is to keep the Leveler cult of Musicology from ever propagating in this country again."

"What about the fact that, despite your best efforts, a sizeable number of people still appear to be secretly listening to banned music right here in the U.S.?" the interviewer persisted. "For example, we've been hearing ongoing media reports of illicit file sharing, using informal networks linked directly to each other through Bluetooth technology. Does this concern you?"

"As you know from these same media reports, our law enforcement agencies are constantly on the watch for these violations," Bibbitt said coldly. "We have electronic scanners deployed across the nation that are perfectly capable of intercepting Bluetooth communications and locating their sources. Investigations are ongoing, and arrests are being made on a daily basis."

"So you disagree with those who think the ban on rock-based music represents an overreaction on the part of the Federal government—or even, as some civil liberties advocates claim, an excuse to silence any viewpoints critical of the Administration and the Republican Congress?"

"If you're referring to Leveler propaganda, then I hardly think we need to apologize for depriving them of a platform for their poisonous drivel," he replied, his speech quickening. "The steps we've taken are not only commensurate with the threat, but essential to our national security. It's been scientifically proven that medium- to fast-tempo music, utilizing amplified instruments and vocals and heavy, staccato percussion—in plain language, rock music—literally *changes the brain chemistry* of listeners in a way that promotes psychological instability, a false sense of individual aggrandizement, and a blindly destructive, anti-social anger against established institutions...including our government *and* the nuclear family."

Bibbitt paused to catch his breath. "My point, Stephanie," he continued in a calmer tone, "is that we are protecting our citizens from a dangerous, proven threat."

"On the other hand, some psychologists speculate that rock music is actually a healthy emotional outlet," said Stephanie, "and that humans have an innate need for this form of musical expression. Take, for example, the thriving culture of rock band channelers in the Urban Zones—a culture that actually seems to be growing rather than shrinking, as the government had predicted."

"Innate? I hardly think that early humans evolved listening to amplified guitars," Martin snorted. "As for the Urban Zones, they are regions where drug addicts, petty criminals and mentally disturbed individuals have unfortunately been allowed to congregate. The laws in these sectors are far too lax. We're in the process of taking steps to deal with that."

"Really?" The young woman's reporting antennae were quivering now. "Can you provide us with any details regarding the government's plans for the UZ? Are they considering a new court challenge to the Zones' free speech exemption?"

Belatedly, Martin realized he'd gone too far. "No, no," he said hastily. "I'm not talking about any formal policy decisions. However, we are continuing to monitor the situation."

"Interesting. Finally, on a more personal note, have you been able to do any composing of your own music recently, given your extensive responsibilities?"

Martin was so angry he was barely listening. "What? Yes...I've been working on a couple of projects. But there's really so little time..."

"I understand. And it appears we're out of time, as well. We've been chatting with Secretary of Cultural Hygiene Martin Bibbitt, guardian of America's artistic sensibilities. Thank you so much for making time in your busy schedule to speak with us."

"My pleasure," he hissed.

His makeup removed, Bibbitt hurried toward his waiting car, three assistants in tow. "Who the *hell* was that?" he asked in a low voice.

"Daughter of some United Electric exec," one aide said guardedly. "She's new, sir. She didn't know what she was doing."

"I want her off the air—permanently," he growled. "Explain to her parents that she'll be far better off in a different line of work. And I want this segment killed, and any recordings destroyed."

"Understood," his assistant replied. "I'll look into it."

"Don't look into it. *Do it,*" Bibbitt snapped. "If this interview—or that young idiot's face—appear on a TV screen in the future, *anywhere,* you'll be looking into a new job. Got it?"

The aide swallowed hard as the color drained from his face. "Got it," he muttered.

FOUR

Over the Hills and Far Away

BLAKE'S PLAN WAS TO DRIVE east and connect with the grid of desert roads leading to the Sierra Nevada. If he could reach the state parkland in the foothills and ditch his car, he should be able to evade any searchers for at least a day or two—enough time to plan his next move.

As he drove, he ticked through the agents' likely actions: By now, they'd have rung the front doorbell of his parents' house. Getting no answer, they would have barged in, arrest warrant in hand, to find the house empty. The note in his bedroom would send them to the nature reserve, a five-minute drive away. Combing the reserve's footpaths for him might take anywhere from thirty minutes to an hour. Failing to find him there, the agents would return to the house, where a more thorough search would reveal that the turntable and records were missing.

At that point, of course, they'd begin to suspect he'd flown the coop. They would go back and question Carter, who would probably feel compelled to mention Blake's homemade car sooner or later—though, knowing Carter, he'd stall as long as possible before "remembering" it. A radio call to other Federal agents in the area—it wasn't Homeland Security's style, Blake knew, to involve local law enforcement on this sort of thing—and they'd begin fanning out over the local roads. Blake's roadster was certain to be spotted on some intersection surveillance cameras. Eventually they'd pick up his trail, maybe even call in helicopters or a drone to assist in looking for him. But that would all take time. He estimated he had at least a two-hour head start—long enough, hopefully, to vanish into the wilderness, where his trackers would never find him.

By half-past noon, he'd climbed 2,500 feet up the western slope of the wooded Laguna Mountains and dropped another half-mile down the other side, speeding into the heart of the Colorado Desert. For the previous hour and a half Blake had been checking his rearview mirror constantly, looking for the growing speck on the horizon that would indicate a car closing fast, but the few vehicles he'd noticed on the road behind him had all been swiftly left behind. The Silver Beetle was running like a champ, hugging the two-lane desert road at a steady 75 mph. He'd counted only a handful of cars driving in the opposite direction and none in the last quarter-hour. Another five minutes and he'd be at the turnoff.

Feeling a surge of elation, he dug into his jacket and pulled out the object he'd taken from the light fixture on the roof deck. It was a portable MP3 player, filled with hundreds of illegal albums. Blake unwound the thin copper wrapper, designed to block any electromagnetic scanners passing through the neighborhood, and stared at the device in his hand. Had the searchers found this, too? He was suddenly struck by the enormity of the risk he'd been running these past few years. Why had he done it? What was the hold that this music had over him?

Whatever the reasons might be, it was too late now. Steering with his left hand, he plugged the player into the car's stereo system, the vehicle's only non-vital piece of equipment—*another testament to my addiction,* he thought—and cued up the album *Fresh Cream*. With a whoop, he pressed harder on the accelerator. Shouting to hear himself over the roar of the wind and the car's motor, he began singing at the top of his lungs to "I Feel Free," as the sounds of Jack Bruce's bass and Ginger Baker's high hat and Eric Clapton's guitar poured out of the speakers and swirled briefly around him, before being whisked away in the hot desert air.

❖ ❖ ❖

"Crown Him with many crowns, as thrones before Him fall..."

The amplified voices of the blue-robed choir, eighty strong, combined with the notes of the electronic organ player, guitarist and bass player to fill the domed auditorium. Across the hall, five thousand worshippers stood on their feet and sang along.

"Crown Him, ye kings, with many crowns, for He is King of all!"

The choir hit the last chord and held it for two bars, then cut out sharply. At a signal from the choirmaster, they dropped as one into their folding seats and looked expectantly toward the lectern.

"Thank you, brothers and sisters," said Pastor Kenmore Jones, gesturing at them with a manicured hand as he beamed his pleasure. From a huge video screen on the wall behind the megachurch's raised altar, a 20-foot-high image of his face did the same.

"That concludes today's service," he continued, turning back to the rows of smiling worshippers. "Go forth into the world filled with the Lord's truth, and do good works in his name—that is my charge to you. As always, there will be church representatives in the lobby, ready to accept your donations. Bless you, my brethren, and may God's love watch over you."

He remained at the lectern while the organist pounded out the recessional and the congregation streamed out the open double doors at the back of the church. When no one remained in the cavernous room but the volunteers collecting discarded programs, he turned and opened a concealed door set into the wall behind him. Stepping through it, he walked briskly along a maze of corridors to his large executive suite overlooking the children's playground and the sun-drenched Texas landscape beyond.

Nodding at his executive assistant, an attractive woman in her early thirties, the pastor strode into his office and shut the thick door behind him. Settling into his chair, he reached for the keyboard of his computer and typed in a series of letters and numbers. As the large screen lit up, he saw nine faces floating on the monitor, each in its own black-bordered rectangle.

"Welcome, Brother Jones," said the face in the top left corner, his baritone voice resounding from a speaker on the pastor's desk. "We weren't sure you'd be joining us today."

"Sorry about that, Brother Crawford," drawled the pastor. "I had a guest preacher delivering the sermon. Seems he was enjoying his message so much, he lost track of the time."

A ripple of knowing laughter came from the computer's sound system as the grid of heads nodded.

"Just be glad it wasn't Brother Raskin," said the first speaker, "or you'd still be sitting there!" The group guffawed again as Reverend Raskin held up his fists, ready to do battle.

"As I was starting to tell the group," Pastor Crawford continued, "today's agenda concerns the Cultural Hygiene laws—which, as you all know, are up for their annual review by the appropriate House and Senate committees this fall."

"That shouldn't be a problem, right?" said one of the on-screen faces. "My understanding is that the election prospects are looking quite good for our friends in the Republican Party—better than good, as a matter of fact."

"That's true," nodded Pastor Crawford. "However, we don't want to take any chances. I'll outline our lobbying strategy in a moment, but first we'll hear from Brother Huguenot, who has the latest results of our coalition survey."

"Thank you, Brother Crawford. I think we all have a clear sense of how powerfully our congregations support the ongoing fight to cleanse our nation of the Devil's music. But it may be helpful to see some actual numbers in this regard. The full results will be emailed to you later today, but the key piece of data to bear in mind is that our weighted sample found *ninety-four percent* of regular attendees at our member churches are either strongly or very strongly in favor of upholding the current Cultural Hygiene laws. What's more, sixty-eight percent actually favor increasing the legal penalties for those who violate them. Our survey of church leaders found a similar level of support. The general consensus is that the government's ban on rock-type music has helped boost church attendance, particularly among families with adolescent children, and has also provided the most potent focal point for leveraging contributions we've have ever had—better than the old Communist threat *or* the campaign against gay marriage."

"I can confirm that from personal experience," broke in another talking head. "We've been holding monthly rallies to promote continued vigilance against the Satanic influence of rock and roll, and let me tell you, they are a cash cow. People can't write checks fast enough!"

"Which leads me to our next point," said Pastor Crawford. "While there's no question about the Cultural Hygiene laws being allowed to lapse, there has been talk among some of the Blue State GOP congressmen about modifying certain aspects of the law. One proposal being actively discussed, for example, is the idea of turning first offenses into misdemeanors—sort of like a speeding ticket. Needless to say, the coalition leadership plans to vigorously oppose any watering down of these laws. If you or any of our colleagues are having doubts in this regard, I hope these latest survey results will ease your minds."

"Listen, if my folks had their way, every one of those hippie-loving scofflaws would do jail time, no questions asked," said one pastor, speaking against the backdrop of a blue lake.

"One strike and you're out!" shouted someone, bringing another round of laughter from the group.

"Yes," said Pastor Crawford, clearing his throat. "At any rate, as Chairman of the Executive Committee, I'm requesting that we vote today to authorize release of a substantial sum of money from our general purpose funds, payable in three monthly installments to our lobbying firm in Washington. These funds will be used for one purpose: convincing our friends in Congress not only to keep the Cultural Hygiene laws intact, but to strengthen them if possible—especially in regard to the Urban Zones. They know how vital the church-going vote is going to be this November. I'm quite sure they'll heed our message."

"How much are we talkin' about?" said the pastor by the lake.

"Our strategic plan calls for investing $50 million in the current lobbying effort," said Pastor Crawford.

"That sounds fine to me," said Pastor Jones, gazing down from his office window at parents pushing their kids on the playground swings.

"But will it be enough?"

"If we need more, you'll be the first to know. All in favor?"

A chorus of 'Ayes' rose from the desk speaker.

"Thank you," Pastor Crawford smiled. "I'll see you all next Sunday. At that time, we'll discuss mobilizing our rank and file for some demonstrations around the Urban Zone Festival. Our plan is to give the pagans a healthy dose of some good, old-fashioned Christian hymns."

"All you need is God," someone sang in an off-key tenor.

When Pastor Jones shut down his connection a few moments later, his colleagues were still chuckling.

Blake's destination was the Carrizo Badlands, an arid stretch of crags and canyons at the eastern end of the 60,000-acre Anza-Borrego Desert State Park. He'd camped there a number of times in his teens. With no paved roads to speak of and hundreds of miles of intersecting hiking trails, it was an area someone could easily lose himself in.

The desert sun was directly overhead now. His eyes shaded by his hat, Blake kept his gaze fixed on the roadbed to his right. At last he spotted the landmark he'd been looking for—a large growth of pink-colored cactus. Steering left across the pavement to the opposite side of the road, he rolled to a stop on the dirt shoulder and killed the engine.

After two hours of air rushing past his ears, the silence was unnerving. Blake stared down the road in both directions through his binoculars, then turned his gaze upward at the cloudless sky, searching for a tiny speck indicating a circling drone.

Nothing.

Climbing out, he pushed the car another few yards off the road to where a three-foot-wide rock ridge ran parallel to the shoulder. On the other side of the ridge, a smooth sheet of sandstone the size of a football field stretched into the desert. Hoisting up the car's front end, Blake propped its two tires up on the ridge and then walked around to the back of the car. With a grunt of effort, he lifted the rear end off the ground and inched forward until the front tires rolled off the ridge and thudded onto the sandstone slab. He kept moving until the back tires had cleared the ridge as well and the car sat flat on the sandstone surface.

Getting behind the wheel again, he used the electric drive to make his way slowly across the slab to its far side, where the rock surface sloped gently downward to meet the hard-packed desert floor. Hearing the soft hiss of earth beneath his tires, he continued around the perimeter of a wide rock formation that jutted a dozen feet out of the ground, finally halting beside a large patch of brambles. He was now on the far side of the rock formation, out of the sightline of anyone driving along the road. Over the years, he'd often stowed his motor scooter inside the dense thicket. Hopping out of the Silver Beetle, Blake walked to the brambles and lifted a low clump of branches to reveal a cave-like space underneath. Holding up the branches with one arm, he began slowly pushing the small car into the opening. A minute later, it was completely hidden in the undergrowth.

Tearing off a small branch, Blake made his way back across the sandstone slab to where it met the roadside. Starting at the pavement's edge, he carefully smoothed over his tire tracks and footprints. When he was done, he walked to the other side of the rock surface and did the same to the tire tracks leading into the brush, then stood pondering his handiwork. To a casual observer, it would be impossible to tell anyone had turned off here. Eventually the authorities might search the area and find his car—but by then he'd have disappeared into the desert.

A wave of exhilaration swept over Blake. He looked west, in the direction of his unseen pursuers. *"Fuck you!"* he screamed, his words floating over the silent plain.

He was being sophomoric, he knew, but there was something empowering about hearing his own voice cutting through the vast emptiness. He opened his mouth and shouted again:

"Rock and roll will never die!"

Feeling a little foolish now, Blake listened as the sound was swallowed by the desert. A light wind had sprung up, causing the scattered islands of plant life to quiver slightly. He took a last glance at the road and then turned to face the foothills, a mile in the distance. "Full speed ahead," he murmured. Settling the backpack on his shoulders, he began striding purposefully over the sun-baked desert floor.

Once in the hills he climbed steadily, following the trail through a series of switchbacks. Every few minutes he paused to study the desert stretched out below him through his binoculars. After an hour and a half, he was rewarded with the sight of a black SUV whizzing along the ribbon of road in the distance. As he watched, it sped past the spot where his car was stashed and disappeared around the bend.

With an abrupt laugh, Blake walked on through a stand of cactus. Up ahead, the trail led through a shallow, winding canyon. He stopped and pulled out his MP3 player from his pack. Placing the attached buds in his ears, he scrolled down the list of recordings to *Black Market Clash*. He hit the play button and then pushed on into the stone passage, propelled by the hoarse strains of Joe Strummer singing "Bankrobber" inside some forgotten Manchester recording studio in the dead of winter, two decades before he was born.

By seven o'clock that evening Blake was deep into the badlands. Even with his heavy pack and the hilly terrain he estimated he was averaging close to three miles an hour, meaning he'd covered nearly 20 miles. He stopped to sip from his canteen, which he'd been careful to refill at every stream and spring he'd passed. The temperature was still close to the 100-degree mark—the end of another typical August day in the Greenhouse Age, as the environmentalists were calling it. One thing Blake had never understood about the Republicans was their steadfast refusal to acknowledge the reality of climate change, even as the sea levels inched up and the earth baked around them. They reminded him of a little kid covering his ears and humming loudly to himself so he couldn't hear his parents admonishing him. *Just one more way they've abused the term conservative,* he thought, mopping his brow.

An hour later, as the sun descended toward the desert rim, Blake felt the heat finally start to ease. Leaving his pack beside the trail he scrambled onto a rock outcropping that jutted into open space, hundreds of feet above the sandy plain. Careful not to get too close to the edge, he stood there for several minutes sweeping his binoculars across the rolling expanse of trails he'd traveled that afternoon, looking for the telltale bobbing of another hiker's head in the slanting light. Seeing no one, he turned and walked on.

During his hours of hiking, the rush of outright panic had slowly dissipated, chased away by The Grateful Dead, Bob Dylan, U2, Patti Smith, T Rex, the Animals, Muddy Waters, and other old friends. Their music was like spiritual food to him, Blake reflected as he strode along. Nowadays, when he saw kids walking across the Berkeley campus with their earphones, nodding to whatever sanitized music they happened to be playing, he invariably felt a pang of sadness at the thought of what they were missing.

"I don't know what I'd do, if I couldn't get back to La Jolla every now and then to recharge on my vinyl and remember what music is really all about," he'd told his uncle Frank a few months earlier. "I'm not sure I could function."

"I know what you mean, buddy," Frank, his musical guide since childhood, had replied. "It's like banning a religion. What the government is doing is criminal, if you ask me."

The longer he walked, the clearer his thinking became. In the late afternoon, somewhere between Bowie's "Station to Station" and Smashmouth's "Walking on the Sun," a rudimentary plan began coalescing in his brain. The key, he decided, was to find some kind of leverage—something that would let him dictate the terms of his surrender, instead of meekly letting the Feds force a future of their choosing onto him.

What was it Lennon said about Presley? *Elvis died the day he went into the army.*

"Not this cat," Blake muttered. "I've got too many lives left."

An hour later, the temperature had plunged and the landscape was enveloped in darkness. Using his flashlight to light the path in front of him, Blake walked another thirty minutes as the hiking trail turned deeper into the foothills, hugging the flank of a high sedimentary ridge. Finally he reached a spot where the rock wall next to the trail cut sharply inward at a right angle about seven feet off the ground, forming a wide, natural roof. It was a perfect place to build a fire without being seen from above.

Blake dropped his gear on the hard earth beneath the overhang. For the past half-hour he had been gathering twigs and branches in his tarp as he walked. Now he took out his knife and shaved off some slivers of wood for tinder, then propped a dozen twigs together to form a small teepee. Pushing the tinder underneath, he lit a match and watched the small branches quickly catch fire. He piled on a few larger branches and held his hands gratefully toward the flames. Even after donning his jacket, he was feeling the chill of the desert night.

Pulling a granola bar out of his backpack, he nibbled it slowly as he studied his topo map by flashlight. His goal the next day was the Salton Sea, an inland saltwater lake twenty-five miles to the east. It would be a full day's walk over open, hot terrain. There was one pay phone along the route that he knew of. If it was still working—a big if—then his plan was to telephone his uncle, who lived an hour to the west, and try to arrange a nighttime meeting in the Salton area, a place they were both familiar with.

Frank, he was sure, would have some ideas about what he should do. Blake couldn't run forever, and he didn't want to. Part of him still believed the whole thing was simply a mistake that could be easily rectified. He was no activist, after all. His only crime was loving music—maybe a little too much, but still…if the government wanted access to his research that badly, they could have simply asked him.

Blake's breakthrough had started as a hobby. His doctoral thesis at Berkeley was a theoretical exploration of the many-worlds concept—the idea, derived from quantum mechanics, that there are a potentially infinite number of parallel universes, and that we are all simply experiencing one possible existence among countless versions of this "multiverse." The idea had always seemed fundamentally untenable to him, in part because he knew that nature, when faced with the prospect of ever-increasing complexity, tended to veer back to its simplest foundations.

Eventually, as he pored over the various aspects of quantum theory, he began to notice that in each swath of probabilities, there was an area at the edge of the mathematical entities where a vanishingly small mathematical constant existed in vector form along the time axis. Time was supposed to be a scalar quantity in a single dimension, though. The presence of the vector meant that it had to have at least two dimensions—which suggested that time could move sideways as well as forward. As he pushed the calculations, he found that when multiple quantum elements were considered in combination, they coalesced around the same vector, taking on a single direction that curved outward from the normal path of time up to a certain point, then curved back toward and across the center line of time again, repeating this process indefinitely. The more particles that were combined together, the more distinct the curve became.

By extrapolation, this meant that all existing quantum probabilities converged on a single, unified future—but one that held a certain degree of variability on the local level. In other words, there was only one possible world, and one ultimate future—a future that had already been determined to a certain extent, but that still had the potential to unfold in a somewhat unpredictable way. *Einstein was right after all,* he realized, as one calculation after another yielded similar results. *In the long run, God doesn't play dice with the universe.*

He gave the name "random convergence" to the theory he'd discovered. Its general thrust was that while quantum mechanics played out in a purely random way locally, on a universal scale the random events largely cancelled each other out, forcing reality onto a single convergent pathway. He'd made several presentations on the subject at conferences, and was putting the final touches to what promised to be a seminal journal article on the subject.

Based on his work, the head of the Berkeley physics department had offered him a tenure-track position on the faculty, and a dozen other leading universities had reached out with informal offers as well.

Blake has politely rebuffed them all. "I can't see myself in academia for the rest of my life," he explained to Mel. "It feels too—"

"Dull?" Mel finished with a sardonic smile. "You may have a point. But don't kid yourself. If you go to work for some high-tech corporation, you'll just find yourself wearing a different set of golden handcuffs."

Oddly, the more progress Blake made on his random convergence theory, the more it bored him. In the evenings, he'd gotten in the habit of putting the mind-bending equations aside and going to the lab instead, where he spent hours fiddling with his true obsession: a quantum communication device. Blake's secret dream was to build a machine that would use quantum entanglement to transmit digital information—including recorded music—in a way that couldn't be intercepted or detected by the authorities. "If I can build a communicator that lets me transmit the Beatles' first album from my house to the beach without being detected by the music police, I'll die a happy man," he told Mel over beers one night.

"Only you, Blake," Mel had laughed. "Everyone else wants this technology to rule the world, and all you care about is taking 'Twist and Shout' surfside."

The more Blake thought about random convergence, the more possible quantum communication seemed. One of the theory's corollaries held that since particles in a quantum state curved sideways through time, this curvature would accelerate the movement of electromagnetic radiation passing over the quantized particles, causing a slight increase in the frequency of the electromagnetic waves. If the same entangled mass got larger or smaller, this acceleration would either grow or diminish proportionally. By getting enough entangled electrons together in one place and then using a Doppler device to measure these tiny changes in frequency, Blake could detect an individual electron collapse without evaluating the actual particles. It was a way out of the closed envelope dilemma.

Spurred by a new sense of purpose, Blake roamed through the school's physics and engineering departments, scavenging parts for a conductor-superconductor apparatus that could generate a continuous stream of entangled electron pairs. After the device was constructed, he added a super-conducting "Y" junction to split the pairs, guiding the newly separated electrons into matching lithium fluoride crystal lattices, where they became trapped inside impurities in the crystal structures.

Once the lattices were full, he experimented on them using a computer-guided laser to interact with selected electrons in the crystals, causing the electrons to collapse out of their quantum state—in which they literally possessed two different spins at once—into a classical state, in which each laser-treated electron took on a single definite spin, while its entangled partner took on the opposing spin.

"Before the entangled electrons collapse, Schroedinger's cat is dead *and* alive. After they collapse, he's either dead or he's not," is how he explained it to Ann once, alluding to the Austrian physicist's famous thought equation from the 1930s.

"Thanks, but I'll take Yeats anytime," she'd quipped. "When I'm reading him, I *know* I'm alive!"

While this laser-driven collapse was occurring, a Doppler meter attached to the other crystal lattice was measuring the frequency of a microwave beam generated by a diode on the other side of the crystal. It was capable of making thousands of precise measurements each second, which meant that in theory it could capture each shift in frequency indicating that another electron had been collapsed—information that the meter's computer recorded as a binary digit "one." By going through the electrons on the sending crystal in a predetermined order and collapsing selected particles, this approach would allow him to send a series of ones and zeros that the computer on the receiving end interpreted as a digital signal, just as if it was scanning a prerecorded CD.

There was a problem, though: The crystals Blake was using could only be coaxed to hold a few hundred thousand entangled electrons at a time—not enough to have a measurable effect on the radiation beam. One warm evening in early summer, he'd been brooding over the problem of how to construct a lattice that could hold more electrons. To occupy himself, he started cleaning out the desk drawers in his office.

Stumbling across an old joint that Carter had given him a year earlier, he went up to the roof of the physics building for a smoke. It was there, gazing over the treetops of the Berkeley campus, that he had a sudden memory of growing crystals in a salt solution as a young boy. *That's it,* he thought. *I've just got to build a better crystal.*

The next day, he approached a chemist friend who supplied him with containers holding dozens of exotic salt constituents. He spent a week growing various types of salt crystals, bombarding them with an ion gun to create vacancies in their crystal lattices, and then feeding electrons into them. He finally struck pay dirt with a salt made of bromine combined with laborium—an artificial metal, recently created in a German lab, that was known for its extreme malleability. To his amazement, the laborium bromide crystal soaked up as many electrons as he could generate. When he stopped an hour later, the lattice held what he guessed to be around a billion entangled electrons—enough not only to generate a detectable wave pattern, but also to transmit multiple megabytes of digital information. *It's a storage battery for entangled particles,* he thought. Just as important, the entangled electrons were remarkably stable. When stored at sub-freezing temperatures, the electron-filled lattices retained their effectiveness for weeks.

Blake didn't tell anyone about his discovery. Working in the evenings, he created several dozen laborium bromide lattices on silicone wafers, filled them to the brim with electrons, and stored them in one of the lab's freezers. Finally he was ready for his first full-scale test. He had already run the audio output from a CD player through an audio-to-digital converter, which was linked in turn to a computer-guided pulse laser that was programmed to move with lightning speed across the lattice in a preset pattern, stimulating only the "one" electrons in the crystal as instructed by the digital input. A few yards away, the receiving crystal was positioned between a microwave generator and a Doppler unit. The Doppler's computer had been programmed to correlate each frequency shift it detected with the original source of the disturbance in the electron array, following the same sequence the laser was using.

It was time to pull the trigger. Putting on a pair of headphones that ran to the receiving crystal, he pushed play to set a CD of Grieg's

"Peer Gynt Suite" spinning, then watched as the laser began pulsing across the crystal wafer. A few seconds later, he heard the strains of the Berlin Philharmonic Orchestra sounding clearly in his ears.

Blake felt suddenly light-headed. *This is it,* he thought. *I'm listening to the future of communication.*

When Blake decided to bring Mel up to speed in mid-August, the professor's first reaction had been skepticism.

"What about causality?" said the older man. He was talking about the main objection to faster-than-light communication—that it meant sending information backwards through time, effectively changing history.

"That's not a problem, according to random convergence," Blake replied. "My theory says the future is already set—that in the long run, it can't be changed. So it doesn't matter if information is sent backwards in time."

"The long run is one thing. How about in the short run?"

Blake shrugged. "In the short run, random convergence says that local history is in flux anyway. Our personal past could be changing constantly but we would never know it, since we can only recall memories from the timeline we're in now."

"Good grief." Mel leaned back in his desk chair, staring wordlessly at the ceiling.

"Hey, it happens all the time with neutrinos, right? And the world hasn't come to an end. Besides, the self-consistency theorem still holds precedence—it's mathematically impossible to change history in a way that negates your own existence. So we're all safe."

Blake's professor held up his hand. "Look, I'm not going to get into a philosophical discussion about determinism. Anyway, it's the practical side of your invention that matters now."

"Which is pretty cool, huh?" Blake prodded.

"If your invention really works, it's historic, I don't have to tell you that. You've beaten the Defense Department at their own game—which could be a problem."

"What do you mean?"

Instead of answering, Mel got up and walked to his office window. Outside, some students were throwing a Frisbee, laughing and cheering at each acrobatic catch. He stood there for a minute, watching the plastic disc skim back and forth over the green turf. Then he turned back to Blake with the air of someone who'd just made a decision.

"Given the nature of this discovery, I've got to report your work to the government," he said. "But I'd like to give the whole thing a rest until school starts up again next month. Why don't you go home and relax for a couple of weeks? All I ask is that you don't breathe a word about this to anyone. Not your parents, not your high school physics teacher—nobody. Understand?"

"Sure," said Blake, not quite sure he did. "I'll see you in September."

❖ ❖ ❖

Blake pulled out his blanket and wrapped it around him, then cued up Pink Floyd's *Dark Side of the Moon* on the MP3 player. Remembering the half-finished joint, he retrieved it from his backpack and fired it up with a match lit from the campfire. As he inhaled, he felt an incongruous sense of peace wash over him. What was it he used to tell himself, when he was worried about a big exam?

"It's all going to work out, Blake," he murmured.

"Breathe" was in his ears now, David Gilmour calling to the fleeing rabbit as it scrambled for its underground lair. Lying back, he looked up at the tapestry of stars in the desert sky, singing softly to Gilmour's caution-filled voice and steel guitar as he drifted into a fitful sleep.

In the DuPont Circle neighborhood of Washington D.C., a young man in white T-shirt and jeans signed out of the secure encrypted network on his classified laptop, then shut the computer down and closed it. Lighting a cigarette, he lay back on the couch of his studio apartment, lost in thought. It was past midnight, and the sidewalk outside his window had grown quiet. After a few minutes he sat up again and began shuffling through the stack of newspapers on his coffee table.

Finding what he was looking for, he took a prepaid calling card from his pocket and reached for his cordless phone. He punched in a series of numbers and then lay back again with the phone to his ear and his eyes closed, pulling deeply on his cigarette.

"Hello?" he said finally. His eyelids snapped open as he quickly stubbed the cigarette out. "Yes, this is John Quincy Adams. I came across something today that I think you'll find extremely interesting." He grunted, shaking his head. "Of course I realize it's Labor Day weekend. That's no problem—I've told you, I'm always on the system, weekends, holidays, whatever. No one will think twice about it." As he spoke, he absently rubbed the tattoo of an American bald eagle on the inside of his right wrist. "So, as I was saying..."

Crossing a small bridge, the man turned down a Venice side street and pedaled to the front entrance of a darkened house. Slowing to a stop, he hopped off his bike and leaned it against the stucco wall, then rapped softly on the door. It opened immediately, and the visitor was ushered into a dimly lit living room where a man sat cross-legged on a low couch.

"Greetings, Gulliver. What brings you out here so late?"

"Some news from our friend," the visitor said. "There's an arrest warrant out for Hawkes—the Berkeley physicist who's been experimenting with quantum stuff. A music possession charge."

"Hmm." The man on the couch thought deeply for a moment. When he spoke, it was in a low, rasping voice, just above a whisper. "He must have made a breakthrough we haven't heard about."

"But they didn't get him."

"What do you mean?"

"They failed to apprehend him at his family home in La Jolla. And now he's dropped out of sight."

"Interesting." The man closed his eyes and massaged his temples. "Someone must have warned him. But where can he go? He won't get far on the roads, obviously. Which means he must still be in the area, unless he managed to cross into Mexico. Any idea who he might contact?"

"I doubt he'll reach out to any of his academic colleagues—he knows the Feds will be monitoring them. He's got an uncle he's close to, a journalist. They're probably watching him, too, but Hawkes might risk getting in touch anyway."

"Yes, I remember. Frank Hawkes. Writes investigative pieces for that indie paper, the *SoCal Sentinel*. Specializes in political and financial corruption—the last of a dying breed. We're connected to him, right?"

"On an informal basis—strictly as needed."

"Well, he's needed now. Let's send someone over first thing in the morning. Give me a few minutes to compose a message."

FIVE

When the Music's Over

Monday, September 2

BLAKE WOKE WITH A START beside the charred remains of his campfire. It took him a few seconds to recall where he was, but the sight of his backpack brought back the previous day's events in a rush.

Got to keep moving. Standing up, he stretched stiffly. As he did, he glanced upward and noticed a two-foot-high crack running sideways where the overhang met the vertical rock wall. Drawing on his old rock-climbing moves, he wedged his feet into some low crevices on the stone face and hoisted himself up to inspect the opening. It extended inward for several feet, and along its left-hand edge another large crack branched sharply to the side, creating a small grotto. Because of the angle it was impossible to see into the space, but it looked about big enough to hold a small suitcase.

Blake dropped back to the ground. After thinking for a minute, he reached into his pack and took out the plastic-wrapped turntable and record albums. Spreading his tarp on the ground, he carefully placed the turntable in the center and laid the stack of records on top of it, then reached into his pocket and added his MP3 player to the pile. Wrapping the tarp tightly around the items, he hoisted the bundle over his head and, standing on his tiptoes, placed it on the ledge. Next, he grabbed a stick of firewood and climbed back up on the rock. Clinging to the wall by one handhold, he grasped the branch in his other hand and used it to slowly nudge the wrapped bundle back and leftward into the hidden space. It took ten minutes of awkward effort, but eventually he pushed the whole bundle far enough into the grotto that it was hidden from sight.

After making doubly certain that no one peering in could see any sign of the cache, Blake spent the next quarter-hour gathering up the remains of his fire and carrying them far off the trail. Once he'd eliminated all evidence of his overnight stay, he slipped on his pack—considerably lighter now—and continued east.

The ramshackle gas station on Route S22 was the only structure for miles. It appeared to be closed up tight for Labor Day, but Blake waited for several minutes in the bushes behind the concrete building to be sure. Finally, seeing no signs of life, he darted across the crumbling apron to the old pay phone on the side of the garage. The last time he'd been through here, two years ago, he had checked the relic out of sheer curiosity and found, to his astonishment, that it was still functioning.

Now, holding his breath, he said a quick mental prayer and picked up the receiver. When the dull hum of a dial tone reached his ear, he exhaled in relief, then punched in the number for the International Communications Hub, an automated service used by the Berkeley Physics Department that allowed members to place phone calls to and from anywhere in the world. To anyone monitoring the call, it would appear to be originating from a switching station in Golden, Colorado. Tracing the transmission back to this particular pay phone would take time, especially on a holiday weekend.

"Hello?"

"Uncle Frank—it's Blake."

There was an almost imperceptible hesitation on the other end of the line. *He knows the situation,* Blake thought. *Probably assumes they're tapping his phone.* When his uncle spoke, his tone was light. "Good to hear from you, buddy—it's been a while. How's life treating you?" It was a code phrase they'd used since Blake's early teenage days, a signal to slip into a form of double-speak in which everything Blake said meant its opposite. They'd hit on the formula as a way of sharing information that Blake didn't want his parents to know about.

"Everything's fine," said Blake. "I head back to Berkeley tomorrow." Translation: *Things aren't good, and I won't be returning to school any time soon.*

"Right. Only, I heard you split from La Jolla a little early—your dad called me last night, and was wondering if I'd heard from you," Frank said. His voice was matter-of-fact.

"Yeah. I decided to leave a day ahead of time in the old Silver Beetle and go driving along the coast," said Blake. "It still runs like a watch, after all these years. If I were closer, I'd drop by so you could take it for a spin." Translation: *I've ditched the car and I'm inland, not that far from you.*

"Too bad. But that's the problem with life in the real world—you can't do everything. How does the ocean look today?"

"Oh, the usual—medium surf, decent breakers. I wish I had just one more day, so I could camp out and so some fishing."

"A nice idea. If I had the time, I'd join you and cook up some of my famous fried flounder. Speaking of which, you've caught me at an awkward spot. I'm on deadline. Can we talk tonight, old salt? You can fill me in on everything then."

"Sure thing," said Blake. "Speak to you later."

Hanging up, he stood for a moment going over Frank's words in his mind. The conversation had gone exactly as he'd hoped. When he was younger, his family used to join Frank and his wife each year for a summer weekend of fishing and camping on the inland Salton Sea, the destination that Blake was heading for now. In their double-speak language, Frank had signaled that he would meet Blake this evening at their old campsite near the town of Salton Sea Beach.

It was noon, and Blake still had 15 miles of hiking in front of him. He filled his canteen with bitter-tasting water from a pump behind the station and drank it down with a grimace, then filled the canteen again. Shouldering his pack, he walked warily around to the front of the gas station and huddled in the shade of the building for a minute, surveying the road and the sky overhead. Satisfied that no cars or planes were in the vicinity, he sprinted across the sun-baked asphalt road to the shelter of the scrub pines on the other side, then began making his way along the rocky trail.

He'd gone about two hundred yards when he heard the unmistakable sound of helicopter rotors in the distance. Throwing himself to the ground, he pulled the tan blanket from his pack and covered himself with it, not moving a muscle. Several minutes later, two helicopters roared directly overhead, flying north. *Is it just a coincidence that they came over this spot, or do they have a bead on me?* he wondered. Blake's scientific training had taught him that the confluence of apparently related yet totally unconnected events was more common than most people realized. He lay still for another ten minutes, but the copters never returned. *Coincidence,* he decided at last.

By the time Blake reached the familiar campground, night had fallen. After hours of walking through blazing heat, the arrival of cool twilight was a welcome change. Even though his khaki clothing blended in with the landscape, Blake felt uncomfortably exposed in the open desert. Twice more, helicopters had appeared on the horizon, and each time he had taken cover until they were well away.

It had been years since he'd seen the campsite, but it looked exactly as he remembered—a half-dozen wooden picnic tables and attached benches, clustered around a stone fireplace with metal cooking grill and abbreviated chimney. Looking around, he felt a rush of nostalgia, recalling the happy times he and his family had spent there. Then he saw a shadowy figure emerge from behind the stone hearth.

"Blake."

"Uncle Frank," he said, wrapping his relative in a bear hug. "Are you a sight for sore eyes!"

"Emily doesn't know I'm meeting you. I told her I was going to interview an anonymous source," said Frank. "I also told her the source was probably hungry, so she made a couple of sandwiches. But first, here." He handed over a liter bottle of water. "There's more where that came from."

"Thanks." Blake downed the full liter, then took one of the meatloaf and lettuce sandwiches and bit in hungrily. All he'd eaten that day were two granola bars—his last. Frank watched as he wolfed down the first sandwich and tucked the second into his pack for later.

"Like I said over the phone, I spoke to your dad last night," he said. "Some Federal agents called him in Laguna, asking where you were. He told them that as far as he knew, you were still in La Jolla. Your parents and Becky are taking it all in stride—you don't have to worry about them."

Blake tried to picture his family's reaction at learning that Homeland Security was looking for him. His father would have been careful to offer no information beyond what was asked for, while inside his gears would have been whirring. Meanwhile, his mom must be frantic with worry. She was an Admiral's wife, though, and used to putting up a stoic front. His 16-year-old sister, Becky, on the other hand, probably viewed the whole thing as a grand adventure, more grist for the short stories she was always churning out.

"Then you have the basic outlines," said Blake. "You understand why I didn't want to discuss it over the phone."

Frank nodded. "You did the right thing," he said. "My line's been monitored for years. It comes with the territory. And if it hadn't been, they would have started tapping it as soon as you went missing. Now, tell me how *you're* holding up."

Frank listened closely as Blake recounted the details of the previous day. When Blake was done, he sat quiet for a moment. "I already knew most of the story, plus a little more," he said finally. "Earlier today, before you called me, I was contacted by some people with access to inside information from Homeland Security. They thought you might get in touch with me, so they filled me in. It seems your recent breakthrough caught the government by surprise. They've been pursuing the same technology with very limited results. Now, they're determined to bring your discovery under military control as quickly as possible. They figured the best way to do that was to apprehend you on a music possession charge, then plea bargain you into an army posting."

"Shit!" It was just as Blake had feared.

"The way I see it," Frank continued, "you have a couple of options. You could go home and turn yourself in—tell them you wanted to take one last trip into the wilderness, and that you had no idea anyone was looking for you."

"Just give myself up?"

"That's right. After all, the military wouldn't be that bad. You'd still be doing your research, just in uniform."

"I don't think I have any alternative," Blake said sadly. "I can't stay out here forever."

His uncle stood rubbing his chin. "There *is* another way," he said. "You could go public—share your knowledge with the world. Your work hasn't been classified yet, so you won't be committing any crime if you do. Once your technology is in the public domain, the government will have a lot less incentive to keep you under their thumb. There's even a chance they might drop the music possession charges and let you go on your way."

"But how can I do that, hiding in the desert?"

"What if I told you that some people are prepared to shelter you, somewhere you're not likely to be found anytime soon?" said Frank.

"What do you mean?"

"The people I've been talking to are proposing to hide you in the Urban Zone."

Blake chuckled incredulously. "You mean, with the lunatic fringe?"

"What better place to lay low? And if the Feds do track you down, you'll have an excuse for being there. It's a natural refuge for someone going through a psychological crisis."

Blake stood in the darkened picnic grounds, thinking furiously. What Frank was saying made a certain amount of sense. If he went back now, it was an almost sure bet he'd be spending a good chunk of the next decade as an Army scientist—assuming they didn't decide to press charges and take him to trial. But if he could somehow manage to evade capture until his research was published and there were some working prototypes in circulation, the authorities would no longer have any reason to sit on him.

There was another attractive aspect to Frank's suggestion, one that he was reluctant to admit to himself: The idea of plunging into the unknown held an innate appeal for him. *What's wrong with me?* he wondered, yet again.

"It's a lot to process," he said.

"Unfortunately, you don't have much time," his uncle replied. "The clock is ticking. Speaking of which, let's make sure your watch is accurate." He pulled out a small flashlight and shone it on the face of Blake's quartz crystal timepiece, then looked at his own digital watch. "On the dot," he said. "Now, here's what's going to happen: At precisely seven o'clock tomorrow morning, and I mean *precisely,* a vehicle is going to pull into the scenic overlook two miles north of here. You need to be there, out of sight but ready to move. Someone will get out of the vehicle and begin taking photographs of the lake. He or she will wait exactly five minutes, then drive away. If you decide to go with that person, you need to approach him within that time frame and say the following code phrase: 'Can you give a stranger a lift?' That person will then reply, 'A stranger is just a friend you haven't met yet.' Got that?"

"Doesn't sound too tough," said Blake, smiling in spite of himself.

"If you go with them," Frank added, "I'll call your parents and tell them I spoke with you, and that you're fine and just need some time on your own to figure out your future. If you decide not to take the leap, I'll come by the same spot two hours later to pick you up. We'll drive back to San Diego, you can greet the Feds politely, and we'll forget everything we just spoke about."

"Okay."

Blake didn't tell his uncle, but he already knew which way he was going to go.

The older man hesitated. "I'm not sure you want to hear this," he said, "but Ann called me, too."

Blake drew in a sharp breath. "We agreed we wouldn't try to contact each other."

"Apparently she spoke with your professor, who mentioned you were coming back early to meet with the authorities. She tried to e-mail you yesterday. When you didn't reply, she called your cell phone several times. You didn't pick up or call back, which wasn't like you, so she got worried and phoned me. I told her I had no idea where you were."

Frank reached out and squeezed his nephew's shoulders. "It's never bad to have people who care about you," he said softly. "Good luck, Blake." He turned and walked through the silent campsite to the pathway that led toward the parking lot below. Then the darkness swallowed him, and Blake was alone again.

SIX

Welcome to the Jungle

Tuesday, September 3

BLAKE'S WATCH ALARM WENT OFF at five in the morning, wrenching him from a dream where he'd been wandering endlessly through the halls of some luxury hotel, searching for a room he couldn't locate. After burying the remains of his campfire he set out on the two-mile trek to the overlook, an oval patch of asphalt located fifty yards from the county road on a promontory high above the lake's surface. Blake got there a little before six, as the sun's first rays were reaching the lake's brown and orange rim. With his pack in his arms, he nestled into a crevice at the far end of the circle, where he had an unobstructed view of the overlook and the road leading up to it.

Fifteen minutes passed, then thirty. Fighting the urge to sleep, Blake opened his canteen and splashed some water on his face. At 6:50, the purr of an engine sounded in the distance. Holding his breath, he watched as a compact car pulled into the rest area and stopped. A young couple sat up front. In the seat behind them, a baby lay sleeping in a rear-facing child carrier. Blake studied the car, debating whether to approach them. Frank had stressed that his contact would arrive at seven o'clock sharp, which wasn't for another ten minutes. They must have shown up early, he decided, and now they were stalling for time.

After a minute or two, the couple got out and spread a map over the car hood. They appeared to be arguing over directions: the man jabbed at the map with his finger and the woman shook her head stubbornly. Striding away from the vehicle, the man stood gazing moodily at the lake while the woman went to check on the sleeping infant. *Any second now, he'll take out a camera,* Blake told himself, getting ready to emerge from his hiding place.

Instead, the man spun on his heel abruptly and walked quickly back to the car. After saying something that Blake couldn't make out, he climbed into the driver's seat and slammed the door shut. The woman hurriedly tucked a blanket around the baby, then walked around to the passenger side and got in. The car drove swiftly out of the rest area, and all was quiet again.

Crouched in his rocky perch, Blake cursed through clenched teeth. Obviously, these were the people he was supposed to meet. Who else would visit this remote spot at the crack of dawn? Somehow he'd gotten his signals crossed.

You blew it! he thought, a wave of despair engulfing him. There was nothing left but to wait for Frank. Thanks to his indecision, his golden opportunity had slipped through his fingers.

Then, in the midst of his self-recriminations, Blake heard it: The hum of another motor in the distance. He ducked down in the rocks, praying for a second chance. A minute later, a pink stretch limousine with mirrored windows cruised slowly into the rest area and eased to a stop. The doors flew open and three long-haired men climbed out clutching beer bottles. With sinking heart, Blake realized it had to be another false alarm. The men were dressed like something out of an L.A. rock magazine from the 1980s, in skin-tight black leather pants and sleeveless body shirts. The first man out of the car had heavily muscled shoulders and a sullen, brooding air. With his opaque sunglasses and black top hat perched high on a mane of curly dark hair, he looked oddly familiar to Blake. The second man wore a billed newsboy cap and had a cigarette dangling from his lips. The third was hatless with mascara-laden eyelashes and a huge shock of almost translucent blond hair that cascaded halfway down his back.

As Blake watched from his lookout, a door on the far side of the limo opened and a fourth man in a leather vest stepped regally onto the asphalt. His bare arms were covered with tattoos and a red handkerchief was knotted around his blonde, shoulder-length hair. Ignoring his companions, he stood gazing around through aviator-style sunglasses, an enigmatic smile tugging at the corners of his mouth.

"A truly awesome view," said the man in the top hat loudly, staring at the lake. "I think I'm turning into a nature lover in my old age."

"Save it for your shrink," snarled the man in the cap.

"James—oh, *James!*" shouted Top Hat. "Could you find it in your cold, cold heart to bring us the fucking *cameras?*"

The driver's door opened and a tiny man in a chauffeur's uniform climbed out, stooping under the weight of four expensive-looking cameras slung around his neck. Bending forward, he stood stock still as the men took turns pulling the straps over his head. While the first three raced back to the overlook and began snapping away, the man in the aviator shades stayed put. Holding the camera's viewfinder up to his eye, he slowly panned the telescopic lens across the rest area until it pointed straight at Blake's hiding place.

Staring at the men with their cameras, the thought hit Blake like a thunderbolt: *Could these nut jobs be my contact?*

He glanced at his watch: One minute after seven. It was a gamble he had to take. Shouldering his backpack, he hopped down from his niche and walked uncertainly toward the group. To his surprise, they barely acknowledged his sudden appearance. The only reaction came from the Aviator, who kept his lens trained on Blake's face as he drew closer.

"Now, *that's* a sunrise," Top Hat was remarking sarcastically. "This shot's going right up on my Facebook page."

"Excuse me," said Blake awkwardly. "Uh...can you give a stranger a lift?"

"Well," said The Cap, turning to stare at him. "Look what the fucking *cat* dragged in! Let me guess: You're a deserter from the Park Service, seeking political asylum."

"Personally, I don't approve of giving rides to strangers," shuddered Top Hat. "I've seen *way* too many horror flicks."

"Easy, my over-exuberant comrades," said the Aviator, lowering his camera at last. "After all, a stranger is just a friend you haven't met yet.

Isn't that so... stranger?"

"I think that's a sound philosophy," said Blake cautiously.

"Sound philosophy?" growled The Cap. "Oh, *now* I get it—you're a rare desert nerd, venturing from your book-lined burrow!"

"The good news," Top Hat continued, "is that we have plenty of room in this palace on wheels, now that our groupies have gone home to their mommies for breakfast. But you've got to promise not to slit our throats and steal our blow." He held out the small finger of his left hand expectantly.

"Sure, I promise," said Blake, shaking pinkies sheepishly. The whole scene was too absurd to take seriously. At this point, though, he had no choice but to see it through.

"What are we waiting for?" said The Cap. "This wilderness crap is triggering my agoraphobia, big time."

"Oh, *James,*" called Top Hat. "If it's not too much to ask of your Satanic Majesty, can we get the fuck out of here, *pronto?*"

Muttering under his breath, the chauffeur gathered up the cameras and climbed back behind the wheel while the other men pushed Blake into the rear compartment and tumbled after him. With a screech of tires, the limousine circled tightly on the pavement and sped back toward the main road.

Inside the limo, a sudden mood of calm prevailed. The Aviator pushed a button and a panel rose behind the driver's compartment, shutting James off from the group. "I hate to do it," he said with a wink. "Eavesdropping is his main pleasure in life, you know." The man in the mascara stretched out on the back seat of the vehicle and immediately fell asleep, as Top Hat immersed himself in the *Los Angeles Times* and The Cap stared out the tinted windows at the rocky landscape. Meanwhile, the Aviator turned his attention on Blake.

"Down to business," he said. "It's time to create the new you."

"The new me?" repeated Blake.

"Your new identity, man! The person you shall *become,* as opposed to the person you will no longer be. First, you need to lose those clothes. Then we'll clean you up."

As Blake peeled down to his running shorts, the Aviator placed each item of clothing into a duffel bag on the floor. "Watch!" he said, snapping his fingers. Reluctantly, Blake took off his prized Citizen quartz wristwatch. "I won this in the Mount SAC Relays—" he started to say.

"Stop it, you're making me weep."

With a pang of regret, Blake handed over his keepsake and watched it disappear into the duffel. The Aviator passed him a plastic bottle. "Sanitizing gel. Full body application, if you don't mind."

Blake smeared himself from head to toe, feeling his skin grow cool as the alcohol evaporated. A hair wash with waterless shampoo followed. Finally, the Aviator reached into the duffel and pulled out a plastic bag. "Especially for you," he grinned. Inside were orange boxer shorts, a pair of bright orange socks, an orange long-sleeved pullover shirt and orange leather pants. Slipping out of his running shorts, Blake pulled on the boxers, socks and shirt, then struggled into the tight-fitting pants.

"Ah, the price of fashion," chuckled the Aviator, watching his efforts. He reached into the bag again and handed Blake a dress jacket colored a slightly deeper shade of orange, along with orange ankle boots and a pair of oval, orange-tinted glasses.

Blake sat in his new getup, feeling thoroughly ridiculous. Lowering his newspaper, Top Hat grinned and flashed a thumbs-up. "Now we're getting somewhere!" he said.

"Last but not least," said the Aviator. Reaching into the duffel bag, he pulled out a battery-powered hair clipper.

"What's this?" said Blake, staring.

"Head forward, please." The Aviator grabbed Blake's hair in his fist and yanked his head over the open duffel bag. Making sure the clippings fell into the bag, he rapidly sheared away the hair on both sides of Blake's head, leaving a four-inch-wide Mohawk running from front to back.

"Next, a dash of color," he announced, taking a spray can out of his jacket pocket. A moment later Blake's hair gleamed fluorescent orange, matching his orange wardrobe.

"And now, the coup de grâce." Pulling a case from his jacket, the

Aviator opened it to reveal a miniature aerosol can, a needle and a gold stud. "Topical anesthetic," he said, brandishing the aerosol.

"Oh no," said Blake, holding up his hands.

"Come on, don't you want to be bohemian like us?" laughed Top Hat. Ignoring Blake's protests, the Aviator sprayed his right ear lobe to numb it, then speared the soft flesh with the needle. Using a tissue to wipe away the droplet of blood, he carefully inserted the gold stud.

"There," he said, leaning back to admire his handiwork. "You are now a rocker—or at least a close facsimile thereof." He passed over a hand mirror and Blake stared at his reflection. In ten minutes' time, he'd morphed from an ordinary-looking grad student into an orange-hued eccentric.

"Now that you're presentable, it's time for introductions," said the Aviator. "I'm Lance. That's Nail, catching up on his beauty sleep, and this is his counterpart Tooth." The Cap gave Blake a royal wrist-turn. "Directly behind you is our resident Neanderthal, Stash."

Top Hat half-rose in his seat and lifted his brim slightly.

"Collectively, we are the Sunset Kidz—that's Kidz with a 'z,' " Lance continued. "Best Guns N' Roses channelers in the L.A. Zone, bar none."

"*Classic* Guns N' Roses," growled Tooth.

"This arrogant turd is our front man, if you hadn't guessed," said Stash, "Tooth and Nail play rhythm and bass, respectively. As for *moi*, I play lead, naturally."

"Sadly, we're between drummers," added Lance.

"So, you all actually live in the UZ?" asked Blake.

"Who would live anywhere else?" countered Stash with raised eyebrows.

"Speaking of which…" Lance handed Blake a laminated card on a lanyard. "This is your UZ ID," he said. "It's your ticket to come and go from the Zone, so guard it with your life." Blake turned the card over in his hands. A name and bar code were printed on it, along with a head shot of Blake in an orange Mohawk.

"Fast work, huh?" said Lance. "Thank you, Photoshop." Reaching back into the duffel, he produced a wallet. "Inside is five hundred dollars in cash. Note the name on the ID. From this moment forward, you are none other than…" —Lance waved his fingers in an approximation of a magician— "...Karl Kliff, audio engineer and self-appointed genius. You travel from one Urban Zone to the next, assisting Zoner musicians of all stripes." He looked at Blake keenly. "Engrave that name into your subconscious, mystery man. They tell me you have the technical expertise to pull the deception off, if it comes to it."

"I can work a mixing board, if that's what you mean," said Blake.

"That's *exactly* what I mean."

"While we're on the subject, can I ask who 'they' are—*exactly*?" frowned Blake.

"Don't shoot us—we're only the piano players," sighed Lance. "A limo full of pretty faces, selected because the Troopers are in the habit of cutting us slack."

"The court jesters," added Stash. "Harmless as the day is long."

Seeing he was getting nowhere, Blake changed the subject. "You said you channel Guns N' Roses. That means you pretend to be them, right?"

"Unlike some other UZ channelers, we don't feel a need to live out every aspect of our heroes' lives," Lance said sternly. "I am *not* into past-life regression. And most of us stay away from hard drugs, despite our public image."

"Except poor Styx," added Stash.

"Our drummer took his role a little too seriously," said Lance. "Which is why he's no longer with us." He clapped his hands. "Enough of this tabloid shit. One more stop, then on to the City of Angels."

The words had hardly left his mouth when the limousine veered off the smooth pavement onto an uneven dirt road. They jounced along for a quarter-mile before pulling into a trash-strewn clearing. As the car lurched to a stop, Blake stared out the window at a group of men sitting on folding chairs beside a large metal furnace. Black smoke billowed from the top of the furnace, partly obscuring the small mountain range of automobile parts and scrap metal that rose behind it.

Lance lowered the car window, letting in a blast of hot air. "Gentlemen," he called out. "Gifts for the fire god!" One of the men ambled over and Lance handed the duffel bag and Blake's backpack through the window to him. Tucking them under his arm, the man walked to the furnace, pulled open a metal door in the side, and tossed the bag and pack into the roaring flames. He peered inside for a moment, watching them burn. Then he slammed the door shut and walked back to the limo.

"For your troubles, kind sir," said Lance, holding out a bottle of vodka. Accepting it without a word, the man returned to his seat.

"Not the chattiest bunch," grinned Stash. As Lance raised the window, James accelerated sharply, steering the car back onto the dirt track. Within two minutes they were on the main road again, bound for L.A.

As the limo sped along, the band began passing around a bottle of champagne along with some pâté-smeared crackers. Blake had just sunk his teeth into one when he heard the whoop of a police siren. Panicked, he whirled to face Lance, only to find the singer smiling back at him calmly.

"Don't get your knickers all in a knot now, Karl," he said in a soothing voice. "Let us do the talking."

Guiding the limo onto the shoulder of the road, James slowed to a stop and shut off the motor. Seconds later, the door opposite Blake opened and a state trooper peered in.

"A little far from home, aren't we?" he said.

"I could make the same observation," said Lance. "Since when do you guys patrol these backwaters?"

"Since when do UZ rockers drive around in the desert?" the officer replied.

"You mean, you've never dropped acid in the wilderness?" grinned Stash. "You haven't lived, officer!"

"I pulled you over because I'm looking for someone." As he spoke, the trooper studied Blake and the others carefully. "Maybe you saw him wandering along the road—a guy in his twenties, college-student type?"

"Sounds like a real dick," snarled Tooth.

"I saw some preppy-looking roadkill a few miles back," said Stash politely.

"Can I have your IDs?" said the officer. He ran a scanner over each card. "Any smartphones, MP3 players, notepads, computers, or other electronic devices?" he asked.

"Not us, officer!" smirked Stash. "The only music we carry is in our heads."

"Good. Then you won't mind if I scan your vehicle. Everyone out!" While Blake, James and the Kidz formed a ragged line next to the limo, the trooper went to his car and returned with a small parabolic dish. He aimed it at each of them in turn, then stuck his head inside the limo and swept the dish over the interior. When he reached the rear seat, a beeping sound came from the monitor on his belt.

"That's a positive!" the officer grunted. Sticking his hand between the seat cushions, he pulled out a small iPod. "Now, who would this belong to, gentlemen?" he asked.

"I was wondering where that had gotten to," said Stash. "I swear, officer, it's loaded with nothing but Sinatra and Garland!"

"Judy Garland?" groaned Lance. "Say it ain't so, Stash!"

"We'll see," the officer said. He plugged the player into the dish and examined the digital display on his monitor. "Okay. Looks like you're clean." He handed the file player back to Stash and watched through narrowed eyes as they climbed into the car.

Back on the road, the limo gradually picked up speed. For several minutes, no one spoke. At last, Lance broke the silence. "Good thing he didn't stop us ten minutes earlier!" he chuckled. While his tone was casual, Blake noticed that the edge of the singer's bandana was dark with sweat.

They reached Interstate 10 a half hour later and joined the westbound traffic, rolling through the towns of Palm Springs, Redlands, San Bernardino and Pomona. As they drew closer to the Los Angeles state line, the sense of relief inside the limo was palpable. Jokes and insults flew, with the conversation eventually segueing into a discussion about the strengths and weaknesses of the various guitarists and drummers Guns N' Roses had run through in its latter-day incarnations.

Exhausting this topic, the group went on to deconstruct G n' R's lurid history of concert riots, then finally launched into a raucous rendition of "Sweet Child O' Mine."

They were still singing when the limo passed a road sign reading: "Welcome to Los Angeles—The Fifty-First State." Through the window, Blake spied the towers of downtown L.A. For the first time in two days, he felt himself relaxing. The rockers' irreverence was the perfect antidote to the tension he'd been under. These guys were more than tribute musicians, he realized: Lance's protestations notwithstanding, they were practically full-time performance artists. Personally, Blake had never cared for Guns N' Roses as a band. He was more familiar with their legend than with their actual music. Now he searched his memory, piecing together what he knew about the odd saga of Axl Rose—how he'd fired his mates and shut himself away for a decade in a hilltop mansion with his pinball machines and video games, recording and re-recording the album *Chinese Democracy.*

Glancing at Lance stretched out on the seat opposite, he sensed a simmering anger beneath the musician's cool facade. Lance must have related to Rose's life story in some way, he thought—otherwise, why go to such lengths to imitate him?

Exiting the freeway, they drove through an area of retail shops and low-rise apartment houses. Pulling into a strip mall, the limo stopped in front of a photography shop. Lance lowered the car window to watch as James got out and handed his armful of cameras to a man standing in the store entrance.

"What's that about?" Blake asked. Lowering another window on the opposite side of the car, Lance pointed at the high concrete wall towering a block away. "No cameras allowed inside, remember?" he said. "Or cell phones, or computers unless their cameras and recording hardware have been disabled."

James guided the limo around the corner to the end of a line of cars, idling as they waited to pass through a thirty-foot-wide opening in the wall. A dozen LAPD officers were inspecting the vehicles and waving them through. Several squad cars were parked nearby, their radios squawking intermittently, and a few yards behind them a small crowd of neatly-dressed men and women stood holding printed signs.

"Now entering the Gates of Hell," proclaimed one. "Rock and Roll is the Root of All Evil," read another. As each entering vehicle passed, the group broke into a chant: "God still wants you…stop and repent!"

"Routine UZ checkpoint, complete with requisite proselytizers," Lance yawned. "Just follow our lead."

Tooth had already joined Nail at the rear of the limo, where they both pretended to be asleep. Taking one of the half-finished bottles of champagne, Lance refilled Blake's glass and then swiftly drained the rest of the bottle himself. Wiping his mouth with his sleeve, he lowered the limo window and glared out at the protestors.

"Be careful what you say—or you may find yourself thrown to the lions!" he called out. Opening his mouth wide, he gave his best imitation of a lion's roar.

One of the men lowered his sign and looked at him reproachfully. "God loves and pities you," he said.

"I'm sure she does," laughed Lance, raising the window again. "Let's brighten these gendarmes' day," he said to Stash. "How does that old Pacemakers song go?" Putting their heads together, they begin singing merrily to the tune of "Ferry 'Cross the Mersey":

Oh take us to the UZ, that sweet place we're dreaming of…

As they sang, the car door opened and a cop ran his gaze over the limo's inhabitants. The duo finished the verse with a flourish, then fell silent.

"You boys behaving yourselves this morning?"

"Morning?" yawned Stash. "The night's young, officer!"

"Not for those two," said the policeman, gesturing to the musicians snoring in the back seat.

"Care for an eye-opener?" said Lance. He turned the empty champagne bottle upside down. "Oops—nothing left!"

Ignoring him, the officer held out his palm. Lance passed over the group's ID cards and the officer looked at each one in turn before scanning it.

"Who's your friend?"

"This is Kliffie, our new soundman," said Lance. "Joined us in the 'burbs. He's from the Frisco Zone. Just itching to be a Lost Angel, like everyone else."

"Don't worry," growled Stash, "he's over eighteen and straight as an arrow."

Blake raised his champagne glass. "Cheers."

The officer glanced at Blake's ID again, then handed back the cards. "God help you all," he said with a shake of his head. Closing the car door firmly, he motioned for his colleagues to let them through.

SEVEN

Hotel California

BLAKE HAD VIVID MEMORIES OF family trips to Los Angeles as a kid, including visits to the areas now walled off inside the Urban Zone. Since the cement barriers went up, though, he'd never actually entered the UZ, despite living practically in its shadow as a UCLA undergrad. Between the hassle of securing a tourist visa and his own busy schedule, it had always seemed like too much effort.

Now, peering out through the tinted windows of the limousine, Blake was struck by how many people he saw on foot strolling down the sidewalks. The car traffic was light by L.A. standards, and most of the vehicles appeared to be convertibles with a half-dozen people or more crammed inside. Many of the riders seemed to know each other, and as their cars passed they waved energetically and honked their horns, blaring out a variety of recognizable song licks.

While the cars and the buildings looked shabby, this was hardly the scene of desolation and despair depicted by the media. The images of the UZ on the evening news always showed anarchic chaos—people shouting belligerently and erupting into scuffles, or nodding off in a drugged stupor inside dilapidated apartments. In reality, the vibe seemed remarkably calm. As the limo made its way through the streets, Blake also noticed that virtually every building had banners hanging from the windows with political slogans scrawled on them: "The 99% is here to stay"... "Set the Music Free" ... and, more times than he could count, "Justice for Fish."

This is not what I expected, thought Blake. *Not at all.*

The limo headed north on La Cienega then turned west onto Sunset, halting in front of a tall building. A glassed-in foyer stretched halfway to the curb, and each floor was covered by blue-tinted windows.

"Welcome to the Dazzle Palace—the Daz, for short," said Lance. "Formerly known as the Andaz West Hollywood and, many centuries before *that,* the Continental Hyatt House—a.k.a. the Riot House of rock and roll legend."

"Keith Richards tossing TVs off the balcony, John Bonham riding choppers through the halls," sighed Tooth. "Those were the days."

"I heard that Little Richard lived here for twenty years," said Stash. "I'm thinking the room service was better back then."

"These days it's a flophouse for local musicians," said Lance. "And there's a room reserved especially for *you,* young Karl Kliff!"

"Time to deliver you to your keepers," added Stash.

"Karl, it's been a blast," Tooth said. "Before you split town, catch our act at the Whisky a Go Go. We go on tomorrow night at eleven. Show up early, we'll get you backstage."

"By the way," said Nail, running his hands through his amazing hair, "you don't happen to play drums, do you?"

"Afraid not," said Blake. Opening the door, he stepped to the sidewalk and was almost knocked over by four mini-skirted young women rushing past him into the limo. It was only after the car pulled away that he realized it was the first time he'd ever heard Nail speak.

"Happy belated Labor Day," said Brash Langley. "A nice enough holiday, if you overlook its socialist organized labor aspect."

"I prefer the Fourth, myself," observed the radio host's sidekick, Wordman.

"Sure. Who doesn't? Fireworks, parades, 'The Stars and Stripes Forever'....Of course, when I was a kid growing up, that field of stars wasn't quite so crowded. There were only fifty states, then—a nice, round, patriotic number," said Langley.

"Half of one hundred," Wordman noted.

"Now today, in the new and improved America, we've got sixty. More states equals greater democracy—that's what the libs keep telling us, anyway. But I have a question for you, sir. Did we gain any actual *land* when we added these ten new states?"

"Not one acre," replied Wordman.

"Did we even gain anything that can actually be considered a *state*, in the traditional sense of the word?"

"Not that I can tell..."

"That's correct, sir. We did not. What we got was ten municipal governments that were tired of being cities, ten cities that wanted to grow up and become big, important states. Except that they aren't, really—they're just warehouses for millions of sniveling whelps, sucking on the teat of the U.S. government. Their very names conjure up images of people standing on line at the grocery store, food stamps clutched in their feverish little hands: New York City... Los Angeles... San Francisco... Chicago... Detroit.... Boston. And the others."

"Don't forget Philly. That's always been a favorite of mine!"

"It would be, Wordman, it would be. And of course there's Seattle, beloved home of heroin addicts, and Baltimore, the city where poverty reigns eternal, and New Orleans, where the local religion is based on booze, pot and laziness...."

"You know, Brash, I never could figure out why they were even *allowed* to become states."

"Because their citizens *voted* for it, Wordman. They were tired of all the mean Republicans running their parent states, so they decided to break off and form their own little mini-nation."

"Alliance, you mean."

"That's right. The Municipal Alliance. Sounds like something Mussolini might have conjured up. Anyway, this is old news, as you all know—happened six long years ago. Then, of course the Urban Zones sprang up inside them, the 'UZs,' which the Federal government had the good sense to build walls around, to protect the rest of us from the druggies and the runaways and the mentally ill—the Fuzzies, I call them, wandering around like zombies in these so-called areas of free expression."

"I was in the New York Zone the other day on an eight-hour tourist pass," said Wordman. "It was sickening."

"Didn't care for the stench, eh?"

"Actually, it was the noise that got me. All that banging around on drums and guitars."

"I know, the last gasp of the commie-hippie-flower child movement. How did it feel, by the way, checking your cell phone at the door?"

"Like I was naked, on a raft in the middle of a putrid sea..."

"Nice image, Wordman—very evocative. Remember, people, no recording or picture-taking or broadcasting is allowed in the Zone. We don't want any of that filth seeping out and polluting us ordinary folk."

"What happens in the Zone stays in the Zone. Isn't that right, Brash?"

"That's right—and I'm sure you prefer it that way, Wordman. Anyway, I bring all of this up because it was announced this very morning that Maxwell Fish—do you remember him?"

"You're referring to Benedict Arnold Fish?"

"One and the same. According to the Associated Press, Mr. Maxwell 'I-am-Not-a-Foreign-Agent' Fish is going to have his house arrest status lifted for two hours, and two hours only to—get this—deliver a speech!"

"Hasn't he done enough talking? I thought that's what got him into trouble in the first place."

"Apparently not. According to the AP, the government is letting him give this address in order to establish legally that they are not infringing on his right to free speech, as a presidential candidate. He's going to give it on September eleventh, no less. But here's the good part: Guess where he's delivering his remarks?"

"Umm...surprise me."

"In the New York Urban Zone, that's where! So at least we'll be spared the spectacle of watching Fish run his mouth off on television."

"What happens in the Zone stays in the Zone."

"I think you just said that, Wordman. Is there an echo in here?

Anyway, I've got another news flash for you—and this one I know you're going to like. It was leaked directly from Republican campaign headquarters. Rumor has it that President Acton—"

"You mean presidential candidate, Brash. He hasn't actually been elected yet, has he?"

"Not yet, Wordman, not yet—but he will be, don't worry your pretty head about that. Anyway, word on the street is that *Vice* President Acton, in preparation for the day when he assumes the top office, is drawing up plans to get rid of the UZ once and for all. He's gonna shut down the Zones—gonna empty 'em out at the point of a gun, if need be. Then he's gonna bring a suit to the Supreme Court to force statewide re-votes that will allow California and the others to reabsorb our ten extra city-states, so-called, and restore our flag to the fifty stars and thirteen stripes that God intended for it to have!"

"Wow—I can't wait!"

"Neither can I, Wordman. At this particular moment, however, I'm afraid that our voyage to return America to its proper glory must take a short detour to the land of our sponsors, who have some important information of their own to share with all you loyal listeners out there."

"The Stars and Stripes, and our sponsors, forever!"

"Well said, Wordman, well said...."

As the Kidz' limousine drove off, Blake heard a raucous banging sound approaching from the opposite direction. Looking east on Sunset, he saw a pickup truck moving slowly down the boulevard. A group of middle-aged men and women in bright tie-died T-shirts were sitting in the back, singing some indecipherable song about universal oneness as they pounded on tambourines, triangles, bongos and assorted other percussion instruments.

The truck halted directly in front of the hotel, and one of the people in the back stood and faced the crowded sidewalk. "Music festival at the Cheatau, seven o'clock!" he announced. "Everybody's welcome—punk rockers included!"

At this, his companions on the truck bed roared with laughter. He sat down again, and a woman and man stood up with acoustic guitars around their necks. Nodding at each other, they strummed a few brisk bars and began singing in two-part harmony.

Ain't it great to be in the UZ—nowhere to go, no one to see,
I'm heading down the road to UZFest, won't you come with me?

Their companions shouted approval, and there was a smattering of applause and cheers from the crowd on the sidewalk. Acknowledging the response with a smile, the duo launched into the next verse:

L.A.'s got a real cool sound, yeah, Frisco has the wind so free,
But soon I will be traveling East—that New York beat is calling me!

Another cheer went up, as the man raised his fist in the air with his forefinger and pinkie extended. "Eight more bars," he shouted. "Sing with us!"

Tall and grey the wall surrounds us; where it ends, we cannot say.
But still the music's all around, so lift your voice and sing today!

With a lurch the truck started rolling again, almost knocking the singers off their feet. As Blake watched it go, two burly men in mirrored sunglasses and black turtlenecks appeared on either side of him.

"Welcome, Mr. Kliff," one of them said, taking hold of his arm. "Hotel security. Come with us, please." His colleague gripped Blake's other arm, and together they propelled him across the crowded sidewalk into the hotel lobby.

Inside, the air was thick with cigarette and marijuana smoke. The place had clearly seen better days: The carpeting was frayed and discolored, the wallpaper torn and marred with graffiti. Outlandishly dressed men and women were everywhere, perched on stools and draped over tattered chairs and sofas. Five wizened men with mod British haircuts glared from a cluster of love seats near the entrance where they sat with four willowy females squeezed between them. Just beyond them, several other women sat with their heads together, laughing over some private joke.

As his escorts walked him across the chipped marble floor to the scuffed reception desk, Blake couldn't help staring at one of the women in the second group, a petite brunette with an uncanny resemblance to Susanna Hoffs of the 1980s group the Bangles. Like thousands of adolescent boys, he'd been infatuated by Hoffs' striking dark-eyed looks as a kid, before the Bangles' recordings had been banned and their photos and videos scrubbed from the Internet.

"Mr. Kliff, checking in," announced one of the men.

"Right," said the desk clerk, glancing at his log book. "Room 301. You're paid up for two nights." He handed Blake a plastic card key. "Enjoy."

Without missing a beat, the two men guided Blake to an ancient elevator that made a clattering ascent to the third floor, disgorging them into a dimly lit corridor. Making their way to the end of hallway, the men pushed open the door to 301. To Blake's surprise, it was a large, attractive suite with a living and dining area, an attached kitchenette, and what appeared to be two bedrooms. A man and a woman sat playing cards at the dining room table. Both were lean and wiry, dressed in identical checkered pants and collarless striped shirts, with the heavy black boots and jet-black, spiked hair once favored by punk rockers.

"Karl, you made it!" the man said, rising to his feet. "Welcome to Los Angeles!" He nodded to Blake's escorts. "Thanks, guys."

Once they'd left, the man walked over and turned the deadbolt on the door. "I'm Blue," he said, shaking Blake's hand. "And this is Serena." He motioned toward the woman, who didn't look up from shuffling the cards. "Not to be too dramatic about it, but we're your bodyguards."

Falling into a chair, Blake stared at the two of them in their punk getups. The situation seemed too silly for words. "My bodyguards?" he said incredulously. "What are you going to do if I'm attacked—fight the villains off with guitars?"

Blue chuckled at Blake's reaction, but his companion clearly wasn't amused. Lifting her head, she shot silent daggers at Blake with her hazel eyes.

"Careful what you say, Karl," Blue said, catching her look. "In the

UZ, things are never quite what they appear. Take Serena, for instance. Before she landed in L.A. and became a rocker, she spent several years with a group called Team Seven. Remind me again, Serena—how many different ways can you can kill someone with your bare hands?"

Blake blinked and swallowed hard. Like most Americans, he was familiar with the exploits of the famous anti-terrorism unit.

"How many ways can you both shut up?" growled Serena, throwing the deck of cards down angrily on the table.

"We thought you might like a nap," Blue said, ignoring her. "We're heading out on the town this evening, and I'm guessing you could use some rest." He nodded toward one of the bedrooms. "You'll bunk in there. Serena will take the other bedroom, and I'll sleep out here on the pull-out couch. I like to be near the front door, on the odd chance we get a surprise visitor during the night."

All this talk of killer bodyguards and nighttime visits wasn't exactly conducive to napping, Blake thought. He *was* pretty beat, though—and hungry. "A little shut-eye sounds great," he said. "So does food."

"I'll dial room service," said Blue. "What do you want?" He picked up the phone and ordered oatmeal, a toasted bagel with lox and orange juice. "It'll be here in ten minutes," he said. "You can eat, then sack out for a while."

A thought struck Blake. "If she was in Team Seven," he said, nodding at Serena, "what unit were you in?"

"Me? I was just a plain old Navy SEAL," said Blue. "But hey, everyone's got to start somewhere."

❖ ❖ ❖

As the final attendee entered the windowless room, Chuck Smyth nodded to his assistant and she shut the soundproof door behind her with a heavy click.

"Sorry to call everybody in. I know you're all busy, post-holiday," said Smyth. "But we've got a Code Red."

"I heard. Your guys screwed up a simple residential arrest," said Marconi.

Smyth shot a look at the short, sharp-featured man across the table. As head of special operations for Homeland Security, Marconi reported directly to him. Lately, however, Smyth couldn't shake the nagging suspicion that he was actually taking direction from someone else.

"As you know from last week's briefing, we've been ordered to take physicist Blake Hawkes into custody," Smyth continued. "He evaded an arrest team on Sunday, and is currently at large. So that you all understand what's at stake, I've invited Major Susan Harris from the Defense Department's research division to bring you up to speed on the technology that's involved."

A woman in a kelly-green jacket and skirt and horn-rimmed glasses opened a folder in front of her. "You'll note on your summary sheet that Hawkes is pursuing his doctorate at University of California, Berkeley," she began. "Over the past two years, he has been doing informal work in the highly sensitive area of quantum communications—a mode of transmission that theoretically enables two parties to communicate instantly with completely security over any distance, through any medium. Our scientists at DOD have been pursuing this technology for several decades. We've also been closely monitoring work in this area at other government labs around the world. The accepted view has been that practical application of this theory is still years in the future."

Harris closed the folder and looked up. "As I mentioned, Hawkes was moonlighting in this area, a fact we became aware of only recently. In so doing, he stumbled on a new approach to the problem—an approach that not only appears to be feasible, but has reportedly resulted in a working prototype."

There was a stir of surprise around the table. "We have the prototype in our possession, and are now analyzing it," Harris added. "As far as we can tell, it seems to be the real deal. We also believe that, given the right resources, Hawkes could reconstruct the prototype in a matter of weeks—which makes it particularly important that we locate him before he can share his knowledge with the wrong parties."

"Thank you, Major," said Smyth.

"Glad to help." Slipping her folder into a leather case, Harris exited the room, leaving Smyth alone with his division chiefs.

"This means we have to move fast," he said. "Hawkes has a two-day head start. We've tracked him as far as the inland California desert, then the trail goes cold. He appears to have gone overland on foot, but we have to figure he may have been picked up by a confederate in a vehicle. We're scanning photos of him to gather some facial-recognition data. We'll have the results to all of you shortly. Mike, I need you to get touch with NSA and have a customized communications filter placed on all U.S. phone and Internet communications. We can also call on drone and satellite surveillance as needed."

As Mike Curtis, his electronic surveillance chief, nodded, Smyth turned to his chief deputy and law enforcement liaison, Gary Piroulis. "Gary," he said, "we need the Border Patrol to be on high alert, in case Hawkes decides to try for Mexico. I also need you to keep tabs on all traffic stops, ID checks, and reports of transients. Our primary area of concentration is southern California, but he could jump to another part of the country at any time. So again, we need a nationwide info sweep. The locals don't need to know any details for now—just tell them we're looking for a person of interest and supply them with Hawkes' description."

"What about looping in Bibbitt and his crowd?" asked Piroulis. "The arrest warrant involves charges related to his department, right?"

"Bibbitt stays out of this," said Smyth curtly. "Dealing with that loose cannon is the last thing we need. All information should be sent directly to me."

"Understood," nodded Piroulis.

Once again, Smyth gave a small prayer of thanks that Piroulis had agreed to move with him to Homeland Security from the Office of Naval Intelligence. They had the kind of deep mutual trust that only comes from a long history together—stretching, in their case, all the way back to the Naval Academy, where Smyth had played starting fullback on the lightweight football squad and Piroulis, a year younger, had opened holes for him on the offensive line. Smyth would have put his life in Piroulis's hands without a second thought—which was more than he could say about some of his other subordinates.

He glanced briefly across the table at Marconi. "That means absolutely no intermediaries. Understood?"

"And *my* assignment?" said Marconi with the hint of a sneer.

Smyth sighed. "Tony, you know we're all counting on you," he said. "Hawkes could be anywhere—the desert, Mexico, Los Angeles...or any points east or north. He's on the run and he knows we're after him. So unless some cop on the beat gets incredibly lucky, your undercover operatives are the ones who'll have to take him in."

"There's something I don't get," said Marconi slowly. "He's supposed to be flying solo, right? So how does he discover you're about to snatch him, and slip away?"

"We're still working that," said Smyth.

"Another question. Are we worried about Hawkes hooking up with some foreign power—or are we more concerned about his potential domestic connections?" Marconi asked, looking around the table.

"At the moment, we have no evidence that he's thinking of connecting with anyone," said Smyth. "Let's assume he's acting on his own until we learn otherwise. We'll reconvene tomorrow at thirteen hundred hours for an update. Thanks, everyone."

Smyth gathered his papers together, then looked up to see that Marconi had lingered behind. "One more thing, Charles," Marconi began. He was the only person in the department who refused to call Smyth by his nickname—another calculated move to get under his skin, Smyth was certain. "When my people get a bead on your whiz-kid—and they *will* get a bead on him, I promise you—it may be more feasible to stop him than to apprehend him. Know what I'm saying?"

"Tony, this guy's father is a respected admiral. He commanded the *George H.W. Bush*, the super carrier, for God's sake. We can't afford a scandal here."

"That's right—I always forget you were a sailor boy," said Marconi. "Personally, I don't give a shit who his father is. *My* old man put up drywall for a living, and he never asked for a break from anyone. Your team had a clean shot at Hawkes and blew it. We aren't going to make the same mistake."

"This isn't just about stopping him, Tony. We need his knowledge."

"Really?" Marconi studied his fingernails. "We already have his walkie-talkie, right? Our folks can figure it out from there."

"I want him alive," said Smyth grimly. "Period."

"Yes *sir,*" said Marconi. Throwing a sarcastic salute, he spun and marched through the open door.

It was late afternoon when Blake woke. He pulled back the heavy curtains covering the windows and blinked at the sundrenched street below. Padding into the bathroom, he saw that shaving equipment had been laid out on the sink. A half-dozen fresh pairs of boxer shorts and socks, all in the same bright orange, lay folded on the dresser, along with a toiletry kit and an overnight bag. Looking in the closet, he spied three sets of orange pants, shirts and jackets identical to what he'd worn in the limo. *My new signature color,* he thought.

After taking his first shower in three days, Blake pulled on one of the orange outfits and made his way into the living room. "I noticed the traveling bag. Am I going somewhere?" he asked loudly.

"Not just yet, Blake," said an unfamiliar voice. He wheeled to see a figure in suit and tie, silhouetted against the backlight from the windows. "I asked your friends to step outside for a bit," the figure said. "They don't know your real identity—just that you're someone being hunted by the Federal government, who we want to keep safe and out of jail. We prefer that it stay that way for now. Okay?"

"Fine with me, I guess," Blake shrugged.

"It's essential that your presence here remains a secret," the man continued. "As we speak, Homeland Security is still searching for you in the desert. Luckily, we extracted you just in time, before they began closing off the roads. It's just a matter of time before they shift their focus here to L.A."

The man motioned toward one of the living room chairs. "Have a seat," he said. Sitting across from Blake, he spread his hands on the coffee table in front of him. "I've been assured that your technological breakthrough is the real thing—"

"It is," Blake interjected.

"If so, then the government is going to do everything they can to find you. Two days have passed since your disappearance, which means the search will start intensifying. As far as we can tell, they don't suspect you're in the UZ, at least not yet. Even if they did, they won't expect you to look the way you do now. With this persona, you should be able move about in public relatively openly. Your security team will be with you at all times. You're in good hands with them—they're the best we have. The important thing is to carry yourself like a normal person, if there is such a thing in the UZ. Remember, you're just down from San Francisco to soak up the scene."

"I'm booked here for two nights. What happens after that?" asked Blake.

"You'll learn more soon," the man said. "If you agree to assist us, that is. We're hoping you'll replicate your discovery for our organization. It's a lot to ask, I know—but if you can pull it off, then at a certain point you'll become superfluous to the Feds. Until that point, however, the authorities will have every incentive to take you out of commission. Do you understand?"

"I think so," Blake said hesitantly. The whole hiding-out thing was suddenly sounding a lot more dangerous than he'd bargained for. What organization was this guy part of, he wondered, and what were they after?

"You seem pretty plugged in," he added. "Can I ask you something?"

"Sure—though I may not know the answer."

"My friend, Carter, the one who was with me right before they tried to arrest me in La Jolla. Do you know what happened to him?"

"He's fine," the man replied. "It's my understanding that they held him for twenty-four hours or so in the San Diego Homeland Security office, until they were convinced he'd told them everything he knew. But they didn't rough him up, if that's what you mean. As far as I know he's home right now, hanging ten at Imperial Beach."

Sensing his uncertainty, the man leaned forward. "This isn't just about you, Blake," he said. "You happen to have come along at a very sensitive time in our nation's history. There's a lot a stake here." For the first time in their conversation, his face creased in a faint smile. "Tonight you're going to meet someone who will put everything in perspective for you, far more clearly than I could ever hope to. Just understand that many eyes are going to be searching for you, so you need to play your role to the hilt."

The man stood to leave. "Thanks for listening, Blake," he said. "Your help would mean a great deal to us. We'll be in touch."

A minute later, Serena and Blue walked back into the room. They'd augmented their outfits with black leather vests, and Serena had put on some rose-red eye shadow.

"So, have all of your questions been answered?" said Blue.

"Not really," Blake replied.

"Well, maybe we can fill in some of the gaps before we push off. Serena, how about updating Karl on his personal history?"

Serena's presentation was concise but thorough. The actual Karl Kliff, she explained, was born in the Bay Area twenty-five years earlier to German immigrants. The family eventually settled in Sacramento.

"You attended Sacramento High School, where you excelled in physics and chemistry and competed in track as a middle distance runner—which is not a stretch for you, I understand." She glanced at Blake, who shrugged noncommitally. "Your profile also indicates you're fluent in your parents' native language," she continued. "Again, I understand this capability matches your own background."

"Sure, I *sprechen sie Deutsche*."

"For whatever reason, you never attended college. Following high school, you've spent the past eight years in the Bay Area, eventually residing in the San Francisco UZ, where you worked off the books as a sound engineer for various musical enterprises." She paused. "The key thing to remember is that Karl is—was—an actual person who resembles you in age and appearance, and who worked in San Francisco in the audio field."

"*Was* an actual person? What happened to him?" said Blake.

"Oxycontin overdose. Last year, never entered into the public record." She paused and fixed Blake with the glare that seemed to be her default expression. "I'm told your own proclivities run to the softer side."

"Guilty as charged," Blake replied, raising his hands defensively.

"Well, we've all got our vices," Blue said briskly. "Would you like to take some time to review? As Serena indicated, it's important that you memorize these key points."

"Karl Kliff, parents from Europe, Sacramento High," Blake repeated. "I've got it down cold."

"Great—a quick study," said Blue, sounding less than convinced. "Excuse me for a moment. I've got to confirm our plans for the evening." He picked up the phone next to the living room sofa and began punching in a number.

"You mean to say you actually use that antique for something other than room service?" asked Blake.

"It's part of a dedicated UZ land-line network," said Blue, "the only way to communicate in the Zone, since all cell phone and Internet service is blocked." He held up his hand for quiet. "It's Blue. Just checking on tonight's reservation. Yes, we'll be there—three of us. Thanks."

Hanging up, he clapped his hands together sharply. "Okay, team. We leave in fifteen minutes. If you need to freshen up, now's the time."

EIGHT

Come on Now

THE PLAN WAS TO HEAD west to the beach, where they'd grab dinner and then catch a musical act. First on the agenda, though, was a drink in the hotel lobby. "You can't hole up too much around here," Blue explained. "Otherwise, people assume you're either using heroin or on the lam from someone."

The lobby was busier than ever. The same five British-looking men were in the same spot, Blake noticed, though they appeared to have a different group of females with them this time. "Stones channelers," said Blue, rolling his eyes. "Local royalty. In their own minds, anyway." They chose a low table in the corner farthest from the entrance with a clear view of the room. "The usual," Blue told their waiter. "Karl?"

"I'll have a lager," Blake said.

The waiter returned with a glass of beer and what Blake guessed were two non-alcoholic cocktails for Blue and Serena. Blake sipped slowly, taking in the activity around him. He picked up snatches of conversation about musical genres, spiritual gurus, and the politics of wealth inequality. In one corner, a woman in a half-mask was strumming a guitar and singing a medley of tunes by The Mamas & The Papas. The tension that had gripped the rest of America for the past decade and a half—everyone scrambling to make ends meet, caught between anxiety over the latest terrorist threat on the one hand, and fear of making some misstep that would draw the attention of the authorities on the other—seemed to exist in another, far-off dimension.

"People have a good time here, don't they?" he said.

"The UZ has its problems, but freedom of expression makes up for a lot," said Serena. "Repression has a lot of faces—political, financial, creative...sexual. They're all aspects of the same power struggle: the few trying to rule the many. A lot of what we do here may seem juvenile to the outside world, but our future as a society depends on it."

Blake was surprised at the force of her statement. He'd always thought of the Zone as a refuge for society's dropouts. He was trying to formulate a reply when he saw Blue glance sharply toward the hotel entrance. "We've got company," he said quietly.

Seconds later, a man and woman wearing Department of Cultural Hygiene uniforms strode into the lobby, parabolic dishes cradled in their arms. As they moved into the room's center, the hum of conversation stopped abruptly.

"Stay right where you are, everybody," the woman said loudly. "As long as no one tries to leave, no one gets in trouble. We're here to do a quick scan. If you all cooperate, we'll be gone before you know it."

The entire lobby watched in dead silence as the officers went slowly through the room, sweeping their dishes from side to side. Suddenly a beep sounded from the male officer's belt. "I've got a reading," he announced, working to contain his excitement. His dish was pointing at a large potted plant. Cautiously, he poked through its leaves.

"Aha!"

With a flourish, he withdrew a small computer tablet. Taking a cord from a compartment in his belt, he plugged the tablet into his detector and studied the display.

"It's only got one file on it," he said in a puzzled tone. Reaching down, he touched the tablet's screen with his index finger. Suddenly, the room was filled with the rasping sound of Keith Richards' opening guitar line from "Satisfaction."

The Cultural Hygiene officer silenced the song with another jab of his finger. Around the lobby, muffled snorts of laughter could be heard.

"Sounds like a hit," said one of the Rolling Stones channelers. The laughter grew.

"You people think you're real comedians, huh?" snarled the

woman. "Just remember, we can close down this shithole any time we want!"

The two officers stalked out of the hotel, taking the tablet with them. As they disappeared down the sidewalk, the entire lobby broke into cheers and applause. Through the noise, the chiming of a clock sounded.

"Six o'clock, everyone. Time to send a message to power!" The speaker was the Susanna Hoffs look-alike Blake had noticed earlier. She was standing in the middle of the floor holding up her right hand with her forefinger and pinky extended, just like the musician on the truck outside. Blake was startled to see everyone in the room stand and raise their hands in an identical gesture.

"It's a UZ tradition—kind of like high tea," said Serena, nudging him in the ribs. "Get up!" Blake stood up uncertainly as the woman spoke again.

"Liberate the music, liberate the nation," she said.

"Liberate the music, liberate the nation," the roomful of people repeated back to her. Then the whole lobby broke into song, clapping to the backbeat:

Set the music free,
Liberate all melody,
Let the music be,
Count together, one, two, three!

The group stamped out four syncopated bars before launching into the second verse:

Set the music free,
Emancipate sweet harmony,
Let the music be,
Sing it out now, you and me!

After a round of wild applause, everyone sat down and calmly resumed what they'd been doing.

"*That* was different," Blake said.

"It's a daily reminder of our mission here," said Blue. "A little show of solidarity. Can't hurt, right? I think the tune's kind of catchy, myself."

"Hey, Serena, Blue...who's your friend?" Blake looked up to see the woman who had just led the singing protest. Up close, her resemblance to the Bangles' singer and guitarist was astonishing. She was wearing a blue fringed mini-dress, cut low in front, over black fish-net stockings and purple high heels. Her luminous brown eyes and hour-glass figure sent a jolt of electricity through the pit of Blake's stomach.

"This is Karl, an old friend. He's down from the Bay," said Serena. "We're showing him around."

"Lucky boy," the woman said archly. She gave a slight toss to her tousled mane of black hair, then reached across the table and squeezed Blake's hand warmly. "I'm Caroline. Nice to meet you, Karl. Have you had a chance to catch our show yet?"

"Caroline's with the Tangles. They channel the Bangles, in case you hadn't guessed," said Blue.

"You don't have to flirt so hard, Car—I'm sure Karl is quite taken with you already," Serena said sardonically. "*All* the new arrivals have crushes on Caroline...don't they?"

"And some of the old ones," Caroline said, flashing a pointed look at Blue.

"Easy, ladies," said Blue hastily. "It's all good, right? I believe we're ready for the check." Summoning the waiter with a wave, he quickly signed the bill and rose to his feet. "Wonderful seeing you, Caroline, as always, but we have places to go."

"It was lovely meeting you, Karl," Caroline called melodically as they made their way out of the room. "Don't be a stranger!"

❖ ❖ ❖

The instant they stepped out the door of the hotel, a taxi pulled up. "Santa Monica," Blue instructed the driver.

The cab cut down Palm Avenue and turned right onto Santa Monica Boulevard, the corridor that connected the UZ's eastern and western sections. The Los Angeles UZ was the largest of the ten Urban Zones in area: It took up most of Hollywood and West Hollywood, then narrowed to a quarter-mile strip that ran along Santa Monica Boulevard for ten miles before widening again to claim large portions of Santa Monica and Venice. As they rode, Serena and Blue chatted casually, but Blake noticed that they were constantly surveying the traffic and the roadway. Two hundred yards away on either side of the street ran the gray, 20-foot-high UZ walls. Most of the buildings between the road and the concrete barriers appeared to be boarded up, and the sidewalks were largely empty except for occasional groups huddled around makeshift fires.

"They call this stretch the Five-Mile Squat," said Blue. "Not a good place for your car to break down." As if to underscore his words, an LAPD cruiser zoomed by them, lights flashing.

As they neared the western end of the corridor, Blake looked south to see another entrance checkpoint with a stream of cars passing through it. "Tourist entrance, right?" he asked.

"People out for big fun," nodded Serena. "They buy eight-hour passes to come inside and see the sights—get drunk, listen to music, maybe score some drugs. Their dollars are what keep the UZ alive. That, and whatever government aid we can scratch up."

Although Blake had never sought out a UZ tourist visa himself, he knew the drill well. Many of his friends at UCLA and Berkeley hit the L.A. and San Francisco Zones on a regular basis. It was a simple arrangement: Once your application was approved and you'd bought that day's pass, you left your U.S. passport at the gate along with your mobile devices, getting everything back when you exited. Those who stayed past the eight-hour limit incurred stiff fines and were barred from returning for a year, so most people were careful not to miss the cutoff.

The cab dropped them off at a small Mexican restaurant in Santa Monica. After they tucked into a booth and placed their order, the conversation turned to Serena and Blue's band, which recreated the music of various 1980s-era L.A. punk groups. As Serena began discoursing on the genre's violent subtext—particularly in its suburban manifestations—it occurred to Blake that the UZ's musicians were concerned as much with the history of popular musical forms as with the music itself.

"That's true," said Blue, when Blake questioned him on this. "After all, you can't really understand the music without knowing its social and political context, can you? We're all amateur music scholars, in a way."

Blue went on to outline how the bands in the Zone were divided between channelers—bands devoted to recreating a single band's music—and broadbanders like their own group, the Microbes, who sampled the music of different bands within a certain musical category. "Since the recordings are no longer available in the U.S., we memorize the exact orchestration of each song," he added. "When someone drops out of a group or a new group forms, the new players are taught the material note by note."

"What made you decide to quit the military and become Zoners?" Blake asked.

"Let's just say that I missed playing bass guitar," said Blue. "And the lifestyle that went with it."

"There comes a point where you've seen enough injustice in the world," added Serena curtly, "and you decide it's time to put your money where your mouth is. This is the only place in America where average people are still pushing back."

"So chatty this evening, Serena!" said Blue, raising his eyebrows. Ignoring him, Serena bit fiercely into her burrito.

Steering the conversation back to the UZ musical scene, Blue began laying out the Los Angeles Zone's topography. The western end of the Sunset Strip in West Hollywood was home base for the glam metal and punk scene, he explained, while the musicians channeling soul, funk, and the American counter-culture rock of the sixties—Crosby, Stills, Nash and Young, Joni Mitchell, the Doors, Frank Zappa—performed mainly in the eastern half of the Strip. Santa Monica was ground zero for the British Invasion and London club genres, and Venice was home to pop, electro music and emo.

When he was finished, Serena glanced at Blake. "You're not a Zoner, and you're not a musician—professionally, anyway," she said. "What got you into rock music so deeply?"

"I don't know. I've just been nuts about it ever since I was a kid," said Blake. "My dad didn't want to know about rock and roll—show tunes and Johnny Mathis are more his speed—but my mom had a huge collection of classic rock CDs. I was sort of a nerd when I was young, and I'd sit for hours, reading science books and listening to albums at the same time."

When he hit his teenage years, Blake had inherited an extensive library of rock and roll books from his uncle Frank, who began collecting them when he was a teenager himself. They were mostly histories and memoirs of old British groups like the Beatles, the Rolling Stones and the Animals. For a boy hungering for something beyond the world of school and southern California beach life, the stories of lower-middle-class English teenagers transforming themselves into international superstars had served as a kind of existential guidebook.

"There was an incredible element of freedom to the British rock scene that really appealed to me," Blake added. "These kids grew up in the most hierarchical society in Western Europe. Their only future was to follow in their parents' footsteps—take up a trade, go to the football games, get drunk at the pub and retire on a pension. But somehow, against all odds, they broke out. And rock music was the tool they used to pick the lock."

As he spoke, Blake realized that this explanation only accounted for part of the hold that rock and roll had on him. It represented freedom, yes, but there also was a more personal aspect to it. At its best—in the bittersweet harmonies of "If I Fell," Duane Allman's soaring slide guitar in "Layla," the hatchet-blow lyrics of "Subterranean Homesick Blues"—it was the closest thing to emotional truth that he'd ever known. He was no Musicologist, but rock was his religion and his touchstone. Like hundreds of thousands of other kids, he'd bought an electric guitar when he was fourteen and formed a band with some friends. He started writing songs and even built a rudimentary recording studio in his basement, always with the vague idea of playing music for the multitudes one day.

Then, with the suddenness of an earthquake, it had all ended.

"I was nineteen, in my sophomore year at college, when the Cultural Hygiene laws were passed," he told Blue and Serena. "I turned in all my CDs and cleaned out my iTunes library, like a responsible citizen. But I couldn't bring myself to hand over my vinyl."

He'd scrounged the old LPs from various back-street record shops around San Diego—tiny, hole-in-the-wall stores run by friendly eccentrics who would gladly spend the day discussing every facet of recorded music under the sun, from scratchy discs of old Delta bluesmen to bootlegs of Dylan and the Grateful Dead. Blake had haunted their shops almost every weekend, soaking up their stories and sampling their wares. In the process, he'd acquired hundreds of 33 ⅓-rpm albums that he would play late into the night on a vintage turntable, listening through headphones long after his parents had gone to sleep.

The night before the official deadline for delivering all illegal music to the designated drop-off locations, Blake had driven to a new subdivision under construction on the east side of San Diego. In the trunk of his car was his record collection and a shovel. Using a GPS locator to record the exact spot, he'd buried the whole collection, packed inside special moisture-proof containers, in a patch of earth between two half-finished McMansions. All, that is, except his two dozen favorites. Those he'd kept, along with his turntable, in the secret compartment on his parent's roof deck.

In telling his story, Blake deliberately left out the part about his loaded MP3 player. To his thinking, that transgression made him seem more like a petty criminal for some reason. "As far as I know, those other albums are still where I buried them," he concluded, "waiting for the day when I can dig them up without committing a Federal crime."

"I'm sure you're not the only one," said Blue. They paused while the waiter cleared away their empty plates, then Blue leaned back in his chair and gave Blake an appraising look. "Now that I know what a British Invasion fan you are, I've got a good idea where we should go tonight."

Serena rolled her eyes. "Like you didn't have this planned all along."

"Serena is such an anti-romantic," grinned Blue. "It's true—I had this venue picked out already. In fact, it was a no-brainer."

Back on the sidewalk, they walked two blocks and then turned down a dark alleyway leading to the rear entrance of a cinder-block building. A black curtain hung across the doorway. Ducking through, they found themselves facing a massive, shirtless man dressed in jean overalls and canvas sneakers, a miniature baseball bat dangling from his fingers. The man gave Blue a familiar nod and Blue grasped his hand in a soul handshake, slipping him a fifty-dollar bill as he did.

The man held open a second curtain behind him and they walked into a half-lit theater with ascending rows of threadbare seats facing a low stage. The air was thick with smoke and the smell of spilled beer. On the stage stood a drum kit with "Conx" printed in script letters across the bass drum, along with three mike stands and assorted amps. The seats were almost filled, with dozens more people sitting in the aisles or standing behind the last row. Somewhere in the back there must have been a bar, because people were coming down the steps clutching armfuls of drinks in plastic cups.

"Thirsty?" said Blue, following Blake's gaze.

"I'm okay." As a fugitive from the U.S. government, Blake thought, it probably wasn't the smartest move to get shitfaced in a strange corner of the Los Angeles UZ.

"Good decision," Blue murmured in his ear. "We've got business later."

The doorman had followed them in. Catching Blue's eye, he pointed to three empty seats in the front row and motioned for them to sit down. Almost at once, the overhead lights flickered off and on several times and the crowd began chanting, "Bray!... Bray!... Bray!"

The chant lasted for a minute or so and then the lights went off for good. As the crowd stirred restlessly in the pitch darkness, a spotlight suddenly illuminated the stage. Into the bright circle leaped a tall, ungainly man with a Fender Telecaster strapped around his neck. He was wearing Beatle boots, a skinny tie and a black suit that was two sizes too small. Leering at the audience, he grabbed the center microphone with both hands.

"Hello, Santa Monica!" he screamed.

"Hello, Bray!" the crowd screamed back.

"I suppose you want to hear some classic rock and roll tonight... and I suppose the *Conx* have to give it to you!" he shouted. The crowd erupted in a mixture of boos, howls and cheers. As his fellow band members ambled onstage carrying guitars and drumsticks, the front man continued talking, clearly in no hurry to start the performance.

"I'm from north London originally," he said, leaning on the mike stand is if too weary to stand upright. "Only I had the terrible misfortune—I'm sorry, I mean the *great luck*—to marry a skanky Yank ten years back. A U.S. citizen now, I am."

The crowd started up a facetious "U.S.A." chant, and Blake realized he was watching a rehearsed act that they all knew by heart.

"But of course, I'm still an Englishman at heart," the man added. Pulling a flask from the breast pocket of his jacket, he took a thoughtful swig. "So tonight," he continued conversationally, "we're going to play some music by a little band begun by a couple of brothers, also from north London. Maybe you've heard of them?"

"We love you, Bray!" shouted someone from the audience.

"Oh, how *they* loved those Saturday night music parties their mum and dad used to throw. They were just little lads then, you know. But they grew up, didn't they?"

"We get you, Bray!" another voice yelled.

The man stopped and peered out into the darkness. "Yes, you—and you alone—get me," he said, stepping back. "You *really, really* get me—so...LET'S GO!!"

The instant the last phrase left his lips, the light widened to illuminate the rest of the stage as the band tore into the Kinks' "You Really Got Me," a hundred raw voices singing along. When the song was finished the band kept going, powering through one high-decibel Kinks hit after another. Every couple of minutes, amid the swirl of guitar licks, vocal harmonies and pounding drums, someone would charge the stage only to be hurled back by one of the bouncers. Finally, as the band shifted gears and slowed into a dreamy version of "See My Friends," a woman was allowed to step onstage and place flowered leis around each of the musicians.

It was controlled madness, and Blake ate it up. He hadn't been to a show with this kind of energy since his teens. "They're fantastic!" he shouted to Blue and Serena at one point.

"Not bad," Blue nodded.

The band played for over an hour, downing beer after beer as the set went on, then withdrew for a lengthy intermission. When they finally retook the stage, something had changed—having to do, Blake guessed, with various substances ingested during the break. Bray's mood had turned dark and snarling, while the musicians behind him alternated between sullen silence and angry defiance. After a ragged version of "Where Have All the Good Times Gone?" the band lurched into the opening riff of "I Need You," then suddenly stopped dead. The lead guitarist whirled to face the drummer.

"What the *hell* was that?" he demanded, as the room fell silent.

"Why don't you go fuck yourself?" the drummer replied in a slurred voice. The guitarist stepped forward and reached over the drum kit, swinging his fist awkwardly at the drummer's head. Rising from his stool, the drummer grabbed his high hat by its metal stand and smashed it sideways across the guitarist's ribs, felling him like a tree. Immediately all hell broke loose: People rushed the stage en masse and began banging on the drums and kicking the amplifiers. In the audience, men flailed at each other wildly while women screamed.

"This is our cue," said Blue. He and Serena each hooked an arm under one of Blake's armpits and lifted him to his feet, levitating him rapidly out of the building the same way they'd come in.

Outside in the alleyway, the cool night air was a soothing balm after the craziness inside.

"Does that happen often?" asked Blake.

"Every show," Serena replied matter-of-factly. "Welcome to the UZ."

"Let's take a stroll in the moonlight, shall we?" said Blue.

They walked down to the ocean and then turned onto the concrete bike path heading toward Venice Beach. The route was crowded with sightseers munching on food from vendors' carts and ogling at the break dancers, jugglers, sketch artists, fortune tellers and buskers who lined the walkway. There wasn't a smart phone in view, Blake realized—no one scrolling through messages as they walked, or talking to some distant person. Everyone's energy was focused on the here and now.

As they continued along the path, Blake spotted a dark gray shape running horizontally across the beach and continuing into the water. Drawing closer, he realized it was the wall marking the southern border of the UZ. The barrier stretched well out into the surf, and a Homeland Security officer with a sub-machine gun stood at the point where the concrete met the waves of the Pacific.

"In case someone tries to slip in," said Blue. "Or out."

Turning back from the ocean, Blake's attention was caught by a long-haired woman in a gypsy dress, strumming an acoustic guitar and singing. Her eyes were closed, and there was something magnetic about her voice.

Went down the wrong road, searching for you.
The way's getting harder every day, but my heart is still true.
Eyes in the sky watching all that I do,
But they can't take my soul, oh no, no, no, 'cause it's promised to you.

After she strummed the last chord she looked up and stared directly at Blake, her brown eyes locking with his. For an instant, some deep understanding seemed to pass between them. A moment later, she glanced away to smile at a passerby who had dropped a few bills into her open guitar case.

Blake felt Blue's grip on his arm as his bodyguard began steering him down the boardwalk once more. "Sounds like she wrote that," he said. "It's nice. She should do something with it."

"Around here, singer-songwriters keep to the street," said Blue evenly. "Best to stay under the radar." Blake nodded, realizing the stupidity of his statement. Under the Cultural Hygiene laws, anyone performing music professionally, inside or outside the UZ, had to submit all original compositions to the government for approval and licensing. Most songs weren't accepted—and once you applied you were placed on a permanent government watch list for your troubles. The whole thing was a total hassle, one that the average garage band or coffee shop composer had no appetite for.

"People come to the Zone because they don't want to deal with authority," added Serena. "That's why most of them stick to busking for cash."

"There's a cool little sculpture garden just up the way," said Blue. "Want to duck in for a quick toke? Then I'll introduce you to a friend of ours."

NINE

Down by the Sea

HEADING AWAY FROM THE BEACH, they walked through a narrow passage between two storefronts, then crossed a road that ran parallel to the shoreline behind the row of beachfront businesses and bungalows. On the other side of the road Blue guided them onto a gravel path lined by tall hedges on either side. They followed it thirty yards to where the path ended at an archway with a fitted metal door set in a tall stone wall topped by concertina wire.

Blue pushed open the door, which was unlocked, and they found themselves in a walled-in garden abutting an unlit ranch house. The garden was filled with carefully tended beds of flowers and ferns surrounding what appeared to be several dozen pieces of modern sculpture. In the darkness, Blake glimpsed what he could have sworn were a Giacometti and a Rodin.

Closing the door behind them, Blue slid home the bolt on the interior side. "Here we go," he said, pulling a sleekly rolled joint and butane lighter out of his vest pocket. "A couple of puffs should set you up—it's strong, and very thought-provoking. You'll like it, I guarantee."

He lit the joint and handed it to Blake. Blake inhaled twice, as instructed, then held the joint out toward Serena, but she shook her head so he handed it back to Blue instead. Stubbing the reefer out on the base of one of the sculptures, Blue slipped it into his pocket.

"You're right, this *is* good," Blake said. *So, I'm the only one smoking,* he thought. He sensed that this was all designed to prep him for his upcoming encounter, but he still welcomed the temporary escape the pot afforded. As a wave of intense well-being flooded through him, he realized he hadn't felt this way in ages. It reminded him of the time he'd smoked some Acapulco gold as an undergraduate and spent the night leafing through the Bible until sunrise, nodding in utter comprehension at every reference to God.

"Doing okay?" Blue said. Blake nodded silently, then glanced at Serena. He'd never noticed how kind her eyes were. He turned to Blue. "Quite okay," he said.

"Good. Then it's time we met our host." Blue eased open a sliding glass door and stepped into the house. Blake started to follow, then froze. His eyes, still adjusting to the darkness of the garden, had spotted the outline of a large man dressed in black, standing silent and unmoving along the garden's inside wall.

"I think we've got trouble," he whispered.

"Get over yourself," said Serena, shoving him forward. "You're not the only one with bodyguards, you know."

The trio passed through an unlit room that appeared to be a library. Blue pushed open another sliding door made of ornately carved wood, and they entered a large room illuminated by scores of candles. The small flames flickered everywhere—in wall nooks, on tables and bookcases, and at the feet of a miniature Buddha.

A woman dressed in a flowing caftan, her hair wrapped in a bun, walked across the Oriental rug to greet them. "Thank you for coming," she said. "He's finishing up a meditation session." She nodded toward a closed door leading to an adjoining room.

"We'll wait here," said Blue. "Karl, you go ahead."

"You're not coming?" asked Blake.

"No. We're just the hired help, you see," said Serena, a hint of peevishness in her voice.

"Hardly, Serena," smiled the woman. "Would you and Blue care for a cup of mint tea?"

"Sounds fab, Tab," said Blue.

"That would be short for Tabitha," the woman said. She glanced at Blake, a hint of amusement in her eyes. Her face could light the world, he thought. "It's a pleasure to meet you."

"Karl," said Blake, putting out his hand awkwardly. "Likewise."

"Go in," she said, motioning again toward the other room. "My husband should be just about done."

Fighting the urge to knock, Blake slid open yet another sliding door. Behind it was a medium-sized room, also illuminated by candles. Two men in prayer robes were sitting cross-legged on mats with their eyes closed. The older one had silver hair cropped in a Marine buzz cut, while his younger companion had shoulder-length black hair and a flowing beard. Between the two men, a Tibetan prayer bell rested on a small stand. On a low table nearby, incense burned in a brass dish.

Blake sat on a nearby couch and waited. A few seconds later, the younger man opened his eyes, picked up a mallet and softly tapped the prayer bell three times, then closed his eyes again.

After several repetitions of this, the older man finally raised his own eyelids and looked at Blake. "Welcome," he said in a half-whisper. "My apologies, but the evening meditation can't be rushed. You understand, I'm sure."

With his eyes open, the shorn head and craggy visage was immediately recognizable. They belonged to Aloysius Branford, the one-time boy wonder of California politics. A decade before Blake was born, he had become the youngest governor in state history. After two terms in office, he'd renounced electoral politics and gone to join the Dalai Lama in exile in India. Eventually he returned to the U.S. to head a citizen's environmental group for a number of years until, disgusted by the government's failure to deal with climate change in any serious way, he quit that post as well. As usual, he did it with a flourish, making a widely-covered speech in which he denounced American politics as "a refuge for thieves, knaves and fools."

The lifelong bachelor promptly departed on a two-year sailing trip around the world with his new love, soon to become his wife. In the course of his ocean odyssey, he somehow managed to find the time and communications capabilities to trade gold and silver futures on a daily basis. By the time he docked his boat back in Marina del Rey in the summer of 2014, he had parlayed his $20 million inheritance from his industrialist father into a $300 million fortune.

It made for a great story, naturally. The media had a field day with "The Flying Yachtsman," as they dubbed Branford. When Blake was in high school, his mother would tease him by saying, "If you're so smart, why aren't you as rich as Aloysius Branford?"

Upon his return to America, Branford donated most of his fortune to a local foundation he established, whose activities included providing free meals and health care for the needy, operating out of facilities in Santa Monica and Venice. When the UZ walls went up, leaving his home and charities inside the Zone, he refused to move. "Never entered my mind," he told Charlie Rose in a famous interview.

In recent years, Branford had gained a reputation as a key advisor to the Municipal Alliance. The Munis—whose very survival was now being threatened by the nation's conservative political forces. *Which must have something to do with why I'm here,* thought Blake.

After one more ringing of the prayer bell, the two men stirred, stretching their necks and shoulders. Branford bowed his head toward his meditation partner, who stood and quietly left the room. Still in lotus position, Branford reached for a wooden bowl on a nearby table. "Have some blueberries, Blake," he said, holding the bowl out. "I hope you won't mind if I use your given name. I realize you're living under an alias at present, but I can assure you this house is secure."

Without waiting for an answer, Branford scooped up a handful of berries himself and popped them into his mouth. "Organic. Healthiest food on earth," he said. "I never touch refined sugar or white flour. They're weapons, deployed by the corporations to keep us weak and sick, sapped of the will to fight. The media is complicit in the endeavor, of course. Disgusting...but that's life in the twenty-first century, isn't it?"

To Blake, the speech sounded like a set piece—a preamble to whatever was coming next.

"I'm Aloysius Branford," the other man continued. "You already know that, of course. And clearly I know who *you* are. You can find out almost anything about anyone these days, if you know where to look." His gaze fixed on the far wall, as if he was reviewing a memorized text. "You're quite a fan of early rock and roll...apparently to the point where you held onto some illicit vinyl record albums, albums that were subsequently discovered by our nation's thought police. The Beatles... The Who... Crosby, Stills, Nash and Young. Real artists, and revolutionaries in their own way. Worth taking a risk for, I suppose."

Branford's eyes focused on Blake again, and he flashed a grin. "I also know that you took a course in modern sculpture as a sophomore at UCLA. You'll have to view our garden in the daylight sometime. As you can see, not everyone in the Zone is a twenty-something, living in a squat with a Stratocaster for company."

Rising from the mat, Branford walked over to his desk and picked up a brown leather briefcase. He was in business mode now, his speech growing more clipped.

"I'm about to trust you with some highly confidential information, Blake," he said, tapping the side of the briefcase. "For the past several years, the Municipal Alliance has been engaged in what might be called a low-level cold war with the rest of the nation. They want us to close down the Urban Zones, stop advocating progressive policies, and basically behave like good boys and girls, giving our unquestioning support to the powers that be—which, of course, has been the deepest wish of the ruling class throughout human history."

Branford stood silent for a moment, running one hand over the back of his crewcut scalp. "As you may have noticed, the Federal government has recently been stepping up their attacks on us," he said. "They see this upcoming election as their chance to close down the UZs once and for all. And maybe go even further—declare the city-states dysfunctional, and begin a legal process to return them to their parent states. We've begun pushing back against their propaganda in every way possible. That's where these come in." He held up the briefcase.

"Wireless mesh networks?"

"Exactly. For a number of years now, our group has been distributing mesh network software that lets people share encrypted Internet connnections over their phones or computers. We've also manufactured thousands of these wireless routers that serve as nodes, each one capable of supporting local networks for a radius of up to a kilometer.

The routers are inexpensive and completely expendable. If the authorities happen to discover one, we simply substitute another."

"May I?" Blake opened the briefcase. Inside were several weatherproof routers with attached antennas, plus a handful of USB drives and a half-dozen smart phones.

"As I noted, we've put thousands of these routers into the hands of people sympathetic to the Alliance. Collectively they're capable of connecting people to the Internet and enabling the transmission of print, audio and video files in most parts of the country, outside the control of the government," said Branford. "They've proven quite effective. Our biggest problem involves disseminating content to these local networks. For sensitive material, we usually employ flash drives sent by courier. As a result, communication on a large scale is excruciatingly slow."

"So you're looking for a better method."

"If we had a technology that could remotely transfer digital data to our nodes in a way that couldn't be blocked, traced or intercepted, it would be a tremendous blow against authoritarian rule—not just in this country, but around the globe," Branford said. "You, my friend, appear to have developed that technology." His voice had been gaining energy as he spoke, and now he was pacing the room excitedly. "Imagine thousands, even millions of your devices, in use around the world. Governments would no longer be able to eavesdrop on their citizens with impunity. People could share ideas freely once again!"

"But they could just as easily use it to hatch plots...commit crimes," said Blake. "Our intelligence gathering apparatus would be hamstrung."

Branford gave him a pitying look. "Of course, criminal activity is a concern," he said. "But Blake, you're an educated man. Surely you understand that in the history of the world, the greatest crimes have *all* been perpetrated by governments themselves. The worst are those that have spun out of control—countries or movements that have been taken over by cabals whose only purpose is to dominate others. But even our supposedly benign democracies are infected by the hunger for power. When you're running the show, no matter how noble your original intentions may be, accountability to the populace becomes a burden to be despised. I know—I've been there."

As if his growing excitement had suddenly depleted him, the former governor sat down heavily on the couch. Blake was struck by how pale he looked. Branford was not a well man, he realized. Closing his eyes, the other man drew in a deep breath before resuming.

"As I was saying, Blake, one day your invention will make this possible. For now, though, I would gladly settle for two working prototypes that could be fully functional by next week."

"Next *week?* Why the mad rush?" asked Blake.

"We believe our nation is at a make-or-break moment," Branford replied. "This November's election will very likely determine the direction of the country for decades to come."

At Branford's mention of the election, Blake suddenly understood why he'd been summoned to the house in Venice. Like most of the planet, he knew all about the Maxwell Fish saga. "You don't seriously think Fish can win, locked away in his Fifth Avenue penthouse?" he said.

Branford's face flushed abruptly. "He not only can, but *will,*" the older man growled, his voice the loudest it had been all evening. "We have our own polling data, showing that Fish's actual support among likely voters is greater than anyone realizes." Branford's eyes were burning now. "You must understand, Blake, that Americans are *sick* of living in fear—sick of watching our leaders mouth patriotic platitudes while doing everything they can to restrict free speech and social justice and empower the rich—not that they need any more empowering!"

Branford closed his eyes again, visibly calming himself. "You're an intelligent person, Blake," he continued in a more even tone. "But you're not particularly interested in politics—I know this from your file. Not that I blame you, the way the game is played these days. As you gain more life experience, though, you'll realize that true electoral governance—democratic rule by the people, for the people—is the most important social tool humanity has ever invented. And effective democracy, at its core, comes down to one thing: using the ballot box to restrain the powerful few."

Blake thought this over for a moment. "There has to be more to it than that," he offered. "Defense of borders. Educating the population.

Pursuit of the scientific ideal..."

"Stalin defended his borders just fine," said Branford tersely. "And his schools and policies turned out some of the finest scientists in the world—more than a few of who ended up in the gulag for their troubles."

He paused and pulled a handkerchief from a pocket in his robe, using it to pat his lips. "No, a healthy democracy exists as a check on power—in government *and* in the private sector. The problem is, our American democracy has been corrupted on both fronts. Over the past fifty years, the wealthy class has been staging a slow-motion coup d'état, through a very cleverly marketed scheme of tax cuts for the rich together with the gradual elimination of government-funded services."

"So you support the Leveler philosophy," said Blake. "No one should be richer or poorer than anyone else, right?"

Branford snorted. "Another nice touch of propaganda. What does making sure everyone has a decent standard of living have to do with 'leveling' anything? We're talking about restraining a wealthy class that is on the verge of buying up the last pieces of the world they don't yet own. Did you know that the richest 20 percent of Americans now possess 96 percent of the nation's total wealth? That's up from 85 percent in 2010, 89 percent in 2015, and 92 percent in 2020. Between exclusive hedge funds and computerized trading, along with the lowest capital gains taxes in the developed world, this country has turned into an institution that ensures the rich get ever richer. Hell, I've been one of the beneficiaries. Meanwhile, the middle class, whatever remains of it, is disappearing fast. All that will be left is one large servant population, working for peanuts and living on credit, just so they can spend their old age scraping by on Social Security—until the Republicans find a way to finally get rid of that, too."

Despite Branford's obvious passion, Blake could feel his mind shutting down. After the stress of the past three days, the last thing he wanted to do was debate economic policy. To his thinking, a lot of what Branford was saying rang true. It was obvious the Republicans were promoting an economy tailored to the upper classes—one that might dampen growth overall but that also drastically pushed down labor costs, resulting in a much higher standard of living for the wealthiest

Americans and a lower standard of living for everybody else. In fact, it seemed to Blake that their ultimate goal was to recreate the economic structure of the Middle Ages, with the masses working dirt-cheap to build castles and cathedrals for the super-rich.

None of this surprised him. As the sociobiologists had shown, human nature was geared primarily to preserving our immediate gene pools. What astonished him most was how the Republicans were consistently able to get so many people lower down on the socioeconomic ladder to vote for them. It wasn't his problem, though: He was a scientist, bent on acquiring knowledge. Politics, to his mind, was a distracting sideshow.

"I'm no economist, Governor," he said aloud. "I just want to be free to carry out my work."

"That's just what I'm talking about," said Branford sharply. "Don't you see what's happening? Our leaders pay endless lip service to the cause of freedom, at the very same time they're working with their corporate allies to forge leg irons for each and every one of us. Why do you think you're a hunted man right now?"

The older man put his hand lightly on the briefcase holding the Wi-Fi devices. "At the present moment, Maxwell Fish is our chief hope for stemming the tide. I don't know if you heard the news announcement today, but the Federal government is allowing him to make one speech before the Supreme Court hearing—and one speech only."

"That's good, isn't it?"

Branford shook his head. "The whole thing is a ploy to weaken Fish's legal case, by demonstrating that he hasn't been silenced," he said. "They're letting him speak on the condition that it takes place next week at the UZ Festival, inside the New York City Urban Zone."

"A political speech—in the middle of UZFest?" Blake shook his head. The annual week-long event was notorious for its mix of music and mayhem. "It'll be a zoo, for sure. But I still don't see what the problem is."

Branford turned to look directly at Blake. The intensity of his full gaze was startling, and it occurred to Blake that this moment was the point of their whole meeting. "With the Urban Zone ban on broadcasting or recording," he said patiently, "Fish's speech will only be heard by a few thousand people inside the Zone itself—unless we can break through the curtain of silence. He's going to be sharing some news that we hope will permanently change the course of politics in the U.S. We've devised a number of ways to spread his message, of course—some journalists who happen to be UZ residents will be allowed to take written notes on what he says, and we also plan to have some operatives there with concealed audio recorders, maybe even a video camera if we can manage it. But the second-hand reporting of his words will inevitably mute their impact, while the dissemination of any recordings will take days, even weeks. The recordings will also have the added stigma of being illegal. Your invention, on the other hand, would let us transmit his speech directly to the nation and the world in real time—increasing its impact exponentially."

"You're saying you want to use the quantum communicator to broadcast his speech to an external location, then relay it from there?"

"That's right. We'd be linked to a secure location outside the U.S., from where we could then transmit Max Fish's words across the globe—including to our own mesh networks here in America." Branford glanced toward the other room, where Blue, Serena and Tabitha were waiting. "Would you mind coming upstairs with me for a moment?"

The older man led Blake into the front hallway of the house, where a spiral staircase rose through a circular opening in the ceiling. Following him up the curling steps, Blake found himself in a small, glassed-in cupola overlooking the garden and the beach beyond. The windows were open to the ocean breeze, and Blake could just make out the sound of voices drifting up from the boardwalk. The room's only furnishings were a writing table, a desk chair and a small bookcase. With no lights on, the room was dark except for the wavering glow from the candle-lit room below.

"I come up here to think and write," said Branford. He stared out over the garden wall at the waters of the Pacific. "We desperately need your help over the next few days, Blake. As I said earlier, our goal is to have two fully operational versions of your invention constructed by the time Fish speaks at UZFest next week. If we can break the communication blackout and broadcast his speech to America, it could change the course of this election—and of history."

Blake didn't know what to say. The practical challenges of constructing a pair of quantum communicators in a few days' time—while fleeing from the law, no less—made the idea seem laughable.

Seeing his hesitation, Branford pushed on. "We can get you access to the finest high-tech manufacturing facilities in the world," he said. "You just have to tell us what you need." Opening a drawer in his writing desk, he pulled out a penlight and a small map of the United States. "Tomorrow, if you're agreeable, you're scheduled to meet with our scientific team here in L.A. to go over your requirements in terms of equipment, materials and personnel," he continued, shining the light's beam on the southern California region. As Blake watched, the spot of light moved up the coastline. "Your next stop will be the Bay Area, where you'll connect with the Silicon Valley group that will be manufacturing the crystal lattices." The light beam made its way further up the coast. "Then on to Seattle, where you'll meet with the people constructing and assembling the computerized laser elements of the device."

He switched off the penlight. "Once that's done, we'll fly you to New York to supervise the transmission from the UZ. Our plan is to keep you constantly on the move, so the authorities can't get a fix on you."

How does he know so much about my technology? Blake wondered. Through the window, he could hear the faint sound of the surf in the distance. He looked at the map, thinking hard. "You're talking as if I've already signed on for this," he said at last. "But I don't know anything about your organization, really. Maybe you want this technology so you can pass it on to China, or Iran, or some homegrown terrorists."

"I'm afraid you'll just have to trust us," said Branford. "You at least know *me* well enough to know that I've committed everything to the vision of a more equal and just nation. If Acton wins this election and the Republicans ride his coattails to another majority in Congress, America is facing a Dark Age with no end in sight."

"What makes you think I'll agree to help?" asked Blake.

Branford reached an arm around Blake's shoulders and gave him an almost paternal hug. As he did, Blake sensed a current of warmth flowing from the other man. *He's devoted his life to this cause,* he thought.

"You already have, Blake," Branford said in his rasping half-whisper. "I knew it as soon as you walked into the room." As he spoke, Branford began to cough, softly at first, then more insistently. The spell continued for a good half-minute, until Tabitha appeared in the curving stairwell holding a paper cup filled with colored liquid. Branford took the cup and downed its contents along with a pill that his wife handed him.

"Allie," his wife said softly, "you need to rest."

He waved her off. "One more minute."

When they were alone again, Branford leaned in closely, speaking so softly that Blake strained to hear him. "This is no game," he said. "We need you…and they don't. It's that simple. I know these people. They have your technology already. If they suspect you're working with us, they'll do everything in their power to stop you—including killing you, if necessary. At this moment, you're in grave danger. But at the same time, the potential rewards are immense. You have a warrior's soul, Blake. That soul will carry you through."

He squeezed Blake's shoulders again, and the younger man felt a surge of emotion. Branford and his own father were different in many ways, but at that moment he felt as if he were in the presence of the Admiral himself, sending Blake off to a track meet with the admonition that he always gave: *Just be yourself, Blake…the very best self you can be.*

TEN

After Midnight

BLAKE FOLLOWED BLUE AND SERENA back through the garden to the gravel path. They lingered there for several minutes, staring up at the night sky as a cool breeze blew in from the beach.

"Branford's something, isn't he?" said Blue.

"He's impressive, alright," said Blake. "But he doesn't seem very healthy."

Serena scowled. "In case you haven't heard, Karl, the bell tolls for all of us."

Realizing he'd touched on a sore subject, Blake kept silent. They walked to the end of the gravel path and paused at the edge of the beach road. Looking south, Blake saw the top portion of the UZ barrier looming above the rooftops.

"Like a modern-day Berlin, eh?" chuckled Blue. "Except that here you're allowed to come and go at will, as long as you're a registered Zoner."

"What if you're not?" Blake said.

"It's estimated that about a third of the people here are undocumented," replied Blue. "They get inside a thousand different ways: swim in from the ocean, come on a tourist visa and never leave, or maybe just hide in a car trunk under some old blankets and hope the checkpoint cops are lazy that day. You can even hire someone to hoist you over the wall."

"Why do people sneak in?"

"Some do it because it's the only way they can get here," said Blue. "There's a lot of underage kids in the Zone who didn't want to wait until their eighteenth birthday to apply for residency status. Others are old enough, but they can't or won't go through the application process—so they find another route." He glanced around. "Our taxi was supposed to be here by now. Maybe he's waiting for us on the beach side."

They crossed the road and started down the alley between the two retail shops. "Heads up, Serena," Blue said casually, "we've got a singleton, armed, at three o'clock."

"I'm on it," said Serena.

An instant later, Blake was flat on his stomach with Blue's knee in his back. Looking up, he saw Blue pointing a pistol toward the darkened building on their right. There was the sound of a brief commotion. "All clear!" called Serena.

"Stay where you are," Blue instructed. From his vantage point on the ground, Blake watched as Blue vanished into the shadows. Seconds later he came out again trailed by Serena and a ragged-looking man. Serena had the man's right arm twisted high between his shoulder blades and was holding a revolver in her other hand. Blue took the gun from her and emptied the bullets in a few deft movements, then shoved the gun and the ammo into the side pocket of his vest.

"You can get up," he said. Blake rose to his feet, his ribs aching from where he'd hit the ground.

"Who are you?" said Serena fiercely. She put additional pressure on the man's arm, eliciting a groan of pain.

"I was just looking to borrow a little cash," the man whimpered. "Honest!"

Blue pulled up the man's shirtsleeve and peered at his forearm, then stepped closer to stare into the man's face. "Tell me your name," he demanded. When the man didn't reply, a movement by Serena brought another moan.

"Lincoln," the man croaked. "Like the President!"

"Listen to me, Honest Abe," said Blue. "Two blocks from here is a place called Venice House. You've heard of it?"

"Sure," the man muttered. "Everyone knows it."

"They can help you there," Blue said, speaking in measured tones. "Methadone, tranquilizers—whatever you need. I know you won't go there tomorrow, or the next day. But sometime, maybe next week, or next month, you'll remember what I'm telling you. When you decide to check it out—and I *know* you will—tell them that Blue sent you. Blue like the sky, blue like you're going to be if you don't get straight. Because if you don't go there, *you will die* in these streets."

He brought his face closer, until the two men's noses were almost touching. "What's my name?" he demanded.

"Sky Blue," said the man. "I'll remember, I swear...."

"We're through here," said Blue. Serena released her grip and the man slumped to the ground. At that instant, a car's lights appeared on the road above them. It was the same cab that had driven them to Santa Monica. The driver peered down the alleyway and tapped his horn twice.

"Good timing, huh?" grinned Blue. The encounter had left him positively cheerful, Blake noticed. Serena didn't reply. She was panting slightly, either from the exertion or adrenaline or both.

"Let's go home," said Blake.

"Can't say I've heard the Daz referred to as 'home' very often," laughed Blue. "But tonight, home sweet home it is!"

Serena sat silently between the two men in the back of the cab, watching as Blue pulled on a pair of latex gloves and took a handkerchief from his jacket. Ignoring the violent bounce the car made each time it encountered one of the boulevard's many potholes, he carefully wiped down the mugger's gun and the six bullets he'd taken from it. "Not really necessary," he said. "But old habits die hard." When he was done, he carefully placed the bullets back into the gun's chamber and slipped the revolver into his pocket.

As the taxi turned off Santa Monica Boulevard onto North La Cienega, Blue leaned forward and spoke in the driver's ear. The driver nodded and made a sharp right-hand turn onto Wilshire. A few minutes later, the car pulled to a stop beside a tall cyclone fence. Blake smiled in sudden recognition: They were at the La Brea Tar Pits—a place he'd visited several times as a boy. In his younger days, he'd been fascinated by the idea of prehistoric creatures venturing into the pools for a drink of water, only to become fatally stuck in the petroleum residue seeping up through the earth's crevices. Sadly, the era when La Brea played host to busloads of wide-eyed children was long gone. It had closed several years earlier, an economic victim of the UZ walls. Now the tar pits could only be viewed through the padlocked fence that surrounded them.

"Sit tight," said Blue. Still wearing the gloves, he got out of the car and sauntered up to the fence. Glancing through it at the tar pits twenty yards away, he fished the revolver from his pocket and hefted it twice, then heaved it into the air with a grunt. The gun flew in a high arc before landing in the center of the oily expanse of black liquid, where it disappeared with a muted splash.

Back in the car, Blue peeled off his gloves as the driver made a U-turn and roared back down Wilshire, heading west. "It's true what they say, you know," he announced to no one in particular. "A bodyguard's work is never done."

At one a.m. the hotel lobby was more crowded than ever, with a hundred conversations going on at once. As soon as they sat down, a pimply kid in a coonskin cap came over. "What's the good word, Danny?" asked Blue, handing him a twenty-dollar bill.

The kid glanced down to check the denomination, then stuffed the bill into his pocket. "Let's see," he said, pretending to search his memory. "Oh, there's a sex party up in the penthouse. Started about an hour ago."

"Keep going," said Blue. He looked at Blake and winked. "Trust me, Karl. When you've seen one orgy, you've seen them all."

"Also, the Tangles are throwing a salon in room twelve twenty-four!" the kid continued.

"That's more like it. We'll stop by, but just for a few minutes," Blue said decisively.

Clanking and shuddering, the elevator took an eternity to reach the twelfth floor. Serena, still preoccupied, stared wordlessly at the elevator doors. "Does anyone ever inspect this thing?" asked Blake.

Blue grinned. "What do *you* think?"

Inside Room 1224, faux rock stars and their hangers-on were standing or lounging in every available space. A young man in a white dinner jacket stood behind a linen-covered table in the living room, doling out wine and mixed drinks. In one corner, a half-dozen people were hunched over a low table, snorting cocaine off the glass surface.

"Hello, Blue. Gonna introduce me to the newbie?" An intense-looking man stood in front of them, peering intently into Blake's eyes. He was dressed all in black except for an oversized pair of yellow, butterfly-shaped glasses.

"Karl, this is Hakim. Hakim, Karl." Blue's introductions were less than enthusiastic.

"Karl, my friend, do you understand about the progression?" asked the man, fluttering his hands like a pair of flailing birds.

"I'm sorry?" said Blake.

"We'd love to chat," Blue began, "but—"

"The *progression*," the man hissed, ignoring him. "I'm talking about how the mad, deep blues of the tormented stratum lay incubating for centuries in the delta swamplands, until they finally rose up and wandered north, where they became immortally electrified—and how that sound was joined to the banjo-laden music of the hill folk, lifted by the pounding pianos of the southern road houses and energized by the twanging three-chord cowboy yodelers of the dusty west—infused, all of this, always, by the rustic ballads of the old country—until finally it reached its ultimate destination: the eternal flower children of America's middle-class diaspora and the crazed, youthful amp-humpers of the British streets, twin aliens on a common quest...while of course, soaring above it all—need I tell you?—forever before and forever after, was the indispensable back-lighting...the impossible brightness...of the throbbing *West African beat*."

Pausing for breath, the man reached for a nearby glass and gulped down its contents greedily.

"I swear he lifted it all from that blackboard diagram in *School of*

Rock," said Blue under his breath. He tried to ease Blake away, but Hakim reached out and grabbed Blake's wrist tightly. "Do you understand all this, young newcomer? Can your bourgeois brain wrap itself around the magical vastness of this promised land?"

"Karl!" Stepping in between them was Stash, gin bottle in hand. "Lance and I just had a *lightbulb moment!*" Lance looked over his shoulder, grinning maniacally. "When you come to our gig tomorrow night, we're going to invite you on stage!"

"To play guitar!" Lance added, slurring his words a bit. "You did say you play?"

"Sure, a little rhythm."

"Shot a flock of rhythm and blues," sang Stash, snapping his fingers and doing a wobbly version of the twist. He wheeled abruptly and wandered off to another corner of the room, bottle in hand.

"Good. Then we'll see you there," Lance said. As Blake started to reply, his vision suddenly went dark.

"Guess who?" Removing a pair of manicured hands from his eyes, Blake turned to see Caroline. "Karl, you made it to my party!" she squealed, throwing her arms around him. She hugged him tightly, pressing her breasts and crotch against his body. "Come on, let me show you around."

Taking his hand, Caroline walked him through the crowd, introducing him right and left. "This is my friend Karl. He's new in town—doesn't know a soul, poor baby," she told a statuesque blonde woman in a full-body pink spandex leotard and matching heels.

"I see," said the woman, raising a knowing eyebrow. "How sweet that he's got *you* for a welcoming committee."

"This is Dee, lead singer for the No-No's," giggled Caroline. "She's jealous because our band blows them off the stage nightly!"

"In your over-lubricated dreams," Dee said calmly.

A tough-looking woman dressed in leather pants and a camouflage shirt walked over with a pair of Cosmopolitans and handed one to Dee. "Thanks, doll," said Dee. "Georgina, meet Karl—Caroline's latest conquest."

"Shush, Dee. I haven't even kissed him yet!" pouted Caroline in mock disapproval.

"Who's the Yank?" interrupted an irritated-looking man with a northern England accent, peering at Blake through round-rimmed glasses.

"Karl, this is Nigel, of the Puddles," sighed Caroline. "God's gift to rock and roll."

"She means the Liverpudlians—but then, if I channeled a derivative, bubble-gum girl band, I'd be vibey too," the man snarled, hooking his thumbs into the waistband of his striped trousers. "Of course, not every band can make musical history." He grabbed Blake's arm and pulled him closer. As he leaned in to speak, the smell of liquor on his breath was overpowering.

"Listen to me, mate—I've had every woman in this room, *multiple* times," he muttered in Blake's ear. "This is *my* town, so don't come in acting like you're some kind of hot shit. Understand?"

"What's he telling you, Karl? How many times he's screwed all of us?" said Georgina with a smirk. "Sorry, Nigel, but I don't swing that way."

"You did that night at the Marmont, love," Nigel replied coolly. "Screamed like a banshee, as I recall."

"Shove it, jerk," said Georgina. With a short, swift motion, she threw the contents of her drink in Nigel's face.

Several partygoers glanced over at the quarreling pair, but no one seemed especially perturbed. "Huck," Caroline called. "Can you give us a hand over here?"

"Alright, folks," said a tall man with sideburns and a cowboy hat, coming up behind Nigel and gripping the back of his neck firmly. "This is *way* too much monkey business. Been hitting the Brandy Alexanders again, Nigel? Say good night to all the nice people."

"Get your hands off me, you bloody has-been," Nigel growled. He tried to take a swing at the man, but Huck held him out of reach with his long-armed grip as he steadily maneuvered Nigel toward the door and out into the hallway. "Don't come back, y'all!" he shouted after him.

The buzz of conversation resumed for several minutes until the lights abruptly dimmed and a spotlight on the ceiling clicked on, projecting a circle of light in the center of the room. Caroline stepped into the light holding a microphone.

"Good evening everyone," she said. "Traditionally, we always like to feature a few performances at these parties. So tonight—here to personally encourage as many of you as possible to join him at UZFest next week, in the Big Apple—is Mr. Sex Appeal himself."

The room burst into applause as a man with traditional African tribal scars carved into his cheeks replaced her in the spotlight, joined by three musicians carrying an acoustic guitar, a violin and a tall African drum.

"It's wonderful to be here with you lovely people," the singer said. "As you know, the Branford Foundation has generously chartered three planes to transport as many Los Angeles musicians as possible to New York City for next week's celebration. Free accommodations are available there as well. Check with our friends at the front desk here, and they'll give you all the necessary information. Now, I'd like to transport you somewhere else, to a special place inside our souls..."

With that, his supporting trio eased into the opening notes of "Kiss From a Rose" while the man with the scars stood listening with his eyes closed. As the introduction neared its conclusion, he opened them again, smiled widely at the roomful of people, and began to sing. All around Blake, people swayed to the music and softly crooned with him. Caroline was singing too, Blake saw. Mesmerized, he watched as she mouthed the lyrics. She looked more beautiful than ever, he thought.

"I know you're having fun," Blue said in a low voice. "But tomorrow's a *big* day."

"Whatever you say, coach." Flanked by his two companions, Blake headed reluctantly for the door. As he passed Caroline he tried to catch her eye, but she was too transfixed by the Seal impersonator to notice. The only person to acknowledge his departure was Hakim, who glared balefully at him from across the room through his yellow frames, then tilted his head forward in a sardonic bow as Blake passed out the door.

In the hallway, a small knot of men and women were embroiled in a discussion of whether groups from the 1960s had been unfairly penalized by the Cultural Hygiene laws because of their later music. "If the Beach Boys had stopped before *Pet Sounds*, they'd be legal today—it's a no-brainer," a man with sun-bleached hair was saying.

"That's complete bullshit! The psychological influence of the surf sound was evident well before Brian Wilson discovered LSD and the theremin," a serious-looking woman in a sari shot back. The rest of the conversation was lost to Blake as the elevator door shut behind them.

Back in their suite, they sat around the dining room table sipping ice water and listening to some formless elevator music with a synthetic click track that Blue had found on the radio.

"The UZ isn't half as bad as it looks on the news programs," said Blake, "although it *is* kind of crazy."

"There's a lot of acting out here," said Serena. "But that's partly because the Zone gives people the freedom to recreate themselves—which is the essential function of art, according to Otto Rank."

"Otto Rank?" Blake thought for a moment. "He's the psychologist who analyzed hero myths, right?"

"That was one of the things he wrote about—recurring themes in the birth stories of legendary heroes," Serena replied. "Did you ever notice, for example, how almost every mythical hero, from Moses to Oedipus, got separated from their original mother and father in infancy and was raised by substitute parents?"

"In case you couldn't tell, Serena was a psych major in college, before she became a lean, mean fighting machine," said Blue. "As long as we're on the subject, Serena, didn't Rank also hypothesize that self-recreation through art always involves a neurotic crisis?"

"Oh-ho—someone's been reading up!" Serena said. She turned to Blake. "Before we left the house in Venice, Branford told us that you hadn't fully committed to the cause yet. He said we needed to pin you down before we can move forward. So, no more beating around the bush...are you going to help us?"

Blake looked away. He'd been hoping to put off this moment as long as possible. From childhood onward, he'd never been much of a joiner. "I just don't want to commit to interacting with a predetermined group at a predetermined time, week after week," he'd told Ann once when he turned down an invitation to join her book club.

"You've got some real issues, Blake," she'd replied, shaking her head.

Now, sitting around the scuffed wooden table in their timeworn Hollywood hotel, that conversation felt like it had taken place a century ago. "I've always felt," Blake began slowly, "that if you just made your way as an individual, trying to be the best person you could be, then you shouldn't have to choose sides."

"In a perfect world, maybe," said Serena. "But in *this* world you're on one side or the other, whether you like it or not. It's the oppressors versus the oppressed—and the oppressors count as their allies all the good people who don't have the stomach to join the fight. The ruling class pours their money into advertising and entertainment and a few public works here and there, all designed to convince everyone that civilization is operating just fine. Meanwhile, billions suffer in their own private corners of hell."

Getting up, Serena went into the suite's kitchenette and took a pack of cigarettes and a lighter from a drawer. Opening a window, she lit a cigarette and exhaled a stream of smoke out into the night air. "Enough talk," she said. "Look, Karl—our movement needs you. Are you with us or not?"

Blake raised the water glass to his mouth and took a drink. Branford had been right: he'd already made his decision, but for his own reasons. People should be free to express themselves without government interference, he thought, including being able to play and listen to any music they wanted. The loss of that freedom—and how that affected him, and Carter's cousin and her friends, and millions of other decent people—was why he hated this government.

"You can both relax," he said. "I'm with you."

Serena nodded and expelled another lungful of smoke out the window.

"I never doubted you for a minute," smiled Blue. "Welcome aboard!" He reached across the table to shake Blake's hand, but Blake didn't budge.

"Just so you know," he continued, "I'm not doing it for your precious political cause."

"No?" replied Blue, unfazed. "Why, then?"

"I'm doing it because the government is made up of a bunch of assholes who insist on telling people how to run their lives. That's why," said Blake.

Blue shrugged. "Works for me," he said. Rising to his feet, he glanced pointedly at his wristwatch. "Whoa—how did it get so late?"

"Bedtime, I know," said Blake. He looked at Blue and then at Serena, still standing with her cigarette by the window. "But first, there's something I've been meaning to ask. Are you two…?"

Serena looked at Blue and laughed sharply. "God, no," she said. "I'm not Blue's type—and he's definitely not mine. That's why we've been able to maintain such a good working relationship."

"So, it's not a White Stripes thing," said Blake.

"Hardly," said Blue. "Serena is neither sister nor wife. Now, what do you say we get some sleep?"

❖ ❖ ❖

Blake woke from a deep slumber to hear Blue and Serena arguing in low, heated tones on the other side of his bedroom door.

"We're not the morality police," Blue was saying. "His love life is his own business."

"It's our job to guard his security. And I say this puts him in potential danger!" hissed Serena.

"Oh, come off it. You know she's been fully vetted. She's one of us."

"Maybe someone got to her."

"In the past twenty-four hours? Highly doubtful. What do you think—she's going to strangle him in the act?"

"I don't like it—and I don't like *her!*"

"Well, I'm overruling you on this one. The guy's been under incredible pressure. He needs to blow off some steam."

"So now you're a stress-relief expert?"

"Would it make you happier if I told her to leave the door open?"

"Yeah, that would make me feel just great. Listen, Blue, I'm out of this. Whatever happens, it's on your head."

A minute later, the bedroom door swung open and a woman's figure stood silhouetted in the light from the living room.

"Who's there?" said Blake, fully awake now.

"I haven't had such a tough time talking my way into a boy's room since our high school's field trip to Disneyland! Who *are* you, anyway?"

It was Caroline.

"What time is it?" said Blake. He rolled out of bed and stood facing her in his boxer shirts. She was wearing the same outfit she'd had on earlier, and her hair was more tousled than ever.

"Four o'clock, five o'clock...who cares?" she laughed. "The way your marine detail is trying to keep you off limits, I figure you must be some politician's kid."

"You're wrong about that," said Blake. "But seriously, Caroline, you shouldn't be here—you don't know what you're doing."

"Spare me," she said. "I'm as sober as a judge, and I know *exactly* what I'm doing." Stepping forward, she pushed on Blake's chest with surprising strength. The unexpected force toppled him backwards onto the bed, where she immediately pounced on him, pinning his wrists down with her hands.

"So, who are you really—*Karl?* And are you ready to fulfill one of your deepest, horniest boyhood fantasies?"

He couldn't have answered if he'd wanted to, for Caroline's lips were fastened over his. As she probed his mouth with her tongue, Blake responded ravenously. He hadn't been with a woman since he'd broken up with Ann a half-year earlier, and he'd been attracted to Caroline from the moment he laid eyes on her. He found the whole Bangles parallel to be an incredible turn-on; Caroline's resemblance to the group's lead singer was uncanny, and it was easy to pretend she was the real thing.

"Whoever you are, I like you—a lot," she said breathlessly. Leaning back, she undid the straps of her dress and let it fall around her waist. Cupping her breasts in her hands, she fed one nipple and then the other to Blake's ready mouth. As he suckled, she reached down and found what she wanted. "Ah...le Grand Orange," she murmured. In one quick motion, she yanked off his underwear, then swiftly divested herself of everything but her stockings and high heels.

"Now, Karl, or whatever your name is," she said, hovering over him in the darkness, "I'm going to show you how to fuck like an Egyptian."

ELEVEN

Crosstown Traffic

Wednesday, September 4

MARTIN BIBBITT LAY ON THE thick shag rug, staring at the ceiling and breathing slowly and deeply, four counts in, eight counts out, as his chiropractor had taught him. Above him, the luxurious notes of Brahms' Symphony No. 1 floated from the quadraphonic speakers on his office walls.

"Mister Secretary," said his assistant, sticking her head through the half-open door, "Your briefer from H.S., Mr. Christie, is here."

Bibbitt struggled to his feet, briefly recalling his resolution to go on a diet in the near future. "Send him in," he barked through the intercom.

"Good morning, sir," said the Homeland Security official, clutching his leather portfolio. Bibbitt, ensconced now behind his mahogany desk, nodded curtly in reply.

"What do you have for me?"

"Let's see," said the briefer, surveying his notes. "We had a strong week, arrest-wise—more than two thousand apprehensions nationwide, mostly for illegal possession of rock-oriented MP3 files. Our agents also broke up a file-sharing operation in New Jersey, as well as an organized-crime ring in Arizona that was smuggling CDs in from Mexico."

"These deviants never learn," snapped Bibbitt. "They're addicts, all of them—sick, sick people. What's new with the Hawkes case?"

"Some leads are being pursued, but we don't have anything definitive yet."

"That's it?" Bibbitt searched the briefer's face. "No details?"

"That's all, sir. Our big effort at the moment, of course, is to ensure that adequate security and surveillance is in place for the Urban Zone Festival in New York next week."

"Oh no!" Bibbitt groaned. "Is it that time of year already? Why can't we shut down that pageant of filth once and for all?"

"As always, we're working closely with the NYPD to monitor all performances and minimize the likelihood of any spontaneous political demonstrations," his briefer continued. "Of course, any attempts to record or film festival activities will be dealt with very firmly. The investigation into the threat of an underground broadcast is also ongoing—" The official stopped short and instantly tacked in a different direction. "The Muni underground, as I was saying, is also the subject of an ongoing surveillance operation by a combined task force of H.S. and FBI agents—"

"Just a moment," Bibbitt broke in sharply. "What's that about an underground broadcast?"

The Homeland Security officer said nothing, his face frozen in the death mask of a government official whose career has just detonated before his eyes.

"Never mind," said Bibbitt. "That'll be all."

The man stood and exited, limping like a man being led to the gallows.

As soon as the door had closed, Bibbitt was on his intercom. "Barbara," he snapped, "get Secretary Jackson on the phone. *Immediately.*"

He waited impatiently, and was rewarded a few seconds later by the sound of a genteel Virginia accent on the other end of the line.

"Robert, so good to hear your voice," said Bibbitt ingratiatingly. "How are Jane and the rest of the family?... Wonderful! Listen, I hate to make waves, but it's come to my attention that there's an ongoing investigation into a possible unapproved broadcast of the Urban Zone Festival activities next week. I was surprised to learn of this, of course, since up until now my office hasn't been told anything about the matter."

The voice on the other end spoke for several minutes.

"I see," said Bibbitt. "So your deputy secretary—what is his name again?... So, Deputy Secretary Smyth hasn't had the basic courtesy to keep our agency in the loop? After we so graciously ceded authority to him on the Hawkes case?" He sighed deeply. "Your department has such a fine reputation for collaboration, Robert. I shudder to imagine what the press would do if they got hold of this—not to mention what the President might think. You know how annoyed he gets when his agencies fail to coordinate."

As he listened to the other man's reply, a smile crept across his face. "Yes, I think a personal meeting between you, Smyth and myself would be an excellent step towards ironing this out. Shall we say tomorrow morning, 8:30, in my office? Thanks so much, Robert. You're a prince."

When Blake woke, Caroline was gone. He put on a hotel robe and shuffled into the living room. On the dining room table was a tray filled with soft-boiled eggs, bacon, fresh fruit and croissants.

"You look like a new man!" said Blue, switching off the TV news. Serena was nowhere to be seen. "I had to send your sleeping companion on her way," he added, seeing Blake glance around. "We've got a full schedule this morning. The last thing we need is the two of you making moon eyes over the breakfast table."

Blake frowned. Once again he felt like he was being manipulated, and he found it profoundly irritating. "Where's Serena?" he said shortly.

"She should have finished her morning kick-boxing session about ten minutes ago. My guess is that she's now downing a mango smoothie. I wonder whose face she was picturing on her boxing dummy—Caroline's or yours?"

"What are you talking about?"

"Get with it, Karl. Didn't you ever see *Bodyguard,* that old movie with Whitney Houston and Kevin Costner? Crushes come with the territory."

"You mean—?"

"No question about it. Beneath that tough gal exterior lies a hopelessly sensitive girl, searching desperately for love in all the wrong places." Blue yawned. "Anyway, eat up, dude. Fuel for the engine." As Blake seated himself, Blue wandered over and plucked a strawberry off the tray. "By the way," he added, "please don't tell Serena what I just said. If you did, I'd have to kill you."

He was kidding, of course.

The lobby and sidewalk outside the Daz were the quietest Blake had seen them since arriving at the hotel the day before. Most of the people out and about at this hour appeared to be drifters lugging their overstuffed backpacks or homeless people pushing shopping carts crammed with precious odds and ends. Blue hailed a cab and they drove a mile down Sunset, stopping in front of a scruffy storefront gym. Serena was waiting outside, an overnight bag slung over her shoulder. Without speaking, she jumped into the car and slammed the door shut.

Blue gave the driver an address in Century City. Then he turned to Blake and Serena. "Better strap yourselves in," he said. Blake was a little surprised at his show of concern, but he dutifully pulled the shoulder belt across his body and latched it.

"Where are we heading?" he asked, recalling what Branford had said about meeting some scientists involved in the quantum project.

Blue didn't answer. He seemed lost in thought, his eyes busily surveying the road ahead. "Watch out!" he suddenly cried, as a truck pulled out of a side street directly in front of them. There was a shriek of rubber on pavement, and an instant later their car plowed into the truck's rear-wheel assembly with a resounding crash.

They sat in silence for a moment, collecting themselves from the shock of the collision. Their car's hood was crumpled and the horn was sounding.

"What the hell?" shouted their driver.

In the distance, a siren sounded. "Everyone okay?" asked Blue.

"Terrific," said Serena sarcastically.

"Karl, you're bleeding," said Blue worriedly. Blake looked at him in surprise. He didn't recall hitting his head, but when Blue pressed a handkerchief tightly against his forehead then pulled it away, it was soaked with bright red blood. "We've got to get you to a hospital," he said.

Pushing open the door, Blue eased Blake out of the car and sat him on the ground. The truck driver was standing alongside their cabbie. Both of them looked at Blake. "Is he going to be okay?" the truck driver asked.

"He'll be fine," said Blue. "We need an ambulance, though."

"I radioed 911 already," the cab driver said. "They'll be here any minute."

The siren grew steadily closer, and a few moments later an ambulance zoomed up, lights flashing. Two paramedics leapt out with a stretcher and a gurney. After a brief examination of Blake's spine and neck, they quickly lifted him onto the stretcher and strapped him into the gurney, then loaded him into the back of the ambulance.

"We'll ride with him," said Blue. He and Serena belted themselves into the bench facing the gurney, the paramedics closed the rear door, and the vehicle accelerated sharply away, siren whooping. Inside the ambulance, meanwhile, all sense of urgency had evaporated. The paramedic riding in the back with them sat leafing through a racing form, ignoring Blake completely. "Relax, Karl," laughed Blue, seeing his puzzled look. He pulled a tube from his pocket and waved it in the air. "Fake blood." He turned to the paramedic. "Could we get a head bandage?" he asked. "Something obvious, but not too dramatic."

Nodding, the paramedic opened his equipment locker, pulled out a roll of gauze and began wrapping it around Blake's head, with Blue reaching in to add several fresh squirts of blood as he worked. They had just finished when the intercom crackled. "Checkpoint ahead." The ambulance braked to a stop and the back doors opened. Two police officers glanced in at Blake, prone on the gurney.

“He’s got a decent gash in his head,” the paramedic said, pressing both hands against Blake’s bandage. “We’ve got him stabilized, and the ER at UCLA has been alerted.”

“Okay, keep moving,” one of the officers said, closing the door again.

“No ID scan?” Blake said after they’d gotten underway.

“If the cops scan someone who leaves the UZ for a medical emergency, they have to file a whole report on the incident—the reason for the accident or illness, the treating clinicians, the medical diagnosis and outcome, and so on,” Blue explained. “It’s a major pain in the ass. For small potatoes stuff like this, they’d much rather just wave you through. It’s a back door in the system that we like to exploit from time to time.”

The group around the table was the same as the day before, minus Major Harris.

“Any updates?” asked Smyth.

“We’ve got something,” said Curtis. “The subject made a phone call to a relative—his uncle, on the father’s side—around midday on Monday, through a third-party routing service. We’ve traced it to a pay telephone in the southern California desert, about a hundred miles east of Los Angeles.” The official glanced at his notes. “According to our analysts, it’s possible they were arranging a meeting.”

“Interesting,” said Smyth. “Any idea why they would want to meet?”

“That’s easy,” said Marconi. “The relative in question, Frank Hawkes, is a journo with known ties to the Muni Alliance. He was hooking his baby nephew up.”

“You know this guy?” said Smyth, turning to look at Marconi.

“Sure,” said Marconi. “We’ve had our eye on him for years.”

“Since Hawkes went on the run, the uncle has also spoken with the fugitive’s father, but the conversation wasn’t substantive,” said the electronics chief. “Beyond that, we don’t have the uncle making phone or e-mail contact with anyone besides his usual friends and business colleagues."

"Is that right?" Marconi sneered. "Did you have his house staked out for visitors? Do you know for sure he doesn't have a disposable cell phone stashed somewhere?"

"I believe that stakeouts fall under your jurisdiction," the other man said calmly. "As for the cell phone, it's certainly possible."

"Please, gentlemen," Smyth interjected. "No need for finger-pointing. We're making good progress here. We have a solid location as of Monday, and a possible theory regarding next steps. If Hawkes did connect with the Alliance, where might that trail lead?"

"The L.A. Zone," said Marconi. "Obviously."

"Anything new from the locals?"

"Possibly," said Piroulis. "We just got notification that the California State Police made a traffic stop yesterday morning, not far from where the subject's phone call originated. The vehicle was filled with some UZ characters, plus an extra passenger—someone who wasn't in their car when they checked out of the L.A. Zone earlier that morning."

"We never issued a state-level alert for Hawkes," said Smyth thoughtfully. "Why would a California trooper be making a traffic stop in the middle of the desert?"

Disregarding the question, Marconi glared at Piroulis. "You didn't tell my office about this," he said sharply. "I'll need an ID on that extra rider, asap."

"I just heard about it a few minutes ago," said Piroulis mildly. A low hum sounded from his jacket pocket. "Hold on." He pulled out his mobile device and glanced at it. "I'm getting word that the same vehicle passed back into the L.A. Urban Zone at the southeast checkpoint, about two hours after the traffic stop," he reported. "The extra rider was still on board."

"Is this meeting over?" asked Marconi, rising to his feet.

"Certainly. Meeting adjourned," said Smyth, striving for an air of authority. "Just keep me posted—" But Marconi had already left the room.

When the office was cleared, Smyth's assistant, Rosemary, poked her head in. "Do you have a moment?" she asked. Recognizing the warning tone in her voice, Smyth's heart sank: it meant some serious shit had hit the fan.

"What now, Rose?" he said wearily.

Walking into his office, she closed the door behind her. "I just received a call from Secretary Jackson's office," she began. "Secretary Bibbitt of Cultural Hygiene has been in touch with him. During his briefing from Mr. Christie this morning, Secretary Bibbitt somehow learned of an investigation into potential underground broadcast activity around the New York Urban Zone celebrations. He was extremely upset at being kept out of the loop, and has requested a meeting with you and Secretary Jackson first thing tomorrow morning."

"Great," said Smyth, burying his head in his hands. "I suppose I'll have to bring that oily fish in on the Hawkes case now." He sat up straight. This was going to make things significantly more complicated. "All right, clear my morning schedule. Oh, and Rose...."

"Yes?"

"Call Christie and tell him to start making plans for a transfer. After a slipup like that, it'll be a while before he works in this town again."

❖ ❖ ❖

The paramedics wheeled Blake into the ambulance bay, where a triage nurse waved them through to the main ER. "We're from the Zone," Serena told the nurse behind the intake desk. "No insurance."

"What else is new?" said the nurse. "Go on back."

A few steps later they were met by a physician in a white coat with a stethoscope around her neck. "Put him in Procedure Room Three and we'll patch him up," she said.

The paramedics rolled the gurney into the room, signed the release form presented by an orderly and departed. Locking the door behind them, Blue removed Blake's orange-tinted glasses and unwound the bandage from his head. Using a damp tissue, he wiped the fake blood away, then unfastened Blake's earring and withdrew it from his ear lobe. From a low cabinet he took out a surgical cap and placed it over Blake's head, hiding his orange-died hair, then handed him a pair of scrubs to pull over his pants and shirt and a pair of booties to cover his orange footwear.

Looking in the room's wall mirror, Blake was startled to see his old self again. With a finger to his lips, Blue opened a door at the back of the room and beckoned Blake and Serena into a white, windowless corridor. Turning right, they walked a dozen yards and came to another door. Blue knocked three times, paused, then knocked twice more. It was opened by the man who'd spoken with Blake in his hotel room. As before, he was dressed a business suit and tie.

"I've got him, thanks," the man said. Serena and Blue nodded and turned back down the corridor. The man ushered Blake through yet another door into a small conference room where a group of people were seated around a table. One of them, a striking, dark-haired woman in a white lab coat, rose and extended her hand. "Blake…so nice to see you again!"

"Maria!" An outstanding physicist and superb teacher, Maria Morakova had been Blake's undergraduate advisor at UCLA: part mentor, part big sister, part mother confessor—and maybe something else, too. There had always been a flirtatious undertone to their relationship. While they'd never crossed that line, Blake had often imagined what it would be like if they had.

"It's good to see you, too," he said. "You look fantastic." As voluptuous as ever, Maria had replaced her eyeglasses with contact lenses and her hair was longer than he remembered.

"I didn't reveal that we were meeting with her former protégé, but Dr. Morakova guessed as much," said a man with a neatly trimmed beard. "Hello, Blake. I'm Neil Cohen."

Blake recognized the theoretical physicist. "Of course, from USC. I heard you speak in Phoenix last year."

"When our friends called me yesterday, asking for a consult on a rush project with some bright young physicist from up north, I had a feeling I knew who they were referring to," smiled Maria. "Your interest in quantum mechanics has borne fruit, I see."

"We don't have much time," Cohen said. "Blake, why don't you sit by me? I'll introduce the rest of our group." Going around the table, he rattled off the names of two other physicists, a chemist and an electrical engineer, all familiar names to Blake. The last person introduced was a computer scientist named Bjorn Bjorkman.

"Good to meet you," said Blake. "Sorry, but I haven't heard your name before."

"I'm with a private company," the scientist said. "My boss prefers we maintain a low profile."

"What we're trying to do here is virtually unprecedented, people," Cohen continued. "Our aim to take a largely untested prototype of a revolutionary communications technology, and turn out multiple working versions in a week's time. The good news is that all the basic steps have already been worked out. Plus, we only need the units to work for one hour."

He looked around the room. "Some of you, understandably, have expressed concerns about the legality of this project. First, I can assure you that this project does not involve any classified information. Second, you are all here in a purely informal capacity, as unpaid advisers. There will be absolutely no data trail connecting you to this project. Understood?"

There were nods around the table.

"Good," said Cohen. "Our goal today is to identify what we'll need for the manufacturing process." He turned to Blake. "We've been briefed on the basics of your device, but that's all. We need you to walk us through the details."

Blake nodded and cleared his throat. After being led around by the nose for the past two days, it felt good to take charge. "Thanks everyone," he said. "First, I want to make it clear that I'm here today because I believe strongly in the free dissemination of scientific discoveries throughout the global community. I trust that's a goal you all share, as well."

He paused for a moment to gather his thoughts, then stood up and moved to the whiteboard on the wall. "There are really just a few essential elements of this technology," he began. "But each one has to be assembled with great precision. The central component is a thermal dosimetry crystal lattice. This is a crystal containing a billion or more nitrogen vacancies, created using an ion gun. In order for this device to work, these lattices have to be manufactured in pairs, with each member of the pair containing identical vacancy patterns. The vacancies in the two lattices are then filled with a series of matching entangled electrons. I've been using an Andreev tunneling mechanism to generate the entangled particles, then passing them through a superconducting Y junction to separate them. These electrons serve as the device's qubits—the quantum particles that will communicate with other."

His throat suddenly dry, Blake stopped and took a long drink from the water glass on the table in front of him before continuing. "The device also requires a pulse laser to stimulate selected 'master' qubits on the transmitting lattice, and a sophisticated computer-guidance system to coordinate the pulse laser's firing pattern. While this laser effect occurs, the receiving unit uses a computerized Doppler device to monitor a microwave beam sent through the field of 'slave' qubits."

Blake blinked at the gathered scientists, conscious of the new terrain he was treading. "That was the really big breakthrough," he continued, "—realizing that the mass of entangled electrons actually accelerated the electromagnetic wave through a slight time shift. By measuring minute fluctuations in this accelerated wave pattern, using my random convergence algorithms, it becomes possible to detect sequential changes in the quantum status of individual electrons. In practical terms, this translates into the ability to send and receive digital messages, in which a stimulated qubit represents a one and a non-activated qubit represents a zero."

He went on to explain each step of the process. "The toughest part is manufacturing the crystal lattices themselves," he added. As the group listened, he described the laborium crystal he'd developed.

"Can we come up with a list of equipment needed to accomplish this?" asked Cohen once he was finished.

Blake ticked through the necessary components while he took notes. When Blake was done, Cohen looked up. "This is an incredibly tight time frame, obviously. But I think we have the resources to pull it off," he said. "One question: Is video transmission a possibility at this point?"

Blake frowned. "In theory, yes," he said. "In practice, though, that would use up the available qubits so quickly that each lattice would last only a few minutes. We can get substantially longer communication times from each crystal by sticking to a digital audio signal."

"You've completed two prototypes, correct?" said Maria. "What happened to them?"

"They're now in the possession of the Federal government," Blake said. "Both devices were good for about sixty minutes of audio transmission time per lattice. If we employed a larger lattice design, that time could be extended somewhat."

"As I mentioned earlier, an hour should be sufficient for this project," said Cohen, "Questions?"

The group peppered Blake with queries about how the crystal lattices were formed, the parameters of the superconductor, and the nature of the laser used to collapse the quantum particles. Bjorkman, the computer scientist, remained silent until the others were done. Then he leaned over the table and squinted at Blake.

"The way I see it," he said slowly, "the weak link here is the laser software. What exactly were you using on your prototype?"

"Actually, I adapted software from a laser surgery device," Blake said with a touch of embarassment. "It was the only pulsed laser program I could get my hands on."

"Pretty clever," said the scientist. "But we could do a lot better with something tailored to this purpose."

The man in the suit, who until now had been sitting quietly against the wall, stood up and wiped the whiteboard clean, then turned to face the group. "I don't need to remind everyone how important it is to maintain confidentiality," he said. "Please keep all communications about this project strictly face to face. No e-mails, no faxes, no phone conversations."

He looked around. "Any other questions?"

"Will our presenter be available for future consultations?" asked Maria.

"That's unclear," said the man. "For now, if you run into a serious issue, contact me and I'll relay the message to Mr. Hawkes." Clasping his hands together, he looked around the table. "On behalf of myself and the Municipal Alliance, I can't thank all of you enough." He turned to Blake. "We have to go," he said.

Blake barely had time to wave goodbye to Maria and the others before being hustled back down the white corridor to the rear door of the medical exam room. Answering the coded knock, Blue pulled Blake into the room. Without speaking, he quickly stripped off Blake's surgical scrubs, replaced his earring and glasses, and then wrapped the red-stained covering around his head. A moment later, the doctor who had greeted them earlier knocked lightly and let herself in.

"Let's take a look," she said, unraveling his head wrap again. "Even more superficial than we suspected. A few butterfly bandages and you'll be as good as new." She swiftly applied several small bandages along Blake's temple and covered them with a longer, flesh-colored strip. "You're free to go!" she smiled.

The paramedics who'd brought them to the medical center were waiting in the ambulance bay. "No stretcher this time, boys," said Blue. The trio climbed into the ambulance and belted themselves in for the drive back to the UZ. "Sorry about the fender bender, Karl," grinned Blue, throwing his arm around Blake's shoulder. "It's lucky you're such a fast healer!"

With the briefing behind him, Blake felt a mixture of relief and fresh concern. Until that morning, the idea of reconstructing his quantum communicator had been an abstract notion. Now that the wheels were actually turning, though, his competitive juices were kicking in and he found himself rooting for the project to succeed.

When the ambulance pulled up to the UZ checkpoint they were met by the same officer who'd let them out of the Zone earlier. "Everything okay?" he asked. "They just brought your car through. It was pretty smashed up."

"Our pal got a little scrape, but he'll survive," Blue replied, patting Blake's arm.

"Glad to hear it," the officer said, waving them through. "Be more careful in the future, will you?"

TWELVE

So You Want to Be a Rock 'n' Roll Star

"HELLO THERE, AND WELCOME TO the Fox News show *American Perspective*. Quite a bit happening on the political front these days, of course. As you undoubtedly have heard, Democratic presidential nominee Maxwell Fish is getting to be let out of his cage next week to give one speech in public. After that, it's on to the Supreme Court, which will decide later this month whether Governor Fish can legally be prosecuted for treasonous activity while running for President—and if so, whether that gives the government the right to curtail his campaign activities prior to going to trial. Who would have thunk it, right? Now, one question we've been hearing a lot from our viewers has to do with *why* Governor Fish has gotten into so much trouble for meeting with a member of the Canadian intelligence community. After all, the Canadians are our traditional friends and allies. Here to provide some American perspective on the matter—if you'll pardon the expression—is our national security correspondent, Sally Wilder. Sally, can you give us some background here?"

"Certainly, Craig. This all traces back, of course, to the Boundary Water Incident of September 11, 2016. On that day—the fifteenth anniversary of the 9/11 attacks, as it happens—the U.S. Border Patrol apprehended five men paddling rubber rafts through what's known as the Boundary Water region, a network of lakes that stretches for hundreds of miles along the border between Minnesota and Canada. The men apprehended that day were ostensibly on a duck-hunting expedition. However, a subsequent search of their belongings revealed that they were actually attempting to smuggle a working nuclear device into the United States from Canada. The device, concealed inside a hidden waterproof chamber in one of the rafts, was estimated to be fifty times as powerful as the bomb dropped on Hiroshima."

"I remember that day well, Sally—one of the most terrifying moments in the history of this great nation."

"It certainly caused a complete rethinking of our anti-terrorist policy. We'd been focused mainly on threats from overseas at that point in time, but these five terrorists were all born and raised right here in the U.S.A."

"All-American types, that was the strange thing about it. Except for the fact that they were over-the-top music nuts, right?"

"Correct. All five belonged to a religious cult that went by the name of Musicology. The cult centered on the worship of rock music as a source of spiritual truth. The terrorists' ringleader, Rick Rogers, was also the cult's high priest."

"And boy, was his arrest high impact! As you know, Sally, many people think the Boundary Water Incident cost Hillary Clinton the presidency that year."

"It's true that she did have a clear lead in the polls at that point in time. And it's also true that President Ballinger, who was then the Republican presidential candidate, passed her in the polls the very next week. Of course, the fact that the Ohio Governor had already named former CIA Director Acton as his vice presidential running mate helped immensely, as well. Following the arrests, news reports surfaced almost immediately indicating that the plot had been uncovered thanks to Acton's aggressive actions in the preceding months, just before he stepped down as President Obama's CIA chief to accept the GOP vice presidential nomination."

"That's right—Obama had chosen Acton to head up the CIA as an olive branch to the Republicans. So much for bipartisanship! Obviously, the Republicans in Congress benefited from the Boundary Water Incident as well."

"That's right, Craig. They solidified their control of both houses in that fall's election, and they haven't looked back since. Everyone understood that this near-catastrophe happened on President Obama's watch, with the Democrats in control of the national security apparatus."

"In short, there was a whole lot of politics around the incident—and a lot of fear, too, plain and simple. If that bomb had gone off in a major U.S. city..."

"I don't even want to think about it, Craig."

"So, where do the Canadians come into all this?"

"The U.S. was never able to prove that Canada knew about the nuclear plot in advance, but there have always been suspicions in that regard. What we do know for a fact, however, is what took place *after* the nuclear terrorists were arrested."

"When Rick Rogers, somehow, inexplicably, escaped—"

"Yes, through the ceiling of a Minnesota jailhouse, in the middle of the night, just two days after his arrest. As I'm sure everyone recalls, he fled across the border to Canada and asked for political asylum."

"Which they gave him."

"Yes, they did."

"Unbelievable. I mean, what could the Canadians have possibly been thinking, protecting this dangerous lunatic?"

"That remains a mystery to this day. Rogers died four years ago from pancreatic cancer, of course, so we'll never know his side of the story. But suffice it to say that our relationship with the Canadians has been strained ever since. For one of our presidential candidates to meet in secret with a Canadian intelligence agent is extremely troubling—particularly since it's a clear violation of the Foreign Contacts Act passed by Congress in 2018."

"Well, leave it to a Democrat to play footsie with a bunch of terrorist-coddlers."

"I'd prefer not to jump to any conclusions, Craig. We'll have to let this play out in a court of law."

"Naturally. That's what we do in a democracy. But, level with me here, which party do you trust more to deal with these threats? It took a Republican Congress to crack down on the Musicologists, for example. Since they passed the Rock Ban back in January of 2017, this has been a markedly safer, saner country. Don't you agree?"

"They certainly took the music-terrorist link seriously, I'll give you that."

"You know that Musical Aggression and Antisocial Behavior scale they use to figure out which music should be outlawed—MAAB, they call it?"

"I'm aware of it, yes."

"Well, someone I know in the Department of Cultural Hygiene was telling me just the other day that my beloved Herb Alpert and the Tijuana Brass almost got nixed by that scale. They just snuck through! I would have been in serious trouble if *they* got put on the no-play list."

"Well, I'm happy for your sake they didn't, Craig."

"I appreciate that, Sally. And thanks very much for stopping by the studio today..."

❖ ❖ ❖

"Tomorrow morning, we head for your hometown," said Blue. They were in the hotel lobby, drinking sodas and listening to a pair of guitarists sing selections from Eels, an L.A. indie band that formed in the mid-nineties and cut a dozen albums over the next two decades.

"San Francisco," prompted Serena under her breath, seeing Blake's look of incomprehension. "Stay focused, Karl."

"Meantime," Blue continued in a low voice, "you've got a job this afternoon, running the mixing board for a review at the Palladium. Their sound man came down with a stomach virus, so we thought this would be a good chance to display your skills in case anyone was wondering. We should make an early night of it, though. We're hitching a ride with the Five Fingers tour bus first thing in the morning." The Fingers were Rolling Stones channelers, the same sullen group Blake had seen in the lobby when he first arrived at the Daz. If they were as nasty as they looked, he thought, it was going to be a long bus ride.

"Sorry if our plans are interfering with your social life," Serena added snidely.

Blake started to say something about the previous night, then stopped himself. Why did he owe Serena an explanation? His hookup with Caroline wasn't just about lust—there had been an emotional connection between them. They'd made love twice: The first time was the pornographic fantasy they'd both had in mind, but when they woke a few hours later, their second coupling had a sweetness to it. Afterwards, Caroline had clung to him as they drifted back to sleep. He'd been feeling a glow from their encounter ever since, car crash notwithstanding.

Thinking about it, Blake felt a fresh flash of resentment at not being allowed to say goodbye to her that morning. And though he'd ditched his faux head dressing, he was also feeling vaguely annoyed at being put through the staged car accident earlier. Now, on top of everything else, he was essentially being ordered to operate a mixing board for the entire afternoon. What did they think he was—a trained monkey?

"So you're telling me I'm supposed to run a sound board I've never seen before, for a bunch of bands I don't even know?" he said.

"It's for your own good, dude," said Blue. "You see those cats over there?"

Without moving, Blake shifted his gaze to the far end of the room. Two thirtyish men in pork-pie hats, loud sports jackets and skinny ties were leaning against the bar, chatting with the bartender.

"Yeah?"

"They just checked in. Supposedly they're part of some Elvis Costello act. Only we've never heard of them. To my thinking, they look a little hard around the edges to be musicians. You agree, Serena?"

As Serena shrugged her shoulders noncommittally, Blue pushed ahead. "For your own protection, we need to clearly establish that you are who you say you are. This is the best way to do it."

Blake sighed. After twenty-four hours in the UZ, he was already feeling like a jaded Zoner. "I hope it's a good show, at least."

With time to spare, they set off on foot down Sunset to the Palladium, stopping for sandwiches along the way. Again, Blake was struck by the number of people in the streets—reading, strolling, talking together in small groups, and playing their guitars, keyboards and harmonicas on the sidewalks. The feeling of energy and creative freedom was a stark contrast to what he'd seen across the rest of America: the desperation and poverty of the underclass neighborhoods, the quiet anxiety in the middle-class towns, and the walled-off paranoia of the wealthy suburbs with their manicured, gated communities. *No wonder they scale walls to get in here,* he thought.

As they walked, a steady river of cars drove past. About half seemed to contain locals, while the other half were packed with boisterous tourists celebrating their eight-hour passes. Reaching the Palladium, they walked around back to where a dozen burly men were busily unloading speakers, cables, instruments and other equipment. Serena and Blue seemed to know everyone.

"Never fear, the engineer is here!" Serena announced when they reached the dressing room area. Surrounded by musicians and roadies, her habitual frown had melted away, leaving her disposition almost sunny.

"Joe Wilson—glad to meet you." A muscular forty-year-old in a Buffalo Springfield T-shirt gripped Blake's hand. "These afternoon shindigs are my baby. Thanks for filling in. I'll show you the console."

Blake followed Joe off the stage and across the dance floor to a small, raised platform at the back of the hall. It held a table with a mixing board not unlike the one Blake had used as a teenager. "Here you've got your master controls for lead vocals, drums, lead guitars, rhythm, keys, ancillary percussion, and background vocals," Joe said, running his hand across a series of faders marked with abbreviations scrawled on masking tape. He pointed to a series of knobs. "Amp outputs are here, PA outputs are here, stage monitors here. You have any questions, have someone send me a message backstage. Otherwise, let your ears be your guide."

With that, he handed Blake a set of headphones and hurried back toward the stage. Hanging the phones around his neck, Blake pulled a stool up to the board and looked over the controls. "You don't need to boost the bass too much—this place is like a cavern," said a voice beside him. "And a nice pan of the vocals and guitars makes for a really full sound in here." Serena had hopped onto the stool next to his and was studying the console over his shoulder.

"I thought you were just a punk rocker," said Blake.

"I'm a Jill of all trades—can't you tell?" she smiled.

"Ready for a sound check?" Up on the stage, Blue was talking into one of the lead vocal microphones, shading his eyes from the overhead lights as he looked out at Blake and Serena. Blue moved from one microphone to the next, counting off test patterns as Blake tweaked their settings. When the mics were all adjusted, he vanished briefly and then reappeared with an electric guitar. Plugging into each of the amplifiers, he raced through a series of deafening riffs as the gathering crowd reacted with a mix of cheers and boos. Blue moved on to the bass guitar amp, then ended up behind the drum kit, banging the kick-drum, snares, toms and cymbals for all he was worth. As he played, Blake listened intently, fiddling with the gain, input and output levels while he eyed the quivering needles on the various gauges.

"What Blue lacks in talent," said Serena dryly, "he makes up for in enthusiasm."

"He's not *that* bad," grinned Blake.

"He's a lot better with a semi-automatic, trust me."

When the sound check was finished, Blue left the stage. A minute later he reappeared next to Blake holding three cups of beer. "Cheers!" he said, handing one each to Blake and Serena. It was the first time Blake had seen the others drink alcohol. For the moment, it seemed, the sense of danger had abated.

The crowd suddenly erupted as a group of musicians bounded onstage. "Good afternoon everybody," a woman in long dreadlocks shouted into one of the microphones. "If you're cool, you rule—and if you're square, the exit is you-know-where!" With a crash of drums, guitar and slap bass, the band launched into a high-volume version of Sly and the Family Stone's "Dance to the Music." Blake's hands flew to the faders. As he began to shape the sounds reverberating off the auditorium walls, he flashed on a memory from his youth, sitting in his basement studio mixing the songs he'd recorded with his garage band.

"How fine is this?" he shouted to Serena. She smiled and nodded. "You're doing great," she said, rubbing his back.

The band rocked out for an hour before yielding the stage to a series of other groups channeling famous L.A. bands—Earth, Wind and Fire, the Eagles, and finally Flyte, a group that reincarnated the Byrds, complete with a Roger McGuinn look-alike in rose-tinted spectacles. Between numbers, the band members took turns reciting historical trivia about the musical groups they were portraying. Meanwhile, the crowd jamming the dance floor was in perpetual motion, singing, dancing, and embracing each other. A young woman caught Blake's eye and waved a fist in the air, and he punched a fist upward in return. The sense of community was palpable—Zoners and suburbanites alike, joined by the bond of music.

The concert lasted four hours. As the afternoon wore on, a parade of musicians, techies and music-business types dropped by their little island to greet Blue and Serena and meet Blake. "You're from the Bay?" exclaimed a man dressed like one of Robin Hood's Merry Men, complete with a lute on his shoulder. "Awesome! How long you here for?"

"He heads home tomorrow," Blue answered for him. "But he'll be back."

By the time the last performers completed their final encore, it was almost seven o'clock. Blake sat back, drenched with sweat. "My man!" shouted Joe, bounding up to him. "You were terrific. Here—" he held out a lit joint, which Blake drew on gratefully.

"Ready to grab some supper, mixmeister?" said Serena, jabbing him playfully in the ribs.

"After that, I suggest retiring early, to prepare for our dawn journey," added Blue.

"But the Sunset Kidz invited me to their show tonight," Blake protested. He felt like a petulant middle-schooler, asking to stay up late on a school night. "Lance said something about standing in with them on guitar."

"You've never played with a real rock band, have you?" asked Serena. "Blue—don't you think he needs to experience that, just once in his life?"

Blue rubbed his chin. "I'm your bodyguard, not your parent," he said. "If you want to skimp on sleep, that's your business."

"Then it's settled," said Serena. "Let's eat!"

At Blue's suggestion, they strolled through the fading light to a Vietnamese place between the Palladium and the Daz. Halfway there, Blue stopped and craned his head, looking upward. Several thousand feet above them, a small grey plane was flying silently in a westerly direction. "Drone," said Blue, matter-of-factly. "The Feds fly them low, just to let us know they care. The ones they really count on are too high to see."

As they entered the restaurant, Blake felt a thrill of excitement. In a booth toward the back, Caroline was sitting with two other women.

"How opportune," muttered Serena.

"Hey stranger," Blake smiled, walking over to the booth. Without a word, Caroline stood up, put her arms around his neck and planted a long kiss on his lips.

"To blow, blow, blow him…" sang one of her companions.

"Is to show, show, show him…" crooned the third woman.

"What you do!" they finished together, dissolving in laughter.

"This must be Karl, the Earl of Orange," said the first singer. "I've heard *all* about you."

"Say hello to my loudmouth friends, otherwise known as Theresa and Darlene of the Tangles," said Caroline. Like her companions, she was dressed in tight jeans and a bustier, with earrings in the shape of peace signs dangling from her lobes. "I missed you this morning," she added softly.

"I missed you, too," he replied.

"Sorry to crash the prom date," said Darlene, "but we have to bolt, Car. We've got a gig, remember?"

"We're opening for the Sunset Kidz over at the Whisky," said Caroline. "I wish you'd come."

"As a matter of fact, that's where we're headed," replied Blake. "Are the Kidz friends of yours?"

"Those delinquents? Not likely," said Theresa. "They do draw an audience, though. Ka-ching!" She rubbed her fingers together and the women laughed.

"Lance told me the show didn't start until eleven," Blake said.

"Naturally, they forgot to mention they'd be sharing the stage with another band," Caroline said. "*We* go on at nine. Here." She reached into her purse and pulled out three tickets. "For you and the Marines. Not that Blue needs a ticket to get in anywhere."

After a protracted kiss goodbye, she and her bandmates retrieved their guitar cases from the coat check and headed for their van parked at the curb.

"What a happy coincidence," scowled Serena. Her bubbly mood had vanished.

"It really *is* a small town, when you get to know it," said Blue cheerfully.

"They know your guy's in L.A.," the man said, speaking rapidly. "They know his alias, and they know where he's staying." He shot a glance around him, then leaned in closer to the pay phone. "It's all there, part of a report filed today.... No, there's nothing about him meeting with anyone." He paused a moment. "They've also updated the arrest warrant. According to current orders, they're planning to take him into custody tonight.... Yeah, that's what it says. This is coming straight from their ops chief to the top brass. I'll let you know as soon as I hear anything more."

Like most of the musical acts Blake had seen in the Los Angeles UZ, the Tangles were superb. Caroline was in great voice, and she had the crowd entranced as they rocked through the Bangles' repertoire of hits. It was almost as if these channelers *became* the musical groups they were imitating, Blake thought, watching from the front row.

Midway through the show, the stage lighting changed to a deep blue as the band segued into a slow instrumental arrangement. "This next song was inspired by the legendary Elvis Presley," Caroline said into the microphone, speaking softly over the music. "Years ago, four young women traveled to Graceland, to pay homage to the departed King. They saw a special altar, constructed in his honor. On that altar there burned a flame—an eternal flame...."

Strumming her guitar, she stared down at Blake and began to sing the song "Eternal Flame" directly to him, as if the thousands of other spectators weren't there. *I love you,* her look said to him. *Do you love me?*

For all her intensity, Blake couldn't shake the feeling that he was a prop in a stage show. In the mirror world of the UZ, it was impossible to tell whether Caroline was expressing heartfelt emotion, or play-acting, or some jumbled combination of the two. On the other hand, he reflected, he wasn't who *he* was pretending to be, either.

After the show ended to delirious applause, Blake, Serena and Blue made their way backstage. The Tangles were sitting in their dressing room, ecstatic and perspiring, sipping champagne and accepting congratulations from a crowd of admirers. Across the crush of bodies, Caroline flashed Blake a happy smile and mouthed the word, "Later."

Walking into the dressing room next door was like entering a different country. The mood was tense and subdued as the members of the Sunset Kidz paced the floor and ran through riffs on unplugged electric guitars. An unfamiliar figure with a mop of curly, purple-streaked hair sat in one corner practicing rolls on a drum pad. The playful bunch Blake had encountered in the desert was nowhere to be seen. Feral and aggressive, each musician occupied his own sullen, brooding space, growling at each other in monosyllables when they spoke at all. Blake was reminded of a wilderness safari he'd taken in Botswana's Okavango Delta as a teenager, where he'd watched a pride of lions spend an hour stalking a wildebeest before finally downing it and tearing it swiftly to pieces.

"Karl—at long fucking last!" snapped Lance. He was dressed in a red leather jacket with no shirt underneath, his hair wrapped in his trademark handkerchief. "We've got your weapon loaded and ready." Pointing to a turquoise Ibanez electric guitar plugged into a small Vox amp, he held out a palm filled with picks.

"It's been a few months since I played one of these," said Blake.

"Can the excuses, Kliff," snarled Stash. "Time to put up or shut up."

Blake flicked on the amp, then slipped the guitar strap over his shoulder and ran through a series of power chords. The guitar handled like a dream. "Jeff Beck, eat your heart out!" he crowed.

"Nice chops," said Tooth with a sarcastic sneer.

"Our set list," announced Lance, holding out a sheet with two dozen song titles scribbled on it. "You'll come onstage ninety minutes into the show, right after 'November Rain,' and play our two closing numbers with us. We're gonna rock straight into 'Paradise City,' finish with 'Nightrain,' and split. If you're any good, we'll bring you back for the encore."

Lance had a no-nonsense air of command—there was no question who was running the band. "These are the chords for 'Paradise,' in C," he continued, grabbing a marker from the dressing room table and scribbling a series of notations on the back of Blake's right hand. "And here's 'Nightrain,' in A minor and A. If you get lost, just follow the bass line. Got it?"

"I think so."

Retreating from the dressing room, Blake saw Caroline walking toward him, her dark eyes flashing. "I don't have much time," she said. "Some people are waiting to go out for drinks. But I'll see you back at the hotel, right?"

"Right," said Blake. It didn't seem like the time to mention that he was leaving town in the morning. They slipped into a narrow space behind the dressing rooms and Caroline wrapped herself around him. As his lips found her neck, Blake tasted the salty sweat from her performance. They clung together for a couple of minutes before she broke free.

"I've got to go!" she said breathlessly. "See you in a few hours. Come to my room. I can't wait!"

Back in the Kidz' dressing room, the rest of the band was poised to go on, but Lance seemed unaware of the time. He sat sipping Jack Daniels and Coke and chatting with two young women while a steady shout of "Kidz! Kidz! Kidz!" drifted in from the auditorium.

The chant stretched on for five minutes, then ten. Leaving the dressing room, Blake wandered out to the stage wing and stole a look at the crowd. The innocent-looking youngsters that had pushed up front to hear the Tangles were gone, replaced by scores of hard-faced men and women who stood sipping from pocket flasks and shouting epithets at the empty stage through cupped hands.

At 11:30, Lance stood up abruptly. "Let's do this fucker," he said. He began striding toward the stage then broke into a run, the other band members hurrying to keep up. Bursting into the spotlight, he grabbed a microphone and let out a piercing howl. "Are you ready to rock?" he screamed. "I can't hear you, Los Angeles—*are you ready?*" As the crowd screamed back in affirmation, the band exploded into "Welcome to the Jungle."

Watching from off-stage, Blake was blown away by the instrumental skill and impact of the music. He'd never especially cared for metal, but now he began to understand its appeal. As the Kidz powered through one number after another, he searched his memory for a description of Guns n' Roses he'd read once in *Rolling Stone*, something about how they embodied the inchoate emotions of the average American teenager. He also recalled that their concerts had frequently been cut short by Axl Rose's angry confrontations with fans. How far, he wondered, would Lance and the other Kidz go in recreating their heroes' performances?

That question was still on his mind when the band paused between numbers and Lance addressed the audience, lungs heaving. "You've been great," he said, wiping his brow and looking out over the sea of faces. "You see how easy it is? When *we* have fun, *you* have fun."

The crowd responded with a dubious half-cheer. After playing for well over an hour, Lance and the rest of the band were shirtless, their skin gleaming with sweat. Lance had already thrown himself twice into the mosh pit that had formed in front of the stage, surfing the crowd for several minutes each time before his security team wrestled him back onto the stage.

"Now I'd like to introduce the other Sunset Kidz," he continued. He called out the names of Nail and Tooth and the new drummer, then turned to Stash, prowling the stage in his top hat and shades. "Last but definitely not least, he lives in a world he did not create, but he walks through it as if it is of his own making....half man, half beast..."

Standing in the wings, Blake had a weird sense of déjà vu. Lance, he realized suddenly, was repeating the same lines, word for word, that he remembered Axl Rose saying on an old concert video.

"Don't be fooled by their act," said Blue, who had been standing at his side since the start of the show. "These guys aren't your typical Zoner band. What they did yesterday, pulling you out of the desert, isn't a job we'd give to just anyone."

"You mean they're ex-military, like you and Serena?"

"I wouldn't want to jump out of a helicopter with any of them, if that's what you mean. But they're UZ operatives—good ones. *And* they put on a decent concert."

Introductions over, Lance settled behind a grand piano that had been wheeled onstage and struck the opening chords of "November Rain." Blake's throat tightened as he realized he'd be joining them in a few minutes.

"One more thing," Blue continued in a low tone. "I didn't want to tell you too early, but there's been a change of plans—so I need you to listen carefully. We aren't leaving tomorrow morning after all. We're leaving town tonight instead, on a different bus. And you will *not* be traveling as Karl Kliff."

"Why the change?" asked Blake.

"You're getting a little more attention than we're comfortable with. Somehow, Karl seems to have gotten on the Feds' radar screen. So we're making him disappear."

"Just when I was getting used to orange," said Blake. "What do you want me to do?"

"You're going to transform again," said Blue. "Head straight for the dressing room as soon you're offstage. We'll do the rest."

Blake felt a knot tighten in his stomach. When would he be able to stop running? Looking down, he noticed his fingers on the neck of his guitar, unconsciously forming the chords of the song.

He was startled back to reality by the amplified sound of Lance's panting voice. "Ladies and gentlemen…we've had more than our share of guest guitarists over the years. But *none* of them, I can safely say, were as fluorescent as the man who's about to come on and play a few numbers with us. Direct from San Francisco, please welcome…*Karl Kliff!*"

Blake bounded onto the stage to a chorus of catcalls. Stash pointed at a waiting amp and patch cord and he hastily hooked up his guitar.

"Now," Lance added, "we're going to play a little song called… Paradise City!"

The audience erupted as the band smashed into the opening chords. Blake's amateurish guitar was clearly superfluous, but he did his best to add to the band's sound, banging out a scratchy back beat. The audience's response felt like a physical wave of energy as they shouted along with Lance's howled lyrics.

Swept up in the song, Blake suddenly realized he was singing the lyrics himself at the top of his lungs. Stash looked over at Blake and stuck out his tongue playfully. Behind them, the drummer was pounding the cymbals and toms like a madman. While the other musicians whirled and stomped to the beat, Lance wove around the stage, shoulders swaying back and forth. To be carried along by the force of the band was exhilarating—every note that Stash was churning out with his flying fingers seemed to penetrate the core of Blake's being. As he began to relax and get into his guitar, he looked up from his fretboard and grinned at the women and men screaming with pleasure. For the first time, he truly understood what it was like to be on the performing side of a superstar rock band—to hold the raw emotions of thousands of people literally in your hands. *It's the greatest feeling in the world,* he thought.

And then he spotted the two men. Wearing the same pork-pie hats they had on at the hotel, they were standing twenty feet from the stage, their eyes fixed on him.

Ripping his gaze away, Blake concentrated on the chords of the song as Lance hopped from one end of the stage to the other, singing something about waking up in an execution chamber.…

As the song ended, Stash took microphone in hand to usher in the next number, "Nightrain." "Despite what you've heard," the guitarist announced, "this song has nothing to do with drinking or drug addiction. It's about a walk in the park—"

The two men were talking to each other now, and another man wearing what appeared to be a radio earpiece had taken up position a few yards from them. He looked around casually and then locked eyes with Blake for an instant. Barely aware of what he was doing, Blake stumbled blindly through the rest of the song.

"Thank you, Los Angeles," screamed Lance as the last chord sounded. "We love you!" The band ran offstage as the audience stamped their feet and whistled.

Blue and Serena were waiting in the dressing room. Standing next to them was a man in a cowboy hat, a scar creasing one of his cheeks and long, braided hair hanging down his back. He could have passed for an extra in some Hollywood Western except for his wardrobe, which was straight out of the Summer of Love: jeans, torn canvas sneakers, and a tie-died shirt under a red velvet vest. Around his neck he wore a knotted bandana and a large metal yin-yang symbol that dangled beside his ID card.

As soon as the door closed, they flew into action. "Strip down!" barked Blue. The man tossed his hat on the counter, then started peeling off his clothes and handing them to Blake, who did the same. Moving like clockwork, Blue took out Blake's earring and passed it to the long-haired man. As they traded UZ passes and wallets, Blake glanced briefly at the man's ID. A digitally altered photo of himself as pony-tailed Ebenezer McEnzie stared back at him.

The band studiously ignored the personality switch occurring in front of them as they downed cocktails from paper cups and puffed on cigarettes. When the wardrobe change was complete, Serena removed Blake's glasses. Handing them to the other man, she reached up and peeled the scar off the man's face, then lifted his hair from his head. It was a wig, braid and all. Beneath it, the man had an orange Mohawk haircut identical to Blake's. With their similar height and facial features plus the outfit exchange, any casual observer would assume that the orange-clad man who had entered the dressing room and the one who'd soon be leaving it were one and the same Karl Kliff.

"Almost done," said Serena. She arranged the wig and hat on Blake's head and artfully stuck the fake scar on his cheek, then stepped back to look at him. Noticing his hand, she shook her head. "I need a marker!" she called in a low voice. Hurriedly she copied the chord sequence that Lance had written there onto the other man's hand, then licked her palm and rubbed Blake's skin clean.

The whole process had taken less than two minutes. Lance jumped to his feet.

"Encore time, you fuck-ups," he announced. "Last one out is a rotten corpse!" The new Karl Kliff grabbed the Ibanez that Blake had been playing and ran onstage with the rest.

"What's going to happen to him?" asked Blake.

"Don't worry—he can take care of himself," said Blue. "You've got a bus to catch."

"Quiet!" hissed Serena. She cautiously opened the dressing room door. Outside were two middle-aged women in hippie dress—floor-length skirts, fringed boots, shawls and granny glasses, with flower garlands in their long, silver-flecked hair.

"Ready to split, Eben?" asked one of them.

"I am," said Blake after a half-second's hesitation.

"Hurry, kitty-cats, or we'll miss the shuttle," said the other woman.

The two women grabbed Blake's arms and began walking on either side of him, pulling downward on his arms so that he was forced to stoop slightly. They inched their way toward the club's side door, picking their way through the cluster of roadies and hangers-on watching the show from the wings.

As they shuffled along, Blake risked a quick glance back toward the stage. His orange-clad replacement was playing guitar in the same spot where he'd been standing minutes before. Turning forward again, he saw two men standing by the side exit dressed in black leather, their eyes glued on the performance. As Blake and his companions passed, the men's gaze flickered over them, then returned to the stage. With an unrushed air, the three hippies eased open the door and stepped out of the club.

THIRTEEN

Nights in White Satin

THE BUS, AN ANCIENT GREYHOUND, was idling on Sunset, a block from the Whisky. The driver lounged in his seat, hardly bothering to look at the tickets being thrust into his hand. By the time Blake and the two women boarded it was almost at full capacity. The women chose seats together on the left side of the bus, two-thirds of the way toward the back. When they motioned for Blake to sit in the empty space across the aisle he quickly obliged, taking the window seat and leaving the aisle seat empty. The passengers around him ranged from fresh-faced youths in their late teens to men and women in their sixties and beyond. About half appeared to be San Francisco types, judging by their colorful, loose-fitting tops and long flowing dresses, and the rest looked to be L.A. hipsters of one kind or another.

A few late arrivals hurried aboard and claimed the remaining seats. "Last call for the Bay Zone Express!" announced the driver. As he reached for the lever to pull the door shut, two final passengers rushed up the steps. The first was a glammed-out Lady Gaga type in bugged-out sunglasses, high stacked heels, short shorts and a see-through blouse showing a black bra underneath. She handed over her ticket with a haughty shrug and walked unsteadily back towards Blake, settling into the aisle seat just in front of him.

The last passenger to board was a dissipated-looking man with a drooping moustache, dressed in ripped painter pants, a stained raincoat and an L.A. Dodgers baseball cap. He handed over his ticket and then broke into a racking cough, finally spitting a wad of phlegm into a soiled handkerchief he pulled from his raincoat pocket.

There were only a couple of seats left, including the one on Blake's left. *Not next to me, please,* Blake pleaded silently, watching the semi-derelict make his way down the aisle. But with the unerring tread of fate, the man walked directly to where Blake was sitting and collapsed wheezing into the seat beside him.

Blake stared out the window, determined not to engage him. A second later, he felt a sharp poke in his ribs. "Drink?" the man croaked. He held out a half-empty bottle of beer wrapped in a brown bag. "No thanks," said Blake, as politely as he could. To his surprise, the man lowered one eye in a slow wink. Blake stared in confusion for a second, then stifled a sudden urge to laugh. It was Blue!

Which meant... He glanced at the woman in the row ahead of him, her face half-turned toward him. Even with sunglasses covering her face, he couldn't mistake the unsmiling profile.

"Name's Pete," Blue said, sniffling into his handkerchief. "Nice knowing ya."

"Likewise," said Blake.

Outside, the sound of sirens was growing steadily nearer. As Blake turned again to look out the window, a pair of black sedans zoomed past.

"Not sure what that means," murmured Blue. "The plan was to play a half-hour encore and have the fans rush the stage at the end. Mass confusion. Plenty of cover. There's a trap door in the stage floor that connects to an underground passage leading out of the club. A few seconds to change his clothing and his hair, and Karl disappears forever."

"Let's hope it worked." The whole identity-changing business was starting to feel stale and forced to Blake. In fact, he was beginning to have second thoughts about the whole enterprise.

"Next stop, San Francisco," yelled the driver. The bus lurched away from the curb. A few minutes later they were at the northeastern UZ checkpoint. The driver leaned out his window and spoke with someone, then turned around to address the passengers. "Sorry folks, the authorities want to say a quick hello."

Groans and curses filled the bus. "Fascism never sleeps!" someone called out.

A moment later, two uniformed police stepped onto the vehicle. Blue's eyes narrowed. "They're Homeland Security, not LAPD," he whispered.

"Just making sure everyone's on the level, folks," said one of the officers. He slowly began making his way down the center of the bus, holding up what looked to be a digital camera and snapping a photo of each passenger in turn, then studying the camera's display screen.

"It's a facial recognition scan," Blue said in a low voice. "They're collecting biometric data. I know it."

Blake felt a bolt of fear flash through the pit of his stomach. *We're fucked,* he thought helplessly.

When the officer was a few rows away, Blue quietly stretched his arm across Blake and tested the latch just underneath the window. For the first time, Blake noticed they were sitting in one of the bus's emergency exit rows.

"If I open this door, I want you to jump out immediately and run straight across the street as fast as you can," Blue whispered. "I'll be right behind you."

Blake nodded, trying to maintain a bland look as the officer began photographing the passengers in the row just before Serena's. He was mentally rehearsing their next steps—yank up the door, leap to the street, then run to...where, exactly?—when the cop's partner suddenly put a finger to his earpiece.

"We just got a positive at the Whisky," he called. "Probable MI. They're requesting all available personnel."

"Okay everyone, we're done here," The first officer said. As he turned and headed for the front of the bus, a woman's voice piped up from one of the back rows.

"Set the music free..."

A few seats away, a man took up the verse:

"Liberate all melody…"

Seconds later the entire bus joined in, singing in unison:

"Let the music be, All together, one, two, three!"

Following the last note, the bus fell silent.

The two officers stood glaring. The one with the earpiece held up his nightstick in both hands like a baseball bat. "You've got ten seconds to get your filthy heads in your laps," he growled.

The passengers in the first few rows swiftly lowered their faces to their knees and covered their heads as the officer strode forward, swinging the nightstick in a vicious arc. With a swift sequence of blows he shattered the first six windows on the left side of the bus, sending pellet-sized glass fragments showering over the passengers.

"Who's singing now?" he shouted, red-faced.

Wheeling around, he walked back up the aisle, smashing six more windows on the opposite side. Back at the front of the bus, he spun to face the passengers one last time.

"Some fresh air for the ride. Enjoy your trip to stinking San Francisco!"

❖ ❖ ❖

Blake felt light-headed with relief as the bus rolled out of L.A. and began the climb toward Tejon Pass. At the same time, he noticed that Blue and Serena seemed distant and preoccupied. Blake had seen a look pass between them when the officer made the comment about the Whisky. Now, they were grimly quiet.

He nodded off for a while then woke again, wishing wistfully for a blanket. The shattered bus windows had been patched with sheets of cardboard but the chill night air still whistled through the cracks, overwhelming the old bus's heating system. He lay his head against his own unbroken window, watching the farmland of the San Joaqin Valley pass in the darkness. The more he thought things over, the more he regretted everything that had happened, starting with the secrecy of his quantum project. If he'd only been more transparent about it—recruited others into the effort, made it a group endeavor—then he wouldn't have been singled out like this.

He'd also concluded that escaping into the desert was a mistake. He had to turn himself in and face the consequences of his actions; it was the only way out. Bucking the U.S. government was simply too hard. He was exhausted, physically and mentally. Blue and Serena might be cut out for this sort of thing—life in the UZ was probably a lark compared to swimming across oceans or parachuting into terrorist strongholds—but Blake was no warrior, despite what Branford had said. Plus, he was losing confidence in the ability of the Municipal Alliance to protect him. Sooner or later, the authorities were bound to catch up with them.

His mind was made up: Once they reached San Francisco, he would make his way to Berkeley, find Mel, and arrange to contact the authorities with his help. *I'm done with running,* he thought. He wondered briefly how Caroline had reacted when he failed to show up at the hotel, but the idea was too complicated to hold onto, and he found himself drifting back to sleep.

The sky was lightening in the east when Blake was wakened by a nudge from Blue's elbow. The bus had pulled into one of I-5's state-run rest stops, and most of the passengers were getting off to use the restrooms and grab a snack. Blue motioned for Blake to follow him. In front of them, Serena tottered down the steps of the bus on her high heels and entered the building.

Inside was a cafeteria and adjoining lounge where an all-news channel blared at top volume from a wall-mounted TV. Trailing Blue into the cafeteria, Blake selected a bag of potato chips and a bottle of juice. Ahead of him, between coughing spells, Blue ordered a coffee from a tired-looking woman behind the counter. *He's staying in character, that's for sure,* thought Blake with a touch of amusement.

An instant later, his attention was caught by Serena. She was standing at the edge of the lounge, signalling to them with an almost imperceptible wave of her head. Grabbing his chips and beverage, he walked quickly into the other room. A group of people were staring up at the news broadcast on the elevated screen.

"...In Los Angeles, yet another casualty of the Urban Zone lifestyle," the announcer was saying. "Karl Kliff, a 25-year-old fringe player in the Zone's upside-down world of phony rock stars, dropped dead of a heart attack last night while playing guitar with a local band at the Whisky a Go Go nightclub. Authorities speculate the death may be linked to drugs that Kliff ingested in his dressing room before going onstage. Kliff was visiting L.A. from the San Francisco Zone, where his taste for prescription narcotics was well-known—as was his odd penchant for wearing only orange clothing...."

Blake watched in horror as the screen cut to footage of medics loading a body onto the back of an ambulance. The body's head and torso were covered with a sheet, but at the bottom of the stretcher a pair of legs stuck out, dressed in orange trousers and boots. The camera panned to a crowd of onlookers gathered around the rear of the vehicle, then zoomed in on one woman, her dark hair obscuring her tear-streaked face. Sensing that she was being filmed, she wheeled toward the camera.

"I loved Karl!" Caroline screamed into the lens. "He was no drug addict! *They killed him!*" As she dissolved into sobs, the telecast cut back to the announcer in the studio.

"California Governor Richard Statler has released an official statement, reiterating his call for federal legislation that would close down the Los Angeles and San Francisco Urban Zones permanently. There has been no response thus far from the Los Angeles state authorities...."

"I don't get it," Blue said, muttering into his handkerchief. "It doesn't make sense."

Too stunned to answer, Blake brushed past Serena and stumbled out of the building. As she followed him through the front door, watching him with concern through her oversized sunglasses, he staggered around the corner of the building and was violently sick.

FOURTEEN

San Francisco (Be Sure to Wear Some Flowers in Your Hair)

Thursday, September 5

THE LAST HOURS OF THE trip passed in a fog of guilt and terror. There was no question in Blake's mind that the fake Karl's death had been engineered by the government agents who were tracking him. All he could think of was that a man had died because of his own stupidity and arrogance. He couldn't bring himself to look at Blue or Serena.

As the bus approached San Francisco and the morning sun cleared the mountains to the east, another realization sank in: As tragic as the substitute Karl's death was, Blake was the one they'd intended to murder. Whoever had killed the other Karl was no longer interested in arresting him, or learning more about the quantum communication device. They wanted to silence him permanently—and as far as the killers knew, they'd succeeded.

This is my chance, he thought. *I can set off on my own, not tell anyone where I'm going. I'll be free as the wind....* Even as the idea formed in his head, though, he knew it was a non-starter. Where would he go, and how would he support himself?

Mulling the situation over in his mind, Blake's fear gave way to a growing sense of anger. Any group that would take someone's life so cavalierly, he thought, deserved to be brought down. Turning himself in was no longer an option: He had to play this out. He owed it to the man whose clothes he was wearing—plus, it was the only way he would ever truly get the target off his back.

As the bus pulled off the freeway, he made a silent promise to do whatever he could, for as long as he could, to help drive the nation's ruling regime from power.

At the entrance to the San Francisco UZ the police did a perfunctory scan of the passengers' ID cards, then waved the bus through. With a loud grinding of gears it made its way slowly over the city's hilly streets, finally shuddering to a stop at the famous intersection of Haight and Ashbury. As the passengers stood to disembark, Blue whispered a street address in Blake's ear. "We'll meet there in an hour," he said.

Descending to the street, the two women who'd helped Blake escape from the Whisky walked rapidly away without a backward glance. Blue ambled after them while Serena headed in the opposite direction, leaving Blake alone on the sidewalk.

To kill time, he decided to take a roundabout route to the address Blue had given him. Strolling through the early morning sunlight, he couldn't stop thinking about his former life in Berkeley—his friends, his work, his apartment, his ex-girlfriend, all just a few miles away across the bay. He'd never felt lonelier.

Get out of your own head, he told himself sternly. With an effort, he lifted his gaze to take in the scene around him. The San Francisco UZ, about six miles square, was a rolling checkerboard of run-down squatters' residences perched side by side with normal-looking houses and shops. The laid-back atmosphere was a marked change from the manic Los Angeles Zone. Pedestrians and shopkeepers smiled warmly at him, and flowers and vegetables sprouted from every available piece of earth. No one seemed in any special hurry.

As Blake walked past a group of youngsters sitting on the sidewalk surrounded by their guitars and backpacks, one of the girls held out a daisy. "Welcome to the universe," she said.

"Thanks." Tucking the flower into a buttonhole in his vest, Blake turned into Buena Vista Park and trudged up the steeply sloping lawn until he reached its highest point. Choosing an open stretch of grass, he sat quietly and watched the sun's rays reflecting off the glass-walled skyscrapers in the distance while his mind drifted back to the image of the orange-suited man on the stretcher. At this moment, hundreds of miles away from L.A. in the glow of a San Francisco dawn, it seemed like a scene out of a movie.

"Great time of day, isn't it?"

Blake turned and saw a man grinning at him from a few feet away. The man was dressed in an embroidered shirt and loose cotton trousers. Long white hair ran down his back, and around his neck was a string of large, pinkish crystals—an aging hippie, thought Blake. "I guess so," he said guardedly. The last thing he wanted to do right now was strike up a conversation with another Zone drifter.

"You look like you've got the whole world on your shoulders," the man said, undeterred. His smile widening, he got up and moved closer. "I should call you Atlas."

"Oh yeah?"

"Just an observation," the man replied. "You live in the Zone, I see." He was staring at Blake's ID card, which still lay against his chest.

"No, I—" Blake stopped himself mid-sentence, remembering belatedly who he was supposed to be. As he yanked off his lanyard and stuffed his ID into his pocket, he felt his wig starting to itch.

"Let me guess," the man continued. "You're slumming on somebody else's card?"

Blake could have kicked himself for being so sloppy, but his newfound companion didn't seem to care. "I assume you're here for the music," the man added. "It's why everyone comes to the UZ. They think living in the Zone is going to somehow transform their lives. But they're chasing an illusion, you know."

Seeing Blake's quizzical look, he laughed. "Don't worry, I'm not some eccentric out to bend your ear. Actually, I'm a clinical psychologist." He fished a card from his shirt pocket and handed it to Blake. "I do a lot of pro bono work with Zoners, especially the young ones who come here searching for the answer to life. I'm guessing you're in your mid-twenties—just coming up on that dangerous age."

"You mean, the Twenty-Seven Club?"

"Sure. The one that claimed Jim and Jimi, and Janis, and the others. All those young rock gods who couldn't make it past that magic moment, when suddenly you realize you can't prolong your adolescence any longer. It's a lot harder to be an adult in the real world than a teen idol in Never-Never Land."

"I wouldn't know," said Blake. "I'm a scientist, not a musician."

"Lucky you," smiled the man. "I'm just kidding—half-kidding, anyway. Still, I'm willing to bet you've got some kind of semi-religious belief in rock music. Otherwise, you wouldn't be sitting at this particular spot at seven in the morning."

"What's wrong with that?" Blake said, a hint of irritation in his voice. "Rock and roll is a window into the mystical, isn't it? At least, it can be."

The man held up a blade of grass and stared at it, fingering his necklace of crystals with his other hand. "Sure," he said slowly. "It's that. And just about anything else you want to make it: The doorway to love and peace. A tool for social change. Underminer of authority, outlet for aggression, hemispheric brain synthesizer, tribal bonding mechanism, portal to the subconscious—or maybe just a good backdrop for driving around town and making out. First and foremost, though, rock music is personal therapy for the music maker. A lot of these famous musicians are on a dead run from depression and anxiety most of the time. It's a fact."

"So, musicians have their share of personal problems. Who doesn't?"

"A song is a chance to hide from your issues for a while," the man continued, as if he hadn't heard Blake. "A way to create a perfect little world—a four-minute paradise where youth reigns eternal, and love once lost can always be reclaimed. And, yes, a place where mystical insights have sometimes been known to burst forth and brighten our drab three-dimensional existence." As he spoke, a far-off look crept into the man's eyes.

Blake was already sick of the man's stream-of-consciousness musings. "Your personal therapy theory sounds pretty reductionist to me," he said curtly.

The man's gaze shifted sharply back to Blake. "You play an

instrument?" he asked.

The abrupt switch in focus left Blake flustered. "Sure...I used to play guitar and write songs," he stammered. "It's been a few years, though." He had the disconcerting sensation of being lured into unwanted self-examination. *This guy really is a shrink,* he thought.

"Tell me this, then. When you took it up—that moment when you first strapped on your guitar and banged out a few chords—were you focused on becoming a famous entertainer, or were you searching for something inside yourself?"

Blake forced himself to think back over the years, to a long-ago summer in La Jolla. "I guess you could say I did it for my own head," he replied haltingly.

"Do you dream about making music?" the man asked. "When you're asleep, I mean."

"I used to...a lot," Blake replied. "Lately I haven't been remembering my dreams much."

The man nodded. "The music connects you with yourself...and you've been missing that connection. Let me guess—you recently broke off a serious relationship. Am I right?"

"No comment." Something about the man's face and voice dredged up a half-forgotten image in Blake's memory. He glanced down at the name on the business card and then at the man's face, trying to picture it forty years younger. "A long time ago, you used to be a rock musician yourself—right?" he said. "You had a different name, though."

"If I told you my stage name, you'd recognize it in a heartbeat," the man smiled. "So I won't. But I will tell you this: My best-known song was about how the essence of love involves two people never committing to each other. An incredibly immature sentiment—but it sold millions of copies."

Like a homing beacon, Blake's thoughts went to Ann. "I'm sure you moved a lot of people with that song," he said.

"Moved them? I don't know," the man replied. "I suppose I offered people an emotion that they could try on for a while, and see how it fit." He rose and stretched, his crystals glinting in the sunlight. "It's great to love music. But to love yourself, not to mention others, takes more than a hit song. It takes self-understanding—and that, in turn, requires growing up."

After he'd walked away, Blake sat staring at the Pacific Ocean in the distance. A stiff breeze rippled up the hillside, raising goose bumps on his skin. Shivering a little, he prepared to move on himself.

"What was he saying to you?"

While he'd been talking with the psychologist, Blake had noticed a number of other people settling onto the grassy slope around him. Now one of them, a woman with short dark hair, had gotten to her feet and stood looking accusingly at him, her long red dress fluttering in the wind.

"Don't tell me," she added in a thick Irish brogue. "I know all too well the shite that flows from that arsehole. The music's all about *therapy.* We create it to work through our *issues.*" She turned her head to face the air flowing from the sea. "Did he also mention that music is *enchanted?* That it transports us to a long-forgotten corner of our souls? That it unites us like no other force on the planet? That it lets us share each other's *dreams?*"

She spun to stare at a man a short distance away, sitting cross-legged on the grass with an acoustic bass guitar cradled in his arms. Nodding, the man began thumping out an eighth-note rhythm. On the other side of Blake, a man pulled a guitar out of a case and began plucking out a dancing lead, while further down the hill someone else took up the driving beat on a small African drum.

Raising her clenched fists to the morning sky, the woman threw back her head, drew in a deep breath and threw herself into a full-throated version of the Cranberries' "Dreams." Her voice, the beauty of the music, and most of all the endless, self-created reality of this world he'd wandered into—it was all too much. Tired of thinking, Blake put his face in his hands and let the song wash over him like a healing tide.

The address Blue had given him on Waller Street led to a row of four connected Victorian townhouses.

"Come in, Eben!" said the woman who answered the door. Her long gray hair hung in a single braid that stretched almost to the floor, and she moved with the grace of a former ballet dancer. "Welcome to the Home on the Hill. We've been expecting you. Claire and your other friend, Leon, arrived a short time ago. Would you like some breakfast?"

Looking around, Blake saw they were in an old-fashioned commune. Someone had broken through the walls to combine the first floors of the townhouses, creating several large rooms that ran the width of the four structures.

"Expansive, isn't it?" the woman smiled. She led him back into a dining area containing several long wooden tables where men and women of varying ages sat eating and talking animatedly. At the far end of the room, several people were working over an industrial-size stove, cooking eggs, pancakes and hot oatmeal. Glancing back toward the tables, Blake spotted Blue and Serena sitting side by side. Blue's moustache was gone and he'd traded his worn clothes for a respectable-looking pullover and khakis, while Serena was dressed in a sweater and blue jeans. Somewhere between the bus and the commune, her hair had turned a reddish brown.

"Your friend has found us," smiled the woman. She sat down beside Serena and gently kissed her cheek. "We haven't seen our dear Claire in years," she said. "I hope you'll sit down with me soon, and relate all that life has shown you."

"I'd love to," said Serena. Turning to Blake, she flashed an uncharacteristically beatific smile. "Melissa is the mother I never had."

"Thank you for your hospitality," said Blue, pressing his palms together. "The energy here is inspiring. It's a precious thing in these difficult times."

"I'm glad you're experiencing it, Leon." Melissa smiled. "That is our mission—to comfort our brethren, and lift them up and sustain them. We were established here long before the walls went up, you know. Claire has told you all about it, I'm sure."

"Of course," said Blue, flashing an angelic smile of his own. "And now her home is ours, as well."

FIFTEEN

Somebody to Love

FOLLOWING BREAKFAST, THE TRIO STROLLED to the Golden Gate Park panhandle—the only part of the park inside the San Francisco UZ's walls. Picking out a small meadow of thick grass, they stretched out full-length and lay there without speaking. As the morning breeze played over them, Blake recalled picnicking with friends on the other side of the concrete divide earlier that summer, a few hundred yards from where they were now. Glancing at Blue and Serena, he felt a flash of anger at their calm demeanor.

"Can someone tell me what the hell we're doing?" he blurted suddenly. "A man's been *murdered,* for God's sake. And now I'm cooling my heels in some park, wearing his freaking *wig*."

"Sometimes you just have to put one foot in front of the other," said Blue, his eyes fixed on the clouds overhead. "You were some kind of champion runner, right? You must know what I'm talking about."

"But what are we accomplishing, banging from pillar to post like a bunch of refugees?" said Blake.

Serena exhaled in disgust. "If you care about honoring the man who died in your place, then how about finishing what you've started? Obviously this mission is important. Otherwise, why would they want to stop you so badly?"

"We have a four p.m. rendezvous with your scientist buddies," said Blue. "Until then, we'll keep a nice, low profile. I'm sorry about Eben.

But as long as he's gone, we need to make sure they keep believing *he* was really *you*. As long as they think you're dead, you've got nothing to worry about."

"You mean they've called off the chase?" asked Blake hopefully. Instead of answering, Blue yawned and closed his eyes.

"Why so glum, chum?"

Startled, Blake looked up see a dozen barefoot men and women dressed in floor-length white robes and carrying instruments. The woman who had just spoken stared at him placidly. Her brown hair glittered with a dusting of gold, and a garland of brightly colored blossoms glowed against her pale clothing. She lifted her tambourine and gave it an authoritative shake. "Can we lift your spirits with a tune?"

The group began walking around the trio in a slow, deliberate circle as the percussionists began tapping out an insistent rhythm and two guitarists plucked a familiar instrumental line. Then they started to sing, the harmonies of "White Bird" floating through the air. It was one of Blake's favorite songs from the late sixties—written, he half-remembered, in the attic of some drafty house in Seattle, where the composing band had gotten itself stuck for the winter.

When the song was finished, the woman took the wreath of flowers from her neck and walked over to Blake. "You are blessed," she said, lowering the garland over his head. "Be at peace." She touched two fingers to her lips.

As the singers moved away through the park, Blue reached out and lifted the flower necklace off Blake's shoulders. "All clean," he announced after sifting through its petals. "No hidden microphones."

Blake felt his annoyance flare again. For all of Blue's show at being a security pro, the whole deal was feeling increasingly like amateur hour.

"I'm sorry—how long did you say I have to wear this guy's outfit?" he said irritably. "I'm turning into a fucking ghoul."

Seeing Blue's face darken into a frown, Blake knew he'd spoken out of turn. He wondered how close Eben had been to Blue and Serena. *I must sound like the world's most ungrateful jerk,* he thought.

"Not too much longer, dude," Blue said frostily.

"Let's just enjoy the sunshine," threw in Serena. "It's a beautiful day, right?"

Around them the park was filling with people. After a few minutes, Blue's chilly mood began to ease. Reaching into a pocket, he pulled out a joint and held it out to Blake along with a lighter. "Take a hit, Karl," he said. "You've been under a lot of pressure."

It felt like a peace offering, and once again Blake had the sense that he was being handled. For the moment, though, he didn't care. Lighting the reefer, he inhaled deeply. Seconds later he was engulfed by the same blissful sensation he'd experienced in the garden in Venice.

"I'll take some of that," said Serena. Surprised, Blake handed her the joint.

"I thought you didn't indulge on the job," he said.

"It's Blue's watch," she said. "I'm on break." She drew in a lungful of smoke and held it, then exhaled lazily. When she handed the joint back to Blake their hands brushed, and a tingling ran up his arm.

After another couple of tokes each, Blake stubbed out the joint and started to hand it to Blue. "Why don't you hold onto it?" Blue said. Nodding, Blake slipped it into his vest pocket. He glanced at Serena and was pleasantly surprised to see her smiling at him. He'd purposely avoided asking any questions about Melissa and the Home on the Hill, but now something compelled him to bring it up.

"So, how did you end up at that commune, all those years ago?" he asked.

"I was alone," she said. "I needed a family, and they gave me one."

"How long did you live there?"

"Two years. Long enough to get my high school degree and somehow get into UCSF. The Home gave me my future."

"When did you stop being Claire?"

Serena shrugged. "I changed my name the day I moved out. A symbol of my new life, I guess."

"How about a walk?" interjected Blue, a hint of restlessness in his tone. "I don't know about you, but I'm curious to see how Frisco is faring these days."

As they were leaving the park, a thought struck Blake. "Isn't Homeland Security going to be looking for you guys, too?" he said.

"Not any more," said Blue. "Our band hopped a train last night to the southern border, bound for a three-week gig at the old Rosarito Hotel in Baja. All of the Microbes were on board. In fact, I hear their new Serena's an even better singer than the old one."

"Oddly enough, I heard the same thing about their bass player," said Serena.

While the San Francisco UZ's vibe was definitely less edgy than that of the L.A. Zone, the energy level was still high. Small knots of people filled the sidewalks, some talking among themselves, others listening to the various speakers who were arrayed along the stoops and street corners, giving oral dissertations on politics and the state of the world. The ground was littered with fliers. Picking one up, Blake read about a Symposium to End Retroeconomic Fascism taking place later in the week. If this kind of political activity was happening outside the walls, he reflected, the police would have hovering everywhere. Here, there wasn't a cop to be seen. Meanwhile, music drifted from every window and doorway. Though it wasn't yet noon, each bar and restaurant they passed had some kind of act going.

Maybe it came from thinking about the police, but as they walked, Blake suddenly felt a wisp of irrational fear on the edge of his consciousness. He tried to ignore it but, like the smoke plumes of a growing fire, the feeling grew more intense with every passing second. From hard experience, he knew exactly what it was: the onset of a cannabinoid-induced psychosis.

Too late, he realized he'd made a serious mistake smoking pot that morning. He was under too much pressure; now, the drug was combining with the stress hormones in his bloodstream to hijack his brain's neural circuitry. It would pass eventually, he knew—but the knowledge did nothing to stem his rising panic. The image of Eben's two orange-clad legs on the ambulance gurney flooded his mind. Everywhere he looked, Blake realized, people were eying him with sympathy, nodding to show that they understood he was a marked man or, worse, glaring at him with quiet menace. Either way, they were all participants in the network bent on destroying him.

Grasping the situation immediately, the street musicians began making veiled digs about his fugitive status. A pseudo-Dylan jeered at him from his storefront perch, inquiring how it felt to be on his own. In front of a tavern, an ersatz Robert Johnson winked knowingly at Blake and bent the strings of his guitar, crooning about the hellhound on his trail. From the leafy depths of a small park, an Arlo Guthrie look-alike flashed a conspiratorial smirk as he sang his tale of airport paranoia.

They're not singing to you, Blake admonished himself. But his attempts at logic couldn't begin to calm the all-consuming terror that gripped him.

Endless, stomach-wrenching minutes later, the three of them sat munching burgers and onion rings in a garden restaurant. Avoiding Serena's worried gaze, Blake struggled desperately to convey an air of normalcy. In one corner, a band of Grateful Dead channelers aimed a mocking lecture at him about the mind-warping dangers of Terrapin Station. When the song ended, the bearded lead guitarist nodded toward Blake.

"We'll see you in the Big Apple in a few days," he said casually.

Blake felt himself starting to hyperventilate. *How does he know I'm going to New York?* An instant later he realized the guitarist was referring to UZFest, and that he was talking to everyone in the restaurant. *I can't smoke this shit anymore,* he thought.

Blake sensed his companions' eyes on him. Then Blue was standing by his chair, his hand on Blake's shoulder. "Let's get out of here," he said. "We could all use some air."

"Hawkes is *dead?!*"

"You're not listening," said Marconi, shaking his head in irritation. "What I said is, someone *posing* as Hawkes is dead. We got some digital photos of him before he keeled over, and ran them through a biometrics check. This guy is a close match to Hawkes, but he's a different person."

"Did it ever occur to you to run a scan *before* you took him out?" said Smyth angrily.

"Charles, you're not focusing here. *We* didn't take him out—not that we couldn't have."

"What do you mean?"

"What I mean is, we were a minute away from snatching him. They had some bullshit escape scheme set up, which we'd already neutralized. So the guy's up there messing with his guitar and suddenly he topples over—boom, right on the stage."

"You're sure he was dead?"

"One of our guys ran a portable EKG while he was performing CPR on him. There was no heart activity. Zilch."

"How did he die?"

"I don't know. Fluke brain aneurysm, maybe, or cocaine-induced V-fib. We're waiting for a report from the hospital. Like I said, though, they'd already pulled the substitution. A few minutes earlier, Hawkes was there—we have those photos, too, and they check out. Then suddenly this guy's taken his place."

Marconi stared at the wall over Smyth's shoulder. "On the other hand, maybe the fatality was no accident. Maybe the Munis wanted to make sure the new guy kept quiet about the switch. It doesn't matter. One way or the other, it bought Hawkes enough time to get away."

"On your watch, this time," Smyth couldn't resist pointing out.

Marconi shot him a chilling look. "If you've got a problem with how I'm doing my job, just say so."

"Of course not. You're doing fine work—as always," said Smyth hurriedly. "Sorry, Tony. It's been a tough few days."

"Better get used to it," said Marconi, rising to leave. "They aren't getting any easier."

At Blue's urging they headed back to Golden Gate. Blake's paranoia diminished a little more with each step they took, and by the time they reached the park he was feeling halfway normal. As they drew closer, the sound of instruments and singing could be heard in the distance.

Walking through a grove of trees, they came upon a band channeling Jefferson Airplane in a small field at the base of the UZ wall. Behind the band's low stage, a massive growth of shrubbery climbed halfway up the concrete barrier.

Listening to the guitarist sing the lovelorn words of "Today," thoughts of Ann returned more strongly than ever. Blake needed to see her—it was that simple. Breaking off their relationship, he realized now, was the biggest misstep of his life. Somehow he had to get to Berkeley and make things right between them.

After an extended, hallucinatory "Embryonic Journey," the band announced a break. As the other members drifted away, the lead singer settled onto a stool in front of the stage.

"I want to share a story with you," she told the ragtag audience scattered across the grass. "It's about a beautiful moment in time, called the Human Be-In. It took place on this very spot, in the nineteen-sixties...." She made a sweeping motion with her arm, taking in the park around her. "The Airplane was a centerpiece of that magical day. It was a time of powerful change—just like today. Can you hear that change? It's in the air all around us. Let's listen together."

The audience fell respectfully quiet. The wind picked up, as if on cue, rustling the leaves in the surrounding trees.

"I've got to pee," Blake whispered to Blue.

It was a lie, but he desperately needed to be alone, if only for a few minutes. Circling around the seated gathering, he walked toward the expanse of vegetation behind the stage. Spotting a gap in the middle of the shrubbery, he bent low and walked a couple of yards into the space. Letting out his breath, he crouched in the darkness, grateful for the solitude. His only thought was how to find his way to Berkeley and reconnect with Ann. Everything depended on it.

Putting his face in his hands, Blake began to form a prayer. He wasn't sure who or what it was directed to, but he knew he needed assistance from a power beyond himself.

"Please, help me get through this," he pleaded out loud.

"You say you want help getting through?"

Blake started at the sound of another person's voice. Peering further into the gap, he saw what looked like the dark shape of a child.

"Who are you?" he said softly.

The shape moved closer, and Blake saw that it was actually a very small man wearing coveralls and a miner's helmet.

"I can help you, but you gotta pay," the man said.

"What do you mean?"

"You've got to pay me to get under the wall," the man replied impatiently. "For one thing, I got the only key to the trap door. And for another, you'll never make it through the tunnel without me." He sidled over until he was almost touching Blake. "It's full of twists and turns. I built it like that on purpose. But for fifty bucks, I'll pop you out the other side like that!" He snapped his fingers.

Blake thought quickly. "Where does the tunnel come out?"

"In the middle of the woods. No one'll see you—guaranteed. If you got the dough, we can go right now." The man held out his hand.

Blake pulled out Eben's wallet and tried to see how much cash it held. The little man helpfully flicked on his miner's lamp, illuminating a pair of twenty-dollar bills.

"Will forty dollars work?" asked Blake.

The man frowned. "No can do, bro. Word gets out I gave you a discount, everyone's gonna want one."

Blake remembered the reefer in his pocket. He pulled out the hand-rolled cigarette and held it up in the light of the miner's lamp. Its fat length was almost completely intact. "What if I throw in a joint of the finest grass you've ever smoked?"

The man stared at the joint. "You say it's good stuff?"

"Best you've ever had—on my great-grandmother's grave," said Blake solemnly.

On the other side of the shrubbery, the band was starting up again. Blake recognized the rising opening guitar line of "White Rabbit." In the darkness of the bushes, the singer's amplified voice came through muffled and distant:

One pill makes you larger, and one pill makes you small…

"Deal!" The man snatched the joint from Blake's hand and tucked it into a pocket of his coveralls. "This way!"

He turned and crawled farther into the undergrowth. The space grew lower and Blake found himself on his hands and knees, scrambling to keep up with the lamp's glow. Forty feet further in, the man paused over a large, flat stone. With a grunt, he shoved it aside to reveal a metal trap door underneath. Yanking a large key from his coveralls, he unlocked the door and swung it open, then slid through feet first.

Go ask Alice, when she's ten feet tall…

Blake stood over the hole, looking into its inky depths. He was a lot bigger than his guide, and it looked like a tight fit.

"Come on!" the man hissed from the darkness.

Sucking in his stomach, Blake lowered himself through the opening, feeling the steel edges scrape against his ribs. He could see from the man's headlamp that the tunnel they were in was about five and a half feet high.

"Shut the door!" the man yelled. Ducking his head, Blake reached up and pulled the trap door downward. As he did, he heard a latch click home.

"Now, stay close!"

Hunching over to avoid bumping his head on the ceiling, Blake followed the man along a curving passageway. Every twenty yards or so, an opening branched off to the right or left. The man ignored most of them, but on three occasions he turned onto one of the side routes. After several minutes, the man stopped abruptly. "Here we are!" he crowed.

In the light of the man's helmet, Blake saw a large cinderblock on the tunnel floor. The man shifted his gaze up to the ceiling, revealing a trap door identical to the one they'd just passed through.

"Listen," said Blake. "If you meet me back here in exactly three hours, I'll pay you another fifty for the return trip. I'll have more money by then."

"You've got it." Jumping onto the cinderblock, the man unlatched the door and pushed it open. "Up you go!"

Blake poked his head and shoulders through the hole. As promised, he was in the middle of a large stand of trees. Feeling a jab to his leg, Blake quickly pulled himself all the way out. Through the opening, the small man's face grinned up at him. "Thanks for the weed!" he cackled. Then he slammed the door shut, leaving a green mossy patch where the opening had been.

Blake peered out through the tree trunks. All around the mini-forest, Golden Gate Park was bustling with activity. He removed his hat and vest and carefully peeled the wig off his head. Remembering his orange hair, he reflected for a moment, then untied his bandana and wrapped it around his head, knotting it in the back. Tucking the wig and vest into the hat, he slid the bundle under some ferns, then walked casually out of the trees. Several yards later he broke into a trot. *Hang on, Ann,* he thought. *I'm coming.*

"What exactly are you saying?"

"I'm saying that Hawkes appears to have left Los Angeles," Smyth repeated. "At least, our operatives can no longer find any evidence of him there."

"How could this have happened?" Martin Bibbitt demanded. He could feel the blood rising in his face, but he didn't care. "What kind of show are you running?"

"We're working around the clock to locate him," said Smyth flatly. As always, his goal was to keep his meeting with Bibbitt as brief as humanly possible, and he was prepared to say whatever was necessary to accomplish this.

"This has something to do with that New York broadcast—I'm sure of it!" Bibbitt studied Smyth's face. "I don't suppose you've found out anything more on that front?"

"Nothing substantive."

"No—I wouldn't have thought so." Bibbitt began tapping his desk with his fingernails. "They're out to destroy what I've built," he muttered. "Don't think I don't know it!"

It's like he's forgotten I'm here, thought Smyth. He quietly rose to his feet. "I'll see you tomorrow, Mr. Secretary," he said. He couldn't be sure if Bibbitt heard him or not.

❖ ❖ ❖

"So, our friend has jumped the fence. They're better than we thought, Tony."

Marconi made a face. "They're good at identity switches, I'll give them that."

"This poses a problem. Our whole enterprise depends on keeping track of Hawkes' whereabouts."

"It's not like we lost him completely. He just got a little ahead of us, that's all. We've had a firm fix on him from Tuesday morning onward, thanks to that favor from my friend in the California State Police. After they staged their little car accident on Wednesday we tailed them to UCLA, where our people got names and photos of everyone Hawkes met with. The Munis don't know this, of course—they think the meeting went undetected."

"Then what happened?"

"We pushed some misinformation that we were going to snatch Hawkes last night, so they didn't think we were slacking off. They had an escape plan set up, and we were ready to tail them on the other side. But they went another direction."

"So, where's our elusive scientist now?"

"A couple of uniforms ran a check on the overnight bus to San Francisco before it pulled out and got photos of all the passengers. They were forwarded straight here, for my eyes only. Turns out one of them was Hawkes in a wig. His minders were on board, too."

"And?"

"I had an operative meet the bus this morning in Frisco, strictly on the QT. I'll let Smyth hear about it in a day or so, once we have a better idea what the Munis' next move will be. Better to let him stew in the dark a little—it'll give us more running room. Besides, we know where the kid's heading. Based on the info we're getting, all roads still point to King Midas."

"Agreed. You've been monitoring his movements?"

"We have—and he's been moving plenty. He coptered down to his floating palace a few days ago. Then yesterday we tracked his undersea jitney from there to Palo Alto."

"Good. So they've brought Hawkes north for a rendezvous with his tech support in the Bay Area. Keep a long-range surveillance on the facility there. Very low profile. When everybody's come and gone, we'll slip some people in for a look around. It's all about gathering evidence right now."

"Understood."

"Oh, and Tony—"

"Yeah?"

"I don't have to tell you that no one can ever know how we're playing this. If it comes to light that we held back from grabbing Hawkes when we could have, there'll be hell to pay. No one else understands that we're playing for all the marbles here."

"I thought you knew me better than that," Marconi said tightly. "As for Hawkes, Smyth is doing your work for you. He's perfect for the job—totally honorable, and dedicated as the day is long. Not the swiftest boat on the water, but he never gives up. He'll give you all the cover you need. At the same time, you can count on him not to make any unexpected moves."

"You're right. And of course I know I can trust you, Tony. That goes without saying. It's just that there's so much at stake." The speaker stared through the windshield of the car, then glanced reflexively to the right and left. Around them, the parking garage was dark and still. "What about the Munis?"

"I'm placing all of our operational updates immediately into the top leadership queue. Whoever's leaking to them is getting everything virtually in real time—almost everything, that is."

"Excellent. That should keep them confident. I guess that's all. You look beat, Tony—you should get some rest."

"Easy for *you* to say."

Blake had been gone five minutes when Blue felt a familiar prickling on the back of his neck. "I'm going to check on our friend," he told

Serena.

"I'm right behind you."

Blue immediately spotted the small opening in the shrubbery. It took him just a few seconds more to find the locked trap door.

"Son of a bitch!" he spat, scowling in the dim light.

"I thought he was with us," said Serena.

"He is," said Blue. "He just decided to take a detour."

"To see his Berkeley babe?"

"Where else?"

As Blue spoke, a thump sounded against the underside of the trap door. An instant later the door flew open and the little man in the miner's helmet stuck his head out. Seeing Blue and Serena, he tried to duck back inside, but they were too fast. Moving with catlike speed, Serena held the door open while Blue plunged his hand into the space below and hauled the man out by his forearm. Rummaging into his coverall pockets, Serena retrieved the key and the joint that Blake had given him.

"It's my tunnel!" the man croaked hoarsely. "I dug it, and it's mine!"

"Don't worry—we're not stealing your business," said Blue, giving his arm a calibrated squeeze. "We just want you to escort me and Alice here out of Wonderland. Can you do that?"

"Sure, no problem," winced the man. "I won't even charge for it!"

"That's big of you," Blue said, still gripping him firmly. "After you, Serena. We'll keep our guide snuggled right between us."

"Let's hope we can find the White Rabbit," said Serena, slipping her legs into the narrow entrance, "before he meets the Queen of Hearts."

❖ ❖ ❖

Sitting on the BART train to Berkeley, Blake felt vaguely guilty. He knew he shouldn't have ditched Blue and Serena, but the need to contact Ann and reconnect with his old life had grown overwhelming. When the tunneling gnome had appeared out of nowhere and offered him that chance, he couldn't turn it down.

The subway car's digital clock read a few minutes past noon. Thankfully, the effects of the marijuana had almost worn off. If he made it back to the UZ as planned and rejoined Blue and Serena, they'd still have time to make their scheduled meeting. He would borrow the money for the return trip from Ann, assuming he found her, or else he'd talk the little miner into letting him pay once he was back inside.

It took fifteen minutes to reach the Downtown Berkeley stop. Climbing the stairs to Shattuck Avenue, the sensation of being back in the city he'd called home for the past four years made Blake slightly dizzy. Several blocks to the north lay his apartment, with its unopened mail and hamper full of dirty laundry. Instead he headed east, down Center Street onto the Berkeley campus. As he walked past the familiar landmarks—the stadium, the Life Sciences building, the computer research lab—he felt like a character in some post-apocalyptic movie, returning to his now-abandoned home planet. The school year hadn't started yet, and the campus was almost empty. Wheeler Hall, where Ann had her office in the English Department, was sure to be deserted except for her and a few fellow workaholics.

Arriving at the large stone building, he ducked in through an unlocked wooden door on the side and ran lightly up a flight of stairs, emerging into the marble-floored hallway he knew by heart. Outside Ann's office, he stopped short. Through the open door he could see her, bent over her desk. She was writing longhand on a lined yellow pad, her cascade of chestnut hair spilling forward and hiding her face from view.

He stood watching her for a minute. Then, summoning his courage, he rapped softly on the doorframe. Ann wheeled in her chair and her eyes widened.

"Blake!" For an instant she remained sitting, paralyzed with astonishment. Then she stood and rushed toward him, enveloping him in a warm hug. Dressed in a light summer dress and open-toed sandals, she looked as wonderful as ever.

"You seem different...like you've aged, somehow," she said, pulling back to look at him. "What happened to your face?"

Blake touched his cheek. He'd forgotten about the scar. "It isn't real," he said. "It's a long story."

"I've been worried about you," she said. "We all have. You were supposed to arrive here two days ago, but you never showed up. Then you weren't answering your cell phone—and no one had any idea where you were..."

"Well, I'm here now. But I can't stay long."

"Then why did you come?"

"To see you."

"Oh." Biting her lip, Ann turned away and stared out the window.

"I just wanted to...connect with you." As the words left his mouth, Blake realized how ridiculous they sounded.

"Connect?" Ann laughed bitterly. "Blake, we *connected* for three years. You were the one who decided to end that. You didn't *want* to connect anymore."

"I know that."

"Then why are you here now? To apologize? Extend your official sympathies for all the tears I've cried?"

"A lot's gone down over the past few days. In case something happens to me, I just wanted you to know that I feel badly about the way things turned out."

Ann heaved a sigh. "Blake, we've been over and over this. I wish things could have been different. But they're not. You don't see a future with me. And that's not going to change."

She was totally right, Blake knew. What in the world had he been thinking, imagining they were somehow going to reconcile?

"I care about you," he said lamely. "And that's not going to change, either."

"I know you do. But we can't turn back the clock." She began stuffing books and papers into her briefcase, then paused and looked up at him. "I don't know want you want out of life, Blake. It's not enough for you to be a brilliant physicist with a great career ahead of you. It's not enough to have someone who loves you. You're after something more—God knows what. Maybe your obsession with rock music is mixed up in it somehow. Maybe you really want to be Mick Jagger, or Paul McCartney, or one of your other idols. Whatever you're after, I just hope you find it. Don't be one of those people who sit around nursing some unfulfilled destiny for the rest of their lives. It doesn't suit you."

Having finished collecting her materials, she slung the briefcase over her shoulder and thrust out her hand. "Goodbye, Blake," she said. "I appreciate your stopping by. And I can't tell you how relieved I am that Mel was wrong."

"Mel?" Blake's inner alarm sounded. "What did Mel say?"

"He was concerned. He and I… speak fairly often these days. He'd heard something might have happened to you. I pressed him, but he wouldn't tell me any more."

Blake's eyes narrowed. "You've been talking to him? What—are you two dating now?"

"It's not like that," said Ann, shaking her head. Her cell phone rang, and she glanced quickly at the incoming number before answering it. "Hi," she said. "We were just talking about you. Listen, I have great news. You were mistaken about Blake!" She listened for a few seconds. "That's what I'm trying to tell you…. He's perfectly okay. How do I know? Because he's standing right in front of me!" She listened for several seconds more. "Fine. See you in a bit."

She turned to Blake. "That was Mel. He's coming right over. He says to stay exactly where you are until he gets here. He has something important to tell you."

"I'll bet he does."

Blake and Ann whirled to see a slender, red-haired woman standing in the doorway.

"I hate to break up the precept," snarled Serena. "But we're leaving—*now*." Grabbing Blake's arm, she hauled him out into the corridor, then stuck her head back inside. "If you really want to help your boyfriend," she said, "you won't leave this room and you won't contact *anyone*. When your other friend shows up, all you know is that he stepped away and he didn't say where he was going. Got it?"

Motioning for Blake to follow, Serena sprinted down the hall, leaving Ann standing open-mouthed in the middle of her office. As they raced down the stairs and out into the afternoon sunlight, Blake heard the heavy oaken door of Wheeler Hall bang shut behind him, closing forever on the life he'd known.

SIXTEEN

Hocus Pocus

IT TOOK THEM LESS THAN a minute to cover the three hundred yards to the western edge of campus. A tan-colored SUV with tinted windows was idling by the curb. Pulling open the back door, Serena pushed Blake in and dove after him as the car accelerated with a squeal of tires.

Blue was in the far back, cradling a pistol and staring watchfully out the rear window. At the steering wheel was the nameless man from the hotel and the hospital in L.A., wearing a plain gray T-shirt and white slacks in place of his usual suit. Driving expertly, he swerved right and then left onto Shattuck, heading south to the freeway.

"I was too late," said Serena. "The world is now aware that Blake Hawkes is in the Bay Area."

Blake was startled to hear his real name. "You know who I am?"

"They decided to fill us in," she said. "It seemed like a good idea, what with you running around on your own and all."

"Anyone spot the car?" asked the driver.

"I don't think so," she said.

"That's a plus," said the man, throwing a glance at the rearview mirror.

"Nobody's following," said Blue tersely. "Do we proceed with the rendezvous?"

"I think so," said the man. "For now, though, let's concentrate on getting somewhere safe."

Merging onto the freeway, they blended in with the stream of cars and trucks for several miles before taking an Oakland exit that brought them into a stretch of strip malls and office parks. As they drove south along the city streets, the business district gave way to a residential neighborhood dominated by scarred apartment buildings and vacant, trash-strewn lots. On every block, groups of adults sat in folding chairs on the sidewalks with children darting around them. Every minute or so a police car cruised by in the opposite direction, drawing sullen glares from the residents. At one point they passed a storefront soup kitchen where several dozen people were lined up outside.

"It never changes, does it?" said Serena, shaking her head.

Eventually they entered a semi-deserted industrial zone. A few blocks later, the man in the T-shirt turned the SUV down a side street and continued straight for a quarter mile, then slowed and swung into the small parking lot of a nondescript two-story building. The first floor looked to be a loading dock of some kind. From the second floor, a wall of mirrored windows looked out over the parking lot. As they braked to a stop, an automated garage door was rising to reveal two similar-looking SUVs parked inside. The man maneuvered their vehicle into an open space beside the other cars and switched off the ignition as the garage door closed again. No one looked at Blake.

"We'll wait here a while," the man said. "I don't know about the rest of you, but I could use some coffee."

Stepping out of the car, he led the group to a door at the rear of the garage. Behind it was a brightly lit stairway, with another door at the top that opened onto a large rectangular room. Along one wall was a row of cubicles with desks and office chairs. A pair of professionally dressed women occupied two of the desks, staring at computer screens as they conversed with unseen voices over their headsets. Neither of them acknowledged the new arrivals.

"John has ordered new stockings for Pauline," said one of women into her microphone. "Please notify when the shipment is en route."

"The party is in full swing," said the other woman. "Toasts will commence at midnight."

After several minutes of this, one of the women glanced at the large clock on the wall. “Okay, that wraps it up,” she said. As her colleague removed her headset, she walked over to a shortwave radio on a nearby table and switched it on. Static filled the room. A minute later, the sound of a brass band suddenly blared from the speaker, playing “(I’m a) Yankee Doodle Dandy.” Once the song was over, a man’s voice could be heard slowly reciting a long string of numbers in a British accent. The women sat in their cubicles, listening intently.

It was clearly some sort of system for sending coded messages. Blake found the process fascinating, but his companions didn’t seem to pay the broadcast any attention. When Blake looked questioningly at Blue, the other man shrugged. “Numbers station,” he said. “Mobile shortwave. Everybody has one.”

On the street side, a couch and two armchairs were arrayed in front of several large picture windows made of one-way glass. The man in the gray T-shirt took a pot of coffee from a warming plate and poured some into a paper cup.

“Anyone else?” he asked, looking around. The others shook their heads. “You might as well relax,” he added, dropping into one of the armchairs. “We have a couple of hours to kill.”

Uncertain what to do, Blake sat down wearily on the sofa. By now the radio had fallen silent. Without a word, the two women gathered up their belongings and headed down the steps, leaving the room to Blake and his companions. As Blake heard their footsteps heading down the stairs, he turned to the man in the T-shirt.

“I guess I screwed up royally.”

The man sipped his coffee thoughtfully. “We all make mistakes,” he said. “You’ve been under pressure, and you felt a need to reach out to someone you knew and cared about. That’s only natural. Unfortunately, in your current situation, following your natural inclinations can be extremely dangerous.”

“So now everyone knows I’m alive,” Blake said.

The man took another sip of coffee. “They knew already,” he said. “All the Feds had to do was scan a photo of your stand-in—I’m sure their operatives took dozens during the few minutes he was on stage—and analyze it using facial recognition software.”

"Oh," said Blake.

"What's changed is that now they also know *where* you are," he continued. "What you have to realize, Blake, is that there are very few people you can trust right now. You can't go heading off on your own—it's too risky."

And I suppose you're one of the trustworthy few? thought Blake, eyeing the nameless man. *Just this morning Blue implied I was safe, because they thought they'd offed me in L.A.*

"Does this mean Mel sold me out?" he said aloud.

"I wouldn't assume that," said the man. "It's my understanding that the Feds contacted your professor about your invention—not the other way around. At that point, he had no choice but to cooperate. Since then, they've probably told him you're being stalked by a foreign power and that they need to bring you in for your own protection. Or something like that."

Blake tried to wrap his head around what the man was saying. After all of their bull sessions and shared confidences, the idea that Mel might have conspired against him, even for what he believed were the right reasons, blew his mind. What had Ann said? *He and I speak fairly often these days.* Did Mel have feelings for Ann—and was that playing into this somehow?

He looked around the large, bare room. "Now that we're alone, and since we're all about trusting each other," he said to the man in the gray T-shirt, "do you mind if I ask what your name is?"

"I never told you?" said the man in a surprised tone. "Sorry about that. I'm Gulliver—but most people call me Gully."

The end of the workday was drawing near, and the usual silence in the analysts' pool had given way to a late-afternoon hum of conversation as the junior employees discussed their plans for the evening.

"Attention, my dear colleagues!"

The chatter quickly died as all heads turned toward their supervisor, a world-weary woman in a navy blue business ensemble.

"I know you're going to *hate* to hear this," she went on, "but you're all looking at a free day."

"What do you mean?" asked a woman from the Asian division. She had been poised to leave, her handbag tucked under her arm, but now she sank back into her chair.

"IT has just informed me that they've detected some infiltration attempts from overseas, so they're ordering a security upgrade on everyone's computers," the woman said. She held up her hands to forestall any further questions. "It's going to take the whole weekend. I want you to leave your laptops here when you go home tonight, and steer completely clear of this place tomorrow. No weekend warrior stuff, either—your instructions are to stay away from the office until Monday morning. Tomorrow's day off will *not* be counted as vacation time—it's a total freebie."

A cheer went up, and a few of the men exchanged high-fives.

"So...we won't be able to do any work over the weekend?" asked a young man in a worn suit and scuffed wingtips. As he spoke, he fingered the inside of his wrist.

"That's right, Phil," said the supervisor. "All computers are strictly off limits. Even *you* are going to have to take some time off." Laughter rippled through the group. "I don't care what you do," she added. "Go to the beach, go to the mountains, stay at home and watch a Three Stooges marathon on TV—it doesn't matter. Just don't come here."

"Don't look so sad, Phil. Maybe you can use the time to get another tattoo," one of the men snickered. "You know, reaffirm your patriotism."

"What are you saying, Steven?" replied the man in the suit. His tone was mild, but something in his gaze made the other man instinctively back up a step.

"Just kidding, Phil," he said quickly. "We all know how dedicated you are."

"Please, no bickering, children," said the supervisor. "I'm giving you a gift here, and I expect nothing but joy and happiness in return. I'll see you on Monday."

❖ ❖ ❖

Throughout their wait, Blue and Serena kept careful watch on the street below through the room's large mirrored windows. At four o'clock, Gully led the group back down into the garage. A nondescript blue van was parked in the space where the SUV had been. Gully climbed behind the wheel and started the engine. Serena rode shotgun while Blue and Blake—once again wearing the wig and hat he'd discarded in the woods—sat in the middle seats.

"One more short trip," said Gully. "After this, Blake, we'll be placing you in much safer hands. No more checkpoints or traffic stops—I promise."

They drove at a casual speed, mingling with the commuter traffic. At one point Serena switched on the car radio, and the van was filled with the saccharine sounds of some newly approved pop song.

"I can't listen to this garbage," Blake said. "Can't you put on the news or something?"

"Why not just enjoy the sound of the rushing wind?" said Gully, clicking the radio off. Blake had almost forgotten his earlier paranoia, but now it reared its head again. Why had his suggestion been rejected so promptly?

"I'd just like to catch the weather, if that's okay," he said. Reaching between Gully and Serena, he turned the radio back on and quickly found the local news station.

"Rush hour traffic is building on the east-bound Bay Bridge and the north-bound Golden Gate," the announcer intoned cheerfully. "And now for the headlines: A manhunt is on for a Berkeley graduate student who went allegedly went berserk on campus this afternoon and assaulted his former girlfriend, also a grad student at Berkeley. The woman, whose name has not been released, was hospitalized and is in serious but stable condition. Authorities say that her assailant, identified as Blake Hawkes, had gone missing several days before. Sources also told KRBS that Hawkes, the son of a retired Navy admiral, has recently been exhibiting signs of mental illness—"

Gully shut off the radio as Blake sat in stunned disbelief.

"What the *fuck?*"

Blue sighed. "They're upping the ante on you, dude. That's all."

"Ann's in the *hospital?*"

"Relax—I'm sure your girlfriend is absolutely fine," said Serena. "At this very moment, she's probably sitting by the pool in some five-star hotel."

"Yeah? How do you know they didn't knock her around, just to up the ante a little more?" Blake asked.

The others said nothing.

"And what if she takes a sudden turn for the worse and, like, *dies* or something?"

"You're worrying about nothing," said Gully, shaking his head. "They just cooked this up to make things harder for you."

"Great. First I'm supposed to be dead, and now the world thinks I'm a violent maniac." Blake clapped his hands over his eyes and groaned. "I can't believe Ann and Mel went along with this!"

"I guarantee they had no say in the matter," said Blue. "Serena's right. The Feds probably have them stashed away in some safe place, just to make sure they can't breathe a word about what really happened."

"If you're trying to make me feel better, it isn't working," Blake said grimly.

"This will all go away soon," said Gully soothingly. "Let's keep our eye on the ball here."

Blue, who had resumed watching the road behind them, turned to face forward. "Seriously, Karl…I mean *Blake*…your honey is perfectly fine," he said. He broke into a mischievous grin. "I know what's really bugging you. You got kicked to the curb, didn't you?"

When Blake didn't respond, Blue began singing a familiar doo-wop line. Despite his feeling of upset, Blake couldn't help recognizing the intro to the old Sedaka number, "Breaking Up is Hard to Do." As Blue hit the verse Serena joined on harmony, a smile tugging at her lips. When they launched into circular hand movements straight out of some vintage Top 40 TV show, even Gully began grinning—and by verse's end, the whole car, Blake included, was convulsed in laughter.

"I have to admit," he said, "you two have pretty good voices for punk rockers."

"I've actually been thinking of ditching the punk scene lately," said Serena. "Maybe start a retro girl band, á la the Shirelles."

"Does this mean you're dumping me, darlin'?" cried Blue.

"Never, baby," Serena said, looking back to blow him a kiss. "We'll always need a bass man!"

"Thank the Lord!" With a whoop, Blue kicked into the song's second verse, the other three joining in at the top of their lungs.

By the time they crossed the Dumbarton Bridge the sun was hanging low over the Pacific, shining directly in their eyes. Reaching the far side, they headed south on the Bayfront Expressway briefly before turning west into the foothills above the Bay. A few minutes later they pulled into a curving driveway and followed it for several hundred yards past carefully tended green lawns, coming at last to a long, windowless white building. There were only a dozen cars in the large parking lot, all clustered near a single unmarked door in the side of the structure.

As they climbed out of the van, Blake noticed a tall, glass-sided tower in the distance, separated from the parking lot by a stretch of woods. There wasn't any road leading to it that he could see. Gully rapped on the door, which was opened by a man in tan slacks and blue Oxford shirt. The man quickly waved them in. "Follow me," he said.

Inside, they passed through several more doors, each manned by a security guard who watched observantly as Gully swiped an ID card through a scanner. Finally they reached a reception area filled with upholstered chairs and a low table piled with magazines and newspapers. An attractive, middle-aged woman rose from her desk.

"Welcome," she said. "Would you care for anything—coffee, tea, a soft drink?"

"We're fine, thanks," said Gully.

"You two wait here," the man told Serena and Blue. He glanced at Blake and Gully. "You'll come with me." They trailed him down another hallway to what looked like a health club locker room. Along one side was a series of smaller rooms, each containing a sink, stool and shower stall.

"Hold on," said Gully. He walked over to Blake and removed his hat, then peeled off his wig and fake scar.

"If you would please disrobe and shower," the man said, indicating the first two washrooms. "You'll find everything you need inside."

As Blake finished showering, another man dressed in an attendant's uniform entered the room and silently placed a hanging garment bag on a wall hook, then collected the clothing he'd just removed and carried it away. Toweling off, Blake peered into the bag. It held tan pants and a blue shirt identical to what their escort was wearing, plus undergarments, socks and a pair of rubber-soled, brown-leather shoes.

Blake wasn't surprised to find that everything fit perfectly. He dressed and joined Gully outside, where their escort opened a closet filled with hooded white sterile body suits. After they each donned a suit along with gloves and a surgical mask, the man pointed them toward an automated air lock.

"Proceed through there, please," he said. Inside was a pristine room where several technicians in similar outfits were examining a rack of thin glass slides. One of them broke away and approached Blake and Gully, a slide in his gloved hand.

"Good timing," he said, his voice muffled slightly by the mask covering his mouth and nose. "This is our first batch of crystal lattices. Have a look." He appeared to be around sixty years old. From his tone of authority, Blake guessed that he was directing the proceedings.

Blake took the slide and held it up to the light, then handed it back. "How does it test?" he asked.

"Don't know yet. It took until now to get the production line set up."

Still carrying the slide, the man took them around the room, showing Blake and Gully the chamber where the laborium crystal sheets were being created. At one station a pair of ion guns were being used to bombard the crystal sheets with nitrogen ions. "Instead of trying to duplicate the firing pattern with a single ion gun, we decided to set up a pair of guns in parallel, each running off the same computer program," the man explained. "It should produce an even better match between the entangled crystals then you were getting before."

He motioned the two of them to follow him through another air lock into an adjacent room. "The source," he said, pointing to a complex array of electronic equipment on a wide, low table. Blake studied the set-up with interest. This was the apparatus that created the stream of entangled electron pairs, then split them apart and guided them into their matching crystals. The assembly was much cleaner and more elegant than the tangle of wires in his lab back at Berkeley.

"You put this together fast," he said.

"We already had it up and running for our own purposes," the man said with a shrug. "It didn't take much tweaking."

Finally they entered a third room where the crystal sheets, now filled with entangled electrons, were being layered together to form wafers, then annealed with an impermeable coating to prevent them from degrading.

"Okay, let's see what we've got," the man said, leading them through yet another air lock into a room containing several white desks and chairs. On the top of each desk was an identical large black box with several appendages protruding from it, including a six-inch binocular eyepiece. A high-definition computer monitor sat next to each device.

Blake gave a low whistle. "Can't say I've ever seen three high-res microscopes in one place before," he said.

"Gotta have 'em," the man said, chuckling. "You can't make what you can't see." He placed one of the wafers into an opening in the back of the device and motioned for Blake to sit in the chair. "It'll take a minute to scan it fully," he added.

"Right." Blake hunched over the eyepiece and peered through it, waiting for the image to finish uploading. "The concentration gradient is very low," he said slowly. "It should be several times denser. And the placement of the vacancies isn't as precise as it needs to be."

"Good to know."

Blake lifted his head to see that the other man had removed his mask and pulled back his hood. Taking in the piercing blue eyes and smooth-shaven skull, Blake suddenly realized who he was. "Peter Matlock," he said. "I can't believe it."

The man looked up from the monitor with a bemused smile. "They didn't tell you?"

"They don't tell me anything," Blake replied, glancing at Gully. Matlock was the co-founder of Star Microsystems, the world's largest maker of computer microprocessors. The company's other founder and longtime CEO, Chet Hillman, was one of the world's richest and best-known men, appearing regularly on television shows and magazine covers across the globe. While Matlock's net worth lagged behind that of his ex-colleague, he was one of the world's wealthiest individuals as well. Although he'd withdrawn from active involvement in Star decades before, he still retained billions of dollars' worth of the company's stock. These days, most of his energies were devoted to Matlock Enterprises, his own mini-conglomerate that included a high-tech company called Vesuvius, various commercial real estate properties, and several professional sports teams. He'd never married and had a reputation as something of a recluse. Rumor was that he'd been struggling lately with a mysterious neurological ailment that kept him confined to his sprawling estate on the banks of Lake Washington, outside Seattle. Yet here he was, 700 miles to the south in some anonymous Silicon Valley industrial park, looking very fit indeed.

"My apologies for ambushing you," grinned Matlock. "A mutual friend asked me to help with your invention, so I decided to supervise the operation personally. I get out more than the media thinks, you know—I just don't advertise it."

"I thought you were in a wheelchair, practically paralyzed," said Blake. He instantly regretted his comment. "Sorry," he added. "It's just one of those things you hear."

"A vast overstatement of my condition," laughed Matlock. "Now, back to the subject at hand. What are we doing wrong? Actually, don't answer that quite yet." He punched a button on a transmitter attached to his waist. A few seconds later, two other people walked into the room. They too were dressed in sterile suits and masks, but Blake instantly recognized Neil Cohen and Maria Morakova.

"Good to see you, Blake," said Neil. Maria smiled wordlessly and squeezed his arm, her violet eyes holding a touch of concern. Despite the incongruous setting, Blake felt his old attraction to his former mentor flare up immediately with an intensity that startled him.

"Hello Neil…Maria."

Neil glanced at the computer monitor, then walked over to the microscope and peered into it for a few seconds. "We're not generating enough vacancies," he said, straightening. "I suspected as much. Any suggestions?"

"Sure," said Blake. "The whole key is to get a higher nitrogen distribution to start with. But you're also having problems with the accuracy of the ion implantation. You need to limit the ion beam more drastically. It's a tweak that has to be done manually, through trial and error. When we go back into the lab, I'll show you what I mean...."

After five hours of intensive effort, they got the production process to a point where Blake was satisfied with the quality of the lattices. "As long as the technicians stick to these specs, they should turn out fine," he said. "I estimate that each crystal should hold about two hours' worth of digital audio data." He was surprised at how quickly the time had passed. It felt good to be working again. He'd been so immersed in the project that he'd almost forgotten about Ann and the whole assault business. Now that he was done for the day, however, the memory of his fugitive status came flooding back.

"Nice job," said Neil.

"He *is* my prize student, you know," said Maria affectionately, encircling Blake's waist with her arm and pulling his body close against hers. The movement forced Blake to put his arm around her as well. Even with the layers of material between them, he felt the stirring of an erection at her physical proximity. Fighting the reaction with every ounce of will-power he had, Blake gave Maria a tentative hug, then let go awkwardly and stepped away.

"What's next?" he asked.

"Our technicians are going to work through the night on these," said Matlock. "The plan is to ship a dozen or so wafers north by courier tomorrow morning, so they'll be there when we arrive." He glanced at his watch. "Ten thirty! Where *does* the time go? To the showers, everyone! Once you're all presentable, a superb dinner awaits."

With a cheerful wave, Maria headed for the women's section as the two other scientists and Gully followed Matlock down the hall to the men's locker area. The same attendant Blake had seen earlier was waiting for them. With a wave of his hand, he steered each of them into a separate cubicle.

Blake's room had been stocked with toiletries and another fresh change of clothes. Matlock had urged everyone to take their time, so he indulged in a long shower, letting the hot water stream over his head as he tried not to think of Maria. Even in their full-body sterile suits, he'd felt an almost overpowering physical pull toward her. Now, standing in the shower's flow, the feeling returned, but he resolutely ignored the impulse. Turning off the water, he stepped out and began drying himself. *Get over it,* he thought with a touch of irritation. *She's your ex-professor, for God's sake.*

He was about to start dressing when he heard a light knock on the wall outside his cubicle. "Yes?" he called out, wrapping the towel around his waist.

"Sir, if I may?" said a low voice.

The attendant entered the room and stood politely with an electric hair clipper in one hand and a safety razor in the other. "I've been instructed to give you a shave," the man said. As Blake ran his hand over the stubble on his chin, the man shook his head. "No, sir. I'm referring to your scalp."

"Oh no," said Blake, holding up his hands. "I've already had one drastic haircut this week. I don't want another."

The attendant took a half-step forward, saying nothing. Suddenly Matlock's large frame loomed behind him, filling the doorway. "It has to be done, old pal," his voice boomed. "That Mohawk of yours has gotten too famous for your own good. Besides, everyone knows I require all of my personal staff to be cueballs, just like me—it's one of my favorite eccentricities!"

"Your personal staff?" But Matlock was no longer around to answer. Smiling implacably, the attendant continued easing his way into the small room. He motioned Blake to sit on the stool, then plugged the clipper into a wall outlet and began deftly shearing the remaining hair off the top of Blake's head. After the last patch was gone, he applied a layer of warm shaving cream to Blake's skull and set to work with his razor. Five minutes later, he stood back and nodded approvingly. "Very nice."

Blake looked at his reflection over the sink, barely recognizing the man in the mirror with the bare, glistening scalp and three-day growth of beard. “I feel like I should tip you,” he joked, “but I’m cash poor at the moment.”

His attempt at irony fell on deaf ears. “Thank you, sir, but I’m very well taken care of by Mr. Matlock,” the man said, backing out of the room. “When you’re ready, I’ll bring you to the others.”

Back in the reception area, a sizeable group had gathered. Along with Matlock, Neil, Maria and Gully, Blake was happy to see Blue and Serena would be joining them. The woman he’d taken for a receptionist was there too, having changed into a stunning evening gown. From the way she leaned into Matlock as they chatted, he guessed that theirs was something more than an employer-employee relationship.

“Nice ’do, Blake,” grinned Blue. Serena ran her brooding gaze over his gleaming skull, then nodded in the direction of Maria, who looked ravishing in a low-cut silk blouse and black midi-skirt with a slit running up one side. “Who’s *she*?” she said in a cutting voice. “Another one of your ex-girlfriends?”

“She was my professor…as an undergraduate,” Blake said weakly.

“You don’t say? How cozy!”

“Good, I see that our party is complete,” smiled Matlock. While the other men were still in shirtsleeves and slacks, he had changed into a formal suit, adding to his already formidable air of authority. “If you’ll follow me….” He ushered the group onto a nearby elevator, which descended briefly then eased to a stop. The passengers filed out to see two security guards standing beside a motorized tram. “Hop on, everybody,” called Matlock, waving to the six rows of double seats.

Gully held Blake back, guiding him toward the last pair of seats. “I need to talk to you at some point,” he whispered in Blake’s ear as the tram started forward. “Alone.”

Matlock sat up front with one of the guards, who steered the tram down several long corridors, finally stopping at another large elevator. Leaving the tram, they boarded it and rose swiftly. When the doors opened again, the passengers were momentarily speechless.

“Wow!” said Blue at last.

"Fabulous," breathed Maria.

They were in a penthouse apartment, high above the dark waters of the San Francisco Bay. They must have traveled underground to the tall building he'd seen earlier, Blake realized. The suite was lined with floor-to-ceiling windows, and the view in every direction was spectacular. Across the bay, the lights of the eastern shore were spread out before them. Thirty miles to the north, the hills of San Francisco glittered in the distance, while on the southern side of the apartment the street lamps of Palo Alto pointed the way toward the Stanford campus.

A long table had been set in the middle of the room with place settings of fine china. In the center of the table were two flickering candelabras and several open bottles of expensive-looking red wine. Two waiters hovered nearby holding appetizers on trays, and a third was working another wine bottle with a corkscrew.

"Welcome, everyone, to my humble pied-à-terre," said Matlock. Assuming the air of a maître d', he bowed to the group. "Please help yourselves to the starters, and enjoy a well-deserved glass of Burgundy. The menu tonight is a salad of mixed greens, potatoes au gratin, lightly steamed vegetables and rack of lamb. Dinner will be served in approximately twenty minutes—and I do hope no one is a vegetarian!"

"Blake—come check out my panorama," Matlock called, once everyone was settled. As always with Matlock, it felt more like a command than a request. Stepping through the sliding glass door, Blake moved with him to the north end of the terrace and stood gazing at the far-off lights of San Francisco. His light button-down shirt offered little protection against the cool breeze blowing off the Bay, and he found himself eyeing Matlock's suit jacket enviously.

"I've got a question," he said. "I understand why Branford is involved in this Muni scene—I mean, his whole life is devoted to progressive politics. But what's in it for you? This government has been terrific for people in your income bracket, hasn't it?"

"In the short run, maybe," said Matlock, staring into the distance. "But it's not sustainable. If this gulf of inequality keeps growing, everyone in the middle is going to be too strapped to buy our products, and the folks on the bottom are going to be dying in the streets. It's a lose-lose scenario: The economy gains a permanent handicap while revolution simmers on the front burner." He chuckled. "I also play a little electric guitar, as you might have heard. If we can get Fish elected and start turning around our police-state mentality, this stupid music ban might finally be lifted. Which means some of my best friends could play in public again."

That's right, Blake thought. For some reason it hadn't come to mind earlier, but now he recalled the news stories of Matlock's over-the-top birthday party jams, where he'd flown in the most famous rockers in the world to accompany him. *He's another rock star wannabe—the one thing money can't buy.*

Lost in reflection, Blake didn't notice that Matlock had jumped tracks. "I want to make you a proposal, Blake," he was saying. "I know you're under some pressure from the authorities right now. But I'm pretty well-connected, and I have a feeling we could work all of this out with the Feds if you decided to sign with Vesuvius."

"What would that involve?" asked Blake cautiously.

"I'm talking about a licensing agreement, giving us exclusive rights to manufacture and market your device," said Matlock. "Your invention has the potential to revolutionize communication. It's completely secure, which means every government on earth is going to want it. Plus, it works over any distance and, just as important, in any medium. Under the ocean, in the most distant part of outer space—it doesn't matter! It's going to be *huge*. If we can use your device to pull off this broadcast under the government's noses, it will be the greatest marketing campaign kickoff in history."

Blake couldn't believe what he was hearing. How could this guy talk about ad campaigns, just hours after his technology had gotten a man killed? The longer he listened to the billionaire, the more convinced he became that Matlock was out of touch with reality.

"I think you're underestimating how much the Feds want to keep this thing under wraps," he said.

"That's impossible," said Matlock with a dismissive wave. "Your discovery is too big to keep hidden. It reminds me of when Chet and I were kids, laying the foundation for the digital era. Quantum messaging is going to shape the direction of civilization itself." He pursed his lips and fixed Blake with an appraising stare. "Have you filed a patent yet?"

"No," said Blake. "I've been a little preoccupied." The conversation was making him uncomfortable, and he was glad to see Gully walking across the terrace toward them.

"Am I interrupting something?" said Gully.

"Not at all," said Matlock. "I was just speaking to Blake about some entrepreneurial possibilities."

"Sure, the sky's the limit—if he doesn't get arrested or murdered first," replied Gully.

"Well, he's under my protection from here on," Matlock said breezily. "Nothing's going to happen to him on my watch."

"Glad to hear it," said Gully.

"Now if you'll excuse me," Matlock added, "I should look in on my other guests."

When they were alone, Blake turned toward Gully. "I know he's one of the world's richest people," he said, "but personally, I think he's a lunatic."

"He's pretty eccentric," Gully agreed. "He's also the only person associated with the Alliance who has the high-tech facilities to pull this off. And Branford trusts him completely. Matlock would never betray us."

"Not intentionally, maybe," said Blake. "But I don't think he fully understands what we're up against. He's so rich and connected, he thinks he can talk his way out of anything. If he's wrong, though, it's my head on the chopping block."

"You'll have to bear with him for now," Gully said. "We need to get you up to Seattle, where another one of Matlock's labs is working on the computerized laser component. The easiest way to transport you there is for you to join him as part of his operation."

"What about you, and Serena and Blue?"

"We'll be close by," said Gully, "but we can't travel with you. It would draw too much attention. The plan is to meet up in New York."

Glancing towards the apartment to make sure no one was watching, Gully reached into his pocket. "I have a couple of things for you," he said. "First, this..."

He handed Blake a small sheet of paper with two vertical columns scribbled on it. The first column was the alphabet. The second was a series of two-digit numbers.

"It's a single-use encryption code," explained Gully. "We're going to be sending you a coded numerical message by shortwave radio, tomorrow evening at the stroke of midnight. It'll be just like the radio transmission you heard earlier today. Write the numbers down carefully, then use this sheet to decode the message. It will refer to a social gathering. If we tell you everything's fine, then you can relax and stay put. If the message says that the gathering is ending, that means there's trouble and you need to split from wherever you are."

"How will I get this message?" asked Blake.

"I'm coming to that," Gully said. "Here." He handed Blake a flesh-colored disc the size of a nickel.

"What's this?" asked Blake.

"A miniature short wave receiver, tuned to our frequency," said Gully. "It has a strong adhesive on one side, so you can attach it to the skin under your armpit where it won't be seen. When it's time to listen to the message, peel it off and press the center for three full seconds to switch on the receiver. Then place it inside your ear, non-adhesive side pointing in."

He leaned forward and tapped the disc as it lay in Blake's palm. "If the message indicates a problem, I want you to leave wherever you are *immediately* and make your way into Seattle as quickly as possible. Go to the Open Door Café, two blocks from the Seattle UZ southern entrance, and ask for Matilda. She'll get you inside. Our rendezvous point is the Space Needle. Do you have all that?"

"I think so," said Blake. "Assuming everything's okay, what happens after tomorrow night?"

"We'll rejoin you in New York the day after tomorrow," said Gully. "You're going to fly there on Matlock's personal jet. One last thing..." He handed Blake a money clip. "There's twenty hundred-dollar bills in here. A little mad money, courtesy of the Muni Alliance."

Blake pocketed the paper, the plastic disc and the cash as Matlock thrust his head out of the open sliding door. "Gentlemen," he bellowed, "dinner is served!"

❖ ❖ ❖

By the time dinner was finished, it was nearly two in the morning. Neil Cohen had left earlier, wishing everyone well. "I've got to get back to Los Angeles," he told Blake, "but I think the execution has gone very smoothly so far. I'll be pulling for you." Now Blue, Serena and Gully were gathering their things and moving toward the elevator.

"This is where we say goodbye," said Blue, turning to Blake.

"It's going to feel strange, traveling on alone," said Blake. "I figured you guys would be with me all the way to New York."

"We'll be nearby, but for now it's safer if we keep our distance," said Blue. "You're heading onto the big man's turf now." He nodded toward Matlock, who was deep in conversation with Maria. "You'll be fine. He's got plenty of hired guns to watch over you."

"I hope so." Blake looked at Serena, but she avoided his gaze. "I wouldn't be here right now, if it wasn't for the two of you," he said.

"Be careful," mumbled Serena. She turned and gazed pointedly in Matlock's direction, then leaned in to give Blake a quick hug.

"I don't trust him," she hissed into his ear.

Gully shook Blake's hand, then tapped his ear. "We'll be in touch," he said. The elevator doors closed, and they were gone.

❖ ❖ ❖

"How thoughtful of Peter, putting us together like this," said Maria. "Now we can catch up properly."

"Very thoughtful," Blake mumbled, his throat suddenly dry. After bidding Matlock goodnight, he and Maria had been escorted to a lower floor, where they were ushered into a luxurious apartment consisting of an expensively decorated living room, a state-of-the-art kitchen, and a single large bedroom with a king-sized bed.

Maria turned to look at Blake in the doorway. "You're as nervous as a schoolboy, Blake," she laughed. "What's the matter? Is there a girlfriend out there somewhere, waiting for your nightly phone call?"

"No," said Blake. He thought of Ann, stuffing her books and papers angrily into her bag. "There hasn't been for a while."

"I thought not," Maria smiled. Walking over to him, she rubbed her hand over his shaved scalp and then continued downward, running her fingertips lightly across his cheek and down the front of his chest. "You're so worried...about everything," she said softly. "Can you stop worrying, for just a few minutes? There's nothing wrong with us being together, you know. You're not an innocent college freshman anymore, and I'm no longer your professor. You don't have to get a crick in your neck, trying to stare down my blouse without my noticing."

"I guess I didn't do a very good job of that," stammered Blake.

"And you don't have to go back to your dorm room and play with yourself, either, fantasizing about me."

How did she know? "Maria, you're making me blush," Blake laughed.

"I was hoping to do more than that." Her hand wandered down to his crotch. "And I think I've succeeded."

"Maria, I don't think—" Blake was stopped by her other hand covering his mouth.

"Tonight, no more thinking," she said. "Sometimes we must listen to our bodies, not our minds. Don't you agree?"

Blake nodded his head dumbly. He felt powerless, hypnotized by her voice and touch.

"And who knows what your body wants better than the woman who has watched you lust after her, year after year, from just a few feet away? Let's get these off you..." She helped Blake out of his clothing, then stood caressing his bare skin for several minutes.

"Yes, I know what it wants," she said at last. Unhurriedly, she opened her bag and pulled out two black, thigh-length boots. Slipping her high heels off, she rolled the boots up over her legs, then unfastened her skirt and blouse and dropped them to the floor. Underneath, she was wearing nothing but a black corset.

"Someone once told me that sexy clothing is all about the spaces in between," smiled Maria. She folded the top half of the corset's brassiere downward so that it formed two cups under her bare breasts. "Isn't it wonderful, to finally see what you've been dreaming of?" Planting one booted foot on the bed, she faced Blake, her thighs spread wide. Then, reaching between her legs, she gently touched herself. "Look at it," she murmured, "how ready it is." Her fingers moved faster. "You've wanted me for a long time, haven't you, Blake?"

"Yes," he said hoarsely. "A very long time."

"Show me what you used to do when you thought about me," she said softly. "How nice. Look at how your body wants me. And look at how mine wants you." A low groan escaped her lips. "There's great pleasure in wanting, isn't there?" she said huskily. "Wait—don't approach yet. Stay where you are for a minute longer. Let yourself feel how much you desire this. How much you *need* this.... Oh, now you're trembling. Don't worry, sweet boy, your wait is over. Come and get what you've been longing for."

SEVENTEEN

Submission

Friday, September 6

THE MORNING SUN WAS POURING through the window when Blake was wakened by the sound of a doorbell. A moment later, Maria walked in with a mug of coffee in one hand and a pile of freshly pressed clothes in the other.

"These were just delivered," she said. "Apparently you are now one of Matlock's crew. You'd better put these on. The butler, or whoever he is, says you must be ready to leave in forty-five minutes. Rather rude of him, don't you think?"

Blake looked over the white shirt and royal-blue jacket and trousers, then picked up the matching billed cap and turned it in his hands. Embroidered on the front were the initials "M.E.," the abbreviation for Matlock Enterprises.

"Another day, another identity," he said, shaking his head.

"He also asked me to give you this." Maria held out an envelope. Blake glanced inside and saw that it contained a Washington State driver's license in the name of Jean Paul Jones along with a short, typed biography.

"Your instructions are to look over the materials before you go," said Maria. She took a sip of coffee, then put the cup down on the side table. "First, though, there's something *I* need to look over." She sat on the side of the bed and drew the sheets back, then reached out to run her fingertips lightly over Blake's stomach. His breathing quickened as her fingers moved steadily lower.

"You're going to be fine, Blake. Everything will work out for you—I know it," she smiled. "I'm going to miss you, my sweet schoolboy. I'll never forget our study session last night. As you may know, however, following any late-night cram session, it's always best to refresh your recollection in the morning."

"I've heard that," said Blake, reaching out for her. "It has to do with consolidating long-term memory, I think…."

"My private submersible," grinned Matlock, gesturing at the 200-foot-long submarine floating in a large metal tank. "Purchased ten years ago. An excellent way to get around without attracting attention. After you—" Blake lowered himself through the open hatchway and found himself in the sub's central compartment where two smooth-skulled crewmen sat gazing at an instrument panel.

"Gentlemen," Matlock announced, "I'd like to introduce my new personal valet, Jean Paul." The crewmen looked up and nodded. Both wore the royal blue uniform of Matlock Enterprises and had pistols strapped to their waists. "Come," Matlock added. "I'll give you the cook's tour."

As they entered the main lounge, Blake was astonished to see a half-dozen electric guitars mounted on the walls. "Those aren't just any axes," said Matlock. "Take a close look." Drawing nearer, Blake saw that each had been signed with a black Sharpie. He made out the scrawled names of Eddie van Halen, Jimmy Page, George Harrison, Jeff Beck, and Robert Cray.

"And here is my Mona Lisa," Matlock said breathlessly, pointing to a guitar hanging over the wet bar. Strung for a left-handed player, it bore the unmistakable autograph of Jimi Hendrix, the crossed top of the "J" swooping over the rest of the signature. "It took me years to track down," added the billionaire. "But I finally nailed him."

"And I thought *I* was a rock fan!"

Thinking of Matlock traveling through the ocean depths surrounded by his collection of autographed guitars, Blake was more convinced than ever that the man had serious psychiatric issues. When they returned to the control room, a man in a captain's uniform emerged from a small compartment and bowed slightly.

"Ready when you are, Mr. Matlock," he said.

"Okay then," said Matlock. "Let's go for a swim."

"Prepare to dive!" the captain instructed his crew.

Matlock turned to Blake. "Care to join me in the observation area? The view's a lot more interesting." Blake followed him through a metal doorway to the front of the submarine, where a thick acrylic window curved across the bow. Sitting in a swivel chair bolted into the floor, Blake watched through the glass as the water line moved slowly up the side of the sub. A minute later, the craft was fully submerged in the tank. Through the sub's hull a faint humming could be heard as a huge metal door at the end of the tank slowly slid open. When the door was fully retracted, the submarine nosed its way through the gap into the gloomy brine of the San Francisco Bay.

"Are you allowed to tell me where we're heading?" asked Blake.

"Sixty miles due west," said Matlock. "A few hours from now, when we reach our destination there, we'll switch to something a bit faster. The *Nemo* can reach 15 knots underwater—not bad for a sub this size. At that rate, though, it would take us take us almost two days to reach Seattle. I'll let you know when we're outside U.S. territorial waters, by the way. Then you can avail yourself of *this*."

He pointed to a large computer screen mounted on the wall. "It's a satellite Internet connection. The signal can reach us even under the water, as long as we're not too deep. Once we're twenty-eight miles from shore, outside the U.S. contiguous zone, we'll have access to uncensored service."

Matlock lifted a pair of wireless headphones off a peg and handed them to Blake. "You'll have all the forbidden music of the world at your fingertips. It's as good as being in Canada."

"Except that Canada doesn't allow Americans to be extradited for Cultural Hygiene violations," said Blake. "Out here in the open sea, I'm still subject to arrest by the U.S. authorities for crimes committed ashore—correct?"

"Now you're nit-picking," sighed Matlock. "Alright, *almost* as good."

❖ ❖ ❖

"The Secretary wants to know why this hasn't been wrapped up yet," said Smyth. "Our butts are on the line here, people. Why's it so hard to nail this guy?"

"After we lost Hawkes in L.A.," said Piroulis, flashing a pointed glance at Marconi, "we put out a general alert up and down the West Coast. Unfortunately, he was gone by the time our people got to the scene of his reappearance in Berkeley. As soon as we heard he'd been spotted there, our division arranged for a local arrest warrant to be drawn up and made sure the media knew all about it."

"So—any guesses where he might be now?" said Smyth, rubbing his chin.

"We know he's getting help from the Muni underground," replied Marconi, more subdued than usual. The fact that his division had let Hawkes slip through their fingers twice in two different cities had dampened his bravado, Smyth noted with a touch of satisfaction. "They're the ones who've been helping him escape. It's a sure bet they've got him tucked away somewhere."

"We also know that he's been on the move," said Smyth. "If we can figure out why, that may tell us where he's heading next."

"Obviously, the Munis are interested in the kid because of his communication device," said Piroulis. "They want to adapt his technology for their own purposes."

"Which takes resources and facilities," Smyth pointed out.

"Right. And the Munis have some pretty deep pockets," said Simpson, the department's finance chief.

"Okay then, let's run review their funding sources and see if we can develop some links," said Smyth.

"Their primary source is an operational fund operated directly by the Municipal Alliance," said Simpson. "They use a couple of bogus political programs to funnel it to their operatives. We estimate it currently contains about fifty million dollars. But they also have significant private backing. According to our information, the Muni's leading supporters are the Branford Foundation in L.A., the Soros sons in New York, and Peter Matlock in Seattle."

"Let's focus on those three for the moment. Do we have evidence that any of them have been in contact with Hawkes?"

"No, to the Soros group," said Piroulus. "Although they're very active in supporting the cultural festival taking place in New York next week—where presidential candidate Fish is scheduled to make an appearance, as you know."

"Any chance Hawkes could be heading out that way?" Smyth asked.

"Maybe he's part of this scheme we've been hearing about," said Marconi. "You know, about the Munis finding some way to televise Fish's speech."

"An underground broadcast is a concern, of course," said Smyth. "But so far we haven't turned up any direct evidence of a plot. Let's go back to Branford. Could Hawkes have met with him while he was in L.A.?"

"Informants have placed him in Venice on Tuesday night, before we started tailing him," said Marconi. "He arrived back at his hotel at one in the morning. That leaves time for a personal meeting at or near Branford's home. We've also established that Hawkes was accompanied throughout his stay in Los Angeles by two security personnel, a man and a woman, both of whom are on the payroll of a shell company funded in part by the Branford Foundation—so there's definitely a connection there. But Branford's influence is pretty much confined to southern California. He also has a serious pulmonary condition that limits his activities."

"What about his people? Are they still guarding Hawkes?"

"In Berkeley, Hawkes was extracted by a woman," said Marconi. "I think it's safe to assume she's the same agent who was with him in L.A."

"Alright then. Let's try to get some names and photos for that pair—they seem to be key to facilitating Hawkes' movements," said Smyth. "Now, what about Matlock?"

"The assumption has been that he's mostly sitting at home, but we can't be sure of that because no one's seen him in months," said Marconi. "He generally avoids communicating by phone or Internet and his estate has extensive ground cover, so drone and satellite photos aren't much help. However, our unit recently began tracking the GPS coordinates of his personal air and watercraft, on the chance he might be connected to the Hawkes affair. In fact, one of his ocean-going vessels is in the Bay Area right now—a submarine, believe it or not."

Smyth started to ask why he hadn't been consulted on the tracking initiative, then thought better of it. "Oh?" he said, leaning forward. "Where, exactly?"

Marconi opened his secure laptop and consulted it. "It passed through the mouth of the San Francisco Bay about an hour ago, heading west at fifteen knots."

Smyth leaned back in his chair. He was pleased that his operative's instincts hadn't deserted him, though he found it slightly disturbing that Marconi had gotten there first. "Let's get a ship on its tail," he said briskly. "We're talking about an extra-territorial operation, so it's your baby, Tony. Nothing too big—a Coast Guard cutter will do fine. When Mr. Matlock comes up for air, we'll be there to say hello."

"We've got company," said the captain. "Medium-sized craft, holding steady at a distance of one-point-five nautical miles, west by northwest."

"Picking up any radio chatter?" asked Matlock.

"Yes sir. It's a Coast Guard fast responder. From their communications, they appear to be on routine patrol."

"How long have they been in the neighborhood?"

"About thirty minutes," the captain said. "I wanted to make sure before I said anything."

"Hmm. A routine patrol that just happens to keep them directly off our starboard bow." Matlock rubbed the back of his neck. "Let's wait another half hour. If they're still hanging around, I'll put a call in to a friend of mine…just in case."

When the submarine surfaced beside Matlock's yacht, the Coast Guard cutter was rocking on the waves two hundred yards away. Before the sub's hatch was open, the cutter's commander and three of his officers were already chugging toward it in a motorized raft.

"Good afternoon, gentlemen," said Matlock, greeting his visitors with a broad smile. Beside him on deck, the submarine's crew stood with shoulders squared, eyes on the horizon. "I was just chatting with your commandant. He told me to expect the privilege of your visit. All of our documentation is below, ready for your perusal."

"That won't be necessary," said the cutter's commander. "Commandant Follette has been in touch with me, as well. He wanted to make sure I was aware of the invaluable assistance you've provided the Guard over the years on our various search and rescue operations. As you heard, there's a high-priority suspect on the loose. We're just trying to cover all the bases in terms of where he might be. To that end, we'd like to do a quick search of your vessel."

Matlock chuckled warmly. "By all means, Commander. I can't imagine there's a stowaway on my craft—but if there's any chance of that, then, as you say, it must be investigated. Please board at your pleasure. My men stand ready to assist."

As Blake and the others stood rigidly, the captain paused to study them. "These are all your regular crew?" he asked.

"I know them all extremely well, and can vouch for their integrity without hesitation," said Matlock.

"Very good," said the commander. "Then if you don't mind, we'll take a look below."

"Absolutely," said Matlock. "Right this way." The captain and his men followed Matlock down the ladder into the sub, leaving the bald-headed crew standing on the hull at full attention.

"I told you it wouldn't amount to anything," Matlock said. He seemed remarkably unconcerned for a man who had just had his personal watercraft searched by the U.S. Coast Guard. Blake didn't reply—he was too busy taking in the sheer size of the billionaire's yacht, the *Squid*.

"The official term is mega-yacht," said Matlock as they stood beside the sub's docking pool. "She's one-and-a-half football fields long. Carries a crew of sixty, with two helicopters and seven launches—plus my personal sub. There's also a spa, by the way, here on the lower deck. *And* a heated pool up top."

"I have to ask," said Blake. "How much?"

"About two hundred million to build, and another twenty million per year to staff and maintain," said Matlock. He was striving hard for a casual tone, but he couldn't hide his grin of pleasure at Blake's shocked reaction. "It's the largest privately-owned yacht in the world. The only bigger ones belong to a Saudi sheik and a couple of Asian heads of state. I keep telling you, Blake, it's good to be rich. Speaking of which..." Matlock glanced toward the upper deck. "Come upstairs with me. I've got a surprise for you."

They ascended two flights to a well-appointed dining room with portholes lining the port and starboard sides. Against one wall was a table holding a spread of fresh fruit, cheese, meat and poultry dishes and grilled vegetables. Bottles of wine stood on a sideboard along with an unopened bottle of champagne in a bucket of ice.

"Help yourself," said Matlock. Aware suddenly of his hunger, Blake reached for a piece of salmon sushi. He'd barely popped it into his mouth when Matlock beckoned him with an impatient wave. Obediently, Blake trailed his host down a plush corridor to a padded door in the ship's midsection.

"My recording studio," said Matlock with a child's gleeful smile, ushering Blake inside. From his tone, Blake was expecting some reasonably sophisticated home recording setup. Instead, he found himself inside the production booth of a spacious, ultra-modern facility. Through the booth's transparent front wall he saw a quartet of gray-haired musicians fiddling with their instruments in the main studio, their sound muffled by the plastic barrier. Beside Matlock and Blake, two engineers were busy manipulating banks of faders.

"I don't have to tell you who recorded a whole solo album here," said Matlock, looking around with pride. He was referring, Blake knew, to the world-famous British front man that Matlock had befriended decades ago.

Noticing their presence, the musicians had stopped what they were doing and were waiting quietly, their eyes on Matlock. "How's it going, boys?" said the billionaire, holding the button that activated the studio's two-way speaker.

"How's it *going?*" asked the man cradling a bass guitar in a sarcastic English accent. As Blake studied the man's close-cropped head, he felt a giddy rush. Here, not twenty feet away from him, stood the schoolteacher turned rock superstar that he'd revered since he was a kid. Shifting his gaze to the others, it dawned on him that he was staring at four aging legends of the pop music world.

"You came back after all, you secretive bastard," said the Bandleader in his Florida drawl.

"I told you he couldn't stay away from his vintage guitars for long," said the man behind the drums. Another Brit, famous for his musical versatility and his production skills, his expression was impassive behind his trademark beard and sunglasses.

"Or his vintage champagne," added the slim rocker known universally as the Artist.

"Where are the ladies?" asked Matlock through the intercom.

"In the spa, of course," said the Producer. "Adding to their already considerable luster."

"What are you waiting for, an invitation?" the Schoolteacher broke in. "And how about your friend here—does he play?"

"Sure, he plays," said Matlock with a hint of cockiness. "Not as good as *me*, of course."

"Don't worry, mate," said the Producer, looking at Blake through the glass. "We're quite used to carrying Emperor Matlock's friends on our backs. Just grab a Gibson and give it a go. You'll have the time of your life."

"Has he been bragging about you-know-who, and how he recorded a whole album here?" snickered the Bandleader. "He's Matlock's one true love, you know."

"Let me know when you housewives are done gossiping," said the

Artist impatiently. He had his guitar on his shoulder and was tweaking the amplifier settings. "We shouldn't waste this precious time on international waters. My deathless music is crying out for release!"

"I like to think of them as a new supergroup in utero," explained Matlock.

"The Traveling Elderberries," cracked the Bandleader.

"Assuming these two can fill the shoes of George and Roy, that is," said the Producer, adjusting the cymbals on the drum kit.

Blake felt like he should join in the banter, but he found himself tongue-tied in the presence of immortality. He was also emotionally drained from the encounter with the Coast Guard. Now that the authorities had connected him with Matlock, he assumed it was only a matter of time before they returned for another look. Meanwhile, he was trapped on this floating funhouse, playing sidekick on a rich lunatic's ego trip.

"Thanks for the invitation, boys, but we'll have to pass," said Matlock, pressing his hand against the glass. "We have an appointment up north."

"You're depriving your young friend here of a once-in-a-lifetime experience—you know that, right?" said the Producer. "But then, what do you care? It must be nice to be richer than God."

"It's not too shabby—and I love you, too," grinned Matlock. "I'll see you tricksters shortly. And now, Robin, to the helipad!"

"Safe journey, Batman," called the Artist softly.

EIGHTEEN

Takin' Care of Business

FROM A PHYSICS PERSPECTIVE, BLAKE had a firm understanding of a helicopter's functional limitations. Because the motion of the blades is faster than the aircraft's airspeed, he knew, each blade generates extra drag on its forward path, inevitably slowing the craft's progress through the atmosphere. The blades also ran the risk of stalling out if the forward velocity was too great. All of which meant that even a top-of-the-line copter like Matlock's had a maximum speed of about 150 miles per hour.

Despite this knowledge, Blake found himself growing increasingly irritated as the endless carpet of ocean unfolded below them for two hours, then three, then four. He kept his gaze glued to the horizon, watching for the Air Force jets he was sure would intercept them any second. He couldn't fathom Matlock's lack of concern over the encounter with the Coast Guard. Did this megalomaniac really think that would be the end of it? Once Blake's hunters heard that Matlock had conned his way out of any real search, they'd be back with a vengeance.

Finally they turned inland, headed on a northeasterly course. "Don't worry—almost there," Matlock shouted over the racket of the rotors as Puget Sound came into view at last. To their left stretched the urban sprawl of Seattle. Flying low over the southernmost waters of Lake Washington, they reached the western edge of Mercer Island, where the aircraft hovered briefly before descending with pinpoint accuracy onto a floating helipad in front of a large waterfront estate.

"Welcome to the house that Star built," said Matlock as the rotors eased to a stop.

❖ ❖ ❖

It was hours later, and Smyth still couldn't get word on how the Coast Guard encounter with Matlock's sub had gone. The executive officer he'd contacted to arrange the stop had gone off-duty, and no one else seemed able to tell him what happened. He finally decided to bite the bullet and go through the office of his boss, Secretary of Homeland Security Bob Jackson.

"Can you hold for a little bit, Chuck?" Jackson's assistant said. "I'll see what I can find out." Five minutes later, she came back on the line. "I just spoke with the Commandant's office. Apparently they did a thorough search of the craft, and everything checked out fine."

"What about his crew?" asked Smyth.

"His crew?"

"Did the investigating officers examine the credentials of Matlock's crew?" said Smyth, struggling to maintain a patient tone.

"Just a moment." After several minutes more on hold, she returned again. "From what I can gather, Mr. Marconi's instructions were to search the submersible watercraft for a stowaway in hiding, and they carried out their orders. He didn't mention anything about checking on official personnel. A full report will be forwarded to you in the morning. Does that answer your question?"

"Yes, thank you," he said grimly. "It does."

So, that's how it's going to be, Smyth thought. His original instructions to Tony had been to follow the submarine closely until it surfaced, and then search the craft thoroughly. He hadn't asked him specifically to vet the crew, but that should have been automatically included in Marconi's orders to the Coast Guard. This latest development confirmed his suspicions: There was a play going down, and he was being cast as the unwitting dupe. Over his long career in national security,

Smyth had learned the hard way that the greatest danger always lay in your own backyard. In the field, at least you knew who your enemy was. In Washington, any one of the smiling faces across the conference table could be masking a hidden agenda.

Regarding the Hawkes case, his bureaucratic radar had been sounding the alarm for some time now. Every aspect of it seemed fishy. For one thing, it was almost too easy how they kept getting a fix on the kid: The trooper who just happened to be patrolling in the desert, for example, and the swift transfer of the scanner information from the L.A. Zone checkpost. Normally it took at least a week for that data to trickle into the Federal computer banks. Then there was the curious fact that Marconi's group had decided, completely on its own, to start tracking the movements of Matlock's submarine.

The other side of the coin was just as troubling: Every time they got close to Hawkes, he found a way to slip away. Smyth knew the Munis had an informant inside his department, but that didn't explain why Marconi's operatives had waited almost a full day to move on him in L.A. And now this fiasco with the Coast Guard. Putting everything together, it added up to a double game: Someone wanted to make it apparent that they were keeping tabs on Hawkes, but at the same time they wanted make sure he continued to run free. There was also no escaping the fact that Marconi was involved, and that he was reporting to someone over Smyth's head—either Bob Jackson or some other Cabinet-level joker.

Whoever that joker might be, Smyth was sure of one thing: it wasn't Martin Bibbitt. Marconi was too smart to get anywhere near that train wreck. Not that Bibbitt couldn't cause trouble all on his own. He was obsessed with the undercover broadcast investigation, and kept pushing the idea that his own forces should join the UZFest security detail—a notion that Smyth had rejected politely but firmly. With Homeland Security and the New York Police Department already involved, plus whoever was sticking their nose in anonymously, having Bibbitt's Keystone Cops poking around was the last thing they needed.

Which brought him back to the central question—who, exactly, was running the Hawkes counter-operation?

I'll give it one more test, Smyth decided, picking up the phone.

"Rosemary, get me the Seattle office," he said. "I need to speak with Associate Director Huntsman, right away."

❖ ❖ ❖

"While we're at it, could I get some different clothes?" said Blake, gesturing to his crewman's uniform. "I'm not really comfortable working in this getup." He and Matlock were in a conference room at Vesuvius headquarters, a few minutes' drive from Matlock's compound.

"Of course, how thoughtless of me—I'll have some brought right away." Matlock's tone was solicitous, but Blake sensed an undercurrent of annoyance. *He likes having me dressed like one of his minions,* he thought.

A minute later someone appeared carrying a button-down cotton shirt, blue jeans and a pair of running shoes. Blake excused himself to change. When he came back, Matlock had been joined by several engineers. Although it was late afternoon, no one appeared ready to go home.

"Good time?" asked a new arrival, sticking his head into the room.

"My head engineer," said Matlock. "I believe you've met." It was Bjorn Bjorkman, the computer scientist from the advisory group in L.A.

"It took a couple of all-nighters," Bjorn grinned, "but we've put together an extremely cool software package."

"Tell him the other good news," said Matlock.

"We've come up with a design to fit the transceivers inside an ordinary laptop computer," said Bjorn. "In any superficial examination, someone would think that's all they are. We've left in a miniaturized circuit board, so each device can still perform some minimal computer functions. Now, however, there's room for two crystal lattices—one for sending, one for receiving—plus a pulse laser, a diode to generate the microwaves, and a Doppler unit, all hooked up to a small but very powerful microprocessor."

He pointed to the side of the laptop. "We've linked each device's transmission channels to these redesigned ports. One port is for input—a digital microphone or line. The second port provides outgoing digital data. They can transmit wirelessly, too. We've also removed the computer's camera and audio recording hardware so they can be taken through a UZ checkpoint without being hassled."

He turned the computer over. "The crystals go here." He slid open the compartment where the hard drive would normally be. "To align them properly, you need to make sure each silicone wafer clicks fully into place." He demonstrated with a pair of dummy wafers. Blake took the wafers and practiced inserting them several times.

"The laser software has been finalized and tested," Bjorn continued. "Each crystal's vacancy pattern was recorded when it was created. The software will automatically read the sending crystal's identification number and calculate its firing pattern accordingly. We've also been working on the pulse laser itself. We've experimented with several models, and like the results we're getting from this one."

Blake watched as the argon laser was put through its paces using one of the crystal lattices shipped in by plane earlier that day. After several minutes, he checked the Doppler readout from the receiving device. "It looks terrific," he said.

"We've got a bunch more on the shelf. Now, we just need to put all the puzzle pieces together," said Bjorn.

"Ready when you are," said Blake.

"Four bedroom Colonial," read the ad in the real estate section of the *Washington Post*. "750K or best offer." It was followed by a phone number. Putting the paper down, the man took his disposable cell phone and dialed the area code, then punched in the final seven digits in reverse order. After two rings, the phone was picked up. There was silence at the other end.

"I'm calling with important news for our friend on the road," the man said.

More silence. "Who is this?" a voice said finally. "I don't recognize the number you're calling from."

"I'm a colleague of Mr. Adams," the first speaker said. "He wasn't available."

"How did you get this number?"

"I knew where to look."

There was a pause at the other end. "Does he know you're calling?"

"No."

"Why should I talk to you, then?"

"As I said, I'm calling with important news. You can do what you want, but I assure you my information is accurate. A major action is scheduled for tonight outside Seattle."

Another pause. "What time?"

"One a.m."

"Remind me again—why should I listen to you?"

"Because you can't afford not to."

The caller punched a button on his phone, and the line went dead.

❖ ❖ ❖

Several hours later, the engineering team had assembled and tested four transceivers. Blake watched carefully as they positioned each laser, then ran the device through its paces. When Bjorn and Blake both agreed they were satisfied, Matlock beamed.

"Fantastic," said he. "That gives us two primary units for communicating between the initial broadcast point and our hub station, plus two backups if something goes wrong with the first pair. We're ready to ship. In fact—" he consulted his watch "—our courier should be arriving any minute now."

For all his doubts about Matlock, Blake was coming to appreciate his ability to move events along at an astonishingly high speed. To have the completed transceivers in hand, just two days after his first meeting with the scientists in L.A., was nothing short of miraculous. To see them actually headed out the door was incredible. For the first time, he began to feel their plan had a real chance of succeeding.

A small white truck with "American Cargo Systems" stenciled on its side panels was waiting in the Vesuvius loading dock. While the driver stood by watching, Matlock's people took the transceivers in their reinforced shockproof cases and strapped them tightly into the rear of the truck, followed by the generator-powered freezer that held the crystal lattices.

Once everything was in place, the driver climbed in and tested the straps to make sure they were secure, then clambered back out again. His face was largely obscured by his shoulder-length, rust-colored hair and bushy red beard. Except for a brown cap with the letters "ACS" on the front, he wore no uniform to speak of—just a polo shirt, chinos, work boots and brown-tinted sunglasses.

"They're a small outfit," said Matlock, "but very dependable." He turned to the driver. "You have your instructions regarding the cargo, correct?"

"Sure do," the man drawled. Turning to Matlock and Blake, the driver touched his cap bill and nodded. "Later," he said. Hearing his voice, Blake couldn't shake the feeling he'd seen him somewhere before. As he tried to make out the man's eyes behind the tinted lenses, he suddenly knew why: From behind the beard and sunglasses, Gully gazed calmly back at him.

He must have flown up earlier that day, Blake realized. *Gully wasn't kidding about sticking close,* he thought.

If Matlock recognized the disguised Muni operative, he showed no sign of it. "Looks like all the pieces are in place," he said gleefully after the truck had driven off. "Have you thought any more about what I said last night?"

Seeing the demonic gleam in his eyes, Blake's misgivings stirred once again. "Why don't we discuss it in the morning?" he replied. "I'm too tired to think right now."

"Super idea. Let's get back to the compound and score some grub. Then I'll show you the guesthouse where you'll be bunking for the night. Tomorrow, after breakfast, we've got a date with a Lear jet—destination, New York City."

The guesthouse was a small, two-story affair about thirty yards from the compound's main building. Following a late dinner, Blake sat alone in the first-floor living room trying to collect his thoughts. After the Coast Guard incident, he was convinced that if he boarded Matlock's private jet he'd be stepping into a trap. The authorities were obviously tracking the billionaire's movements; once they learned he was headed cross-country, they'd go over his plane with a fine-tooth comb. And despite the amazing progress that had been made on the quantum project, he still didn't trust Matlock's motives. The billionaire seemed driven more by business interests than by any great desire to aid the cause of political freedom.

Looking at the clock, Blake saw with a start that it was almost midnight. The shortwave transmission! Reaching into his shirt, he pried the miniature receiver from his skin, pressed the center for a long three seconds, then placed it in his left ear canal. As the disc came alive with a crackling sound, he grabbed a sheet of stationery and a pen from the desk in the living room.

At first there was nothing but static. Then, on the stroke of midnight, the white noise was replaced by the faint but clear sound of a brass band playing the same marching music he'd heard on the shortwave radio in Oakland. There was a short pause, followed by a woman's voice, crisply reciting a series of numbers in an unrushed cadence: "Ten…twenty-three…sixty-seven…fourteen…ten….eight-five…"

This went on for several minutes as Blake carefully wrote down each number. Finally, there was silence. Leaving the disc in his ear, he took out his encryption sheet and began deciphering the message, his heart pounding harder with each letter that was revealed:

Party ending early due to excess noise. Police are on their way. Please join us across the lake immediately. You'll find transport 600 meters to the north.

I knew it, he thought grimly. *When I'm with Matlock, I'm a marked man. Time to ditch the asylum.* In a way it felt like a relief, the idea of distancing himself from Matlock's antics.

Blake stuck the disc back under his arm, then got up and walked casually onto the front porch of the cottage. He had already surveyed the grounds when he'd first arrived, worried that he might have to make a sudden exit. Now he knew exactly what his next move was going to be. Taking a deep breath, he stepped down lightly onto the lawn. With a nod to the guard patrolling the waterfront—*just another houseguest, out for a late-night stroll*—Blake ambled across the lawn toward the nine-foot iron fence that ran along the estate's perimeter. While the area outside the fence had been carefully cleared, the vegetation on the interior side was fairly thick. Nearing the fence, he began walking slowly away from the lake until the main house blocked him from the guard's view. Once he was certain he couldn't be seen, he reached for the branches of a sizeable pine tree and swiftly climbed until he was even with the fence's upper cross bar. Planting one foot on the bar, he let go of the tree and pushed off, landing hard on the rocky earth outside the compound. As he darted into the woods he heard a shout somewhere behind him, and then the blast of a horn cutting through the night air.

Standing at a lighted control panel in a glass-encased room at the top of the main house, Matlock stared at the patch of trees where Blake had disappeared. Without shifting his gaze, he grabbed a microphone from the table beside him and held it to his lips.

"Come back, old friend," he said. "You're making a mistake."

In the surrounding woods, Matlock's amplified words thundered like the voice of God. "BLAKE, WHY ARE YOU LEAVING ME? I CAN HELP YOU..."

Blake pushed deeper into the forest, intent on putting yardage between himself and Matlock's madness. The voice boomed again: "WE COULD HAVE MADE BEAUTIFUL MUSIC TOGETHER—LISTEN TO WHAT YOU'RE MISSING!"

The amplified voice gave way abruptly to the ear-splitting sound of an amateurish electric guitar. It was Matlock, playing the lead to "Free Bird." Like a bad dream, the screech of his guitar solo followed Blake as he pushed on through the woods, circling gradually to the northwest in the direction of the lakefront.

You'll find transport 600 meters to the north.

When Blake finally spotted the dark lake waters again, he estimated that he was a few hundred yards above Matlock's helipad. A kilometer away, on the far side of Lake Washington, he could just discern the outlines of Seward Park. Working his way along the shoreline, he passed one large house with an expanse of green lawn, then another.

On the second house's northern side a dock jutted into the water, with several sailboats and a motor launch moored to its posts. Drawing closer, Blake spied a kayak sitting on top of the wooden planking. Stepping softly, he crept onto the dock and looked inside the craft. In the light of the half-moon, he saw a double-bladed paddle resting on the bottom, along with a weather-beaten Seattle Seahawks cap.

Gully! Blake couldn't help smiling as he rubbed one hand over his shaved skull. He picked up the cap and put it on, then grabbed the paddle. For a moment he stood stock still, listening. Through the trees, he could still hear the PA system booming from Matlock's estate. The billionaire's guitar solo had been replaced by a recording. In the calm night air, Blake could make out The Guess Who's lyrics clearly:

She found a mountain that was far too high,
And when she found out she couldn't fly,
It was too late....

The guy doesn't quit, he thought. Holding the paddle in one hand, he eased the kayak into the water and climbed carefully in. Then, moving as quietly as possible, he shoved away from the dock and glided silently out into the moonlit lake.

A quarter-hour later, Blake felt the front end of the kayak nudge against the shore of Andrews Bay on the lake's western bank. Pulling the craft out of the water, he carried it forty yards into the underbrush and began covering it with dead leaves. He had just finished when he heard the sound of sirens wailing in the distance. Walking back to the beach, he looked to the north. Several miles away, a stream of police cars was pouring across the I-90 bridge onto Mercer Island, roof lights flashing. As Blake watched, the procession swung south off the bridge in the direction of Matlock's compound.

He didn't wait to see any more. Moving quickly, he located the darkened entrance to the park's hiking trail and began half-walking, half-running toward the city of Seattle, seven miles away.

NINETEEN

Come as You Are

Saturday, September 7

"I'M LOOKING FOR MATILDA."

Trying to affect a bored tone, Blake leaned against the counter of the coffee house in the Seattle business district, a few hundred yards from the southern entrance to the Seattle Urban Zone. As he spoke, he kept one eye on the street outside, where Homeland Security and SeaTac State police cars were passing by every few minutes—looking for him, he was certain. Ducking out of sight every time a cruiser appeared, it had taken him over an hour to make his way from the edge of town to where he was now. A light rain had been falling since dawn, and he was damp from head to toe.

"Over there," the barista said, nodding at a young woman in jeans and a down vest, hunched over her computer.

Clutching a medium roast coffee, Blake sauntered across the room and sat down at the table next to her.

"I've had all the coffee I can drink, so keep your money," the woman said without looking up. "And I don't date. So whatever line you're planning to lay on me, you can save your breath."

"I need to get inside," said Blake. "Gully said I should talk to you."

"How do I know you're not with the Feds?" she asked, still staring intently at the computer screen.

"That's who I'm running from," he said. "Let me go online. I'll prove it."

Wordlessly, she pushed the laptop toward him. Blake called up a search engine and typed in "Berkeley," "grad student" and "assault." He was startled to see a full page of local and national headlines, all reporting on his supposed crime and the manhunt to find him. "Cops Seek Berkeley Grad Student in Sexual Battery," read the San Francisco *Chronicle* entry. He clicked on the link and pulled up the full story, including his official school photo.

"That's me," he said, handing the computer back to the woman. She studied the screen for a moment then looked at him, her eyebrows raised. "It says you tried to rape this woman and that when she resisted, you beat her up."

"It's a lie. The Feds planted that story," he said. "That's why I need to get into the Zone."

Matilda resumed surfing while Blake sipped his coffee and waited. After several minutes, she closed her laptop with a decisive snap.

"Well, you don't *seem* like the violent sex offender type," she said. "It'll cost you three hundred—cash, up front."

"No problem," Blake said, reaching for his wallet.

"Not here," she said. "Northeast corner of Third and Yesler. Fifteen minutes." Slinging her laptop case over her shoulder, she walked out the door into the misting rain.

The truck was backed into a narrow driveway between the brick walls of two industrial buildings.

"Once I close this up, I'm gonna need you to stay real still—okay?" With his toe, the man nudged a four-foot high wooden crate in the center of the truck's cargo hold. The box was open on one side, with sacks of Brazilian coffee beans stacked around and on top of it. "If everything goes smooth, I'll let you out in twenty minutes."

"And if it doesn't?" asked Blake.

"The cops ever find you, I got no idea how you happened to end up in here." The man frowned for an instant, tugging at his moustache.

Then his face brightened. "But that'll never happen. Even if they bring their dogs around, those mutts can't sniff a thing through all this coffee."

Blake crawled into the box and sat with his arms wrapped around his knees. "Relax," the man chuckled. "I've done this a thousand times. There's plenty of air holes. You'll be fine, long as you don't mind the smell of Mundo Novo!"

As the man nailed the front panel into place, the interior of the box went dark except for some hairline streaks of light between the slats. A minute later, Blake heard the thud of more coffee sacks being thrown in the back of the truck. There was a metallic shriek as the truck's rear door was pulled down and locked. Then he felt the floor shake as the engine roared to life and the truck rumbled forward.

A few minutes later, the vehicle lurched to a stop. Blake heard the rear door being opened.

"How many dead bodies you carting in today?" a woman's voice asked.

"Just the usual two or three," chuckled the driver.

"Easy boy, easy." Outside the truck, a dog was whining anxiously. "Believe it or not," the woman said, "this is one German Shepherd that actually likes the smell of coffee. You don't happen to have any brewed, do ya?"

"Fresh-made, as usual. Got a cup right here."

"You the man!" The door rattled shut, and all was quiet.

After another ten minutes of fitful starts and stops, the truck halted for good. The rear door opened and Blake heard the sound of sacks being moved, followed by a wrenching noise as the front of his crate was pried off. He blinked in the sudden rush of daylight.

"Here we are," the driver said. "Now skedaddle."

Blake hopped off the truck to find himself in another alleyway. He walked to the entrance and peered out at the sidewalk filled with pedestrians. Bending over, he pretended to tie his shoe, then rose and began walking down the sidewalk. He saw that he was on the edge of the Queen Anne district, an area he'd visited during his college years. Unlike the L.A. and San Francisco Zones, the neighborhood looked much as it did back then—a low-key mix of working-class grit and artistic creativity. Cargo pants and ripped jeans appeared to be the local fashion of choice, topped by oversized sweaters, hoodies or flannel shirts.

As far as Blake could see, there were no police around. Chilled from the rain and conscious of how his Matlock-issue button-down shirt stuck out in the world of grunge, he ducked into a thrift shop and shelled out a few dollars for a gray University of Washington sweatshirt. Feeling semi-invisible in its snug embrace, he set off for the Space Needle a half-dozen blocks away.

He'd nurtured a fantasy that Blue, Serena and Gully would be waiting for him at the old tourist attraction with open arms, but the pavement around the structure was wet and empty. Disappointed, he turned and headed back for Queen Anne, trying to figure out how he could safely pass some time. Like the other Urban Zones, the Seattle UZ teemed with musicians. People of all ages were busking on the street, banging away inside coffee shops and bars, or jamming in basement apartments, their amplified notes floating up out of ground-level windows. From what Blake could hear, all the famous Seattle-area groups were prominently featured: At least a dozen bands were channeling Nirvana or Pearl Jam, and he was also picking up snatches of Soundgarden, Alice in Chains, and Screaming Trees. Compared to San Francisco, many of the people seemed aloof or downright hostile, but the political activity was the heaviest he'd seen. Signs calling for a populist uprising were plastered on virtually every wall and lamppost, and the sidewalks were filled with men and women soliciting donations or collecting signatures for petitions.

In one small square, a woman stood on a milk crate giving an impassioned speech about the economy. "The super-rich are siphoning dollars out of the middle-class service sector," she screamed, "and what are they doing with it? Putting it into transnational companies that pay no taxes, and speculating in the markets with their supercomputers—skimming more money every day off the investments held by everyone else. They have just one goal, people: to make the rest of us poorer and poorer! Why? So we can be hired by *them* for next to nothing! Listen to me, Seattle, when I tell you that their collective assets are the modern equivalent of the Pharaohs' pyramids. Their boats and houses and private planes are temples to a religion of greed! Meanwhile we, the non-rich, stand here exposed to the rising waters and growing heat—the heat *they* refuse to do anything about, as they sit in their air-conditioned offices and homes!"

It was actually a decent summary of the Leveler philosophy, thought Blake, as he listened to the crowd murmuring agreement. Heading down the street, he came on a group staging an impromptu demonstration outside a second-hand music store, chanting the same "Set the Music Free!" song he'd heard in L.A. Half-wondering whether they were protesting the Rock Ban or the prices of the instruments in the store window, Blake kept walking, scanning the landscape for any sign of the police.

On the next block, a thin youth sat alone on a stoop playing an acoustic guitar. Blake stopped to listen as the kid leaned over the fret-board, singing in a plaintive tenor voice.

Did you ever lose your mother's love?
Did you ever lose your mother's love
And cry for her in vain?
Did you ever lose your mother's love?

Closing his eyes, the boy launched into a soulful refrain:

How can we maintain…
In a world with so much pain?

As Blake tossed a five-dollar bill into his open case, the youth set down his guitar on the steps beside him. "One day when this Rock Ban gets deep-sixed, I'm gonna be famous," he said. He eyed Blake shrewdly. "You're new in town, right? How'd you like a guided tour? I know all the legend spots."

"Legend spots?" Blake repeated, unsure what he meant.

"Sure. I can show you where Nirvana recorded *Bleach*, and where Pearl Jam played their first gig. I even know where Jimi lived when he was little."

"What's the charge?"

The boy shrugged. "Whatever you can pay."

As the kid stowed his guitar into its case, Blake noticed his hands trembling. Then he saw the needle bruises on the boy's inner arms and felt a pang of sadness. He hesitated, considering his options. He had plenty of cash, and there was no telling when Gully, or Blue, or whoever he was supposed to meet would show at the rendezvous point. Riding around in a taxi seemed safer than wandering the streets of a city he barely knew.

"Sure," he replied. "Why not?"

Hailing a decrepit-looking cab, the two of them climbed into the back seat.

"My name's Champ," said the kid. He turned out to be a chatterbox, directing the driver into one neighborhood after another. True to his word, he led them to the old Reciprocal Recording Studio, followed by the Off Ramp Café, a series of flophouses where he claimed Jimi Hendrix stayed during his early childhood, and other points of varying interest.

Ninety minutes later, they found themselves back in Queen Anne. As Blake paid the driver, Champ tapped his shoulder. "We've done a lot of looking," he said. "How about doing some listening instead?"

"To who?"

"Best Nirvana channelers in the Zone, that's who." Turning down a side street, Champ rapped on the small center window of a black metal door set into the side of what looked to be an old, abandoned factory. The door cracked a few inches and Champ quickly grabbed the edge of it, pulling it open to reveal a scrawny man in a Green River T-shirt, perched on a folding stool puffing a cigarette.

"We're going to Paradise," said Champ with a grin.

"Ten each," the man said, holding out a grimy hand.

Blake forked over one of his hundreds and collected the change—Champ's hungry eyes tracking every movement of the bills—then followed his young guide up five flights of a graffiti-lined stairwell, their footsteps echoing on the metal steps. At the end of the last flight, another door led onto a large tar rooftop. In one corner, under a canvas awning, a makeshift plywood stage held a guitarist, bass player and drummer playing a spot-on imitation of Nirvana's "All Apologies." Several dozen people sprawled on sofas and chairs or sat upright on yoga mats. Above their heads, wooden trellises covered with flowers and vines stretched across the width of the roof.

Blake was struck by the magical feeling of the place. Near the stage, a group of young women twirled in a slow-motion dance. A couple clung together kissing deeply on one of the couches, while directly in front of him a circle of kids in their late teens sat passing a joint and speaking in low voices. A few of them nodded to Champ, but he didn't notice—he was too lost in the music, swaying with his eyes closed, singing the lyrics softly as the song moved from its primary chord verse into the four and five chords of the refrain.

As much as he admired the rooftop's sense of community, the tight-knit vibe sent a wave of loneliness through Blake. He'd lost his friends, his family and his career, and caused a man's death—and for what? A half-baked mission that was almost certainly doomed to fail, in the name of a hopeless cause he didn't fully understand. For all he knew, the whole game was up already, thanks to the previous night's raid.

The bittersweet music drifting across the tar surface only added to his sorrow. Blake felt his eyes welling with tears. What was the point of it all? What would become of Champ, and the rest of these people?

"Do you hear us, Seattle? Can you *comprehend* what we're trying to say?" The song had ended, and the guitarist was riffing at the microphone to the mild amusement of his audience. A moment later the rain began to fall again, lightly at first, then more heavily. Everyone seemed to know the drill: they quickly pulled out plastic tarps and covered the furniture, then scurried to the stage and stood huddled together under the canvas awning, watching the raindrops pelt the roof.

"Let's go," yelled Champ, pulling Blake into the stairway. They made their way down several flights of steps before pausing on the second-floor landing. "Did you like the tour?" he asked.

"It was great," said Blake. He reached into his wallet and pulled out another hundred-dollar bill. "Here you go. Thanks."

"Thank *you!*" The boy snatched the bill and stuffed it in his jeans. Licking his lips, he gave Blake a sideways glance. "You sure there's nothing else I can do for you?" Blake didn't know if he was referring to drugs or sex—not that it mattered. His sense of sadness deepened.

"No, I'm okay," he said. With a wave of his hand, he headed down the last flight of stairs, then turned for a last look at the slight figure in the stairwell, clutching his guitar.

"Good luck with your music, Champ," he called out.

"You're gonna hear about me one day!" the boy shouted.

Blake felt a lump in his throat. "I believe you," he said. "Take care of yourself."

Wrapped in a cloud of depression, Blake wandered aimlessly through the rain for several blocks. As he walked, his thoughts wandered first to Ann—now lost to him forever—and then to Maria. Their tryst the night before last had been exciting and intensely pleasurable, but he knew the fleeting bond they'd shared was nothing more than a moment in time.

Stumbling along the puddle-filled sidewalk, Blake's mind went suddenly to Serena, and the way she'd looked in the moonlight in Branford's sculpture garden. Maybe it was the circumstances that had brought them together, but there was some deep connection growing between them, unlike anything he'd ever known.

Is she the one I've been searching for? he wondered.

Looking up, he was startled to find himself in front of the stoop where he'd first heard Champ playing. He walked to the next block, looking for the second-hand music shop he'd passed earlier. The crowd of protestors had gone, and the storefront was deserted. As he got closer, he could see a guitar propped in the window—an Epiphone acoustic, polished to a golden sheen. Next to it was a hand-lettered sign: "Labor Day Special—$200.00."

Blake pushed open the door and glanced inside the shop. Behind the counter, a young woman with two rings in her lower lip sat reading a magazine.

"I was wondering about the guitar in the window," he said.

"What about it?"

"I'd like to give it a try."

Wrenching her gaze away from the page she was on, the woman eyed him suspiciously. "Do you have any *money?*"

"Sure." Blake reached into his pocket and placed two hundreds on the countertop. Satisfied, the woman nodded toward the window.

"Knock yourself out."

Cradling the instrument in his hands, Blake began playing the introduction to "Here Comes the Sun." The guitar's action was smooth and responsive—it felt more like he was caressing the strings than plucking them.

"It comes with a case," said the woman. Sensing a potential sale, she'd abandoned her reading matter for the moment. "I like the way you play," she added.

"Thanks," said Blake. "I'll take it." The woman brought out a fleece-lined hard-shell case from the back of the shop and Blake laid the guitar carefully inside. "Could I get a few picks?" he asked.

"No problem." The woman dropped a half-dozen picks into his open palm. "On the house."

Blake stowed the picks and snapped the case shut. "Good doing business with you," he smiled.

"Have fun," she grinned in return. Holding up her hand, she gave Blake a resounding high-five.

Like a magic talisman, having the Epiphone in his hand dispelled Blake's depression instantly. It felt great to be walking along with a guitar case banging against his thigh. The rain was easing to a light drizzle, and by the time he reached the Space Needle it had stopped altogether. For a long moment, he stood looking upward at the famous structure, lost in thought.

"You've just got to wonder how such a *major* tourist attraction ended up inside the wall."

Blake started with surprise at the voice behind him. Turning, he saw a figure in dark glasses, plaid lumberjack's coat and a John Deere cap, holding a bagful of sunflower seeds.

"God, is it good to see you!" he said. "This Seattle scene is one fucking downer."

"Yeah, well," said Blue, spitting a seed husk onto the sidewalk, "I don't recall anyone ever accusing Kurt Cobain of being Mr. Cheerful."

"Is Serena with you?"

"She's around here somewhere. We've taken a room just up the street. Say, where'd you get the axe?"

They'd been apart less than 48 hours, but the moment Blake rejoined Serena he knew something had changed between them. At the first sight of her, curled over a book at a sidewalk café, his heart leapt. When she looked up at him, her smile said everything.

"Karl!" she called softly, then caught herself. "—I mean, Blake!" Then they were hugging each other tightly, as Blue watched with the studied indifference of someone who had just stage-managed a highly successful blind date.

For the next hour, the three of them sat sipping soft drinks and catching up. After describing his encounter with the aging rock stars on Matlock's ship, Blake was now recounting his nighttime paddle across Lake Washington.

"Pretty sweet, how that kayak was right there when you needed it," said Serena.

Blake didn't have to ask, but he did anyway. "Gully?"

Blue nodded. "The man who foresees all."

"I saw him at Matlock's plant," said Blake.

"I thought you might. He and I are going to shepherd the transceivers on their trip east. Now we just need to get *you* to New York to make sure they're operational. Since your pal Matlock is the Feds' new favorite target, we're going with Plan B."

"It's great to be with you guys again," Blake said, only half-listening. As the glow of reconnecting faded, he felt his spirits sinking once more. *Those orange boots.* "I'm just not sure why I'm doing all this."

"Not sure? Dude, you're on the brink of an amazing victory!" said Blue. "According to Gully, your gizmo is coming together before our very eyes. With a little luck, we can pull this whole thing off. You'll make history!"

"But what about the raid last night?"

"From what I gather, Matlock presided over the whole thing like a pasha. He told the Feds you'd been recommended to him as a consultant, and denied knowing anything about your being a wanted man."

"And his lab?"

"They only had a search warrant for his home. When it was all over and done with, I heard the Feds ended up apologizing to him."

"Leave it to Matlock!" Blake shook his head in wonder. "That's really good news. I just wish..."

"You wish what?" said Serena, putting her hand on his forearm.

"I can't stop thinking about Ebenezer. And how I'm responsible."

Serena looked at Blue. "He doesn't know," she said.

"How could he? We haven't seen him," said Blue. To Blake's surprise, his two companions burst out laughing.

"What's so funny?" he demanded.

"It's not funny, really," gasped Serena. "In fact, it's *wonderful.*"

"The thing is," said Blue, wiping tears of laughter from his eyes, "the thing is—Eben isn't dead! The whole thing was faked!"

"Faked?" asked Blake "But how...?" In his relief, he found himself laughing along with them.

"One of the Kidz injected him, right there on the stage, with some kind of drug that slows your heartbeat down to practically nothing," said Serena, after catching her breath. "After he was in the ambulance, the medics gave him a shot of adrenaline and poof! He's alive and well again."

"You see how it is?" said Blue. "Everyone's playing everyone else. The Muni wanted the Feds to think you were dead, so you could make it out of L.A. And in some half-baked way, it worked!"

"They kept us in the dark, too," said Serena. "We just heard the news from Gully yesterday."

"Damn," said Blake, giddy with relief. The government wasn't trying to kill him after all! For the first time in three days, he felt the knot of fear in his stomach start to dissolve.

"Long live the spirit of the real Karl Kliff, wherever it may reside," said Blue, raising his glass solemnly. “Rock on, brother!” The three of them dissolved into laughter once more.

“So, what’s this Plan B?” said Blake, once they finally settled down. “How am I getting to New York?”

“We’re going overland—you and me,” said Serena. “In fact, as we speak, our chaperones are holding an executive meeting.”

“Speaking of which,” said Blue, “how are you on a motorcycle?”

“I’ve ridden one a few times. I’m okay, I guess.”

“Well, you’re about to get a lot more practice.” Blue paused. “One other thing,” he added. “Apparently Homeland has decided to bring in the FBI on your case. It doesn’t really mean anything—it’s mainly a public relations move, to build up your notoriety.”

“How so?”

“You know how people are,” Blue shrugged. “Nothing says ‘scary criminal’ like being on the Bureau’s Ten Most Wanted list.”

“Ten Most Wanted!?”

“Now look what you’ve done,” frowned Serena. “Just when we had him in a good mood again.”

Back at their boarding house, Blue and Serena sat in the parlor watching a game show on the television while Blake took a shower in their room.

“So,” Blue said, “this is what you look like when you’re in love.”

“What of it?” said Serena. Glancing over at her, Blue could see a mix of defiance and anxiety in her eyes.

“He’s a kid,” he said. “Not to mention a civilian.”

“And?”

“I’m just worried about how you’re going to do your job,” said Blue. “You can’t be at your sharpest when your mind is filled with visions of a white picket fence and rug rats. Admit it.”

Serena fixed him with a stony stare. It was a look Blue knew well: *Don’t get in my way—or else.*

“Where he goes, I go,” she said curtly. “You can tell Gully that. If they want to bring another person on board, that’s fine. But I’m sticking with him.”

"Okay, okay," said Blue, holding his hands up in surrender. "I was just playing devil's advocate, that's all."

"Well, this court is officially adjourned."

"You told me Smyth could be trusted not to make any unexpected moves," the Secretary said in an icy tone. The ordinarily unflappable Virginian was in a cold fury.

"I don't what he was thinking," said Marconi, choosing his words carefully. "It's not like Charles at all, to order an operation unilaterally like that."

"If they'd snared Hawkes in that raid, it would have ruined everything!" Jackson sat staring angrily through the windshield into the gloomy depths of the Arlington parking garage. "Thank God the orders made it into the leadership queue in time. If the Muni's mole hadn't gotten word to his people to extricate him, you and I would be having a very different discussion right now."

Marconi started to reply, then stopped himself. "I'm sorry, Mr. Secretary," he said. "I dropped the ball."

"Not only that, but now Hawkes has disappeared again. This is the third time we've lost touch with him—first he almost ducks us in L.A., then he vanishes in broad daylight in Golden Gate Park. Now he's adrift in the vapor, somewhere in the Pacific Northwest. We're supposed to be the professionals here, Tony. Why do these amateurs keep running rings around us?"

"We've still got tabs on Matlock," said Marconi. "And we've got the New York end covered tight as a drum."

"Now that Smyth's blundered into Matlock's front hallway, how do we know they won't call the whole thing off?"

"Matlock doesn't scare that way. He believes he's invincible. And they can't afford to call their plan off. It's their only hope. I think we can safely assume the broadcast is still on track, and that they'll try to spirit Hawkes into New York sometime over the next couple of days." He waited a beat before delivering the kicker. "We also got a report from Europe. Somebody's contacted several major broadcasters there, asking them to hold the time slot when Fish is supposed to speak on Wednesday."

"That clinches it, then. They're going full speed ahead. Which means we are, too."

"Again, Mr. Secretary, I feel terrible about the Seattle business."

"I know how committed you are to what we're trying to do here, Tony. If I'm upset, it's because the stakes are so high. If that socialist somehow managed to take the White House, it would mean the destruction of this nation as we know it. Do you understand?"

"Of course. We're not going to let that happen."

"No, we're not. Thank you, Tony. You're a fine American."

"I appreciate that, sir—very much."

For the past two days, SeaBUZ—a.k.a. the Seattle Bikers of the Urban Zone—had been gathering in preparation for their annual transcontinental ride to UZFest. Three hundred group members were decamped in Denny Park, their parked bikes clustered around makeshift villages of tents and tarps.

"Check it out. One Harley and one Sukuki, as ordered." The biker stroked his Fu Manchu, looking with pride at the two motorcycles standing side by side in the dirt.

"Fast work, Juan," said Blue. "I can't thank you enough."

"You know how it is, man. Cash makes things happen." The bearded man grinned, rubbing his hands over the small campfire in front of him. "Are these the ones riding with us?" he added, nodding toward Blake and Serena.

"That's right," Blue replied. "If anyone asks, they're friends from L.A."

"Got it. Your clothes are in there." Juan pointed to two large paper bags leaning against the bikes. "Leathers, helmets, boots. Licenses and UZ cards, too. Bedrolls and a tent are tied on the back. If you want, you can camp here tonight. We leave tomorrow at sunrise."

Blue pulled the other two aside. "Another parting of the ways, I'm afraid," he said in a low voice. "I'm meeting Gully for the drive east. Be careful, okay?"

"Don't worry about us," said Serena. "Just keep your cargo safe."

"What day is it, by the way?" asked Blake.

"Saturday, September seventh," said Blue. "Why?"

It had been six days since Blake had driven the Silver Beetle into the desert. "Could you get word to my parents—let them know I'm alright?"

"That shouldn't be a problem," said Blue. Holding out his hand, he bumped fists with both of them. "Happy trails, kids."

As evening fell, Serena and Blake shared a meal of hot dogs and corn on the cob with Juan and the other SeaBUZ chiefs. The plan was to camp outside Gillette, Wyoming the first night, then split into smaller groups for the rest of the drive. On the second day of their journey, one of these groups would escort Blake and Serena to Chicago, where they'd board an overnight train to New York City. "Just pray it's a sleeper," sighed Serena.

A few gang members were still trickling into the park. As the twilight deepened, there was the rumble of another late addition.

"The Experience!" someone shouted.

A chopper appeared, driven by a man dressed in black leather with an electric guitar strapped to his back. The bike wove through the maze of tents, campfires and parked bikes, then skidded to a stop as its rider leapt to the ground. A folded red bandana was tied around his forehead and a cigarette hung from his lips.

"Behold," he shouted, taking off his guitar and holding it high above his head. "I am here!"

A large, battery-powered Marshall amp had been lashed to the rear of the chopper with lengths of clothesline. The man reached back and switched it on, then plugged the attached patch cord into his guitar. Pulling a pick out of his bandana, he let loose with a soaring sequence of rapid, high-pitched notes. A throng of bikers crowded around the guitarist, cheering him on as he sank to his knees and brought the guitar behind his neck, fingers flying. He was playing left-handed, Blake noticed.

"Next he'll bring out the lighter fluid," he quipped.

"Don't think he hasn't," said Juan, without cracking a smile. "One of our assignments is to make sure The Experience makes it to New York in one piece. He tends to get into trouble when he's unsupervised."

The solo lasted another five minutes, concluding with a final string of arpeggios that had the bikers roaring and waving their fists in the air. "Thank you, my buzz brothers...you're too kind," said The Experience, panting for breath. "And now...in a foreshadowing of my upcoming performance at the noble UZFest...I will provide some inspiration for the journey ahead." Leaning intently over his guitar, he proceeded to perform a slow, distortion-filled, undeniably beautiful version of "My Country 'Tis of Thee."

That night, Serena and Blake stayed up tending the campfire after the bikers had retired to their tents.

"I'm going to bed," Serena said finally. "We've got a long day ahead."

"I'm glad you're here," said Blake.

"Me too." Serena turned and gave him a long kiss on the lips. "When this is over," she said, "we'll have time for everything."

Picking up a stick, Blake stirred the glowing embers. "You remember the night I told you and Blue that I was joining your cause?"

"Yeah?"

"There was one thing I wasn't completely straight about."

"What's that?" asked Serena, her eyes narrowing.

"When I said that my decision had nothing to do with the arguments you and Blue were making. I really *do* care about building a fairer society. But I always assumed there were enough smart people running things, and that they'd eventually figure it all out. And that the best thing for us non-political types was to keep the world functioning in the meantime."

"And now you're not so sure?"

"Being chased by the government makes you re-think things."

"So?"

"I'm still thinking it through, but it comes down to the idea that having a workable society is about maintaining a balanced environment—the Founding Father's checks and balances, incorporated as a systemic principle."

"You're talking political theory now?"

"I guess so. Human life is a competition—there's no getting away from it, at least with the current state of human psychology. So everything depends on how the rules of the game are set."

"And who sets them," said Serena with a yawn. "I've got to tell you, professor, none of this is exactly news." They had moved into their tent by now, and she was climbing into her bedroll.

"I know that. But if we applied game theory to politics in a rigorous way, we might be able to develop a whole new approach to creating democratic institutions."

"Well," Serena said, reaching for his hand, "I hope you get the opportunity to work it all out. Just not tonight!"

TWENTY

Born to Be Wild

Sunday, September 8

THE NEXT MORNING AT DAWN, an armada of motorcycles roared out of the Seattle UZ in two long columns, waved through the crossing point by the local police as each biker held out their ID card to be scanned. No one looked twice at the helmeted man on a Harley in the middle of the pack with an acoustic guitar strapped to his bike, or the Suzuki-riding woman beside him.

The man studied the chessboard for several minutes, then nodded at the 11-year-old boy sitting across from him. “I respectfully resign,” he said. “That was a masterful Silician Defense, Theodore. I’m very proud of you.”

“Thank you, Grandfather,” the boy said with a half-bow. “I learned from a good teacher. May I go play in the pool now?”

“Of course.”

The man strode out to the sunroom to greet his visitor. “Let’s walk,” he said. He led his companion across the back patio and down a series of slate steps. Passing through an open gateway, they entered a grassy field. Beyond it, gently rolling hills stretched out into the

Virginia countryside.

"Remind me again, how many acres do you have?"

"A little over a thousand," said the man. "Jane and I have been very blessed."

They walked through the warm September sunshine until they reached a small brook where a table and chairs had been set up under a weeping willow tree. On the table was a pitcher of lemonade with two ice-filled glasses beside it. Motioning for his guest to sit down, the man filled the two glasses from the pitcher.

"You'll be happy to know that everything is proceeding in letter-perfect fashion," the man said, sipping from his own glass. "The cat chases the mouse, while the mouse, always one step ahead of the cat, continues to pursue the cheese. And at each point along the merry chase, we've been gathering airtight evidence—including detailed information on everyone who is assisting said mouse. The end result will be one of the largest mass conspiracy prosecutions this country has ever seen."

The other man sat quietly for a moment, savoring the late afternoon breeze. The fresh-squeezed lemonade was quite delicious, he thought.

"So, you're not worried that the process might potentially get out of control?" he said finally. "What happens when the mouse does, in fact, reach the cheese?"

"We'll have the area covered like a blanket," his host replied. "I've requisitioned over six hundred officers from our riot control division, who will be supported by half as many undercover agents. They'll all be on hand at the speech site, ready to close down the entire venue just before Fish commences his address. No one knows this yet, except for myself and one trusted colleague—and you and your associates, of course. The company commander will be informed of the plan at the last minute."

The other man shifted uncomfortably. "Still, aren't you taking a chance, letting things progress that far? What if Fish actually launches into his speech, and the Muni manages to transmit his words through this network they've developed? It will give him the very status we're trying to prevent."

"I promise you, our forces will move in the instant Fish takes the stage. As a backup, I'm also arranging to cut the PA system at the same time. It will be impossible for him to get out even a sentence. Don't worry—I'll be onsite, overseeing everything personally. I assure you, Fish will be completely discredited once the Muni's conspiracy to flout the UZ broadcast ban is exposed, and people learn of his involvement."

"And both the cat and the mouse are unaware of what's going on?"

"As for Smyth, I stay informed of every move he makes. He's beginning to suspect that someone on the inside is alerting the mouse, but it doesn't matter—I'm about to shift his assignment. In the end, his man will be apprehended and he'll get his full share of the glory."

"What about Branford and the Muni Alliance?"

"Sickness has dulled his antennae. And the rest of the Munis don't have a clue. They're convinced they're getting legitimate information from their mole."

"Which, up to a point, they are."

"True." The man chuckled and downed another swallow of lemonade.

"Well." The visitor stared at the flowing stream. "I admire your confidence."

"The strategy can't fail. Once we're done exposing their treason, the entire top leadership of the Muni Alliance will be under indictment. Meanwhile, the quantum technology will be under wraps, and we'll be poised to sail into the White House virtually unopposed. The Leveler movement will never recover."

"You seem to have thought of everything," said the visitor, rising from his chair.

His host held up his glass and bowed his head in mock humility. "It's what I do," he said with a smile.

In Gillette, the motorcycle caravan set up camp on an empty fairground a mile off the Interstate. They parked their bikes in a dozen long, neat rows in the large asphalt parking lot next to the hard-packed earthen plain, then began spreading out their bedrolls and tents. To Blake, the patch of dirt looked like heaven: Fourteen bone-rattling hours on the Harley had left every joint in his body stiff and aching, and all he wanted was to lie down and rest.

A few yards from where Blake and Serena staked out their tent, some bikers had lit a kerosene stove and were cooking some food. After a week in the cell phone-free UZ, Blake was startled to hear a mobile ringing in Serena's jacket pocket. She glanced at the caller ID and stood up.

"I'll be back in a few," she said.

As she slipped off through the sea of bikers, someone handed Blake a Coors. He squatted on his heels, enjoying the smell of grilling chicken and the taste of cold beer. Some local vendors were hawking their wares, and a cowboy busker sat on a folding stool cradling his guitar.

"Before I begin, I want to certify that all the old cowpoke songs I'm about to perform are completely and one hundred percent legal," the cowboy announced, squirting a mouthful of tobacco juice into a paper cup. "Every one of 'em has been thoroughly reviewed and approved by the almighty powers who strive so tirelessly to protect our hallowed land!"

The singer had just begun strumming the opening notes of "The Old Chisholm Trail" when Blake felt a sharp jab in his spine. Thinking Serena was back sooner than expected, he began to turn around, only to hear the sound of a man's voice a few inches from his left ear.

"Keep looking straight ahead," said the voice. "Long as you don't make any sudden moves, I can just about promise this gun won't go off."

Blake remained rooted in place, his heart racing. No one around him seemed aware of what was happening. He thought about shouting for help, but as if reading Blake's mind, an unseen hand pressed the gun barrel harder into his flesh. "Ain't no one gonna say squat if the likes of you gets shot by a lawman in these parts," said the voice. "Now, when I count three, I want you to put down your beer and stand up nice and slow. Start walking toward the parking lot, like you're getting something from your hog. Pull any funny stuff, like signaling a buddy or hollerin', and I'll blow a hole in your back faster'n you can say 'dead man's bluff.' If you believe me, nod your head."

Blake moved his head up and down slowly.

"Good. One...two...three...and away we go."

Blake rose to his feet and headed toward the parking lot at an unhurried pace, the sound of footsteps directly behind him. "Let's go find your ride, in case someone's watching," the voice added.

Numb with fear, Blake made his way among the rows of motorcycles to his own bike, offering a silent prayer that Serena had seen them leaving the campground. When they got to his Harley, a hand snaked around him and slid two cans of Modelo beer into the saddlebag.

"Now, reach in and pull those back out, one in each hand," the voice said. "Hold 'em up nice and high, so anyone looking can see them. Then wheel around toward me."

Holding the beers as instructed, Blake turned to face a tall, potbellied man in his fifties with thick white hair and sideburns and a full white moustache. He wore a wool poncho over his Western-style shirt, and from under its front edge Blake could see the tip of a revolver protruding. With his free hand, the man pulled the top of the poncho aside to reveal a gleaming star pinned to his chest.

"Say hello to your friendly county sheriff," he grinned.

"What have I done?" Blake asked. "You want my driver's license?"

"Don't need it. I know who you are," chuckled the sheriff. "Faces are my specialty, you see." Keeping his gun trained on Blake's chest, he used his other hand to pull a folded sheet of paper from his pants pocket and shake it open. The large type across the top read "FBI's Ten Most Wanted." Beneath it was a photo of Blake—the same one that had run in the *Chronicle*.

"Fax came through this morning," the sheriff said cheerfully. "According to this, you're wanted for anti-government activity *and* assaulting a lady. A two-fer!" He shook his head disapprovingly. "I got a call into the G-men now. I expect they'll phone back pretty quick." He stuffed the flier back in his pocket and nodded toward a four-seat pickup at the far end of the lot. "Be a friend and carry those beers to my truck, would you?"

When they reached the pickup, the sheriff took the two beers from

Blake and set them on the hood before quickly handcuffing Blake's wrists behind him. "In you go," he said. He pushed Blake into the rear compartment and locked the door, then walked around the truck and climbed into the driver's seat. Yanking open one of the Modelos, he drank it down in several large gulps. With a contented belch, he pulled a cigar from his shirt pocket and lit it, sending a thick stream of smoke out his lowered window. As he did, his cell phone rang.

"Speak of the devil," the sheriff chortled. "Hello?" He listened for a moment. "Yeah, I've got him right here, in cuffs. Oh, he's your fella, alright. He's with one of them biker gangs, only he ain't no biker.... Okay, see you soon."

Hanging up, he swiveled to look at Blake. "The G-men are gonna meet us back at my office. Pretty good service for a Sunday night, huh? They sound kind of excited."

Puffing on his cigar, he started up the engine and switched on the radio. A country music station came on, playing a song about a man who lost his truck, his hunting dog and his woman in the same late-night poker game. The sheriff tapped his cigar in time to the music, then tilted back his head and started singing along:

As he lay that last hand down, a distant church bell pealed,
And when I saw the Ace of Hearts, I knew my fate was sealed.

So, this is how it ends, Blake thought. *In the middle of nowhere, being serenaded by a badge-happy drunkard.* What would Serena do when she found him gone, he wondered—and what about the Fish speech, and the quantum transceiver?

When the song was through, the sheriff opened the second beer and wedged the can into the cup holder on the dashboard. "The jailhouse is just up the road," he announced. "We've got a couple hours before the big boys get here. Plenty of chance to spend some quality time together." He moved to put the truck in gear when a female voice stopped him short.

"It's such a turn-on to see a *real* man driving a *real* vehicle in these parts!"

The woman standing at the driver's side window seemed to have materialized out of thin air. Startled, the sheriff put his hand on the butt of his gun.

"Relax, sugar," the woman said. "You act like you've never seen a lady before."

From the back seat Blake could see that Serena had her leather jacket opened wide and that she wasn't wearing anything underneath.

"I hate to disappoint you, honey, but I'm sort of busy now," the sheriff leered, eyeing her breasts. "I could meet you back here in a few hours, though. How's that sound?"

"That sounds nice," said Serena. "You're sweet. How about a kiss?" She reached for the sheriff's face with both hands. A second later, he was slumped unconscious over the steering wheel. Leaning through the window, Serena covered the man's face with a cloth and held it there for a full half-minute. "That'll put him out for a while," she said. She began sorting rapidly through the keys hanging from the sheriff's belt.

"Jesus," said Blake. "Where did you go?"

"I can't leave you alone for a minute, can I?" Opening the rear door, she moved behind him to unlock his handcuffs. As Blake flexed his wrists, Serena replaced the cuffs on the sheriff's belt, then shoved his limp form over to the passenger's side and climbed behind the wheel.

"Our biker days are over," she said, guiding the truck toward the parking lot entrance. "And not just because of the folks that lover boy here has been speaking to. There's been a change of plans."

"What about our cycles?" asked Blake.

"Someone will take them over. It doesn't matter."

"And the Epiphone...?"

"Don't worry, I haven't forgotten your precious guitar." In front of them, illuminated in the headlights, he saw the case resting on the asphalt. After Blake had retrieved it, Serena gunned the motor, driving out of the parking lot and turning west onto the two-lane state road. Hearing a rumbling behind them, Blake looked back and watched headlight after headlight flick on, as three hundred motorcycle engines roared to life and a river of bikers began wheeling out of the fairgrounds. They were all going east, in the opposite direction from the one Serena was taking.

"When I explained that we'd had a little brush with the law, everyone agreed it made sense to hit the road early," she said.

Leaving the stream of headlights behind them, she drove another mile down the highway before cutting off onto a brush-lined dirt road. They bumped along it for a hundred yards, to where the track widened slightly. Serena turned the pickup around so that it was pointing back toward the main road and then killed the engine, leaving the headlights blazing and the radio volume turned up. It was still tuned to the country station, now featuring an up-tempo female vocal about a romance gone bad.

"I'll never understand how people listen to this stuff," Blake said.

"That's Patsy Cline," shot back Serena. "One of the all-time greats. For your information, a lot of your beloved British rock has the same roots as this 'stuff' you like to knock so much. Did you ever hear of skiffle?"

After Blake helped Serena wrestle the sheriff's body back behind the steering wheel, she took the beer from the cup holder and emptied its contents over the front of his poncho. Slamming the front door shut, she stood facing Blake. "He can have fun explaining *that* to the FBI." Reaching for his hand, she drew it inside her jacket and pressed his palm against one of her nipples. It was rock-hard.

"Are you excited by me, or by what just went down?" asked Blake.

"Both," she said.

Together they trudged back toward the highway, their shadows stretching before them in the truck's high beams.

"You made a good point back there," said Blake. "About skiffle, I mean." Serena grunted and kept walking, as the distant strains of "Heartaches" played on beneath the dark Wyoming sky.

They'd been standing on the shoulder a few minutes when a pair of headlights appeared down the road. Serena stuck out her thumb and a large Winnebago slowed to a stop.

"You kids need a lift?" asked a man, peering down from the

window on the driver's side.

"We'd be much obliged," said Serena.

"Don't keep them waiting, Henry. It's chilly out there!" scolded the woman sitting beside him.

"You heard Nell—hop in," the man said.

Blake followed Serena into the roomy interior of the RV as the man steered back onto the road. He and his companion were both attired formally, the man in jacket and tie, the woman in a knee-length dress with matching hat and fur stole. After they'd settled into the cushioned bench seats, the woman turned and beamed at them.

"Serena, I'm always running into you in the most *unusual* places," she said. "Although this is certainly quieter than Beirut."

"Or Nairobi," said Serena. "Or Kiev."

"Stop it, you two," growled Henry. "You're making me jealous."

"You know each other," Blake said, stating the obvious.

"It's true. I was with the State Department for many years," said Nell, "and Serena was our department's security liaison. Whenever trouble popped up, so did Serena."

"We've been fully briefed," Henry said, clearing his throat. "I think the best thing is for us to get into character, in case we encounter any friendly inquiries in the near future."

"Of course, dear," replied Nell. She shot a knowing look at Serena and Blake. "Tradecraft, tradecraft—he's something of a broken record, if you ask me. Anyway...if you could hand me your latest collection of driver's licenses and credit cards, please?" Pulling a small box from the glove compartment, Nell plugged it into the car's cigarette lighter, then fed the cards into an opening in the side and pressed a button. A low whirring sound could be heard for several seconds. When it stopped, Nell unplugged the box, opened her car window and held it outside, releasing a cloud of dust particles into the rushing air.

"Quite a handy gadget," she said with satisfaction. "Now, here are your new Illinois driver's licenses, along with two credit cards each, as well as library cards—a nice touch, don't you think? And of course your Urban Zone IDs, to be used at the appropriate time."

She handed the cards over with a canary-eating grin. "Here's your back story, children: You are Felicia and Donald Hill, a young married couple, both born and raised in Highland Park—wholesome, church-going folk. We are your equally spritual former neighbors, Nell and Henry Jamison. We've never gotten over the fact that you gave up the North Shore suburbs for the madness of the Chicago Urban Zone—but thankfully we were able to persuade you to join us for a glorious two-week road tour of religious sites in the Western states."

"From which we are now returning, praise the heavens!" interrupted Henry.

"In actuality, Henry is an atheist," sighed Nell. "To continue: Once we reach Chicago, the two of you will be boarding a train to New York, where you hope to bring our brand of religious music to the heathens at that dreadful-sounding cultural festival. That reminds me—I have some new clothes for you." She rummaged around her feet, then handed back two packages.

"Once you're fresh and clean," she said, "*and* you've gotten a little sleep, you can change into these." Pawing through his bundle, Blake saw it contained an outfit similar to Henry's: Pressed dark trousers, white dress shirt and conservative necktie, a gray blazer, a fedora, and a pair of polished black dress shoes.

"If you'll hand me your current outfits," said Nell, "I'll happily dispose of them at the next rest stop. Although part of me hates to see them go—they're so *wonderfully* butch."

"You want us to get undressed...here?" asked Blake.

"Don't be shy on my part," said Nell, winking broadly. "I've always enjoyed a little beefcake on the side." Glancing at Henry, she added in a stage whisper: "He pretends to be upset—but secretly it excites him!"

Ignoring her, Henry focused on the road as Serena unzipped her jacket and removed it. "Bareback under our leathers, are we?" squealed Nell. "That's my sexy girl!"

She turned to Blake. "Come, young man," she said briskly, "this is no time to be bashful." Reluctantly, Blake stripped off his clothing under the woman's watchful eye. "My, but you two youngsters are so *attractive*," she gushed, studying Blake's bare torso. "An athlete, I see. Maybe we can train together sometime."

"Nell, you haven't changed a bit," laughed Serena.

Removing her hat and stole, Nell slipped on a pair of black stiletto heels, then rose from her seat and walked toward them. "Come along, darlings." Taking each of them by the hand, she led the nude duo to the back of the vehicle.

"Henry," she called over her shoulder, "Can you put in the CD, please?" She smiled at Blake. "To get into character, as my faux husband would say, I brought along some recordings of hymns—eighteen hours' worth, enough to last us straight through to Chicago!"

As a choir's rendition of "Rock of Ages" poured from the RV's speakers, Nell pulled back the shower curtain to reveal one bucket of soapy water and another filled with fresh water for rinsing.

"We'll drive in shifts," she explained. "Henry will take the wheel until morning, at which point we'll start alternating, four hours each. Which means the three of us need to get some rest—and I know *just* the right activity to get us sleeping like babies."

"Let me guess," said Serena. "This house on wheels has only one big bed, right?"

"Serena, you know me so well!" smiled Nell, dipping a sponge into the soapy water and squeezing out the excess fluid. "Anyway, returning to our back story: For the rest of our trip together, I will be playing the part of an outwardly proper, yet in reality *hopelessly* debauched Midwestern housewife—who, several years ago, seduced the sweet young couple next door into the *lewdest* sort of three-way relationship. For our own safety, it's absolutely vital we all play our parts to the hilt."

"What is she talking about?" Blake asked Serena.

"I think she's saying she wants to have her way with both of us," said Serena.

Nell replaced the sponge in the bucket. "Now that we've cleared that up, my dears," she said, "I might as well make sure this nice frock stays dry." With an apologetic shrug, she stood up and let her dress fall to the floor. "There!" she exclaimed, striking a pose in heels, stockings and matching red-silk bra and bikini briefs. "There's a handrail on the wall beside you, in case your knees get wobbly."

She picked up the dripping sponge and knelt in front of Blake. "You'll find that my touch is second to none. If you doubt me, just ask Serena." Throwing back her head, she began singing along lustily with the recording:

Simply to thy cross I cling
Naked come to thee for dress…

Once she'd finished thoroughly washing Blake and Serena—a task she stretched out far longer than necessary, while providing a steady flow of admiring commentary—Nell produced two pairs of pajamas for them, then led them to the RV's pull-down double bed. After tucking them in, she planted motherly kisses on both of their foreheads. "You two make a *lovely* couple," she purred. With a fluttering wave of her fingers, she headed back to the front of the Winnebago.

"She would have done each of us, if I'd let her," said Serena after Nell left. She rolled over and stared at Blake. "Are you relieved or disappointed? Be honest."

"Both."

With a laugh, Serena wrapped her arms around him and they fused together in an embrace. "More later," she said at last, pulling away. Feeling the highway rushing by beneath them, they drifted off to sleep.

❖ ❖ ❖

It was three in the morning, and the small panel truck was the only vehicle on the four-lane divided highway. Gully drove in grim silence, his eyes fixed on the pavement in front of them as the darkened Ohio landscape rolled by.

"Four miles to Upper Sandusky," announced Blue cheerfully, looking out the window. He used his forefinger to flick the screen of his smartphone. "Population 8,000," he continued. "Named for its location on the upper reaches of the Sandusky River—not to be confused with the city of Sandusky, situated fifty miles to the northeast on the banks of Lake Erie."

Undeterred by Gully's stone-faced stare, he surfed the Internet for another minute. "Did you know," he said, "that Route 30 was the first paved transcontinental roadway in the United States, back when it was known as the Lincoln Highway?"

"Don't you ever go to sleep?" said Gully sharply.

"Gigi, sweetheart, what's got you so bugged?" Blue pouted. He reached an arm out and rubbed Gully's shoulder. "Come on, you can tell the Blue Man." They were approaching the town, and shuttered auto repair shops and 24-hour fast food joints were beginning to line the roadway.

"The whole setup, to tell you the truth," replied Gully. "Why have the Feds put us on the side burner all of a sudden? Our guys aren't picking up any chatter about our situation at all. We probably could have waltzed down Interstate 70 towing a brass band behind us."

"What you're saying is, they want us to make it to New York."

"Brilliant deduction, Watson."

"And *you* think they want this because they're cooking up something major."

"I don't think, I know." Gully's grip tightened on the wheel. "There are significant additional security forces headed for the New York Zone. All off the books—highly classified."

"Oh." Now it was Blue's turn to brood silently. "When were you planning on sharing this particular insight?" he said finally.

"I'm sharing it with you now," said Gully.

"What does it mean?"

"They know about the broadcast, and they're letting it go forward."

"Because…?"

"Because they've got a plan to stop it at the last minute."

"How are you so certain about all this?"

"Our mole has been doing some digging. Our moles, I should say. Which is another problem."

"So, Seattle Man's been in touch again?"

"Briefly. Just to report the force expansion, and to say he'll call back with more information when he has it."

"How do we know he's on the level?"

"We don't. That's the trouble. He was accurate the last time…but I'm sure he had his own reasons for wanting Hawkes to run free."

"What does John Quincy say?"

"He hasn't heard anything about anything. Nothing about the extra troops—nothing even to indicate they're worried about an illegal broadcast."

"Guess they're playing this one close to the vest." Taking a bar of dark chocolate from the glove compartment, Blue broke off a square and sucked on it thoughtfully. "With these additional forces, our little gang is going to be seriously outnumbered."

"Correct. Plus, the more boots there are on the ground, the easier it is for the whole thing to blow up in our faces," said Gully. "All it takes is one soldier to get trigger-happy, and they'll call the whole show off. Fish will never even make it to the microphone."

"That would be a shame," nodded Blue.

"What it would be," Gully said flatly, "is a fucking catastrophe—for America and the world."

TWENTY-ONE

Truckin'

Monday, September 9

NELL HAD REGAINED THE REST of her wardrobe by the time she shook Blake awake the next morning to inform him that it was his turn to drive. While Henry went to the rear to nap—there was, in fact, more than one bed on the vehicle, Blake discovered—she sat beside him for the next hour, regaling him with jokes and stories. When Serena poked her head into the driver's compartment, Nell finally excused herself and retired to catch some sleep herself.

Riding shotgun, Serena fiddled with the radio dial until she found a news station. The national stories were all about the Presidential campaign—reports on Acton's post-Labor Day barnstorming tour of the South and Midwest, and updates on Fish's legal case and his upcoming speech in New York.

"Rumors are flying that Governor Fish will use the speech to announce his withdrawal from the race," said one announcer. "But there's also another school of thought, which says that Fish may up the political stakes instead, by calling on Congress to allow all U.S. residents unrestricted access to the Urban Zones—thereby challenging Vice President Acton to take a stand on the issue."

A commercial came on and Serena turned the volume down. "Are you okay about last night?" she said.

"You mean with Nell?" asked Blake. "Did you hold back on my account?"

"No—on mine. I didn't want us to start that way." Serena glanced at him. "Nell and I have had an off-and-on thing for years. I'm not saying I prefer women, because I don't. I'm just telling you this because you need to understand that if you're looking for a relationship out of *True Romance* magazine, then I'm the not the right person for you."

"I already knew that," said Blake.

"I'm not saying I wouldn't like to settle down, maybe even have kids," she continued. "But I've come too far in life to be anything but who I am."

"I wouldn't want you to be anything else."

"Good," Serena said with a hint of a smile. "I feel the same about you, by the way."

Serena hadn't asked him about Maria, but Blake sensed that it didn't much matter. Her earlier flashes of jealousy, he realized now, were an expression of her uncertainty. His fling with Maria, like his night with Caroline, had been a one-time event, the mutual fulfillment of a fantasy. This was different.

As Blake guided the Winnebago down the Interstate, Serena turned up the radio again. Suddenly she leaned forward.

"Listen—they're talking about you!"

"This in from the West Coast," the newscaster was saying. "Authorities in Berkeley, California have announced they are dropping assault charges against U.C. Berkeley graduate student Blake Hawkes, son of retired Navy Admiral Cameron Hawkes. Following accusations several days ago that Hawkes attacked a fellow grad student, the alleged victim has now come forward to deny that any assault took place. The student, Ann Montgomery, held a press conference this morning at Berkeley City Hall to announce that the allegations were the result of what she calls a misunderstanding."

The report cut to a sound bite from the press conference. "It's true that Mr. Hawkes and I met in my office that day to discuss our relationship—our former relationship, that is," Ann was saying. "At no time, however, did he lift a hand to me, or threaten me in any way. Due to the stress I was under, I did seek hospitalization afterwards—a fact that was unfortunately misinterpreted by the police and the media. But I want to emphasize that I sought medical care voluntarily out of concern for my emotional well-being. I had no physical illness or injury whatsoever, and my hospitalization was in no way the result of Mr. Hawkes' actions."

The newscaster's voice returned. "Hawkes is still being sought by Federal authorities in connection with alleged violations of the Cultural Hygiene laws."

"Well," said Blake, switching off the radio, "that's something, at least."

❖ ❖ ❖

"I don't understand—why aren't they doing more? *Why??*"

A half hour earlier, his new Homeland Security briefer had left Martin Bibbitt's house after sharing the unhappy news that Blake Hawkes was still at large. Now, as his masseuse, Yuki, applied trigger-point therapy to his upper back, he couldn't keep from venting his frustration through the face hole in the massage table.

"You work hard," Yuki assured him, rubbing her oiled hands across his trapezius muscles. "Everything will be okay. Just breathe."

Bibbitt followed her instructions as he tried to focus on his conundrum. For some reason the Department of Homeland Security seemed utterly incapable of apprehending this Hawkes fellow, despite the fact that the young man had the brazen gall to consort openly with the notorious Peter Matlock, a known supporter of the Municipal Alliance and their treasonous associates.

He cared less about Hawkes himself—although Bibbitt knew from reading his dossier that the young man was a deeply disturbed individual—than the possibility that Hawkes was somehow in league with Maxwell Fish, the Democratic pretender to the Presidency. *Fish,* who had vowed to roll back everything that he, Martin Bibbitt, had worked so diligently to achieve. The prospect of seeing everything fall apart, after all that he'd accomplished over the past seven years—the idea of opening the door once more to the music of the antisocial and the mentally ill, after he'd struggled so hard to protect the American citizenry from being exposed to it....

"Never!!" he screamed.

"Martin, you shout so loudly—I think you are having a bad dream," said Yuki softly.

"Sorry," Martin replied sheepishly. He hadn't realized he was speaking out loud.

"I'm finished here. Shall you roll over now?" Yuki said.

"Whatever you say," Martin replied. This was a time-honored ritual, one they both knew well. As he turned onto his back, she slipped out of her robe and rested one hand on his stomach, letting him drink in the sight of her unclothed body.

"You are very stressed," she continued. "I think you could use some special TLC."

"Yes," Martin nodded. He closed his eyes and exhaled slowly. "I think that's a very good idea."

"You've done great work, Chuck—tracking Hawkes to L.A., then linking him to Matlock as quickly as you did." As he spoke, Secretary Jackson picked up the small bust of J. Edgar Hoover from his desk and examined it. "You were absolutely right to bring in the Coast Guard, too. It's a damned shame they didn't grab Hawkes then and there, when they had him in their grasp!"

Jackson clenched his fist tightly to underscore the point, then opened his hand again and sighed deeply.

"But the thing is, Chuck, when you went back at Matlock a second time on the same day, in his own home no less, and you came up empty again... well, that was a step too far. Matlock's an important man—not to mention richer than sin—and he has a lot of influential friends."

Smyth shifted in his chair. "We didn't come up empty, sir. Matlock admitted Hawkes had been on the premises and that he'd left of his own volition." *Because he was tipped off,* he added silently. *In the nick of time, too.* "We've also established that Hawkes visited Matlock's engineering facilities in both northern California and Washington State. Which means that Matlock is almost certainly helping Hawkes reconstruct his communication device."

"Matlock claims he didn't know there was an arrest warrant out for Hawkes, and that Hawkes was simply doing some general consulting for him."

"If you believe that, then—"

"I know, I know." Jackson waved his hand dismissively. "The point is, we have no hard evidence to the contrary. And the last thing we're going to do is drag Peter Matlock in and start questioning him."

"Well then, what are you saying?"

"What I'm saying, Chuck, is that I'm switching your assignment. You gave it your best shot with Hawkes, but you're radioactive now."

"Who's taking over?"

"I'm tasking the Seattle and San Francisco offices jointly. That way they can both pursue the Matlock angle and try to connect his operation with this quantum technology. I've also asked the Bureau to see if they can pick up any leads on Hawkes in the heartland."

"I understand. What shall I focus on then?"

"I want you to head for New York and help secure the venue for Fish's speech."

"I thought everything there was under control."

Jackson shrugged. "Fish's staff has expressed some concerns, so we've decided to expand our presence. They're worried some plot's being hatched against their guy."

"Based on what?"

His boss waved his hand again. "Paranoia, as far as I can tell. Everyone has to pass through a high-security checkpoint just to get into the New York Zone for this festival. Plus the speech site will be crawling with cops—ours and the NYPD's. It'll be the safest place on earth."

"What do you want me to do?"

"Oversee the final prep work, make sure Marconi's undercover operatives coordinate with our uniforms on the ground there—and keep your eyes and ears open, like you're doing already. A driver will be at your office in two hours to get you there by late afternoon. I'm coming up tomorrow evening. Having you there in advance will be immensely helpful."

Smyth looked at his boss in surprise. "HS is putting in uniforms? How many?"

"All of 'A' Company. Just to make sure everything stays copacetic."

"That means almost a thousand of our people in and around the park—six hundred Federal security officers with insignia, plus several hundred in plainclothes. How does NYPD feel about this?"

"Come on, Chuck, you know better than that," Jackson grinned. "When we say jump, their only job is to ask, 'how high?'"

Instead of returning to his office, Smyth decided to take a stroll and grab an early lunch. The sidewalk outside Homeland Security headquarters was spotless as usual, its white squares set off by the perfectly manicured strips of green grass on either side. *Everything neat as a pin*, he thought. He loved that about the Federal offices in Washington, D.C.—the sense of cleanliness and rationality that emanated from the massive buildings and their surroundings.

Buying a gyro from a street vendor, he continued walking to a small pocket park nearby. There was an open spot on a bench in the sun, and Smyth settled there to eat while he sifted through the conversation that had just taken place. The picture was now crystal clear: The person protecting Blake Hawkes was his own boss. For whatever reason, Robert Jackson, Secretary of Homeland Security, wanted the Muni Alliance to successfully transport Hawkes' completed communication device to New York City. Jackson had probably been tracking Hawkes since he emerged from the desert. That was why that California trooper had been patrolling so far inland. And Marconi must have been clued in every step of the way—the little weasel!

At the same time, though, Jackson had to protect himself by demonstrating that he was trying his hardest to capture Hawkes. That was where Smyth came in—except that he'd gone too far with his latest move: The Matlock raid had upset the delicate balance the Secretary was trying to maintain, and now Jackson was using the episode as an excuse to take Smyth off the case. He was also making sure there would be no more monkey wrenches thrown in the works. Asking two regional offices to share responsibility for finding Hawkes might sound good, but in fact it was a surefire way to stop the whole process in its tracks. Pulling in the FBI was another piece of window dressing: In the short run, it accomplished nothing beyond getting Hawkes' photo posted in a bunch of backwater post offices.

But why was Jackson doing it? As Smyth continued to munch methodically, that answer stood out clear as day to him as well. "Acton!" he muttered.

Earlier, during his conversation with his boss, Smyth's gaze had wandered over the power wall behind the Secretary's desk—every inch covered by photographs of Jackson posing with various government officials he'd known over his career. One photo in particular had caught Smyth's eye: Taken almost eight years ago, it showed the newly-confirmed Secretary shaking hands with former CIA chief and recently elected Vice President of the United States, William Acton.

"To my good friend Bob," read the inscription, "New arena, same great show!" It was signed simply, "Bill."

Of course, thought Smyth. *This is all about the election.* Acton and Jackson had come up through the ranks of the CIA together. If Smyth remembered correctly, Acton was even godfather to one of Jackson's children. Now Jackson was helping his old pal in his quest for the ultimate prize, by torpedoing the only man who stood between him and the White House.

Smyth thought for another minute. Jackson must have concluded that putting Fish under house arrest for his Canadian escapade wasn't enough. He was planning to scuttle Fish's candidacy once and for all, by letting Hawkes, Matlock and their cronies go ahead and attempt an illegal broadcast of the UZFest speech. Jackson's people would swoop in at the last minute and expose what was happening, allowing them to scoop up Hawkes and anyone in the Muni Alliance who'd helped him. Most important of all, Fish would be tied to the broadcast conspiracy as well—putting the final nail in his political coffin.

That was why Jackson was assigning such a large force to the speech in New York: He was planning the largest sting operation in history! It also explained Smyth's new assignment. Jackson wanted Smyth at his side in New York to keep an eye on him and make sure he didn't interfere.

At any rate, Smyth reflected, now that he was going to be there at Tompkins Square Park in person, he could at least do his best to ensure no one got hurt—unintentionally or otherwise. As he stood up, he glimpsed the Capitol dome in the distance. It was a sight he always found immensely reassuring. *Remember, Chuck,* he told himself, *you took an oath to protect everyone—not just whoever happens to be in power at the moment.*

The wooded glen in Rock Creek Park was deserted, as Hutch had known it would be on this Monday afternoon in September. The park had never looked more beautiful, he thought—a fact his companion clearly didn't appreciate. It was interesting, he mused, how people who were uncomfortable in their own skins were often uncomfortable in natural environments as well.

Hutch prided himself on his ability to read not only people's likes and dislikes but also their motivations. As for the man sitting beside him, Hutch judged that he had once been spurred mainly by ambition, the desire to make a mark and taste the world's acclaim. Lately, though, through some combination of factors—dissatisfaction borne out of life's disappointments, perhaps, or anger over enduring one slight too many, or maybe just mental disintegration from age and stress—he had been slipping further and further into the realm of the fanatic.

Fortunately this didn't affect his value to Hutch as a client, so long as he could still meet one essential criterion: the ability to pay.

"Of course, we never had this conversation," Hutch was saying amiably. "Since we're here, though, let me play contrarian for a minute. My firm has helped advise you on some, ah, outside-the-box assignments in the past. But we've never considered anything as dramatic as the scenario you're hinting at. You're an important man—a respected man. Someone in your position generally doesn't want to take such a radical step."

Martin Bibbitt's face was impassive. "I didn't come here for a lecture," he said. "What I want to know is whether your firm might have any thoughts on how to make an intractable problem disappear—permanently."

"My firm? Certainly not! I'm astonished that you'd raise such a possibility. If you won't take my advice, however, I can't stop you from calling a number scribbled on some random park bench—but that's totally up to you."

Hutch looked up and down the tree-lined path cautiously. "This is a nice, secluded place," he said. "Once I leave, I suggest you take full advantage of the privacy it affords and engage in some reflection. I'm sure you'll end up following the route you're meant to take. Be well."

Martin watched the other man walk off through the dappled sunlight. When Hutch had vanished from sight, he sat for several minutes with his lips pursed in thought. Finally, looking in both directions to make sure the trail was empty, he stretched and glanced casually behind the bench he was sitting on. On the back of it was a phone number scrawled in white chalk over the green painted wood. He committed the number to memory, then, wetting his palm with his mouth, he carefully wiped the surface clean.

"Welcome aboard the Blues Train, son," said the Reverend, as the aging string of cars began pulling slowly out of Chicago's Union Station. "If you're looking for the road to redemption, you're on it! We, which is to say, my traveling companions and I, are the Midway Minstrels—"

"Otherwise known as the Way Out Wastrels, when we're in places more agreeable to our primary musical form, that being the *electric* Chicago blues," grinned a man seated across the aisle from Blake and Serena. He had a slide guitar at his side and wore a dark purple suit with lavender dress shirt, white shoes and purple-and-white striped tie. Reaching into his jacket pocket, the man took out a small bottle of Jim Beam and held it out to Blake. "They call me Stringfellow," he said. "Care for a touch of the holy spirit?"

Blake held up his hand. "No thanks."

"Your mistake," said Stringfellow, pulling the bottle back. "We have time for one more blues number before this train officially leaves the Chicago UZ limits. After that, it's nothing but God's music from here to New York—and believe me, brother, that requires fortification!"

"Blessedly, we have plentiful refreshment to comfort our souls on our pilgrimage," said the blind man sitting just behind Stringfellow, patting the seeing-eye dog at his feet.

"Can I hear a hallelujah?" shouted the Reverend.

"Hallelujah!" called the passengers in the seats around them. The blind man reached for his own guitar and hit a twanging chord, then jumped into the "Diving Duck Blues." The rest of the car's inhabitants grabbed their instruments and began playing and singing as Stringfellow rose to his feet and did a waltz with his bottle of whiskey. As they hit the last notes, a voice came over the train loudspeaker:

"Attention—we are now leaving the Chicago Urban Zone. Passengers will be expected to obey all local laws and regulations."

Hearing this, the Reverend stood up and waved for silence.

"Enough of this nonsense," he said gruffly. "I'll be damned if I get thrown off this train before we even reach Cleveland. Ms. Franklin, an F major, if you please—"

Two rows down, a woman with a small electric keyboard across her lap pressed her fingers on the keys to produce an organ-like chord.

"All together now," the Reverend boomed. In a bass voice, he began to sing,

Go down Moses, way down in Egypt land...

He paused and glared at the rest of the group. For a long moment they stared silently back at him. Then, with an abrupt shout, the assemblage picked up the tune as one, singing with the fervor of a gospel choir bent on the salvation of all mankind.

The train pulled out of Chicago in the late afternoon. Fueled by a stream of old spirituals and baskets of food, the first hours of the trip passed swiftly. An hour into the journey, Blake pulled out his Epiphone and started to strum along. In recent years, with the pressure of work, he'd rarely picked up a guitar at all. Now, pressing his fingers on the frets and feeling the humming vibration of the strings, the constant worry of the past week was replaced by something approaching a sense of peace.

Serena joined the singing as well, and even took the guitar from him at one point to pluck out some counter-melodies. As midnight approached they dozed off together. Blake slept fitfully, dreaming he was carrying a quantum transceiver through a maze of city streets while being chased by mysterious masked men. Waking with a start, he passed a hand over his face, feeling the tacky stretches where Nell had coated his forehead and cheeks with invisible paint earlier that day. According to her, the paint contained a microscopic carbon filament that would distort these portions of his face on any video or photograph.

"To keep you two darlings from being identified by those nasty surveillance cameras," she'd explained over the rumble of the speeding Winnebago, as she began applying the same pattern to Serena's face. "The railway stations are full of them, you know."

TWENTY-TWO

Aladdin Sane

Tuesday, September 10

WHEN BLAKE WOKE AGAIN, the sun was rising. Serena was still asleep, her head on his shoulder. Careful not to disturb her, he shifted his eyes to look at the green landscape outside the window. As he watched the countryside gliding past, feeling Serena's breath against his neck, Blake went over the details of the quantum transceiver again and again, probing for any weak points. In his mind's eye, at least, every element seemed to check out. *Let's hope there are no surprises tomorrow,* he thought.

It was noon when they passed under the Hudson River and rolled into Manhattan. Filing off the train with his fellow passengers, Blake was shocked at the dilapidated condition of Penn Station. The walls and floors were lined with cracks, and electrical wiring dangled from gaping holes in the ceiling. Everywhere he looked, panhandlers held out cups beseechingly.

"Come along, brothers and sisters," said the Reverend. The group climbed the stairway to Seventh Avenue and walked east through garbage-strewn streets to the subway. When the downtown express finally arrived, it was filled to bursting. Through persistent pushing, the entire choir forced their way inside along with their instruments. With a resigned sigh, the blind guitarist's guide dog lay on the subway floor, pressed against his master's legs. As the packed train moved away from the platform, Blake heard the hummed strains of "Nobody Knows the Trouble I've Seen" rising around him in three-part harmony.

Ten minutes later they exited into the sunlit expanse of Union Square. Again, Blake was startled at the rundown condition of the park and the surrounding buildings. There was a feeling of danger in the air that hadn't been there when he'd visited a decade earlier—a reflection of the poverty that seemed to have seeped in everywhere. The upscale food, clothing and appliance shops that once lined 14th Street had given way to discount retailers and down-at-the-ears grocery stores, while apartment buildings that had boasted doormen and landscaped entrances were now unmanned and unkempt-looking, the residents hurriedly opening the locked lobby doors with keys as they arrived home.

"Brothers and sisters, I can't tell you if this is the wilderness or the promised land—but either way, we have reached our destination," said the Reverend. "Can I hear a song of praise?"

"Swing low, sweet chariot," crooned the blind guitarist.

"Coming for to carry me home..." sang the others in response. Voices ringing, the Midway Minstrels carried their song east toward the UZ entrance at 14th Street and Third Avenue.

Just outside the UZ wall, a cyclone fence had been erected along the curb of Third Avenue. As they stood inside the fence, waiting to pass through the entry checkpoint, Blake saw an open white tent with wooden flooring a few yards away. Along the near edge of the tent, a low set of risers faced outward toward the UZ entrance. Several dozen neatly dressed men and women sat in the tent's interior on folding chairs, fanning themselves and listening to a man in a clerical collar as he paced in front of them, speaking into a microphone.

"Are you ready to make your voices heard by the unwashed multitudes?" the man said loudly. The listeners nodded their heads and shouted assent.

"What are we waiting for?" someone yelled.

"Before we begin this hour's singing of His praises, let us bow our heads and pray," the preacher continued. Halting in place, he lowered his chin and closed his eyes. "Dear Lord, lend our lungs and voices the power and might of your divine goodness, and grant that the music we create be filled with your heavenly light, that it may pierce the darkness which blinds our fellow human beings to the truth and glory that is your path."

"Amen," the group responded.

"And now, if you'll turn to page two hundred forty-one, let us loose His mighty sword!"

Clutching their hymnals, the group rose and filed onto the risers as the strains of an electric organ rose from inside the tent, sounding the opening notes of "Oh Sinner Come Home."

With the hymns droning in the background, the security queue inched slowly forward. To pass the time, Blake watched the activity swirling around the various TV news vans parked inside the fence. A young NBC reporter stood by the nearest one, clutching her microphone and staring into the camera.

"Ready when you are," said the cameraman.

"We are outside the entrance to the New York City Urban Zone," began the reporter, "where tens of thousands of UZ residents from across the nation are taking advantage of their Zoner status to gain entry to one of the most unusual cultural events of the year—the annual Urban Zone festival, commonly known as UZFest."

The camera panned to the checkpoint entrance where the officers were searching each person in turn and checking any electronic devices they were carrying. Above the entry point was a sign that read:

> ***Absolutely no cell phones, video or still cameras, or audio recorders. All personal computers must have their cameras and recorders disabled. Any illegal devices found will be confiscated.***

"As usual," the reporter continued, "the awarding of UZ tourist visas has been suspended for the duration of the festival. Since it's illegal to broadcast any audio or visual images from inside the Urban Zones, the rest of us can only imagine what's happening inside. But if the past is any guide, there's sure to be plenty of music and a fair amount of trouble—the kind of antisocial behavior that the Zone is notorious for, and that the rest of the nation is happy to keep within these concrete walls."

As she finished speaking, the camera moved away from her again, this time panning over the outside of the UZ wall, where a fresh piece of graffiti had recently been spray-painted on the gray concrete in large, red letters:

FREEDOM WILL NOT BE SILENCED

Inside the checkpoint, Blake and Serena exchanged goodbyes with the Minstrels. "May God watch over you, my children," said the Reverend, passing his open palm above their heads as his companions hummed an augmented seventh chord, "and safeguard you on your journey."

For someone who had spent the past eight years living exclusively in the tightly-controlled world of mainstream America, walking into UZFest 2024 was like entering an alternate universe. The Zone, which encompassed the entire East Village and Lower East Side of Manhattan, had been converted into one huge fairground. Thousands of people wandered around in clothing ranging from the minimal to the outlandish, with every era of pop fashion represented. Along the avenues, each block had several raised platforms where different musical acts performed in rotation. On the side streets between the platforms, dance troupes staged acrobatic routines, some set to music or rap, others to poetic monologues. Other groups engaged in street theater, most of it sharply political. The remaining space was taken up by buskers. In one storefront they passed, a large video screen was broadcasting recorded greetings from famous musicians. Blake paused to watch an UZFest salute from one of the top pop performers of the previous decade, known for her shifting hair colors and stylized costumes.

"I can't wait until I'm able to perform in New York again," said the superstar. "I'm with you in spirit, and I'm praying for change. Let's make it happen together!"

On First Avenue between 6th and 7th Streets, a woman stood on one of the temporary stages, vigorously channeling Adele. As she launched into a high-energy version of "Rumor Has It," Serena and Blue stopped to listen. When she was done, the audience applauded wildly.

"What I'd give for those pipes!" said a woman's voice in the crowd. Blake looked over his shoulder and then quickly turned forward again, pulling his fedora down lower on his forehead. It was Caroline, standing with her fellow Tangles and the Sunset Kidz. Clearly just arrived themselves, they were sipping cocktails out of plastic cups, their suitcases and backpacks on the pavement beside them.

Nudging Serena with his elbow, Blake began edging down the street. He was too late: From behind him, a hand grabbed the hem of his blazer.

"Hey—don't I know you from somewhere?" said Caroline. "You're from L.A., aren't you?"

"Sorry, you're mistaken," he sputtered, trying to pull free.

"You don't have to run away," she cooed. "I don't bite!"

She stepped closer and stared teasingly into his face. An instant later, she sucked her breath in sharply. "Holy shit," she said in a low voice. "It can't be! I saw you on that stretcher. You were *dead*."

Caroline was backing away now, eyes wide, her hand covering her mouth. "It's Karl," she told her companions, pointing at him with a trembling finger. "I know it's him!"

"Caroline, baby," crooned Lance, "it's been a long day. You know how New York is—you're always seeing people you think you know."

Ignoring him, Caroline looked straight at Blake. "What's this all about, Karl?" she demanded, her voice rising. "What the *fuck* is going on?"

"We need to find our hotel," Stash announced loudly. Over the heads of the other L.A. musicians, he frowned at Serena and Blue and drew his finger across his throat. "Time to go, *everybody!*"

“Follow me,” Serena muttered. “And don’t look back!” She turned and sped east down 6th Street. Despite her dress and heels, she walked so quickly that Blake had to half-trot to keep up. They covered three full blocks before she finally slowed to a normal pace.

“Well, *that* was interesting,” she said coolly, using her hand to smooth her hair as she glanced behind them. “I wonder what other old flames of yours we’ll run into.”

Their designated rendezvous was a walkup apartment on East 5th Street and Avenue C. Serena and Blake climbed the three flights to Apartment 4-A and pushed the doorbell. A rasping buzz sounded, and a second later the door was opened by a short, goateed man in knee-length shorts and sandals.

“Hello?” he said, his blinking eyes magnified by his eyeglasses.

“We were told you had a spare bedroom for visitors,” said Serena.

“Yes, of course,” said the man. “Before anyone passes through this portal, however, they must pay a tariff, in the form of a poetic verse. Any scrap will do, large or small.” He waited expectantly, eyebrows raised.

“Ever since middle school, it’s been my dream to join the poetry club,” said Serena drily, rolling her eyes at Blake. She thought a moment, then recited: “2 little whos (he and she) under are this wonderful tree.”

“Hmm, Edward Estlin Cummings,” the man said, blinking faster in his pleasure. “Very nice—and quite apropos. Enter, please.” He waved Serena into the apartment’s interior, then placed his hand against the doorframe to prevent Blake from following. “And you, young man?”

Blake’s mind was a blank. “I come to this city to wander the streets,” he said haltingly, “breathing the air that inspired the Beats.”

Pressing his lips together, the man gazed up at the ceiling. “An original couplet—coined on the spot, if I’m not mistaken,” he pronounced finally. “For the effort alone, I bid you welcome, sir!”

Blake walked into a living room with large windows overlooking 5th Street. One of the walls was taken up by a massive oil painting of abstract blue, pink and green pastels. Across the soft colors ran two rows of words in stark black paint:

> ***Would there be any freedom of press or speech if one must reduce his vocabulary to vapid innocuous euphemisms?***

Around a low table, Gully, Blue, and a man Blake had never seen before were sitting on cushions, drinking tea from small china cups.

"Can I offer you anything?" asked their host.

Serena shook her head. "I'm fine, thanks," said Blake.

"Then I'll leave you to your discussions," the bearded man said, bowing deeply. "I'm due at a gathering of my fellow poets. We'll be presenting our annual reading of 'Howl' as part of UZFest." He studied Blake through his glasses. "My name is Mac, by the way. My father was there, you know...with Alan, at the first reading back in '55."

"I'm sorry?" said Blake, not comprehending his meaning.

Mac shook his head in disappointment. "From your allusion to the Beats, I thought that perhaps you had a stronger grasp of modern literary history than you apparently do. Rock musicians don't have a patent on cultural transformation, you know. Ah, well. Gentlemen—and fair lady..." Grabbing a beret from a hook on the wall, he waved it at the group and marched out the door.

"Topic A has been finalized. Topic B we're still working on."

"What's the holdup?"

"We have to take the enhanced security into account, for a start. And we need a plan for covering our tracks and disposing of all equipment. We've never had a job traced back to us yet, and I don't want to start now. This sort of job also takes a special person on point—someone willing to take a big risk for a big payoff. That's partly why it costs so much." The speaker paused. "Remember what I said. You don't have to go through with this."

"Why would I have given you...what I gave you...if I didn't want to go through with it?"

"I'm just restating the deal: You get seventy-five percent back if you change your mind. And you can do so right up to the last minute."

"Why the pushback? I've done all that you asked, left the money in the storage unit as instructed—"

"I know. Everything's fine."

"Do you have what you need, in terms of information?"

Over the phone, the man's laugh was mirthless. "Don't worry. We know right where Topic B is gonna be. And assuming Topic A is in the New York Zone, we'll find him before the day is out."

"You sound pretty certain. Some highly trained intelligence officers haven't found it so easy."

"The difference is, our people are on the street. They see everything. We can find anyone, unless they're hiding out in a cabin in northern Canada—and maybe even then."

"Alright then. And I do understand what you're saying. It's possible that, in the end, the assignment may not need to be carried out after all."

"Why don't we play it this way: You've got my number. One hour before the show is due to start, you give me a ring and let me know if it's a green light."

"Agreed. And...thank you for all your help."

"Sure, pal—any time!"

❖ ❖ ❖

"Good to see you both," said Gully. "Glad you made it in one piece."

"Where are the transceivers?" asked Blake.

"Two of them are here," said Gully. He gestured toward the stranger at his side. "Alex has been tending to them. One will serve as our primary transmitter, the other we'll run as a backup. The crystals are in a portable freezer in the kitchen."

"And the other two?"

"They're in a secure location outside the United States, ready to receive whatever we send them. From there, we'll beam the audio in real time to the Web and to TV and radio relay stations in Europe, Asia and Africa. All the major international networks have been alerted to watch for an audio transmission with maximum news value. If it all works out, we could end up with quite a large audience."

"What about the U.S.?" asked Serena.

Gully tapped his fingertips together lightly. "I won't go into details," he said, "but during the speech, we're taking the unusually risky step of beaming an Internet data signal directly into our mesh network nodes across the continental United States."

That sounded like they'd be using communications satellites, thought Blake—which suggested that Matlock's companies were involved. He' d been wondering when the billionaire entrepreneur would reenter the picture.

"Even though they're disguised as computers, we thought it was important that the transceivers be concealed," Gully was saying. He walked to a trunk in the corner of the room and opened its combination lock. Lifting the lid, he took out the two simulated laptops.

"We've devised two different carriers," he said. "A knapsack and a woman's handbag." He reached into the trunk for a khaki backpack and an oversized leather shoulder bag. "They each have hidden compartments lined with shock-dampening material, to keep the transceivers stable and protected. The microphones are concealed in these—" Gully pulled out a bushmaster hat and a wide-brimmed straw hat festooned with silk flowers. He turned to his companion. "Alex, maybe you could explain how the microphones work."

"Right." Alex picked up the bushmaster hat and pointed to a mesh opening at the top. "The mics are sewn into the crowns of both hats. They're miniature, supercardioid directionals, incredibly good at picking out a single pinpointed audio source—a person's voice, for example. The key is to keep it focused tightly on the desired sound. Swing it a fraction of an inch one way or the other, and you'll pick up something completely different."

He put the hat down on the table. "Each mic connects to a dedicated wireless audio input inside one of the transceivers. Whoever is carrying the devices will be wearing a flesh-colored earpiece with an identical wireless connection, letting them monitor what the microphone is picking up."

"Nice setup," said Blake. "Who's going to be carrying them?"

Gully and Alex glanced at each other. "We thought it should be

Blue and Serena," Gully said. "You'll be right alongside them, in case anything goes wrong. No one knows the technology better than you do, and no one's in a better position to trouble-shoot if something goes haywire."

"No way," said Blake firmly, shaking his head. "This is my project. I'm going to do the primary transmission."

"That's a bad idea, Blake," said Gully softly. "You don't have the skills to protect yourself."

"Then Blue can stick with me," said Blake. "But I'm working the transceiver."

The silence around the table was finally broken by Blue. "I think he can handle it, Gully," he said. "The kid's been through a lot. We know he can think on his feet."

"I think it could work," agreed Alex. "Having Serena on the second device gives us an extra edge. She can serve as the backup transmitter *and* added security for Blake. And this way Blue is free to move if he needs to."

Gully clenched his jaw for a moment then smiled tightly.

"Okay," he said. "Even a stubborn mule can change its mind once in a while. Blake is on Transmitter One, Serena's on Two, and Blue sticks to them like white on rice."

"We shouldn't run into any trouble," said Blue. "We'll be well disguised, and we only need to stay undetected for an hour. Fish is scheduled to speak for thirty minutes, starting at four p.m. And he's known for being prompt."

"The plan is for you to stand about forty feet from the stage, directly in line with the microphone that Fish will be speaking into," added Alex. "He's going to be using public-address speakers, but we want your directional mics to focus on his actual voice, which will provide the clearest audio signal."

"We'll leave the apartment at three-thirty," Gully said. "We want you in place by three-forty-five. You'll start transmitting at five minutes of four, to make sure all of Fish's address is covered. It's going to be crowded in front of the stage, but we'll have operatives on all sides creating a zone of protection around you."

Leaning forward, Gully looked around the table. "This is our one shot, folks," he said. "If we do this right, the entire globe will be listening to Fish's speech. It could be a tipping point. Our top priority—our *only* priority—is to maintain a safe space for Blake and Serena to handle the transmission."

"You sure you're ready for this?" said Blue, turning to Blake. "It could get dicey out there."

"More than ready," said Blake. "I've been sitting on the sidelines way too long."

That night, after a meal of stir-fried broccoli rabe, tofu and bulgur that Mac prepared in a huge wok over his gas stove, Blake carefully examined both transceivers, then took the four test crystal wafers from the freezer and inserted them into the devices. At five minutes to eleven, he switched on both transceivers. At eleven sharp, he spoke softly into the attached microphone of the first device. "This is Alice, calling Bob. Do you read me?"

A man's voice sounded crisply in the headphones. "This is Bob. We read you, Alice. The connection is successful."

"Very good. Please note that our next transmission on this device will utilize sending component A973, that's Alpha, 9, 7, 3. Please confirm."

"Roger, that's sending component Alpha, 9, 7, 3, repeat, Alpha, 9, 7, 3."

"Confirmation received. Over and out."

Inwardly elated, Blake put on a second set of headphones and repeated the process with the backup unit. "They're both good to go," he said, trying to contain his excitement. "Let's hope they work as well tomorrow."

Next, they took the hats with the built-in directional mics up to the roof for some target practice, as Gully put it. Their sensitivity was amazing: Swinging them in any direction brought an entirely new crop of sounds, including scraps of conversation from the street and other apartments, all picked up with perfect clarity.

Curious about the microphones' range, Blake pointed his across the rooftops toward the East River, where a series of band shells had been erected. As he swept it across the horizon he caught an amplified female voice singing the same Cranberries song he'd heard on the grassy slope in San Francisco, half a lifetime ago. Listening to the rich-toned Irish accent, he felt sure it was the same woman.

It was late at night when they were finished, but everyone was too keyed up to sleep. Blue joined Blake and Serena in one of the back bedrooms, where Serena sat strumming Blake's guitar.

"Some day we'll all have to play some music together," said Blake.

"Whenever will we find the time?" Serena riffed, running through a series of minor chords. She turned to Blue. "Blake writes songs—did you know that?"

"Serena, you're sounding more like a girlfriend every day," grinned Blue. "No, I didn't know that. But I'm not surprised."

"Here," said Serena, handing the guitar to Blake. "Play something of yours."

"I thought you'd never ask," said Blake. Cradling it in his arms, he struck a G chord. Shooting a look at Serena, he began to sing.

I'm just a fool, it's true. 'Cause I can't stop loving you.
Don't know what I will do—I'm so in love with you…
So in love with you.

When he was finished, Blue applauded lightly. "Very nice," he said. "A bit on the sentimental side, but still…"

"Tomorrow night," interrupted Serena, reaching to take the instrument back, "you'll play us another."

TWENTY-THREE

Heartbreaker

Wednesday, September 11

WITH A DEEPENING SENSE OF anxiety, Martin watched the pale light of dawn creep across his patio. He'd taken an amphetamine at four a.m. and had been pacing the ground floor of his house ever since. His mind seemed to be moving in several directions at once. Closing his eyes, he struggled to focus his thoughts.

"Concentrate, Martin, concentrate!" *How long have you been talking out loud to yourself?* part of him wondered. "Oh, shut up!" he replied.

He couldn't shake the sense that he was making a monumental error—but what alternative did he have? If only he could talk to Hawkes personally, make him understand why he was so mistaken in pursuing the path he was on....

"That's it! I'll speak with him!" he cried, pounding his fist into his hand. He thought for a moment more, then picked up the phone and dialed.

"Hello...Robert? It's Martin—Martin Bibbitt. I apologize for calling you so early, and on your personal line. It's just that I couldn't sleep, worrying about how things were going in New York.... Ah, you're out on the streets already, preparing security for the Fish event? Good for you, good for you—that's wonderful.... I'm glad to hear things are well in hand.... Of course, I trust you implicitly. I know everything will go perfectly.... Me? I'm fine, couldn't be better. Thank you, Robert, you are a true gentleman—a gentleman and a patriot. Take good care. Yes, I'll do the same. Goodbye."

He looked at the clock, calculating the earliest time that he could reasonably call the West Coast. He'd wait another two hours, he decided. Pressing a button on the wall, he sank into an armchair, his face breaking into a half smile as one of his earliest works, a synthesizer piece of gradually shifting half-tones, began playing over the room's sound system. He had written it when he was twenty-six—the same age as the Hawkes boy, he thought. Fighting off a wave of despair, he closed his eyes and focused on the music. As he listened to the soothing progression of intricately linked electronic notes, silent tears began trickling down his cheeks. What happened, he wondered, to the earnest young man who had composed them?

At 6:30 a.m. Pacific Time, the phone beside the bed of Tabitha and Aloysius Branford chimed softly. "Hello?" said Tabitha. "Oh. Certainly." She handed the phone to her husband, a look of warning in her eyes.

"Good morning," said Branford in his rasping half-whisper. "Why, hello there. No, we've never had the pleasure.... Yes, do tell me why you called."

Branford listened with a furrowed brow. "This is a most unusual request," he replied at last. "I have acquaintances in many different circles, of course, and there's an outside possibility I might be able to make indirect contact with the person you're seeking—if, as you say, it really is a matter of life and death.... If you'll give me a number where you can be reached, someone will be back in touch with you within the next few hours. I'm not promising anything, you understand.... Yes, of course. I appreciate you reaching out to me, as well. Good day."

At 10:15 on the East Coast, Martin Bibbitt got the call he was waiting for. "Everything is arranged for one p.m. Eastern," said an unfamiliar voice. A series of details followed in rapid-fire succession. "You'll have ten minutes," the voice added. "Not a second longer."

"That's perfect," said Martin. "Thank you—you won't be sorry."

Now there was just one more phone call to make, to the West Coast again.

Sitting with his newspaper by the front window of the 5th Street apartment, Gully listened to a man and woman arguing loudly on the sidewalk, three floors below.

"If you can't discuss this rationally," said the man in an angry tone, "what's the point of discussing it at all?"

"I'm happy to talk," the woman retorted. "Just not here."

As the couple drifted down the sidewalk, Gully stood up. "I'll be back in a few minutes," he told Blue.

Walking out the front entrance of the apartment building, Gully barely glanced at the unshaven homeless man asleep on a grate, a stench of urine rising around him. A minute later, a man walking a Dalmatian on a leash paused to let his dog sniff the pile of garbage next to the passed-out vagrant.

"Anything?" the dog walker said. His lips hardly moved as he spoke.

"The head guy just left," the homeless man said, also barely moving a muscle. "The package is still inside."

"Good boy." Pulling on his pet, the man continued down the sidewalk whistling an aimless tune.

When Gully returned twenty minutes later he was carrying an attaché case under his arm. "Team meeting!" he called.

"I think this is insane, frankly," he said once the group had gathered in the living room over cups of green tea. "But here goes: Martin Bibbitt, the U.S. Secretary for Cultural Hygiene, has asked for a video conference with Blake. He claims he wants to offer Blake some kind of deal—clemency, or a plea bargain for a suspended sentence, or some such thing." Gully's frown deepened. "My professional opinion is that this is some kind of a trick."

"If it's a trick, what's the goal?" said Blue. "Confirm that Blake's in New York? Get a fix on his location?"

"There's no danger of that," said Gully, patting the case he'd brought back with him. "There's a mesh network laptop in here. If this conference happens, it'll be relayed through a dozen other nodes across the country. The transmission will be strictly limited to ten minutes. There's no way anyone could track even the first few relay points in that time period."

"Our hypothesis is that Homeland is already operating on the assumption that Blake and his technology are here in the Zone," said Serena. "My question is, what does Blake gain by talking with this guy?"

"What if he really can make the music possession charges go away?" said Blake. "I could go back to Berkeley and take up where I left off. Everything would be just like before."

As Blake looked around the table, Serena, Blue and Gully all examined their cups of tea intently. *They're leaving this up to me,* he thought.

"Let me get this straight," he continued. "Bibbitt is the one who's been spearheading this whole drive to ferret out illegal music, right? The little composer on TV, who thinks rock music represents some kind of mental illness?"

"That's him," said Blue.

"You know what?" Blake said. "I'm going to do it—just so I can look this fruitcake straight in the eye."

❖ ❖ ❖

"Hello, young man. I'm Secretary Bibbitt. Thank you for agreeing to speak with me."

"Sure," said Blake, studying the rapidly blinking face on the computer screen. "How can I help you?"

"The question is, how can *I* help *you?* I know we don't have much time. I also know that you have some very serious charges pending against you, arising from your illegal possession of certain dangerous forms of music. I wanted to let you know that I'm prepared to personally intervene on your behalf. If we can come to an agreement, I'm sure I could get your sentence reduced to a period of community service."

"You mean, no compulsory military service?" asked Blake.

"No threat of military service or jail time," said Bibbitt. "I'm taking them completely off the table."

"What do I have to do?"

"Do? Why, that's easy. I'd like you to immediately cease whatever activities you're currently involved in, particularly those concerning any potential illegal broadcasts out of New York City, and turn yourself into the authorities at once. And, of course, publicly renounce your allegiance to the deranged music that's already caused you so much unnecessary trouble."

"And you can guarantee that the only consequence I'll face is community service?"

"Young man, I have many friends in high places. As you know, criminal charges related to possession of illegal and unhealthy music fall directly under my jurisdiction."

"But my case has been taken over by Homeland Security, right? Are you speaking for them as well?"

"Well, I—no, I'm not saying that. But I'm sure I can reason with them, help them understand that you're merely a deluded young man, who doesn't pose any serious threat to society."

"Let me ask you another question," Blake said. "Why do you keep referring to rock music as unhealthy and deranged? What have you got against the Beatles—or Boy George, for that matter?"

Bibbitt looked flustered for a moment. "I have no doubt that these outlawed groups included many talented musicians. But they've chosen to put their energies into the most manipulative drivel, made up of simplistic melodies and an incessant drumbeat. My dear boy, to anyone who understands true music, rock music is sickening. You're an educated fellow. Surely, you must be starting to realize this yourself!" Bibbitt paused to wipe a fleck of spittle from the side of his mouth.

"Mr. Secretary, I appreciate your offer," replied Blake, shaking his head. "But with all due respect—when it comes to your views on music, you're out of your freaking mind!"

Bibbitt's face hardened. "You think so?" he hissed. "How would you feel to know that one of your closest relatives agrees with me?"

"What are you talking about?" Blake felt his stomach tighten.

"I didn't want to do this," growled Bibbitt, "but you've forced my hand!" He reached forward to punch a button on his computer, and the image on Blake's computer suddenly switched to a split screen, with Bibbitt on the left, and on the right...

"Uncle Frank!"

Blake's uncle looked pale and tense. "Hello, Blake," he said in a strangled voice. "I'm so sorry—so, so sorry...."

"Your uncle understands the evil of this music," sneered Bibbitt. "He's the one who alerted the authorities to your secret horde of filth! *And* he kept the authorities informed when you decided to co-exist with the vermin in the so-called Urban Zone of Los Angeles!"

"Blake, when he asked me to link in today, I thought he'd be offering you a real way out," said Frank weakly.

Despite his shock, Blake felt an odd lack of anger at his uncle. He looked so wan and defeated, he thought.

"They had me against the wall," Frank said, answering Blake's unspoken question. "The government wanted me to reveal the names of certain sources for my corruption reports—sources whose lives would have been at risk. If I didn't cooperate, they were going to send me to prison. I had to give them something. They told me they'd treat you well, let you continue working in an Army laboratory—that it would be the best thing for you in the long run. Again...I'm sorry." He dropped his head.

"Time's up," came Gully's voice from over Blake's shoulder. "Blake, have you made a decision?"

"I'm sorry too, Uncle Frank—and Secretary Bibbitt," said Blake. "But this conversation is over." He punched the button to close down the video link.

"That must have been a shock," said Gully. "Are you okay?"

Blake didn't answer. He was too busy turning this new reality over in his mind. His uncle, the man he'd turned to for advice and comfort all his life, had betrayed him. He felt an emptiness inside, as if part of his childhood had just vanished.

"I never saw it coming," he said.

"We're all flying blind here," said Gully, resting a hand on his shoulder. "We just have to feel our way through. Speaking of which, I have something else to show you."

He fished a flash drive out of his pocket and plugged it into the USB drive of the laptop. "I was going to play this for you earlier today, before we got sidetracked. Your father contacted Branford a couple of days ago and asked him to get this message to you. A courier brought it in last night."

Gully clicked open a video file and the screen filled with the faces of Blake's mother and father.

"Hello, Blake," his mother said. "If you're watching this, then I trust you're safe. We got your message...we were so glad to hear that you're okay. Please know that we're sending you our love and prayers." Her eyes started to well up, but she caught herself. "Becky sends you her love as well. She also requests that you keep careful notes of everything you're experiencing, because she plans to write a book about it." She smiled, then glanced sideways at her husband. "That's all from me. I love you."

Staring into the camera, Admiral Hawkes cleared his throat before speaking. "I haven't been filled in on the details of what's taken place, Blake," he began, "but I have an idea of the general outline. All I want to say is that I have the utmost faith in you and whatever course of action you've chosen. Your mother and I stand behind you, one hundred percent. Stay strong, Blake, and trust your instincts. They've never let you down before. They won't let you down now."

As Blake watched, his father put his hand to his forehead in a military salute. "Godspeed, son," he said. "We'll see you when your mission is complete."

Closing the computer, Blake turned and faced Gully. "Thanks for passing that along," he said. "Now, let's rock and roll."

Alex, it turned out, was a makeup artist as well as an electronics expert. He had transformed Serena into some kind of avant-garde librarian, with cat-eye spectacles and a floral-print dress that might have come from a 1950 Sears Roebuck catalog if it had been a little less form-fitting. It matched the flowered hat with the microphone perfectly. Blue, in a stroke of genius, had been done up as a white-faced mime, complete with bowler hat and a plastic lapel flower that squirted water. Now, Alex was putting the finishing touches on Blake.

"All set?"

Blake looked at himself in the mirror one last time, then nodded. "I think I'm running out of personalities, though." His nose was augmented with putty, his skin had been died a deep olive, and he'd sprouted a short, dark beard. With the addition of his bush hat, Blake's latest disguise was complete.

As the appointed time drew nearer, the tension in the apartment mounted. Mac made a point of burning incense and playing recordings of indigenous South American folk songs, featuring a variety of flutes and gentle rain sounds. In the kitchen, Gully had turned on a small television. Wandering in, Blake found him watching a local newscast intently. The correspondent was standing outside the New York UZ entrance. In the background, Blake could see the white tent where the religious group had been gathered when he first arrived. Where the scene had been calm and orderly before, the area was now crowded and chaotic, with many more people milling about. In the background, a low chant could be heard: *"Kill the Devil's music!...Kill the Devil's music!"*

"We're talking with Reverend Val Lawson, one of the leaders of 'God's Voice in Protest.' They've been gathered on this spot since the start of UZFest '24, several days ago," the correspondent said. "Reverend Lawson, your group has been the model of good behavior up until now. But clearly, the atmosphere is becoming more charged. Can you assure us things won't get out of hand?"

"I think people are understandably upset that the government permits this festival of paganism and, frankly, Satanism, to go on, year after year," said the minister hoarsely. "No one wants disorder. But if there is trouble, it will be the government's responsibility for allowing this untenable situation to exist."

"So, you're not guaranteeing you can control your organization?" the correspondent asked.

"It's not up to me..." the Reverend's voice trailed off as shouting erupted behind him. The camera swung to record a knot of screaming protesters being pushed against the cyclone fence by a group of police officers. "Excuse me," he said. "I have to go."

Gully switched off the TV with a grimace. "Looks like the circus just gained another sideshow."

Before they headed out to the park, Gully drew Blue aside. "As promised, our friend has been in touch," he said softly.

"What does he have?"

"He was very detailed. I've mapped it all out for you." Blue leaned over the paper Gully was holding. "The uniformed detail will assemble at this point, here. Their plan is to deploy along these lines, shortly before Fish begins to speak. There are also going to be sizeable groups of Federal undercover operatives located in each of the indicated spots. Our people should be able to identify them by their earpieces."

"Good. I've already touched base with all our people," said Blue tersely. "I'll start spreading the word as soon as we hit the street."

"I have an absolutely awful feeling about this—I wish you would simply cancel the speech!"

Maxwell Fish looked at his wife and sighed. As a former legal counsel to the Senate Judiciary Committee, Beth wasn't ordinarily one to shrink from a fight, and he trusted her instincts implicitly. But this was one time he couldn't follow her advice.

"That's impossible, my love," he said gently. "First, if I turned down this opportunity, I'd badly weaken whatever legal case I have. Second, I've been sitting on this information for too long as it is. This is the time to get this out—we both know that."

"Why can't we follow the alternate plan, and let our friends in the media handle everything? It'll be just as big a story that way."

Fish shook his head. "We've discussed this already. If the public learns about this secondhand, it will give the right-wing media time to pick it apart, start smearing the source and me, begin dropping innuendoes about phony recordings and hidden motives. No, this has to come straight from my mouth."

"But your speech isn't being broadcast..."

"There will be plenty of journalists there to report on it. We'll also have transcripts available for the press. There are even likely to be a few people out there with illegal recording devices, although of course I can't condone that."

"I know all that." His wife shivered. "I just have a premonition. There's something in the air. Something malevolent...."

Fish glanced at the closed door leading to the living room, where his four-man Secret Service contingent was stationed—ostensibly to protect him but also, he knew, to help ensure he didn't violate the conditions of his house arrest.

"We have to trust that things will work out," he said quietly. "The future of our country hinges on this. That's far more important than the fate of one individual."

Jim Marshall's voice came from the other side of the door. "Time to get going, Governor!" Elizabeth Fish grasped her husband's hand tightly.

"I love you so much," she whispered.

"I love you too, darling," he said, squeezing her hand in return. "Have faith."

Martin Bibbitt's hand was trembling as he punched the buttons on the pay phone. "It's a green light," he told the man who answered. "You can move forward with both assignments."

"Understood," said the man. "We'll proceed as planned."

"One more thing," said Bibbitt. "I want to send a personal message to Topic A. When that little bastard sees the end in sight, I want him to know who's responsible. Tell him this..."

When he finished, there was a moment of silence on the other end. "You sure you want to put that out there?" the man said.

"I'm the one paying for this," Bibbitt snarled, "and that's how I want it done."

"Okay," said the man cheerfully. "It's your funeral."

The crowd screamed their approval as the singer stared impassively back at them through his dark glasses, shouting his own take on the words from the Statue of the Liberty. Every foot of Tompkins Square Park was packed, and the atmosphere was testy: A half-hour earlier, the Chattering Skulls' versions of "Psychokiller" and "Burning Down the House" had met with only a moderate reception. The proto-punk offerings of Lou Reed were a better fit for the audience's disgruntled mood, but the people jammed together at the front of the stage still seemed to be waiting for something more. As the last chords of "Dirty Boulevard" faded away, they pushed in expectantly.

"Thank you," said the MC. "Thank you, Stu Bleed, for channeling the music of the man who *fired* Andy Warhol as his band's manager..." The crowd roared a mix of approval and catcalls. "...Who told David Bowie to go screw himself—then ending up doing a *fucking record* with him!" This elicited a warmer reaction. "...Who survived electroshock therapy at *age fourteen*, then went on to pave the way for countless other great New York City musicians—including four kids from the borough of Queens, four young rockers who shared a love of fast, raw music...and who, to prove their undying devotion to each other, even took the same last name...*Joey*...*Johnny*...*Dee Dee*...and *Tommy*...give a big UZFest welcome to *The Regrowns!*"

The crowd congealed in a scrum of delirium as four skinny, black-haired men raced onto the stage and tore into a breakneck version of "I Wanna be Sedated."

"Timing is critical here, men," the commander told the lieutenants gathered around him. "We don't want to move in too soon, but it's absolutely essential that we're in position *before* Fish begins speaking. Understood?" He looked up to see nods all around. "When I give the word, you'll head out from the staging area to your stations on the perimeter. Once you're in position, wait for my radio signal and then move in *fast* with the cordon fences. Every human being in the park gets arrested, without exception. They can sort it out later in court. I mean *everyone*—no matter what their story is or who their daddy knows. They all get the plastic cuffs and a free bus ride.... All right now, *let's go!*"

He glanced at the man in suit and tie standing by his side. "Good to have you here, sir," he said. "You do understand, though, that I'm taking orders only from Secretary Jackson himself."

"Of course," said Smyth pleasantly. "I'm just here to help any way I can."

In front of them, six hundred Homeland Security riot troops stood in formation, stretching west down 9th Street. They had been in place only five minutes, but word of their presence was already filtering through the crowds of people thronging the park and the surrounding streets.

"They've brought the Army in....Word is they're shutting the festival down....It's all about stopping Fish....No, they're after the music, they want to silence all of us...."

Over the next several minutes, imperceptibly at first and then more and more rapidly, people began drifting into the intersection of 9th and Avenue A to gawk at the collection of law enforcement officers.

"Set the music free!" someone shouted. The crowd took up the chant, clapping their hands in rhythm to the words. After a minute, the words gave way to singing: "Set the music free...liberate all melody..."

The entire street took up the UZ anthem, raising their voices to be heard over the amplified music coming from the stage. Thousands of people were crowded into the intersection by now, packed so tightly that people were wedged against each other and jammed against the park's fence and the sides of the adjacent buildings. In just minutes, the sheer mass of bodies had created an impassable wall of humanity between the assembled riot officers and Tompkins Square.

"PLEASE CLEAR THE STREET," the commander ordered through his loudspeaker. "YOU ARE INTERFERING WITH POLICE BUSINESS. YOU *WILL* BE ARRESTED IF YOU DO NOT MOVE." The ever-growing crowd responded by singing louder:

"Set the music free...Emancipate sweet harmony!"

"Jesus Christ, where are all these doped-up assholes coming from?" the commander grumbled to his second in command. "This is going to cost us some serious time." Raising his loudspeaker again, he turned and addressed his troops: "Alright men, shields up—begin moving forward, slowly now. We don't want any dead hippies on our hands if we can help it."

"And now, before I introduce the next President of the United States," the MC said, eliciting another loud roar from the audience, "we have a special tribute, in honor of what our country has been, can be, and *will be again*. Straight from Seattle, Washington, the guitarist you have to hear to believe....Ladies and gentlemen, *The Experience!*" The MC nodded to the side of the stage, where a drum circle began pounding out an anticipatory beat.

Forty feet away, in the tightly packed crowd at the front of the stage, Blake was picking up the MC's words perfectly through his earpiece. He nodded to Serena, standing beside him in her garden club getup. Blue, watchful as ever, stood just to their left. Directly behind them, four young Muni operatives were arrayed shoulder to shoulder, forming a barrier against the surging crowd.

As the drums subsided, The Experience roared up a ramp and onto the stage on his chopper. Banging his kickstand down with his heel and plugging his guitar into his mobile amp, he stood and faced the audience with arms upstretched while the MC held a microphone to his lips.

"Thank you, kind people of New York," the guitarist said breathlessly. "You are truly fabulous.... And now, for your listening pleasure, I'll play the song that the great patriot...Kate Smith...made famous so many years ago, back in the days of wine and roses. Here we go…."

Bending over his guitar, The Experience began playing an excruciatingly slow, distortion-filled, undeniably beautiful version of "God Bless America."

❖ ❖ ❖

"Greetings everyone, and good evening," said the BBC announcer. "As reported earlier, we are taking the unusual step of standing by for a broadcast that may or may not take place over the next few minutes. America's embattled Democratic Party candidate for president, Maxwell Fish, is scheduled to address the public today in New York, from inside that city's designated Urban Zone—an area normally off-limits to television and radio crews, except in special cases where an exemption has been granted by the U.S. government. It's our understanding that such an exemption was *not* granted for today's speech. However, we've also been told that a live audio transmission of the speech may be forthcoming anyway. As I said, this is not definite, but we are holding airtime open on the chance that we will indeed be able to bring you a live broadcast of today's address by the American presidential candidate. So please, stay tuned…."

The Indiana backyard was empty, although the grill was still warm. A folding table held half-finished plates of burgers, hot dogs, potato salad and baked beans. Inside the house, in a darkened basement den, the picnic's host had her laptop's volume set on high. A dozen people huddled closely around her, faces illuminated by the light of the computer screen.

"There's nothing but static!" someone complained.

"I'm still trying to connect with the streaming audio, if you'll just wait a goddamn minute! There, got it…."

"Hello friends," came a voice over the computer. "Thank you for joining us on the Free America network. Today's special, live broadcast presentation will begin in ten, nine, eight…"

❖ ❖ ❖

"He's coming—I see him!"

"I hear it's the first time he's been out in a month..."

"*I* heard they wanted to put him in solitary, but Ballinger vetoed it—"

"He's so pale. I hope he's okay..."

When Maxwell Fish took the stage, a raucous cry swept through the crowd. He stood waving for several seconds then walked slowly to the microphone as his Secret Service detail took up position on either side of him. He waited another minute for the pandemonium to die down, but when it became clear the cheering showed no signs of abating, he began to speak into the microphone over the audience noise.

"Thank you... thank you very much... you're too kind..."

His efforts did no good. The cheering and yelling went on for another minute, then evolved into a chant of "Max... Fish!... Max... Fish!"

Raising his hands high, Fish finally managed to quiet the gathering.

"Hello, New York City," he said. "Hello, Urban Zoners.... And hello, America." A murmur went through the crowd, and Fish nodded.

"You all know the circumstances surrounding my appearance here today," he went on, eliciting a chorus of boos. "I'm grateful for the opportunity to address this wonderful gathering. It's my fervent hope that you are able, through word of mouth, to share my words with the millions of people beyond these walls who share your love of music, of creative expression, and of freedom...."

From the edges of the park, Blake could hear the half-shouted, half-sung notes of a song. It was many people's voices, he realized, singing a familiar tune and lyrics. *Set the music free*. The UZ liberation song! There wasn't any time to think about it, though. Another roaring wave of cheers and shouts washed over him, and the "Max Fish" chant resumed. Seized by the excitement of the moment, the drum circle started up again, adding their throbbing rhythm to the swirling ocean of sound that filled the park.

Outside the UZ entrance, the ministers had been conferring tensely for the past half-hour as the crowd clustered around them grew increasingly restless. Most of the NYPD officers who'd been monitoring the portals had been redirected to Tompkins Square, leaving just a couple of cops at each doorway.

"If you don't lead us in there, *Reverend,*" shouted a ragged voice, "we'll go in on our own!" An angry roar rose from the jostling throng.

Reverend Lawson nodded grimly at his colleagues, then turned and spoke through his megaphone. "Our time has come, my brethren!" he shouted. "The forces of evil are rising within. It is our sacred duty to confront them with God's righteous wrath. Follow me!"

With a rousing cry, the evangelicals, now several thousand strong, began to pour through the wall's openings into the Urban Zone, led by a large, heavily muscled man holding a crucifix above his head.

"Where do you think you're going?" shouted a frightened-looking young policeman. He rested his hand on his holstered pistol and then removed it again as the stream of humanity swept by and over him, singing "Onward Christian Soldiers" at the top of their lungs.

Blake's microphone was picking up every syllable with crystalline clarity, but he had no way of knowing whether Fish's words were actually being transmitted out into the world. He caught the eye of Blue, who stood at his side busily scanning the crowd. Blue leaned toward him. "Stick with it," he shouted over the noise. "Just concentrate on the words."

With the candidate's speech halted temporarily by the chanting, Blake decided to go off script. Turning to the left, he swept his microphone over the throng of people to pick up some random comments from the crowd.

"What do you think you're doing?" said Blue sharply.

"Livening up the broadcast," Blake yelled back.

"That's not part of the plan!" Blue barked, shaking his head, but Blake was too focused on his audio input to hear. As he moved his head, the microphone picked up a series of conversation fragments—

"...can't believe they've kept him cooped up like this..."

"...Save some of that water for me, would you?..."

"...I can't get a clean shot from here. I'm shifting position...."

His attention caught by the last phrase, Blake swept the microphone back over the same location.

"I'll have time to get off two rounds, maybe three. We'll do the transfer at the left end of the stage. I'm moving now." The speaker was conversing in a quiet tone, as if talking to someone over a high-powered radio. Peering in the direction his mic was pointing, Blake spotted a man in a green army jacket twenty feet away. He had a large bouquet of flowers in his arms and was slowly pushing his way through the crowd toward the left side of the stage. As Blake watched, he noticed another man pushing through the crowd in the opposite direction, heading directly towards Blake himself. The two brushed shoulders and seemed to acknowledge each other with a glance. As the second man drew closer, Blake saw that he was carrying a large black umbrella despite the sunny day.

Blake nudged Blue with his elbow. "I caught something strange," he muttered. "Someone talking about getting off two rounds. And there's a guy in a green fatigue jacket holding a bunch of flowers, moving toward the uptown side of the stage."

Blue's jaw tightened. "I'm going to check it out, just in case. Meanwhile, keep the microphone directly on Fish. Remember, Serena's got your back. Do whatever it takes, but *stay on him.*"

Motioning with his hand, Blue began swiftly working his way through the tightly-packed crowd, two of the four other Muni operatives following closely behind. *We just lost half of our protection,* Blake realized. He glanced at Serena but her attention was on Max Fish, who was preparing to speak again.

As the crowd quieted, Fish began once more. "We are here today to celebrate the joy of music and creativity. And I want to make it very clear that if I am elected President of this great nation, I will do everything in my power to end the ban on certain forms of music that has burdened our country for the past seven years!"

Cheers erupted again as the drum circle banged gleefully.

"Please understand that I do not minimize the threats we face as a nation," he added. "As we all know, today marks the anniversary of an unspeakable attack on this city and its residents—an attack in which three thousand of our mothers and fathers, sisters and brothers, daughters and sons were consumed by a fiery inferno of hate. But as we remember that tragedy, we must also recognize that our own fears can threaten our freedom, as well."

Cheers rose, mixed with boos.

"To this end, we must remain ever-vigilant against those who would exploit our legitimate security concerns," Fish continued, "by raising false alarms, and even by going so far as to manufacture false evidence."

The crowd stirred. "What are you saying?" a woman's voice shouted loudly.

The candidate's tone, measured before, began to grow in intensity.

"In my conversations with the intelligence agencies of Canada," he said, "...those same conversations that led to my arrest, I was made aware of information that up until now has been a closely guarded secret—shocking information, information that warrants a full and aggressive inquiry by an independent prosecutor. These findings relate directly to the Boundary Waters Incident—an affair that the current Administration and Republicans in Congress have used to justify the most far-reaching encroachments on our own civil liberties."

The crowd was buzzing now. A new chant went up: "Speak... truth... speak... truth!"

Jostled by the people around him, Blake fought to keep his microphone directed at Fish. Suddenly, an amplified voice boomed across the sea of humanity.

"THE PARK IS NOW BEING SECURED. THIS IS A POLICE ACTION. STAY WHERE YOU ARE AND SEAT YOURSELF ON THE GROUND IMMEDIATELY."

At the same instant, something went wrong with Fish's

microphone. The candidate was still speaking, but no sound came from the public address system.

Just keep talking, thought Blake frantically, *I can broadcast your voice even without a PA*. As Fish looked around helplessly, there was a movement at the far end of the stage: The Experience was wheeling his motorcycle toward the podium, only to be stopped by one of the Secret Service agents. The two men spoke heatedly for a few seconds and then the Secret Service agent stepped back. Reaching for his bike, The Experience retrieved a microphone, jammed its cord into his Marshall amp, then handed the mic to the agent who passed it on to Fish. The candidate nodded his thanks and started speaking again, his voice now coming from the amplifier on the back of the guitarist's bike.

"Thank you, young man," said Fish, clearing his voice. "Apparently, the authorities are trying to stop this speech, just as they've been trying to stop me every step of the way. But I won't be prevented from sharing this with you." His voice had now risen to a near-shout. "I have evidence clearly showing that certain elements in our government not only knew about the Boundary Water operation ahead of time, but *staged the entire incident*—including arranging for Rick Rogers' escape. My evidence is this audio recording I'm holding in my hand, made by Rogers himself. He gave it to the Canadian authorities shortly before his death. I'm going to play it for you, here and now, so that you can draw your own conclusions."

"STOP ALL PUBLIC ACTIVITIES AT ONCE AND SEAT YOURSELF ON THE GROUND,"

boomed the loudspeakers again…

"THIS IS AN OFFICIAL POLICE ORDER. ALL VIOLATORS WILL BE ARRESTED."

The crowd at the front of the stage countered with another round of "Speak…truth…" until Fish's waving quieted them. As he held a portable cassette tape player to the microphone, the sound of a man's recorded voice could be heard clearly.

"You have my word of honor," the voice was saying, "that if you carry out this patriotic duty, we'll make arrangements for you to get political asylum in Canada. We'll also see to it that your colleagues are treated as leniently as possible. I promise you, we won't forget what you've done for us."

Concentrating intently on Fish, Blake was dimly aware of a rising commotion at the edges of the park. There was widespread shouting, and a tide of people seemed to be pressing inward, causing the crowd to pack together even more closely.

"They're going to kill us!" someone behind him screamed. The crowd abruptly surged forward, almost knocking Blake off his feet. Struggling to stay upright, he strained to keep the microphone trained on Fish.

"And if I don't go along?" another man's recorded voice was saying.

"In that case, with the tax evasion case we've got on you, you'll rot in jail for decades.... We're not asking you to hurt anyone. We just want you to carry a piece of equipment across the border."

"You promise we'll all come out of it okay?"

"I swear it."

"Alright then. You can tell Mr. Acton that I'm on board."

Amid the chaos, Blake's brain was reeling from what he'd just heard. The crowd was in full panic mode now as the ring of police slowly closed in on the park's center. Across the river of swaying bodies, he saw Blue standing by the edge of the stage, almost at Fish's feet. Then a nearby motion caught his eye and he spun his head to the left. The man with the umbrella was standing three feet away, staring straight at him. Feeling a flash of terror, Blake looked for Serena, but her attention was still focused on Fish.

A scream rose from the stage, and Blake's microphone picked up a man's shout: "He's got a gun!" He watched Fish crumple to the floor as Blue's white-faced figure leapt onto the stage to cover the fallen man. Racing to the side of the platform, one of the Secret Service agents fired his revolver into the crowd while another agent moved toward Blue and the candidate. Another shot must have been fired from somewhere nearby, because Blake saw the cloth suddenly ripped from the back of Blue's shirt as he lay on top of Max Fish's prone body.

Above the din came another sound—the heavy rise and fall of a new group of voices in unison, singing a song Blake remembered from the church-going days of his youth:

Christ the Royal Master, leads against the foe
Forward into battle, see his banners go….

At that moment, he felt a sharp pain in the side of his thigh. Glancing down, Blake saw the black umbrella's tip pressed against his pants leg. As Blake looked up at the man holding the umbrella, the man grinned.

"Personal greetings," he said, "from Martin Bibbitt."

An anguished cry sounded from Blake's right. He saw Serena lunge toward the man with the umbrella, driving her fingers into his throat. A second later, the man slumped to the ground.

"What have you done?" she screamed. It was the last thing Blake heard before everything went black.

TWENTY-FOUR

Sky Pilot

OPENING HIS EYES, BLAKE SAW blue sky and sunlight. There was a loud mechanical clacking sound. He lay back, listening to it. He was in a helicopter, he realized, and Serena was next to him. She looked down at him and smiled. He smiled back at her, and slept for a while. Somewhere, the R.E.M. song "The End of the World as We Know It" was playing on an endless loop.

When he woke again, he saw two men sitting in front of him, the pilot and another person. As he watched, the other person turned around and grinned, flashing a thumbs-up. Studying the face, Blake saw that it was Peter Matlock. He turned this fact over in his mind as Matlock took off his ear protectors and leaned down to speak to him.

"Great to see you, Blake," he shouted over the sound of the helicopter blades. "I told you we'd make beautiful music together!"

Blake nodded. He couldn't speak, he noticed. Then Serena waved Matlock off and rested her hand against Blake's face, and he slept again.

❖ ❖ ❖

"An umbrella gun? I didn't think that sort of thing actually existed." Rays of sunlight were bouncing off the surface of the Atlantic, creating a dancing pattern on the wall of Blake's stateroom. An untouched lunch sat on a tray beside his bed. A few feet away, the Epiphone was propped against the wall inside its case.

"More syringe than gun, really," said Blue, lounging in a nearby armchair. "Designed to inject a pellet straight into your leg. Smaller than a BB, but with enough potassium cyanide to kill you in a few minutes once the sugar coating dissolved." Popping a handful of peanuts into his mouth, he munched on them with gusto. "Luckily, it took Serena less then thirty seconds to dig it out of you with her penknife. Otherwise, you might not be here. As it was, you spent two days in the ship's infirmary on an IV drip." He glanced around. "I've got to say, your new room looks a lot more comfortable."

Blake touched the bandage on his thigh, then reached for a paper cup of water and drank it down before lying back again. "So," he said, staring at the ceiling. "The transmission worked."

"Yep. Both of them. Yours and Serena's. The whole world heard Fish's speech in real time—what there was of it. Followed by screaming, gunshots, and a whole lot of other exciting stuff—including a surrogate confession by the person who tried to have you murdered."

"Bibbitt." Blake shook his head. "But why?"

"He just plain snapped, is my guess—though I doubt that argument will hold up in court. When the police went to Bibbitt's house, he was curled on the floor in fetal position."

The door of the stateroom opened and Serena walked in, drying her hair with a towel. "That's some spa! The gym's not bad, either." She fell into a second armchair. "A little more of this and I might start liking that crazy Matlock. You say he's got *two* of these things?"

"The one in the Pacific's even bigger," Blake said.

"Cripes!"

"I was just filling in Blake on a few details, now that he's rejoined the living," said Blue.

Serena stood and walked over to Blake, planting a kiss on his forehead. "All I can say is, thank God cyanide has an antidote," she sighed. "The original umbrella gun victim wasn't so lucky." Seeing Blake's blank look, she added, "It's an old Cold War story. I'll tell you about it someday."

Blue wiggled his eyebrows, whistling a few bars of "Waterloo Sunset."

"What I'd really like to know," said Blake, "is how all this has affected the campaign."

"You sound pretty interested for a guy who couldn't have cared less about politics two weeks ago," grinned Serena.

"The impact has been *unbelievable,*" said Blue. He stood up and began pacing the room. "Acton's approval ratings are in the toilet. Fish jumped to a ten-point lead in the polls overnight. The Democrats are showing big gains across the board in the Congressional races, too. Now people are saying they might take the Senate back, maybe even the House. There's been pressure on Acton to quit the race, but so far he's resisting. It doesn't look good for him, though. The Canadian government refuses to deny the authenticity of the audio recording, which in the media's mind is as good as a confirmation. Plus, the Department of Justice announced this morning that it's dropping all charges against Fish. So he's free to campaign his little heart out."

Blake searched his memory, trying to piece together everything that had happened in the park before he'd blacked out. "Then, Fish didn't get shot after all?"

"Oh, he got clipped all right. The shooter got off two rounds. The first bullet grazed Fish in the shoulder. Just a scratch, basically—but you'd think he made it back from Iwo Jima, the way the press is carrying on."

"And the second shot hit you—in the back. I saw it...."

Blue pounded his chest with his fist. "Bulletproof vest, my boy. Never leave home without it."

Blake's eyes widened. "Really!" he said in surprise. "I don't recall anyone offering *me* any body armor!"

"Why don't we take a break from the blow-by-blow?" said Serena. "Let Blake rest a while. Maybe he'll be up for a stroll on deck later."

"Wait a minute," said Blake. "What about *my* charges? Are they going to be dropped too?"

"Sorry, dude. That's going to take a little more time," said Blue. "But at least we were able to haul you out of the UZ before Homeland Security swept you up in their dragnet."

"Yeah—how did you manage that?"

"Thank Martin Bibbitt, first, and the holy rollers, second. The Secret Service killed Fish's shooter dead as a doornail, but not before he handed off his gun to some other mojo who took off like a scared rabbit. Half of the Homeland contingent went chasing after the bag-man. They caught him just before he tossed the pistol into the East River. A bunch of other cops were sidetracked by the religious nuts, who were looking to rumble with anyone they bumped into."

"Did Bibbitt arrange the hit on Fish, too?"

"That's only speculation at this point, but I wouldn't bet against it," said Blue. "The FBI has been working overtime, looking for links between the dead shooter and the man who tried to off you. It's lucky that guy can still talk after what Serena did to his voicebox."

"Enough!" cried Serena, rising to her feet. "We've only got a couple of days left on this tub, and I want to enjoy them."

"Where are we sailing to?" Blake said.

"Branford and Gully want you kept out of harm's way for a while," said Blue. "Matlock owns an island in the Bahamas. He's offered to put you up indefinitely."

"Can I be extradited to the U.S. from there?"

"Technically, yes. But I'm told it would take a lot of doing."

As if on cue, an intercom on the wall sputtered.

"How's the patient?" asked Matlock's disembodied voice.

"Just fine," Blue said loudly.

"Good. Please give Blake my apologies, but I'm afraid there's no recording studio on this particular vessel."

"I think he'll survive," said Blue, winking at Blake.

"Wonderful. I'll be down shortly to greet the hero in person. I believe Governor Branford is hoping to Skype with him later, as well."

"There's no hurry!" called Serena, but the intercom had already gone dead.

Blake rolled over in bed to look at the two of them. "Are you guys coming to the island, too?"

"I'll drop by at some point. Right now, I've got a few other things I need to take care of," said Blue. "I think Serena might be prepared to hang out for a while, though."

"Hey, it's up to you," said Serena in a bored-sounding voice. She was standing by the stateroom window, staring out at the ocean. "I just figured, now that I've been a special-ops soldier and the member of a punk-rock band, it might be fun to play at domesticity for a while. Who knows? If it works out, maybe we can try the real thing."

❖ ❖ ❖

The next morning, Blake asked for a laptop computer. As soon as it arrived, he set to work.

"What are you doing?" asked Serena.

"What I should have done weeks ago," said Blake.

Eight hours later, he was still hunched over the computer, typing as rapidly as his fingers could move, taking only occasional breaks to scribble batches of equations on pieces of scrap paper. Serena and Blue wandered in and out of the stateroom, moving quietly so they wouldn't disturb him.

"Time to hit 'Send'," said Blake finally, glancing at Serena, who was nestled in an armchair reading a book. He clicked on his email account then leaned back. "This paper is now heading out to Berkeley, Oxford, Moscow State University, the Technical University of Munich, the University of Science and Technology in Beijing, and Kyoto University," he said. "Within forty-eight hours, the entire physics community is going to know everything that I do about quantum communication."

Gully flew in the following day on one of Matlock's helicopters. It was the first time Blake had seen him since the day of Fish's speech. Blake sat on the deck wrapped in a blanket, and Gully joined him there.

"Any more thoughts about the stunt your uncle pulled?" Gully asked.

"It might sound strange," said Blake, "But I understand why he did it. There were other people he had to protect. He thought this was a reasonable alternative. The system's the real villain here—repressive government turning ordinary people into criminals."

"That's pretty forgiving of you," said Gully. "I'm not sure I'd be so generous."

"What I don't understand, though, is why he helped me escape after turning me in."

"By that time, the Feds had already decided to give you some running room. After the Munis approached Frank about helping you, his handlers in Homeland Security told him to go along with the plan."

"So they knew I was in the L.A. Zone?"

"Yeah. They didn't plan on capturing you there, but they wanted to keep a close eye on you. Just as important, they wanted to *look* like they were trying to bring you in. You fell off their radar screen when you bolted down the rabbit hole in San Francisco, but they were already tracking Matlock, so they were able to catch up with you in Palo Alto. They lost you again when you split from Matlock's place on Lake Washington, but by then it didn't matter. They'd collected all the information they needed, and were just waiting for the end game to play out in New York."

"And you guys never knew about any of this."

"We figured it out with a couple of days to spare. Until then we thought we were outsmarting them every step of the way. Matlock was so proud of how he used his connections to get the Coast Guard off his back!" Gully gave a rare chuckle. "The joke was on us, I guess."

"Except that we won in the end."

"Thanks to our sources in Homeland Security," Gully said. "They'd known for a while that we had an informant inside their organization, but they could never find out who it was. So they decided to make the mole work for them—make sure we got fed all the information about the Blake Hawkes manhunt. They wanted us confident, so that we'd keep moving forward with our plan. Meanwhile, they kept their Tompkins Square scheme under wraps. It wasn't until very late in the game that our informant—or one of his colleagues, actually—found out about it and clued us in."

"You mean you have *two* moles?"

Gully frowned. "That's still a mystery," he said. "Our second source was anonymous—very helpful, as it turned out, but completely opaque."

Something in Gully's voice told Blake it was time to switch subjects. "So it was this late information that led to the Zoners' flash mob?"

Gully nodded. "That's right. Those are America's real heroes—every person out in the park that afternoon. They're the ones who gained us the precious time we needed."

"When you analyze the whole thing," said Blake, "My uncle did all of us a huge favor. If not for Frank, Max Fish might still be under house arrest. And I'd probably be sitting in some corporate conference room this very minute, bargaining my life away."

"Instead, you're a free agent," nodded Gully. "A national celebrity, too, once your role in all this comes out."

"The funny thing is, I thought all along that it was Mel who betrayed me. I couldn't figure how else the Feds would have known about the quantum device. Since Mel knew about my record collection too, I figured he was the one who dropped the dime on me."

"I can reassure you on that point," smiled Gully. "Your esteemed mentor stayed true throughout."

"Then how did they hear about the communicator?"

"The old-fashioned way," Gully replied. "The janitor who cleaned your lab every night was on the Homeland Security payroll. He was giving them daily reports on your progress."

"No shit!"

"So you can tell Professor Morrison all is forgiven," said Gully, rising to his feet. "By the way, you also might want to give him the okay to date your ex. My sources tell me he's developed a real thing for her. And while I don't want to deflate your ego, they also inform me that, given your newfound interests and all, she's basically over you—to the point where their feelings have become, as they say, mutual...."

Epilogue

BLAKE LAY WITHOUT MOVING, LISTENING to the gentle splash of waves on the beach. Since taking up residence in the Bahamas, he'd been waking every morning at dawn. *Nice of Matlock to loan us this island,* he thought, not for the first time. "Stay as long as you want—a year, ten years, I don't care. I never use it," Matlock had said with a wave of his hand. "Besides, it's about time my security force down there earned their salary."

Blake's thoughts floated to the day's projects. After a lengthy discussion, he'd finally persuaded Matlock to launch a not-for-profit company that would license his quantum communication technology and then use the revenues to support scientific research. He had some fresh ideas for refining the device that he wanted to explore before lunch. Then there were e-mails he needed to respond to, plus a Skype media interview that afternoon, hopefully followed by a run on the beach. That evening he was sitting in on guitar with the local ripsaw group at an outdoor bar across the channel, and tomorrow Blue and Caroline were arriving for a week's stay in one of the guest cottages. Serena had also said something about Nell and Henry visiting later in the month—for a "spiritual retreat," whatever that meant.

His attention was diverted by the smells coming from the kitchen: Bacon, toast, eggs and freshly brewed coffee.

"Still in bed? You'd make one pitiful soldier!"

"Thank God for that!" said Blake. He turned to look at Serena standing in the doorway. "Do we have a few minutes before breakfast?" He patted the mattress invitingly.

"Have you already forgotten our conversation?" Serena folded her arms. "I told you when I agreed to set up house with you, I'm not one of your rock-and-roll nymphos or cradle-robbing Russian professors. If we're going to have a non-sexist, non-manipulative relationship, that means intimacy takes place on a case-by-case basis."

"When can I present my next case, your honor?"

She rolled her eyes. "Maybe after lunch. Now stop acting like a frat boy. You have responsibilities."

As she spoke, Blake moved to a desk by the window and began reading from the computer screen. "Two weeks since Fish took his oath of office, and things are already going to hell," he announced. "Yesterday, the Senate had to stay in session past midnight to pass the new legislation repealing the Rock Ban. The Republicans kept threatening to filibuster but the public pressure was too great, so a bunch of them finally caved."

"That's good, isn't it?" said Serena. "You'll be free to go home."

"Sure. But it's going to be like this every step of the way," Blake said, shaking his head. "The Republicans are already saying that Fish's election was a fluke. Passing his economic justice package is going be an all-out battle."

"He said, living free on a billionaire's island," snorted Serena. "Anyway, what about the Boundary Water Commission? That should help the progressive agenda."

"Except now the Republicans are trying to walk back the whole scandal. The latest story they're peddling is that Rogers was on the CIA payroll, giving us information about other terrorist groups—and that the nuclear attack scheme was a reverse sting operation gone wrong."

"It's a long fight," said Serena, walking back to the kitchen. "Nothing changes overnight."

"At least they aren't trying to get rid of the UZ anymore," Blake called after her. "Can you imagine the Zone with no blackout, no IDs—and no walls?" His mind wandered to his buried trove of records in La Jolla, and the plastic-wrapped package in the desert. *Some day soon...*

"That's right," Serena's voice piped up. "In fact, when you get down to it, it won't even be the UZ anymore."

"Hmm. I hadn't thought of it that way."

Pulling on a pair of pants, Blake walked to the front door and looked out at the ocean, framed by a grove of palms. Serena had a point: What would become of the Kidz and the Tangles and the rest of them, now that the Rock Ban was lifted and there was no need for channelers anymore? It was hard to envision.

"So if we can't believe in radical change, what *can* we believe in?" he asked.

Serena came to stand next to him. "Empathy...communication... the emotional connection between human beings," she said, slipping her hand into his. "And probably some other things I'm forgetting." Looking toward the dining alcove, Blake saw that she'd placed the eggs and bacon under covered warming dishes. Still holding his hand, Serena began to tug him toward the bedroom.

"But I thought..." he began.

"I changed my mind," said Serena, shaking her head in exasperation. "Haven't you heard? It's a bodyguard's prerogative."

"Thank you so much for this wonderful sendoff," said the man at the podium. "The opportunity to serve as our nation's Director of Homeland Security for the past seven and a half years has been the most singular experience, and honor, of my life. After this week, however, the only security I'll be directing is that of my own home—something my wife is definitely *not* looking forward to...."

As laughter washed across the banquet hall, Smyth drifted to the back of the room. Glancing around to make sure no one was looking, he slipped through the door into the hotel foyer, then turned and headed for the circular bar at the end of the lobby.

"Chivas on the rocks," he told the bartender, settling into one of the wicker-backed stools.

"Hitting the good stuff, eh? Well, I guess you've got a lot to celebrate."

The speaker was hidden by the wall of bottles at the center of the bar, but Smyth recognized the voice. Carrying his glass, he walked around to the opposite side where Marconi sat nursing a vodka tonic.

"Mind if I join you, you duplicitous S.O.B.?" he asked.

"I'll take that as a compliment," said Marconi. "Besides, as the saying goes..."

"Hardly. Compared to you, I'm just a bumbling civil servant," replied Smyth, sampling his Scotch. Except for the bartender, they were alone.

"Nice event, huh?" said Marconi, gesturing with his head toward the ballroom. "The bigger you are, the easier they let you down."

"Not always," said Smyth.

"No," said Marconi, smiling. "Not always."

"I hear you're retiring, too."

"Yup. Gonna spend some time fishing in the Gulf of Mexico. But word is, you're staying on."

"I thought I'd give the new regime a chance."

"Why not? You've always had a socialist streak," the other man chuckled.

They sat silently for a minute, sipping their drinks.

"You know," Marconi said finally, "Jackson's plan wasn't all that bad. Especially for something dreamed up on the fly."

"On the fly?"

"Don't sound so shocked," said Marconi. "It was plain bad luck that Hawkes got away in the first place, of course.... Once the kid was on the run, though, Jackson realized it was an ideal chance to roll up the whole Muni underground once and for all—*and* shut down Fish permanently in the process. He never knew about the audiotape. If he had, he would have taken a whole different approach and started playing some serious defense. Still, his plan might have worked, if only..."

"If only Bibbitt hadn't decided to get so ambitious?" said Smyth.

"Bibbitt's stunt sent the operation to hell at the end, for sure. And the sympathy boost Fish got from the attempted hit was huge. But the damage was already done," said Marconi, biting into a pretzel. "No, the only thing that would have saved the day was if Jackson had lowered the boom before Fish started speaking, like he'd planned. Let's say the speech never gets past Fish's first hellos, and instead Jackson swoops in—scoops up Hawkes and his walkie-talkie, and everyone else associated with the illegal broadcast."

"Okay," Smyth said. "Let's say he does."

"So now Fish has to go with Plan B, and give the tape to the press. If Acton catches a break, maybe he even snags the tape from Fish and gets a head start. Either way, when the Rogers recording surfaces, Acton goes on the record immediately to swear that the recording is a fake, put out by a man who is his bitter political enemy and has just been linked to a major criminal conspiracy. At the very least, he's now on an even playing field. And since the shooter never gets to pull the trigger, Fish doesn't get his big bump from the assassination attempt. In fact, *Acton* might have gotten some sympathy votes from Fish's attack on him. He could have weathered the whole scandal and be President right now. Max Fish would just be a footnote in history."

"That's a lot of ifs."

"Yeah. But it all boils down to the fact that Jackson's men got slowed up that crucial ten minutes by the protestors."

"Funny how ten minutes can make such a difference," Smyth said evenly.

"What's funny," continued Marconi, "is how fast the word spread once those officers showed up outside the park, and how quickly everyone mobilized. They even jammed up my undercover squads—glommed right onto them, like they knew just where they were. As if there were Muni operatives in the park with inside information, who were telling people exactly where to go and what to do."

"Interesting theory."

Marconi crunched a piece of ice between his molars. "Remember how upset you were when you thought Hawkes had been killed?" he said thoughtfully.

"Of course. I wanted to take him alive, to get any information he might have had."

"Here's something I've always wondered about how the original arrest went down. How come those officers were instructed to grab the friend if they saw him with Hawkes' black box, but were never told it was a communication device? And while I'm at it, why did it take the backup team so long to get into place?"

"Slip-ups like that happen all the time. You know that, Tony."

"Sure they do. And I won't even bring up the bureaucratic glitch that sprang Hawkes' buddy from the Congo a month early. Now, here's another thing I could never figure out: How were the Munis able to warn Hawkes to get out of Matlock's compound?"

"It's obvious, right? Either their mole told them the raid was coming, or you contacted them directly."

"A nice thought. Except that for some reason, the order never made it into the Department's computers until 11:00 Eastern Time that night—the time's listed right there in the leadership queue. I didn't hear about the raid until the next morning. Jackson assumed that still left the Munis' mole enough time to alert them. The only thing is, our leaker was temporarily out of commission that day, thanks to a coincidental computer overhaul—which Jackson didn't know about."

"But you did. Why didn't you say something to Jackson?"

"The oldest reason in the books: I was covering my own ass."

"Jackson was pretty cheesed off about that raid, wasn't he?"

"Furious. It almost ruined everything. But it also removed any doubts he had about you. He knew then that you were dead serious about nailing the kid—and that if he wanted to make sure the plan went forward, he had to remove you from that end of the case *and* make sure you didn't make any other surprise moves. Which of course meant sending you to New York, where he could keep an eye on you. Again, Charles, it's funny how everything worked out."

Smyth finished his drink. "I'll take one more," he told the bartender. There were certain moments, he thought, when absolutely nothing beat a good Scotch.

"The biggest riddle of all, though, is how Jackson came up with his scheme in the first place—the notion of letting Hawkes and the Munis play out the whole game, right to the end."

"I suppose we'll never know."

"Yeah, I suppose. I did ask him about it once. He said the idea just came to him while he was playing chess. Which isn't that surprising, since he makes a point of playing a few times a week. In fact, Piroulis is one of his regular partners. They've got a standing match every Sunday night. Were you aware of that?"

"You know Gary," chuckled Smyth. "He'll do anything to get in good with his superiors."

"One last thing," added Marconi. "I happened to be in Annapolis the other weekend. I had some time on my hands, so I did a little digging in the Naval Academy archives. The file on Admiral Cameron Hawkes, specifically."

"That was enterprising of you," said Smyth quietly.

"The file contained copies of all his old citations, including one from the second Iraq war, when he was lieutenant commander on a destroyer in the Gulf. He got a Bronze Star for saving the life of a young ensign who'd been hit by fire from an Iraqi attack boat. Crawled out on the deck through a hail of bullets and pulled him to safety. It had the ensign's name in there, too." Marconi tilted his head back and swallowed the last of his drink, than brought the glass down hard on the bar. "It's a small world, isn't it?"

Smyth raised his glass and half-turned in his stool. "Getting smaller all the time. Cheers, Tony. It's been good working with you."

Leaving the bar, Smyth strode slowly across the lobby. A rock tune was playing on the hotel's sound system, he noticed, some old Rolling Stones recording. He paused for a moment to listen. Then, still holding his drink, he pushed through the revolving door and walked into the Washington night.

Original Songs Featured in *Soundscape*

(Recordings of these songs can be heard online by visiting the website www.soundscapebook.com)

Set the Music Free

Set the music free,
Liberate all melody.
Let the music be,
All together, one, two, three!

Set the music free,
Emancipate sweet harmony.
Let the music be,
Sing it out now, you and me!

The Road to UZFest

Ain't it great to be in the UZ—nowhere to go, no one to see,
I'm heading down the road to UZFest, won't you come with me?

L.A.'s got a real cool sound, yeah, Frisco has the wind so free,
But soon I will be traveling East—that New York beat is calling me!

Tall and grey the wall surrounds us; where it ends, we cannot say.
But still the music's all around, so lift your voice and sing today.

Ain't it great to be in the UZ—nowhere to go, no one to see,
I'm heading down the road to UZFest, won't you come with me?

Pathfinder Blues

Went down the wrong road, searching for you.
The way's getting harder every day, but my heart is still true.
Eyes in the sky watching all that I do,
But they can't take my soul, oh no, no, no, 'cause it's promised to you.

Climbed up a high hill, heading for you,
Trail's getting steeper on the way, but I'll make it through
The night is so dark, and my thoughts are blue, oh so blue,
But I know the sun will shine again when I'm back home with you.

Did You Ever?

Did you ever lose your mother's love?
Did you ever lose your mother's love
And cry for her in vain?
Did you ever lose your mother's love?

Did you ever feel your father's rage?
Did you ever feel your father's rage
Like a prisoner in a cage?
Did you ever feel your father's rage?

How can we maintain…
In a world with so much pain?

Did you ever take your brother's side?
Did you ever take your brother's side
And give a place to hide?
Did you ever take your brother's side?

And did you ever think about your age?
Did you ever think about your age
And try to make amends?
Did you ever think about your age?

How can we maintain…
In a world with so much pain?

Did you ever lose your mother's love?
Did you ever lose your mother's love
And cry for her in vain?
Did you ever lose your mother's love?
Did you ever lose your mother's love?
Did you ever lose your mother's love?
Did you ever lose your mother's love?

Ace of Hearts

Wandering through a lonely town, I saw an open door
Walked into a poker game with room for just one more.

My money went and then my truck and last my hound dog Abel.
But deeper still that hole I dug, for the sake of my love Mabel.

Ace of Hearts, you faithless card that stole my life away
I played my part, now have a heart, for it's my dying day.

I'd promised her we'd marry soon, when I had a home at last.
But on that fateful night in June, my dreams were fleeing fast.

With one pot left, the biggest yet, I took a final stand.
I bet the one thing I had left—my dear sweet Mabel's hand.

Ace of Hearts, you faithless card that stole my life away
I played my part, now have a heart, for it's my dying day.

I drew three kings, and hope grew strong when the next card made it four.
Across the way three aces lay, and the dealer dealt two more.

As he lay that last hand down, a distant church bell pealed,
And when I saw the Ace of Hearts, I knew my fate was sealed.

Ace of Hearts, you faithless card that stole my life away
I played my part, now have a heart, for it's my dying day.

So in Love With You

I'm just a fool it's true
'Cause I can't stop loving you.
Don't know what I will do,
I'm so in love with you,
So in love with you.

Maybe one day I'll see
Another way to be.
Until that day is here,
I'll keep dreaming of you, my dear,
I'll dream of you, my dear.

I hope you'll hear me now,
As I try to tell you how
A new day is dawning here,
The sun's shining bright and clear,
Shining bright and clear.

I'm just a fool it's true
'Cause I can't stop loving you.
Don't know what I will do,
I'm so in love with you,
So in love with you.
So in love with you,
So in love with you.

www.ingramcontent.com/pod-product-compliance
Lightning Source LLC
Chambersburg PA
CBHW020257030826
48979CB00026B/1373/J

* 9 7 8 0 9 9 0 8 8 2 8 1 7 *